I0603616

The Good Doctor

Kerry Rogerson

FOREST ROOM PRESS

First published by Forest Room Press in 2021
This edition published in 2021 by Forest Room Press

Copyright © Kerry Rogerson 2021
forestroompress.com.au
The moral right of the author has been asserted.

All rights reserved. This publication (or any part of it) may not be reproduced or
transmitted, copied, stored, distributed or otherwise made available by any person or
entity (including Google, Amazon or similar organisations), in any form (electronic,
digital, optical, mechanical) or by any means (photocopying, recording, scanning or
otherwise) without prior written permission from the publisher.

The Good Doctor

EPUB: 9780648923411
POD: 9780648923404

Cover design by Christabella Designs

Publishing services provided by Critical Mass
www.critmassconsulting.com

For Janice

PROLOGUE

'You bloody goose, Jarrod, I could have shot you.'

Sophie had already lowered her gun. Hands shaking, she re-holstered.

The probationary constable seemed to be holding his breath.

'What were you doing coming around the other side?' she went on, heat still prickling beneath the neck of her uniform. 'You were supposed to be behind me.'

'I thought I could head them off,' he said, finally breathing.

'Head who off? There's nobody here.'

'But the alarm's still sounding.'

'Look, you can't just make up your own rules. You stick with me, okay? Do exactly what I tell you.'

'Yeah, sorry.'

Sophie turned away and spoke into the microphone attached to her jacket collar, telling the operator that the warehouse appeared intact and there was no sign of any person in the vicinity.

'Key-holder is on their way to your location.' The operator's voice was mixed with radio static. 'They'll reset the alarm.'

'Copy that.'

The rain started again. Sophie headed to the police car. The probationer followed. She could hear his boots scraping on the gravel.

Idiot.

He'd only been out of the academy two weeks. She shouldn't even be out here tonight with him – she wasn't his buddy – that was

Maria. But as usual her colleague had complained of a headache and changed the duties around on the roster so that Sophie had to take her place on the car crew. Maria would be sitting back in the station, drinking coffee, keeping warm.

And tonight of all nights.

Sophie knew she should be home sorting her marriage woes, not out in the drizzling dark with a useless freckle-head who'd spent the first hour spouting his philosophy about women in the job.

They waited in the car for the key-holder: an elderly man who stuck his face in the passenger's side window, looking past Sophie to the probationer. 'Happens a fair bit, alarm going off. Third time this month I've been called to reset it. Still, keeps me employed.'

'Tell whoever, if it keeps happening they'll be fined,' Sophie said, drawing the man's attention. *Yes that's right, I'm in charge.*

'Might do them some good,' the old guy said. 'Anyway, thanks for coming out. You got better things to do, I know.'

Jarrod drove. He was quiet since his close-up with Sophie's Glock. Rain sprinkled across the windscreen. The wipers creaked left to right. Everything was fogging up. Sophie reached across to hit the demist switch, Jarrod eyeing her remorsefully.

'Are you going to report me?' he asked. 'For what happened back there?'

Correct procedure required an incident report. Jarrod would have to go for retraining, maybe get rapped over the knuckles for insubordination. But she hadn't really come close to shooting him. Fourteen years on the job had taught her to keep her finger off the trigger and identify her target. Still, she'd pointed the gun at him and that probably wouldn't bode well for her either.

'We've had our serious talk. Let's leave it at that.' She flipped open a folder and reached for the radio handset in the centre dash. 'We better get this paperwork delivered before it gets too late.' She used a small pocket torch to read: *Interim restraining order, 42 Bakerton Street.* 'Take the next right.'

Jarrod parked two houses down as Sophie spoke into the radio. She gave the address and the nature of their business. The radio operator responded, asking them to wait. A police pursuit had just started in the Royal National Park.

Sophie swore and chucked the handset onto the dash. 'We haven't got all flaming night.'

'What are we waiting for?' Jarrod asked. 'It's just paperwork for a restraining order.'

'Officer Survival. There might be warnings on the address or the person named in the order. Radio will look it up, get back to us. And they need to know where we are. That's the main thing.'

Jarrod peered through the windscreen at the house. 'Doesn't even look like anyone lives there. It's a bit derelict.'

Sophie flashed her torch briefly over the papers again. 'Ray Waddington... back to his old tricks, no doubt. I don't suppose he'll be keen to open the door.'

'Offer us a cup of tea?' Jarrod tried to laugh.

'It'll be a no-show.'

They listened to the pursuit for a while. It was a high-speed chase involving at least three highway patrol vehicles and a Ford Falcon with bent number plates.

'They'll call it off,' Sophie said. 'Too dangerous.'

Almost immediately the radio operator terminated the pursuit. Sophie smiled smugly at Jarrod and took up the handset again expecting her response. But another urgent job was being called and took priority.

She groaned and sat back, looked out at the rain-spattered evening and thought of Sam. She owed him an apology. Strange that she should think of it that way after the names he'd called her earlier today. There'd been no chance to sort things out and she'd left for work in a fever.

'I should call him.'

'What?' Jarrod said.

She shook her head. 'Sorry, thinking out loud.' Tiredness was creeping up on her. She took the papers from the folder and undid her seatbelt. 'Stay here, I'll just go and see if anyone's home.'

'You don't want to wait?'

'We'll be here all night at this rate. Besides, I need coffee.'

Sophie was glad to be free of the probationer, away from his scrutiny. Earlier she'd let slip about her argument with Sam. Nightshift tended to do that – driving around in the dark, making conversation for the sake of keeping awake. But she regretted having said anything. Rumours could start from far less. And an academy-fresh nineteen-year-old was hardly the best choice as a confidante.

Feather-light rain flitted onto her cheeks as she made her way up the slope towards the house. Flaking paintwork and tattered curtains – Jarrod was probably right, nobody lived here. Bogus addresses were common amongst thieves and villains.

But then the porch light came on, startling her. She squinted at the stark whiteness of the bare globe as she reached the base of the stairs. The moisture on the timber railing sat up high like beaded pearls. Absently, she touched one, dissolving it into the grain.

The screen door squealed open as she started up the steps. She caught an impression of a figure – more of an apparition, an aura beneath the blistering light. The pump action of the shotgun was clear.

Sophie stopped.

A loud explosion ripped through the air, and she was hurtled backwards onto the rain-drizzled grass.

Blood gushed from the hole in her chest as her body jerked several times. After a final shudder, she was still.

ONE

Four years later

She was crying.

Dr Samuel Tyler let out a tense breath and checked his watch. Then he leant forward in the armchair and tapped the low table between him and the young woman, trying to get her attention. She'd emptied the box of tissues and was now destroying the last of them. He frowned at the dusting of tissue lint on the rug.

'Sorry,' she gulped.

'It's all right,' he said. But it wasn't all right. He took her file from the armrest of his chair and headed for the door. 'I'll be back in a moment.'

Leah, the receptionist, beamed a smile at him that vanished as Sam slapped the file on the counter in front of her.

'Check the records and find out how I ended up with this patient.'

'Alice Lacey,' she said, glancing at the file. She tapped on the keyboard. 'She was Glenn Whittaker's.'

'I know. I just broke the news of Glenn's death to her. My question is, how is it that she's sitting in my office? She's a cop – I don't do cops. You've been here long enough to know that.'

Leah shook her head. 'I didn't allocate her to you. Richard did. He took care of Glenn's patients. It's nothing to do with me.'

'Is Richard still in his office?'

Before she could respond, Sam grabbed the file and headed down the hall to the door marked *Dr R. Madden*. At the same time, a stout man with a harried look on his face came rushing out, shoving papers into a briefcase.

Sam stepped in front of him. 'Richard, I need a word.'

'I don't have time for this, Sam,' he said, pushing past into reception where he hit the button for the lift. 'It'll have to wait.'

'It can't wait. It's about Alice Lacey, one of Glenn's patients. She's in my office now.'

Richard frowned, so Sam spelt it out. 'She's a cop.'

'She's a special case. No other psychiatrist was suitable to take her.'

'*I'm* not suitable.'

'I can't talk about it now. I'm already late for a meeting.'

The bell chimed on the lift. As Richard stepped inside, Sam put his hand against the door to stop it closing. 'We need to sort this out now.'

'We'll sort it out later,' Richard said, checking his watch. 'You shouldn't keep her waiting. You don't come cheap.'

The shiny metal door slid shut. Sam stared at it blankly then thumped the twisted version of himself staring back.

'Is there something I can do, Sam?' Leah asked as he passed the reception counter.

He shook his head and returned to his office.

Glenn Whittaker's patient had stopped crying. She looked at Sam with eyes so bloodshot he couldn't tell what colour they were. He sat, put the file on the low table between them and leant forward, resting his elbows on his knees.

'Alice,' he began, but she burst into tears again. Sam sat back. He wasn't going to have the patience for this.

'I'm sorry, Dr Tyler.'

He felt a brief softening, but only, he told himself, because none of this was her fault. And maybe because she'd addressed him formally. Patients tended to call him by his first name and without any prompting.

'Don't worry,' he said. 'It's a shock about Dr Whittaker, I know.'

'We only had a couple of sessions, but he seemed like such a nice man.' She dabbed her eyes. 'Do you mind me asking how he died?'

Glenn had been found slumped over his desk by the night cleaner almost three weeks ago. There was nothing unusual in him working back so late. Sometimes Sam had wondered if he even went home.

'It was a heart attack.'

Alice twisted a charm on her bracelet. 'Another death. It seems to follow me. Maybe I'm a bad omen.' Her eyes sought his as though inviting renunciation to the claim. He gave her no relief. Instead, he sighed and went back to her file.

Glenn's handwriting was on the front cover and clearly marked *in-house therapy only*. That was odd – or maybe not, knowing Glenn. He'd always tended to have his special patients – and special treatments to go with them. Sam wondered where he should take the rest of the session, given it would be their last.

'Are you able to continue?'

She cleared her throat. 'Yes.'

The digital clock on the bench behind her indicated there was still half an hour left. Alice had cried for at least twenty-five minutes and someone was paying for this. Richard was right: psychiatric sessions didn't come cheap.

He leant back in his armchair and positioned her notes on his knee, flicking through a few pages.

'It's been hard,' he said. 'Lots of distressing pictures in your head.'

She bit down on her bottom lip.

He added quickly, 'I want you to know that we won't be discussing any of that today.'

'So does that include the train crash?'

'It includes every bad job you've ever been to.'

She nodded and breathed relief.

Sam produced a pen from the inside pocket of his jacket and clicked the end with his thumb. 'Let's just check a few details.' A ploy to fill time. 'You've recently moved from Coffs Harbour to Sydney.'

'Yes, a few months ago.'

'Right on the beach at Cronulla.'

'You know it?'

He knew it. He lived three streets back from the ocean at the other end of the southern Sydney suburb. Not that he would tell a patient that. There was nothing worse than being stalked or having a patient drop in for tea and a free session. Instead, he nodded and returned to her papers.

She answered other generic questions, things that were already noted in the paperwork. But they kept her talking, kept the session moving.

'Married?' he asked.

'Single. I used to be married.'

'So, you're divorced,' he corrected her, making a note.

'I hate the term *divorced*,' she said. 'I mean, what difference does it make? You're either married or you're not.'

He detected her bitterness. If she were staying then he'd be looking to see how her situation might have affected her relationships. That was the most common thing with cops – all they experienced in the job usually spilt over into their personal lives.

He went as far as the police record. Length of service, rank, departments and locations. She confirmed what was already written. A senior constable with fourteen years' service – all of it in uniform. She'd never branched into anything else. A few failed attempts at making sergeant. She seemed bright, but that typical cop persona had washed into her tone: formal, direct, brief.

He noticed his hand was shaking as he ticked off her responses.

The next question was not listed. 'Fourteen years of service – makes you twenty when you joined. So, why did you become a police officer?'

'To serve my community and uphold the law,' she said, a flicker of irony crossing her lips. She paused and looked down at her hands. 'Actually, I thought I'd be helping people. That was the plan. A bit naïve, really. Instead, I got a whole lot more than I bargained for.' Her gaze lifted but didn't settle on him. 'There should be a disclaimer in the glossy brochure they hand out from recruitment; you know, the one with the glamour shots of police in helicopters or smiling as they walk the beat and being well received by a grateful community; making a difference. What they leave out is the part about wrestling with drunks in the gutter, being spat on, abused, assaulted, shot at...'

Without warning Alice jerked backwards in her chair. Sam stared in bewilderment, then realised he'd just slammed her file down hard on the small table between them, scattering papers onto the rug. He could feel the perspiration beading on his forehead. He had to get out.

Sam found himself at the water cooler in reception. Damn it, his hands were shaking like he had the DTs. The water missed the cup and trickled over his fingers. He could feel Leah's eyes boring into the back of his skull. He managed to fill the cup and then gulped the contents like it was medicine.

He got a fresh cup and filled it.

When he turned around Leah was all smiles. She poked a strand of black hair behind one ear.

He smiled back, begrudgingly.

Back in the office, Alice was standing by the window at the far end of the room. Layered blonde hair fell over one shoulder, with darker regrowth that was either neglect or style. She was curvaceous although hadn't packed on the kilos like a lot of shift workers did. Her mid-length summer dress seemed to belie her station as a cop. Most of the off-duty female cops Sam knew wore trousers, gym gear, or jeans.

She turned as the door clicked shut but stayed where she was.

'Come back over,' Sam said, moving towards his armchair.

She hesitated then approached slowly, looking at him expectantly.

Green. Her eyes were green.

He handed her the cup of water.

'Sorry,' he said, not sure what to add to that.

He indicated the other chair and she sat. He picked up the fallen papers and smoothed down the front of his tie before also sitting.

'So, you're taking over my matter,' she said, putting the water, untouched, on the table between them.

'Well, things are still being worked out at this stage.'

Ten minutes to go on the clock.

The file papers were out of order. He pretended interest in one of them, clicked on his pen and made a mark in the corner.

'Well...' He made a show of checking his watch. 'We might call it a day.'

Alice stood with him and shook the hand he extended.

'Same time next week?' she said as he walked her out.

'Um – Leah will sort that one out.'

He was about to close the door when she turned back and smiled. It was quite a contrast to the sadness he'd seen earlier. He didn't know what to make of it except that Alice Lacey was the sort of woman whose smile was worth waiting for.

But this would be their last meeting.

'Thank you, Doctor.'

He closed the door, leant back against it and exhaled as if he'd been holding his breath for an hour. His eyes darted to the window. The vision of Alice standing there was uncomfortably clear in his mind. She hadn't been admiring the view; he'd frightened her and she'd retreated to a safer place. It bothered him how close he'd come to losing control. He let his sight drift to the long bureau holding the neat row of psychiatry books. He walked over and opened the first drawer.

The framed photo was face down. He turned it over and his heart began to race. It could have been one of those pictures that came with the frame – a black-and-white close-up of a happy couple.

'Sophie,' he heard himself whisper.

They'd had an argument about the whole photo thing. Sam hadn't seen the point of it – the expense or the time. But Sophie had insisted it would be something nice to look back on.

Looking back now only brought him pain.

His thumb traced over her image. Dark hair parted in the middle and pulled tight. Well-defined cheekbones and wide eyes with thick lashes. He was the grump, smiling only because he'd been told to.

Suddenly his eyes were burning, his body trembling the way it used to.

Sam put away the photo and thumped the drawer closed. He grabbed Alice Lacey's file, glared at it, then dumped it in the outbox tray on his desk.

TWO

The track through the Royal National Park was gone, destroyed by fallen trees and the rubble of a recent landslide. Sam readjusted his backpack and moved up the escarpment, hoping to go around the problem and pick up the track further along. Lengthening shadows reminded him he'd have to turn back soon. A few minutes later he stopped climbing and looked around. Nothing was familiar.

Why had he left it so long to come out here? Not once, since he'd set Sophie's ashes free, had he returned to honour her memory. If he had, he wouldn't be facing this conundrum.

Frustrated, he slammed a tree trunk with the palm of his hand, grazing his skin on the bark. Specks of blood appeared.

'Shit.'

Sitting on a boulder at the edge of the track, he shrugged off his backpack to get his water, drank half the bottle and poured the rest over his hand. His conscience was screaming at him.

Sophie, you deserved better than this.

Last night he'd woken in fright, thrust forward in his bed, clutching his chest, and yelling her name. He'd gone to the bathroom cabinet, found the bottle of pills, shook out two and swallowed them dry. Then he'd roamed the house like a sleepwalker, imagining her ghost in the eerie light from a flickering streetlamp. He'd climbed the spiral staircase and stopped at the barricade guarding the unfinished extension. It had been Sophie's dream – spacious rooms with full-length windows to take in ocean views they were missing one level down. The extension remained an empty shell. He hadn't been able to face it after she'd gone. Eventually, in the early hours of the morning, he'd sat exhausted on the top step and tried not to think.

A lyrebird wailed like a siren from somewhere deep in the bush.

Sam put the empty water bottle in his backpack and stood up. His legs protested.

At thirty-eight, he wasn't as fit as he used to be. That was one of the pitfalls of his job: an office-bound pen-hugger who sat and listened to the woes of a population seemingly glad to wallow in its own misery. He'd become locked into that life; set himself in the standard of all highly paid professionals – clean nails and laundered suits and silk ties with embroidered initials. The four flights of stairs to his office were about the only exercise he got these days. And that was only when the lift was out of service.

Further up the slope, his shoes skidded in the dry leaf mulch and he stumbled against a rock, scraping his knee. It was bleeding but he didn't stop. He pushed himself harder, aware of the fading light. He came out onto a fire trail. This was better. He started to run and took the first signposted track – *The Leap* – weaving his way through the spindly foliage, watching his step, alert to how close the cliff edge was.

The trail opened onto a flat area of rock shelf. A sheer drop was just a few steps ahead. Catching his breath, he took in the view. Deep valleys of dense bushland stretched all the way to the ocean. White water smashed against the distant coastal rocks.

Was this the place?

He squeezed his eyes shut and tried to remember. It was all a blur. But what he was sure of was that his head had been bowed as he'd clutched the urn containing Sophie's ashes. And the prayer. What was it?

'Panis Angelicus'.

He opened his eyes again. It didn't feel right. But it had to be the place. Sophie had loved it here.

Dammit. Why was his memory so fissured?

This whole excursion had been an abysmal failure. Sophie's ashes lost to the wind in that time long ago. He couldn't even re-member if he'd cried.

He headed back.

By the time he reached the coast, dusk had settled and the tide cut off his path. He turned towards the hills. It was dark by the time he reached his BMW parked outside the surf club at Garie. The place was deserted. Tired, his calf muscles aching, he drove five kilometres to the main road only to find a wide metal gate blocked the exit.

'You're kidding me.'

Sam got out of the car and checked the large padlock and chain illuminated by his headlights.

He returned to the car, moved it over to the side and turned the engine off. Reaching into the backseat he found a hooded wind-cheater and pulled it on. There was nothing else he could do.

*

A tap to the driver's window woke Sam. It was just coming on first light. He blinked and wiped the grit from his eyes, then let his window down.

The park ranger leant in. 'You should have called the police, mate. They've got keys to all the gates in the park.'

Call the police – what a joke, Sam thought. As if they'd come to assist *him*.

He sat up straight and turned the engine over. 'Yep, well I'll remember that for next time.'

He made it home just as the sun was lifting out of the Pacific, driving up to the unfinished Cape Cod monstrosity at the top of the street. Nestled into the slate-grey tiles of the roof, the arched upper windows seemed to stare down at him like two bulbous eyes. It wasn't possible for him to hate the house any more than he did. He'd tried to sell it but nobody wanted an ugly half-finished extension, especially when the owner's wife had met an untimely and tragic death. 'Bad karma,' the real estate agent had said. Now it sat there to remind him what a mess he'd made of everything.

Sam tossed his keys on the sideboard and fell into the wide armchair that faced the window, tilted his head back and groaned.

It was then he remembered the cut on his leg. The blood had dried, but a patch of redness under the skin indicated the brewing infection.

Well, serve himself right if his whole bloody leg dropped off.

*

The supermarket car park seemed to be doubling as a speed track in the afternoon. Sam manoeuvred his trolley around the impatient and blatantly rude. A station wagon stalked him for a moment, creeping behind him as he made his way to his car – but sped off seconds later.

He offloaded two weeks' supply of frozen meals and a case of South Australian merlot into the boot. It would be a competition to see what got him first: alcohol poisoning or a poor diet. Maybe the combination would quicken the process.

'Hello, Sam. I thought that was you.'

Sam closed the boot, biting on the inside of his mouth, then turned around and forced a smile. 'Maria.'

Leaving her shopping trolley aside, the tall brown-haired woman stepped in and kissed Sam on the cheek. They both tried for something of a hug, but it all became awkward. Sam ended up patting her shoulder, which didn't feel right either.

'Rob and I were only talking about you the other day,' she said.

'How have you both been?'

'We're good. Rob's working with the major crime unit in the city now, but I'm still at Gymea Police Station.' Maria paused, took a breath and touched the small gold cross on her neck chain. 'We've missed you, Sam.'

'Yeah, time gets away…'

They used to be so close, the four of them. Sophie and Maria had worked the same shifts. Sam was always the odd one out.

Three cops and a shrink – great name for a sitcom, Rob used to say.

'I heard about Glenn Whittaker,' Maria said. 'It's really sad. I couldn't make it to his funeral – nobody would swap shifts with me. But Brian Heath said he saw you there.'

Sam recalled the moment, coming face to face with Brian just as they were leaving the chapel. It had been uncomfortable. Sam hadn't said anything to the detective, just put his head down and walked outside.

'Heart attack, wasn't it?' she added. 'I know Glenn wasn't a spring chicken, but he was such a presence. And a terrific psychiatrist. Always turned up at the police station during a critical incident to offer support. I don't suppose you'll be taking over that role now?'

Sam's stomach muscles tightened. 'It wasn't a role. Glenn visited the stations off his own bat.'

'God help us all then. We'll be lost without him.'

Sam pointed to Maria's trolley. 'Anyway, I won't keep you – looks like you've got frozen stuff too.' He stepped in and kissed her cheek. 'Say hello to Rob for me.'

She touched his arm, and before he moved away he saw the pity in her eyes. 'Maybe we could get together one day, you know, for old time's sake?'

He didn't answer, simply lifted his hand in farewell, pretending he'd missed her suggestion. As he walked around to the driver's door he took his keys from the pocket of his shorts and crunched them inside his fist – the sharp ends digging into the soft flesh of his palm.

Sam couldn't face going home. The towering edifice with its unhappy history, made worse by Maria's condolatory expression. He'd all but blotted her from his mind these past years. Now she was snaking her way through old memories, as though picking out the more hurtful ones to throw back at him: Maria consoling Sophie and shouting abuse at him for being an unfeeling drunkard; collecting Sophie with an overnight bag after one of their many fights...

He parked his car at the deserted end of Wanda Beach, pulled off his shoes and t-shirt, and walked into the ocean. The thrashing surf matched the rush of blood pumping through his body. He dived under every wave until he was past the breakers, and then turned to face the shore.

His mind conjured images of Sophie on the beach, turning cartwheels and laughing at him because she knew how much he hated public displays.

'*Samuel, it's only the beach,*' she called across the waves to him. '*Nobody cares.*'

A swift moving cloud covered the sun, and the image of Sophie was gone by the time the rays fought their way out again.

A wave belted into the back of his head, forcing him under. Muscles relaxed, he drifted. Maybe the undercurrent would tow him further out, so that by the time he resurfaced he'd be closer to the treacherous Kurnell rocks, no chance of escape.

Instead, the waves took him back to shore, the last tumbling him about in foamy grit. He emerged with twisted shorts, the crotch laden with sand.

He dropped close to the edge and laid back, the salt and sun prickling on his lips.

And he waited for the burden to ease.

THREE

Dr Cranston Jones stood sentry in the doorway of Glenn's old office. A scrawny man with a red-veined nose and a comb-over, he scowled as Sam helped their other colleague, Diane Briggs, drag in the last of several big boxes.

Sam had been watching the antagonism brew all morning.

'It's not right,' Cranston grumbled.

'Get used to it, Jonesy,' Diane said, sneering up at him from under a long fringe. 'I've been working out of a cupboard for the past eight years. About time I got to spread things out. And don't whine just because you didn't get up early enough to do it first.'

'The police might want to come back, take another look around.'

'For what? Glenn wasn't murdered. He croaked it from a heart attack. Anyway, what do you want me to do, turn the place into a shrine, burn candles?'

'Oh, it's all right for you, but I was the one who got called in to identify the poor bastard. He was dead at that very desk, still with a pen in his hand.'

Diane lost her patience. She grabbed at pens in a tray and held up a handful. 'Well, come on, which pen was it? I'll have it set in bronze and mounted for you.'

Cranston stormed across the hall and into his office, slamming the door.

Diane grunted and turned to Sam. 'Hey, I tell you what, I'd sell my soul for *your* office.' She grinned, revealing the wide gap between her front teeth. 'All that space complete with sitting area. I reckon my clientele might pick up with an office like that.'

'If I cark it, it's yours, no argument,' Sam said, absently fingering the framed picture of Diane's black Cocker Spaniel.

'And the furniture?'

'I'd have no use for it where I'm going.'

'Pearly gates I'm guessing.'

'More likely that other place.'

'Not you, good sort. You're squeaky clean.'

Unimpressed, Sam left the room.

His first patient was running late. Leah had a pile of correspondence for him to sign, so he stood at reception and checked each page carefully. He found a mistake on every one and handed them back. She glared at the last page where Sam had circled an errant comma.

'She likes you, you know,' Richard said when Sam cornered him in his office later that afternoon.

'Leah? I know.'

'Not interested?'

'I don't have time.'

'Sam, you're still a young man. You should get out more.'

'Things are fine for me. A distraction is the last thing I need.'

'You make it sound like an inconvenience. People generally enjoy being together.'

'Yeah, well I'm in the lower percentage that prefers my own company. Anyway, I didn't come in here to talk about Leah.'

Richard sighed. 'I know what you're going to say. About Alice Lacey, the cop. But I did my research on her. All her duty was up north in Coffs Harbour. She never worked in Sydney, only moved here recently. Too many bad memories for her up there. She won't be going back – she's done with the job. Post-traumatic stress – that train disaster near Bellingen last year. Eleven killed, twenty-odd injured. Nasty business.'

Sam took a deep breath. 'I want her off my books. It's not a request.'

Richard tapped a pen thoughtfully on the papers in front of him, his eyes fixed on Sam. 'Listen to me – you're the most capable psychiatrist in this practice. You're good at what you do. My decision is in the best interests of the patient. She's had a hard time.'

'Haven't they all,' Sam said sarcastically. 'Why not give her to Cranston or Diane? They're always looking to increase their numbers.'

'I've divided as many as I dared between those two. Sure, they were pleased for the clientele, but you know as well as I do that the honeymoon period will be over before long. We'll end up losing more than we'll keep. Besides, I only gave you Alice.' Richard paused. 'Glenn marked her file as in-house therapy only. So, he wasn't planning to send her to a clinical psychologist. He must have had his reasons for that, to keep everything here. I feel like I owe it to him, to make sure this one is okay.'

Sam recalled the note on Alice Lacey's file and understood there would have been a good reason for Glenn's decision. But he wasn't prepared to acknowledge it. 'Glenn always got too involved – treating most of his patients like they were family.'

'And they loved him for it. You've got to admit, he got results.'

Sam stood and walked to the window behind Richard's chair, parted the venetians with his fingers but realised the futility of staring at a brick wall.

His colleague swivelled on his chair, the heavy creak of metal and plastic seeming to threaten the manufacturer's warranty.

'I don't work the way Glenn did,' Sam said. 'I don't have that same level of... demonstrative compassion, whatever you want to call it. I prefer to keep the boundaries well in place.'

'That's what makes you the best choice for Alice. She needs stability now. Glenn went and carked it after just a handful of sessions, and she'd be feeling the pinch of that. Come on Obi-Wan, you're her only hope.'

'This is not some joke.' Sam turned from the window, releasing the blades of the blind so that they swung and clattered. 'You're messing with people's lives. Start thinking about what you're doing.'

'Steady on.' Richard tossed his pen aside and adjusted his bulky frame. 'What's got into you? Is this because of Sophie?'

Sam leant against the wall and folded his arms across his chest. 'What do you reckon?'

'Mate, it's got to be... three, four years ago?'

Sam pointed a warning finger at his colleague. 'I was the most hated man in the eyes of every one of Sophie's colleagues. They blamed me for what happened. And now you want to go and throw me under the bus with it all again. I've come a long way, pulled myself together. I don't want to unravel what I've made of myself here.'

He started to pace, somehow found his way back to the chair, sat heavily.

'It was unfortunate about what happened to Sophie,' Richard said cautiously. 'But come on, nobody could ever say it was your fault. You never know, working with cops again might prove cathartic. At least it's worth a try.'

'Try? I had trouble staying in the same room as Alice last Friday, and that was without hearing about any of her problems.' Sam thumped the desk with his fist to make his point. 'You don't know what it's doing to me, and I haven't even got started.'

'Why, what's it doing to you?'

Sam thought of the nightmares, the images of Sophie that were plaguing him again even while awake. Then there was the drinking and the pills. He shook his head. 'I'm not up to it. I can't work with damaged cops.'

'They're *all* damaged. For some reason the healthy ones don't want to see us.'

Sam knew he needed a different tactic. He forced a cooler tone. 'Richard, I'm asking you as a good friend – *please* – give Alice to someone else. I'll take on extras, work weekends if I have to, just not with police. I know I'll get there in the end. But not now, not *her.*'

The open laptop to Richard's left beeped. 'I've done it again,' he said. 'I'm supposed to be somewhere.' He snapped the laptop closed, heaved himself out of the chair, grabbed his jacket and searched for his keys. 'Leave it with me, Sam. I'll look into it.'

At reception, Sam was surprised to find Leah still at her desk. She handed him the corrected documents. Without even trying he saw a typo on the first page.

'I'll sign them tomorrow,' he said.

Leah sighed and leant across the counter towards him to take back the papers.

He returned to his office and shut the door. When he heard her leave he went out to the computer and pulled up the electronic copies. He fixed the problems, reprinted the documents, and signed them.

The house was cold when he arrived home. It took ten minutes for the reverse cycle air-conditioner to kick in. But the hum of the motor bothered him and he turned it off. It protested with a metallic clang, the fan shuddering to a halt.

Sam poured his wine, sat in his armchair, and stared at the bland walls and meagre furniture.

This is my life, he thought. How did it come to this?

*

Sam jolted awake. He'd been dreaming. Something about being out at The Leap – and stumbling at the edge.

It took him ages to settle back on the bed, trying to force his mind into meditation, listening for the distant thrum of waves against the rocky coastline.

A soft creaking noise overhead alerted him. He didn't move but his eyes traced the ceiling as though he might be able to see through it if he stared at it long enough. And there it was again – soft but with definite movement – like someone was up there walking around.

His skin crawled as he remembered a time before Sophie died when she would wander through the unfinished rooms, usually following a late shift. He would hear her right from where he lay now. On one occasion when she came back to bed he'd pretended to be asleep, unwilling for the conversation. But he remembered it now as clear as if she were right beside him.

'Sam,' she whispered. *'Are you awake?'*

He groaned and rolled away.

'It's so beautiful up there.' Her breath was soft against his bare shoulder. *'The sea breeze comes right through the front windows.*

We'll sleep under a canopy of stars. And the back room would be great for a nursery.' She paused. 'Sam, we should talk about that, starting a family.'

He made no response, fudging sleep.

She kissed his ear, gently hummed, tuneless but pleasant.

Sam emerged from the memory, flipped the sheet back and, still looking towards the ceiling, got out of bed. The cold air chilled him through his damp singlet as he ventured slowly down the hall towards the spiral staircase.

The sounds remained faint and distant as he put his hand on the rail. He looked up to where the top of the spiral disappeared into a boxed cavity in the ceiling. There was supposed to be an opening into the new rooms. But he'd had the whole thing filled in, plastered like walls – a staircase to nowhere.

He started up, although his footfall on the triangular grate of each step caused the metal to creak. Stopping at the barricade where the opening should have been, he touched it and then pushed to check its strength. It was as firm and tight as the day it had been constructed.

He put his ear to the plasterboard. There was a whispery sound, like the wind had found a gap in the building and was flowing through the upstairs rooms, forming words, softly like prayers. He thought he heard his name.

And... *crying.*

Sam pulled away, feeling ridiculous. What was he thinking – that Sophie's ghost was wandering around in there? That she was sad and lost, calling to him from an unearthly realm?

He went back to bed.

Sophie was gone. And there was nothing left of her.

FOUR

Patient is a police officer seeking counsel. She presents as neatly dressed and is quite articulate. She indicates symptoms of depression: crying, despondency and despair regarding the decline of her marriage. She has searched for explanations inside herself and also by talking to friends, but this has not brought her any relief or insight. She has not consulted her husband in regard to her feelings or fears. She is unaware if he has similar concerns.

Plan: patient to commence a diary for future in-session examination. For now, medication has been deferred.

G. Whittaker

Sam had left Alice Lacey in the waiting room. He'd been trying to reach Richard on the mobile for the last ten minutes.

Leah stood in the office doorway, wringing her hands.

'Honestly, Sam, I don't know anything about Alice Lacey being reallocated to another psychiatrist,' she said, keeping her voice down. 'Richard never mentioned anything to me.'

'He's not answering his mobile.'

'Same for me. He might be in a meeting.'

'Keep trying. And when you get him, put the call through. Or if he comes in. Either way, I need to speak to him urgently.'

She nodded. 'Should I send Alice in anyway?'

He groaned and rubbed his forehead.

'Sam?'

'Um… okay. Send her in.'

He didn't stand when Alice entered; he remained at his desk, examining her, deciding what to do.

She hesitated on the threshold as Leah closed the door behind her.

'Have a seat,' Sam said, indicating the consultation chairs in the centre of the room.

She took a deep breath and moved forward.

Today she was wearing a blue cheesecloth dress with a denim jacket and lots of beads. Her hair was drawn into a high ponytail, accentuating the darker roots. She didn't appear to be wearing makeup, apart from a soft pink on her lips.

Sam brought her file over and sat in the opposite armchair. 'I'm sorry to have kept you waiting, but there's been a bit of a mix-up.'

She blinked rapidly. 'But this is my appointment… Friday.'

'Yes, but I'm not your doctor.'

'What?'

'I'm sorry, but since Dr Whittaker's death, all his patients have had to be reallocated. And even though I saw you last week, it wasn't—'

'But I like you,' she interrupted. 'No. I'm not going to be messed around, pushed from one doctor to the next.'

Sam was surprised by her outburst. 'It's nothing that won't be done without your best interests at heart.'

'I'll decide what my own best interests are.'

He didn't want to upset her. He'd already been down that arduous road with her last week. 'Try not to worry about it.'

'Too late for that.' She stood, grabbed her handbag. 'We may as well forget the whole thing.'

He could see her tears and was annoyed with himself.

'Don't go.' He also stood, held out his hand.

'It's hard enough summoning the will to get in here, let alone being turned away.'

'I'm not turning you away. I just don't want to lie to you – make you believe I'm going to be your doctor when that's not the case. But if you'll take a seat, there are a few things we still need to go over.'

'I hardly see the point.'

'Please, Alice.'

She sat with a reluctance that stiffened through her shoulders. Sam settled back in his chair and took up the notes. This hadn't been his intention, to make something of a session out it. But he was forced by her reaction and his insistence that she should stay.

He cleared his throat. 'Now, what medication are you on? I can write you up a fresh prescription if you need it.'

'I'm not on anything.'

'Didn't your GP start you on antidepressants?'

'I don't want to take any.' She folded her arms defensively, as if she'd had this argument before.

It would be remiss of him not to say anything. 'Why not?'

'I don't like drugs.'

'Medication.'

'What?'

'Medication. Not drugs.'

'Please, you're wasting your breath. I've done my research and I won't be swallowing any mind-altering pills. Dr Whittaker was aware of this. And now so are you.' She added sarcastically, 'For all the good that's going to do me.'

Sam let it go. Her next doctor could take it up with her. There was nothing else he needed to cover, but he could hardly push her out the door either. He stared at her, the moment becoming a little awkward when the silence went on too long.

Finally, he said, 'So, how are you finding Sydney?'

'It's pointless making small talk, don't you think?'

'I'm interested.'

'No you're not. You're being polite. There's no need.' She stood and this time she meant to leave. Sam didn't try to stop her. After she closed the door behind her, he leant forward in his chair and rubbed the back of his neck. He hadn't handled that well at all. But he wouldn't deny his relief at her leaving.

After the last patient of the day Sam returned the files to Leah at reception. He was making a final notation on one of them, aware that the young secretary was staring at him from across the counter.

She gasped. 'Oh, I nearly forgot, Richard finally got back to me. He's not coming in.'

Sam looked up sharply from the papers. 'When did he say this? Why didn't you put him through to me?'

'You were with a patient and he said not to bother you.'

'I gave you specific instructions.'

'Sam, I can hardly go against Richard. He said he'd see you tonight anyway at my housewarming.'

'Housewarming?'

She pouted and twisted on her swivel chair. 'I told you about it weeks ago. Tonight at seven.'

He vaguely remembered the conversation. He'd never had any intention to go.

'I've got a couple of nice red wines for you,' she added with a hopeful smile. 'Richard said you like red wine.'

*

Sam let himself into Leah's house shortly after nine o'clock. The television in the corner was blaring, and a total of four people sat squashed on the lounge staring at him as if he'd just walked into the wrong house.

Leah came into the room and nearly leapt on him.

'Sam, you made it. I was starting to get worried.'

She linked her arm through his, turned him towards the centre of the room and made an introduction – then steered him out to the kitchen where bottles of alcohol were set up on the bench.

'Do you live here alone?' Sam asked as she handed him a glass of red wine.

'Gosh no. I'd never be able to afford this place on the wage Richard pays me.' She giggled and seemed to wait for his response.

He didn't say anything.

She went on. 'I'm here with my brother and his wife. This is their place. But they travel a lot. So I often have run of the house – just take care of the cat for them and keep the place tidy.'

She smiled and flicked the gold chain at her neck. 'Don't you recognise it?' she asked.

Sam frowned.

'It's the locket you gave me for Christmas.'

'I gave you a locket?'

'Well, it was from everyone at work. I wear it all the time.'

One of the female guests came and asked Leah if she could show her where the bathroom was. While she was distracted, Sam stepped outside onto the rear deck. The first thing he noticed was the open view down to the Georges River. Sprinkles of residential lights outlined the foreshore on both sides of it. Shadows of moored cruisers rolled gently on the blackened waters. Sam put his glass down on a small metal table and went to the railing, and leaning over it caught a waft of brine.

'Good to see you finally out of the office. I was beginning to think you were fused to your desk.' Richard slapped Sam hard on the shoulder as he came to stand beside him at the railing. 'Well, how's that for an impressive view. Looks like Leah's landed on her feet.'

Sam straightened. 'Where the hell were you today?'

'What is that sinus clearing smell?'

'I got stuck with Alice Lacey. You told me you'd reallocate her.'

'I said I'd look into it. And I did that, but I can't place her anywhere else.'

'Then *you* take her.'

Richard almost laughed. 'Me? Nobody wants to be treated by me. I'm better off with the paperwork.'

'You still practise. You've got clients.'

'A few old fogies who've been coming to me for years. I'm not in touch like I used to be. You know that.'

'Well I don't care what you do with her. But she's off my books.' Sam turned back to the view, making it clear that the matter was now at an end.

Richard grunted and went to walk away, but seemed to change his mind. 'What's the matter with you?' he snapped, pointing his finger at Sam. 'Alice is not Sophie. She's just someone who needs help.'

Sam stepped up as though there was a challenge, knocking Richard's hand aside.

But his colleague wasn't backing down. 'You're so uptight. You don't allow any chance for feeling, and I mean proper feeling – not this pompous indignation you choose to hide behind. It might serve you well in your doctor's chair, but it's not a shovel to bury the past. And at some point you have to face it. I thought I was actually doing you a favour. One cop. Just *one* cop.'

'Who are you trying to cure here, Richard?'

Leah shoved her way between the two men as though she were a referee in a boxing match.

Richard grunted again, much louder, before walking off.

'What was that all about?' she asked.

'Nothing.'

Sam turned back to the railing and stared out at the dark waters but his mind was filled with Richard's accusations. It was true; he *did* hide behind a facade of professionalism; he *did* suppress his emotions. But what his colleague needed to understand was that it kept him sane, in control – and it gave him a reason to go on. For a while, after Sophie died, he'd stayed with his sister and brother-in-law in Queensland. He was a drunken mess for almost a year. Then one day the booze ran out, so he went down to the ocean and tried to drown himself – except he couldn't even get that right. But he'd made a decision. If he had to live with this then it would be on *his* terms and *his* only.

Leah didn't seem to mind his silence. She leant against him now, her perfume coming into his senses. It reminded him how much he hadn't had a woman around him in the years since Sophie was gone.

Four years. Four *long* years of this macabre, silent grieving.

He looked at Leah. She was reasonably attractive with dark shoulder length hair and some highlights he hadn't noticed until now.

She smiled lightly, the breeze catching a few strands of hair that lifted and danced around her face. She made no attempt to move them. He did it for her, eventually tilting her chin with his fingers.

And he kissed her. She tasted faintly of toothpaste.

When he was done, her head dropped back like she no longer had control of it. 'Oh, Sam,' she breathed. 'You don't know how long I've waited for this moment.'

Her reaction bothered him. He'd made a decision to sleep with her but now he knew it wouldn't be tonight. Maybe never.

'I'm going to head off,' he said.

Leah halted her dreamy expression. 'But you just got here.'

'I only came to talk to Richard.'

Her bottom lip quivered. 'Is that all?'

He forced a half smile and lightly pinched her chin before dropping a quick kiss on her nose.

'The rest was a nice surprise.' He wasn't sure he meant it. But it made his retreat easier.

Her tears splashed down onto his hand. 'Oh, look at me. I'm as bad as the cop. She was bawling at the counter today after she saw you. Any wonder you want rid of her.'

Sam shifted uneasily, shoving his hands into his trouser pockets. 'Bawling?'

'She wasn't sure whether she was supposed to book for you or someone else.'

He let out a heavy breath, released his hands. Somehow he'd made two women cry today.

'So what did you do?' he asked.

'I put her down for next week with you. Was that right? You were on the phone so I couldn't ask.'

'It can be worked out later.'

He touched Leah's arm and made his farewell, passing Richard on his way to the front door.

'I've sorted it,' the older man called sharply to Sam, pocketing his phone. 'Cranston's going to take your cop.'

Sam nodded and kept walking.

*

The next morning Sam followed the footpath north from the rocky coastline to the pale sands at Wanda. Normally, walking on the beach was therapeutic. But he'd drunk too much wine when he'd got home from Leah's last night and his hangover was making sure he remembered the reason why.

A fitness group charged past him, kicking up sand in their wake. He veered down to the shoreline where he stopped and looked out to sea. In the distance, white caps rose like peaks of meringue as the wind picked up, carrying the salty spray to his lips. An albatross hung in the sky and Sam watched it as it drifted on the slipstream – then with wide wings it tilted and swooped low before heading north.

As Sam's gaze dropped back to the shore, he saw her in the distance – Alice Lacey. He remembered she lived nearby. Her head was bowed as she sat hugging her knees – a sad and lonely figure.

He watched her for a while, trying to shake off his guilt, the reason he'd drowned his sorrows last night. There was nothing he could do, he told himself. She was a police officer and he'd come too far to risk the distraction. Cranston was her doctor now. That was the end of it.

He left the beach, building to a swifter pace. But the notion of Cranston taking over Alice's matter continued to trouble him. She had been in good hands with Glenn.

But Glenn was gone.

Sam groaned, frustrated by the turn of his thoughts.

He couldn't backpedal now; it was too risky. But damn it, Cranston Jones, of all the psychiatrists Alice should end up with. The man didn't exactly endear himself to clients with his scarecrow features and whiny voice. And he'd do a lousy job of pretending not to look down Alice's blouse during the sessions.

It's not my problem.

The house loomed from the top of the T-intersection like it was getting ready to digest him as soon as he came through the door. For the moment he tried to imagine it ablaze, razed to the foundations, nothing left but the mangled spiral staircase. That would solve a few problems. A new house in a new location. Maybe an apartment so he wouldn't have to bother with lawns.

His thoughts returned to Alice. Why on earth did she pick Sydney to move to? She could have escaped to anywhere else in New South Wales. But Sydney with its crime and pollution and unfriendly population? There was nobody here for her. Nobody now except Cranston Jones.

Damn.

There were several missed calls from Leah on the home phone when Sam got in. He listened to the recorded messages. Her voice sounded as if it had been dipped in sugar as she invited him first for coffee, then to the movies, and finally for a stroll. She rang twice more, this time on his mobile phone, and Sam decided on the last call to put them both out of their misery.

'Leah, you're very sweet, but we have to work together. It would make things awkward if we started anything.'

'But you kissed me last night.'

'And I'm sorry, I shouldn't have done that.'

'Well I'm not sorry,' she said sulkily. 'And nor should you be. Forget about work. We shouldn't allow something as silly as that to get in the way of how we feel about each other.'

Irritated, he tapped the phone against his forehead. It seemed to reignite his hangover.

'I'm trying to be practical,' he said. 'I'm not looking for a long-term relationship with anyone. And I don't want to drag you along in some casual arrangement either, not when we have to face each other Monday to Friday.'

'Maybe casual suits me too.'

He doubted it. 'It would only complicate things.'

When he hung up he felt bad for being so cold towards her. But it had to be kinder than giving her false hope. He shouldn't have kissed her last night and he wasn't really sure why he had now. Maybe it had been Richard's accusation that he had no proper feeling.

Or maybe it was simply because he'd wanted to feel a woman in his arms again.

FIVE

Unmanageable crying at the start of session. Patient indicates feelings of loneliness and abandonment. Distress during interpersonal conflicts has caused her confused and scattered emotions. There is a sense of subterfuge which she appears unwilling to discuss. This may be relieved in later sessions. For now, she has begun supplying her diary notes in loose-leaf form so she can continue writing, but at this stage therapeutical discussion of the notes has been suspended.

Plan: continue fortnightly sessions. Treatment remains supportive.

G. Whittaker

Even though Sam assured Alice she was going to stay under his care, she eyed him cautiously.

'I didn't say anything – well, it wasn't to make trouble,' she said. 'I mentioned to your receptionist last week that I wasn't sure what was happening. If it came out that I was complaining…'

'No, it was nothing like that. Things were up in the air with Dr Whittaker's patients still being divided, and I didn't want to mislead you at the time. But it's all sorted now.'

Her smile seemed one of relief. She had even teeth except for the slight overlap of an eye-tooth. Sam wondered if she'd been the sort of kid who'd worn braces. She bit onto her lower lip, reminding him that he was staring.

He cleared his throat, took up the notepad and clicked on his pen. 'Now, let's talk about your therapy.'

She seemed to sink into her seat, twisting one of the charms on her bracelet.

'Nothing to get upset about,' he added. 'I promise it won't involve thumb screws or stretching racks.' His joke fell flat. 'Whatever we do, Alice, it will all be with your full knowledge and approval. No surprises.'

Sam was aware that after all the messing around, he needed to build her trust, not distress her unnecessarily. As her doctor, her wellbeing was paramount.

Her doctor. Well, maybe it wouldn't turn out to be so bad.

'Time to face your demons?' Richard had asked when Sam told him earlier in the week that he'd decided to keep Alice on his books.

'It was the thought of Cranston taking her on.'

'I agree he doesn't have the same bedside manner as you. And staring at his ugly dial every week, she might have lost the will.'

'Well, it's done now.' He'd paused and then followed through with an apology for his earlier behaviour, but Richard waved it off.

'You're a good bloke, Sam. I don't blame you for baulking at the prospect of dealing with a cop. But unfortunately it's a growing concern. Someone's got to look after the poor souls.'

'As long as you don't expect me to take on the same load as Glenn. I don't want to specialise in police.'

Richard had looked as if he'd wanted to say more, but Sam gave him no further opportunity.

Right now, Alice was getting worked up. It had been since the mention of therapy.

'I'll guide you through the process,' Sam said calmly. 'We'll be going at a slow and steady pace. Nothing accelerated in my methods.'

'What will it involve?'

'Some psychotherapy to address your symptoms. And eventually exposure therapy. The aim is to get you talking about the train crash.' Noting the rise of tension in her demeanour, he said, 'So, tell me about your hobbies.'

She pursed her lips and leant forward slightly. 'Are we back to small talk?'

He smiled. 'We need to get you involved in something. You'd have to admit that sitting around at home all day on your own isn't good. And it will help, believe me, if you can get out and socialise with others.'

She sat back and sighed. 'I used to be interested in things. Not anymore.'

'Tell me some of them.' He repositioned the notepad on his knee and tested his pen in the corner of the page.

'Nothing to tell.' She became thoughtful as he watched her. 'Nothing relevant, anyway.'

'How about you take the time to think on it. And we can discuss it in our next session. Writing a few things down might help.'

'Write it down. You sound like Dr Whittaker.' She went to smile but seemed to think better of it. 'Sorry,' she added. 'I didn't mean that to come out the way it did. It's a good idea, but I'm not much of a writer. Not about myself, anyway.'

'A list will be fine. We can look at it next time.'

He picked up her file from the table in front and flipped through some pages. He really needed to go through this properly. There was a notation by Glenn about recurring nightmares. Sam asked Alice about them.

'I'm always being chased, but I can't see who it is. All I know is they have a gun.'

Sam knew how that went. Guns featured prominently in *his* sleep. 'How often do you experience these nightmares?'

'Most nights. I stay up as late as possible to avoid sleep. It's like *Nightmare on Elm Street* – except Freddy Krueger without a face.'

They went over the allocated hour, but Sam had needed to catch up. He'd keep her on weeklies for the same reason. He stood and walked with her to the reception counter and told Leah to book every Friday for Alice from now on.

Leah's eyes widened.

'What's the deal with Alice Lacey then?' she said to him at the end of the day. 'I thought you wanted rid of her.'

'Change of plan.'

He made some final notes in the last patient's file while Leah leant across the reception counter. He could smell her strong perfume. It was different to Alice's. He was surprised that he could even tell that.

The session with Alice had gone better than expected and had proven he could handle it. Maybe he would take on more police in time. And where better to start than with a gentle, lonely soul. Richard was right. Sam had let the whole cop issue get in the way, consume him. He had to step out from behind that shadow now. Really move on with his life. The decision made him feel good.

'What are you smiling at, Sam?'

He looked up from his papers at Leah, surprised by her comment.

'You fancy a meal tonight?' she almost blurted out.

Without knowing why, he said, 'Would you like that?'

She seemed to stumble on the spot. 'Oh yes,' she answered at the same time. 'I'd like that *very* much.'

*

Leah was waiting at the front of her Sylvania Heights house, shivering against the southerly that had whipped up in the last hour, chilling the late-March air. Sam thought she was a little formal in a tight black dress, her hair swept high. He'd opted for jeans.

'Wow, such a gentleman,' she said when he came around to open the passenger door of the BMW. 'I could get used to this.'

'I'm just thinking, dressed like that, maybe I ought to be taking you to the theatre.'

Her smile grew larger. 'We should arrange that for next time.'

He took her to an Italian restaurant in Brighton with a nice view over the bay. They ordered their meal and the waiter recommended a sangiovese to wash it down.

'So, what kind of music do you like?' Leah said after a minute of awkward silence.

Sam shrugged. 'I don't really listen to music.'

'Everyone likes music, Sam.' She started to rattle off a list of bands and performers she favoured; most he'd never heard of before.

'What about movies?' she urged enthusiastically.

He knew he should offer her something. 'Foreign films are all right.'

'*Foreign films*,' she said as though he'd disappointed her. 'But it's another language and you have to read the subtitles.' She sulked as her fingers found the base of her wine glass. 'Well, do you want to hear my favourite films?'

'Sure,' he said, but her voice became a background drone as he watched the planes take off and land on the bay runway. Maybe he could spare a week and head north, stay with Julia and Paul at their bed and breakfast. His sister hadn't emailed him in a while, but she was probably tired of making the offer.

'So, what do you think about a movie night?' Leah interlaced her fingers – red varnish on stubby nails. 'We could do it at your place or mine. I'll provide the chips and dips.'

Sam realised he should have stuck to his original resolve not to get involved with the office secretary. He'd fended her off for the last six months. Now he was just digging a bigger hole. They really had nothing in common. He tried to perk up, for her sake, but steered the conversation away from another get together.

During the drive home Leah put her hand on his knee.

'Do you want to come in for coffee?' she asked when he pulled up outside her house.

'I better not. I've got some uni essays to mark this weekend. Need to make an early start.' It was a lousy excuse and he knew he could have done better.

'I didn't know you lectured.'

'It's just for this semester. Finishing it up for Glenn.'

'Is it any wonder that man had a heart attack.' She didn't make a move to get out. Instead, she tapped his knee. 'We could catch up after you finish with your essays. I could come over.'

'I'm a grumpy bastard after reading the shit students write.'

She leant across the car but he got out and came around to her side. She took his hand as he walked her to the house. On the first step of the porch she turned back and kissed his cheek, her mouth lingering at his ear.

'Archie and Anne are away this weekend,' she said a little breathlessly. 'Are you sure you don't want to come in?'

Sam had no doubt where the rest of the evening would go. All he had to do was walk inside with her and break the four-year drought. But it was the consequences that held him back. Sex with Leah was never going to equate to casual, despite what she'd said to him last week. She was after a relationship.

He wished her goodnight.

Not bothering to hide her disappointment, she tightened her lips, stamped her foot, and then slammed the screen door so hard behind her it shuddered.

*

Richard rang in the early hours of the following morning.

'Sorry about this, Sam, but I just got a call from the cops. Apparently one of your patients is threatening to do a high-dive act without a net from his apartment block.'

'Who is it?'

'Three tours of Afghanistan.'

'Minh Luong.'

'That's him.'

Sam sat up in bed and rubbed his brow. 'What's the story?'

'Well, he's been asking for you. Had a fight with his missus and wants to end it all. I don't know, huge problem this post-traumatic-stress business. Our soldiers, our cops. Makes you wonder what kind of world we've created. Wars overseas, on our streets. There's no getting away from it, no solution either. The things they've seen... and here I was whingeing last night about the Dragons first game of the season, like it was the end of the world when they lost—'

'Shut up and give me the address.'

Rain fell on the dark, deserted city streets. Sam parked behind a police car, trying not to let his mind wander back in time. A young uniformed constable queried his presence and then directed him into the forty-storey building.

There were several more police officers in the foyer and one of them spoke into a microphone attached to his lapel. A minute later a thickset man in a bad suit stepped out of a lift. Sam recognised him. Detective Sergeant McGuire, or Mac to his friends, he'd worked with Sophie in the southern suburbs.

An image of the past flashed into Sam's mind, of the police-station Christmas party just over four years ago; Sophie yelling at Mac to keep his hands off her; Sam asking what the hell was going on and Sophie telling him it was nothing, just a work thing. He'd known better at the time but he hadn't pushed it because she'd begged him not to make a scene.

'So, *you're* his doctor,' the detective sergeant said, scowling.

'It would seem that way,' Sam replied in the same tone.

'He's on the fifth floor with one leg over the balcony railing. You trained up in negotiation or what?'

'Yes. But I'll need more information before I go up and speak with him.'

The detective led Sam into the lift, and the two men stuck to opposite sides during the slow ascent to the fifth floor.

'Minh Luong – twenty-nine years of age.' McGuire said it as if he were bored. 'His wife tried to leave him tonight and take the dog with her. I'm not sure if he's more upset about the dog, or her. Maybe it's because nobody can pronounce his name. Who knows? But he's been posed over the railing for the last couple of hours. He's more than likely *tired*. So you might want to take that into consideration when you talk to him.'

Sam bit down on the inside of his mouth and tasted blood.

The detective seemed to be watching him for a reaction. 'How long has he been seeing you, Dr Wilde?'

Sam didn't correct the detective's error. Sophie had kept her maiden name.

'I'm not sure. I'd have to look at his file.'

'What, you don't know?' It came out as a criticism.

'Less than three years, more than six months. Hope that helps,' Sam said, not bothering to disguise the sarcasm.

McGuire grunted but said nothing more.

The lift door pinged and opened. Sam was shown to the apartment where Minh Luong straddled the narrow balcony rail. He was directed to go no further than speaking distance to Minh, so he remained just back from the open balcony door. A small group of uniformed police officers stayed out of sight.

Despite Minh requesting Sam's presence, he clammed up and wouldn't speak. It remained a standoff with Sam trying to get at least a version of the events from Minh, something to open communication. He was acutely aware of what McGuire had told him too – several hours of hanging over the edge of the railing – add tiredness into the equation and there was potential for errors. He tried hard not to think of something going wrong. But it was inescapable. Right now the responsibility for Minh's wellbeing lay solely with Sam.

Damn, he wished he hadn't come.

After a while Sam risked moving closer into the opening of the balcony where he was in arm's reach of the young man. He hoped the cops wouldn't haul him back. Leaning on the door frame, he drew on Richard's words from the morning call. 'Disappointing first season game for the Dragons. Did you watch it?'

Again, no response.

Sam could tell Minh was getting worked up, looking over the edge at the roadway below, sucking in air as though filling his lungs before a deep-sea dive.

This is bad, Sam thought, feeling the heat of panic sting at the back of his neck.

'Minh, you asked for me to come here. Why don't you move over properly onto this side of the balcony so we can talk.'

The young soldier shook his head, dribbling spots of rain from the ends of his black hair. 'I'm done talking this time.' He turned glazed eyes towards Sam. 'I just wanted you here so you could be the one to tell Cara...' He slowly shook his head again. 'You know how it is, the way I am. But I just can't live without her. Could you tell her, Doc? Tell her I'm sorry, that I never meant to hurt her.'

'Come back over, talk to Cara.'

'No. It's better this way...'

Minh let go of the railing and opened his arms wide. As he leant into the moist night air, Sam yelled and lunged forward, grabbing for the young soldier. His hip jammed hard against Minh's leg on the right side of the balcony, but the momentum of their upper bodies began to draw both men over the edge.

In a flash, three or four police officers had hold of Sam. Working together they helped him drag Minh, kicking and screaming, back onto the balcony. They all fell through the open doorway of the apartment, landing in a heap on the carpet. The officers wrestled the soldier onto his stomach and handcuffed him.

Sam was out of breath. For the next five minutes he sat where he'd landed, wondering at the foolishness of his actions. But God, he couldn't have let Minh go. It had been close. So close.

On the way out McGuire stopped him. 'Hey, I didn't really think he was that serious.'

'Dangling over a balcony? It looked serious to me.'

'Yeah, but five floors up? If he'd have meant it, he'd have gone to the roof.'

'It would have been the same result,' Sam said, unimpressed. 'Just get him to hospital. And get them to take the handcuffs off him. He's not a prisoner. I'll be in to see him through the week.'

McGuire huffed.

Sam walked on, left the building and headed for his car. Except it wasn't there. He went back inside and spoke to a constable who told him it had been towed.

'Towed?' Sam was outraged.

'It's a police-vehicle-only zone out there,' the constable said, not making eye contact with Sam.

'At four in the morning? It wasn't in the way. You knew it was my car. Why didn't you stop them?'

McGuire was staring at Sam from nearby. 'Lose something did you, Doctor?'

'My car. It's been towed.'

'Where was it?'

'Parked outside behind one of your police cars.'

'Well, see, there's your problem. Police vehicles only.' McGuire made an exaggerated gasp. 'You're not suggesting that we had your car towed on purpose?'

'This is bullshit,' Sam snapped.

McGuire stepped up to him. 'You better watch your language, Doc. There are families in this building.'

Sam met the challenge. 'You did it on purpose.'

'Yeah, well good luck proving it.'

'You're going to pay for this.'

'See you in court.'

It was all Sam could do to pull himself away. He stepped out into the rain but then wondered what the hell he was supposed to do now without a car. He turned to go back and confront McGuire again, but the detective sergeant had beaten him to it. The two men sized up to each other on the pavement as the rain started to fall harder. Sam was two inches taller, but McGuire was broader and heavier.

'You're a piece of scum, Tyler.'

'So now you remember my name.'

'I remember every fucking pathetic detail about you. And most of all I remember what you *did*. You don't know how lucky you were just now with that bloke on the balcony. If he'd have gone over, you'd have had more blood on your hands.'

'You would have enjoyed that, wouldn't you? Or maybe you were hoping he'd take me with him.'

Mac raised his fist. Sam half wished he'd swing at him – he'd like to put this lump of meat on his arse, like he should have done years ago.

'I wouldn't have been that lucky,' McGuire spat. 'Hell, the only inconvenience would have been the double paperwork. But I reckon I'd have been cheering anyway.'

Sam could no longer contain his anger. He shoved the stocky man with both hands and was surprised when he didn't retaliate. McGuire dropped his fist and rolled his shoulders as though to settle himself.

'Won't give you the pleasure,' the detective sergeant said, and backed away.

Sam moved off before he did something he'd really regret. He pulled the collar up on his jacket and shoved his hands into the pockets.

How on earth was he supposed to get a taxi? It was dark and pelting down. But as he turned the corner he saw his car. It had only been moved, not completely towed away.

Fuck you, McGuire.

SIX

Sam struggled to break free. Four or five police officers were grappling with him, shouting, pulling his arms behind his back. It was happening so slowly. His legs, which felt as if they were filled with lead weights, betrayed him as he tried to run. Somehow he got one arm free, swung it and hit an officer in the face with the back of his knuckles.

'Where's Sophie? Oh God, what have I done?' He managed a few steps before they took him down. He hit the ground hard. They hauled him to his feet, an officer on each arm. McGuire was in his face.

'Payback,' the detective said before stepping aside.

Sophie was there with the shotgun, raised and pointed at Sam's chest.

'No!' he screamed.

She pulled the trigger.

Sam woke and bolted so far forward on the bed he was up on his knees, clutching at the gaping hole in his chest, blood pumping through his fingers. Gasping and yelling, he staggered to the bathroom and hit the light switch.

There was no blood. His body was wet only with perspiration.

He sank against the cold tiled wall.

'Christ almighty,' he moaned, putting his head into his hands.

The pill bottle was empty. He went back to the bedroom and rummaged through the jackets in the wardrobe until he found the sample pack he'd pocketed from work. It was enough for ten days, a fortnight if he went easy. Glenn Whittaker had prescribed the antidepressants for him – without counsel or consultation. Glenn had understood. It wasn't as if Sam could write his own prescriptions now. These things were monitored, recorded on a central database.

I just need to get through this.

*

Alice was ten minutes late for her appointment on Friday. Her cheeks were tinged with pink when she finally came in, and she was slightly out of breath.

'I'm so sorry,' she said, falling into the usual client chair. 'I hate public transport. Three different buses and road works. I thought I'd never get here.'

Sam remembered the notation in Alice's file about an aversion to train travel since the Bellingen accident. It would be something to explore later in therapy.

He undid the button on his jacket, smoothed his tie and sat down. They began by talking about her symptoms of depression.

'I'm crying a lot at home,' she admitted, fidgeting with a charm on her bracelet.

'What are your strategies for dealing with it?'

She shrugged. 'Isn't that what I'm here for? Aren't you going to tell me what to do?' He waited, and then she added with a sigh, 'Well, I tend to sit in the dark, curl into a ball and hope Freddy Krueger can't see me.'

'Why do you choose the dark?'

'I don't know that I *choose* the dark. It just gets dark after a while and I don't bother to turn the light on.'

Sam discovered that her support network was practically non-existent. She didn't like to trouble her parents on the other side of the country in Perth. Her brother was over there too, married with kids. But they hardly spoke. Sam talked to her about simple strategies to help deal with the depression, the tears, and the nightmares. She smirked at the suggestion of meditation, but nodded to beach walks.

'And from now on,' he added, 'turn a light on when it gets dark. It will give you perspective.'

When the session finished he stood and shook her hand. Her skin was soft, the bone structure finely sculptured. She had the hands of a lady, not someone who'd dealt with drunks and drug addicts.

He walked her to reception. 'See you next week, Alice.'

'Thank you, Doctor.'

He watched as she stepped into the lift, and caught her faint smile as the door closed.

Leah was staring at him. He ignored her and called in the next patient.

Richard came to see him at the end of the day. 'How's it going?' he said, slumping into the chair on the other side of the desk.

Sam's eyes narrowed. 'What is it?'

'Why does there have to be something other than me popping in to see how you are?' Richard rolled his knuckles on the desk. 'Well, there is that conference in the Blue Mountains next month that Glenn was supposed to do. We have to send someone. Glenn was signed up to do a lecture about PTSD and police...'

'No.'

'... and I half nominated you to go in his place.'

'I said no.'

'I'd rather you do it ahead of anyone else – you've got the right kind of... let's say, *poise*. And it will be easy because Glenn wrote the lecture before he died. You'd just have to read his notes.'

'Find someone else. I don't do conferences and I certainly don't do lectures about police.'

Richard grunted and held up his hands. 'You don't have to give me an answer now. Think about it.' He went to stand but changed his mind. 'Hey, a little birdie told me you've been dating.'

'A little birdie by the name of Leah?' Sam said apathetically.

'She's a nice girl. Took you long enough to get around to asking her out. All this mystery around you.' Richard waved one hand as though conjuring a spell. 'But maybe that's the appeal.'

Sam closed his laptop. 'I wouldn't say we're dating. We only went out once, just a meal at the Italian down on the bay.'

Richard gave an approving wink. 'So, how was it?'

'The food's always good there.'

'You know what I mean. Come on, amuse me. Lie if you have to.'

Sam let out a bored breath. 'We ate and I dropped her home. An hour and a half tops. That's it.'

'That's it? Doesn't even sound like you were trying.'

'It was impromptu. I'm not sure we'll be doing it again.'

Richard rolled his chair in closer to the desk and leant across. 'Don't you think you've done your penance? It's time you got back out there in the real world. And Leah isn't a bad sort. She's keen, that's for sure.'

'We don't have anything in common. The conversation the other night was flat.'

'Why, was she on the wrong side of Nietzsche and the philosophy of existentialism? Or did she pronounce his name wrong?' Richard sat back, hooked his foot across his knee. 'Come on, you can't tell by one date. Give it another go. She'd be good for you – drag you out of the doldrums.'

'She's very attractive.'

'But?'

'Do you really wish that on her, to get tied up with me? I'm only good sitting behind this desk. Socially, I'm a pariah. She's young and she could do a whole lot better than some old diehard psychiatrist who lives for his work.'

'So, you're Methuselah now.'

'I don't want to hurt her.'

'Then don't.'

At that moment Leah walked in and the two men fumbled at the desk: Sam opening his laptop and Richard picking up papers, pretending interest in them.

She hesitated for a moment. 'I was just seeing if you'd finished with those files, Sam. I was going to put them away.'

'It's fine. You can go home. I'll sort the files.'

'You're not working back are you?' Richard said, discarding the papers and staring at his colleague.

'I've got a pile of reports to get through.'

'But it's Friday night. You two ought to go out and have fun. You do know the meaning of the word *fun*, don't you, Sam?' Richard stood. 'Come in early Monday and get the reports done then, if you must. But don't waste your weekend.'

Sam heard his colleague click his tongue at Leah as he passed her in the doorway. He turned and gave Sam another wink before he left.

Leah was grinning. 'I know a great steakhouse two blocks away. Did you want to go home and get changed? Or should we go from here?'

'I really should get this work done.'

'Oh Sam, come on. It's Friday night. Those reports will keep.'

She sauntered to his desk and sat on the edge. Her skirt rode up slightly to reveal long legs beneath silky stockings. It was hard not to imagine them wrapped around him.

'Well, I suppose I could come in early on Monday...'

*

The steakhouse Leah took him to had an inane outback theme that didn't belong in the city. Sam wanted to say something, suggest a different venue, but was reminded of Richard's Nietzsche comment. He wondered if that was how he really came across – as some pompous elitist. It wouldn't be the first time he'd been accused of it. Sophie had told him more than once to get his head out of his backside and try acting a little human. He'd never considered his wife anything less than his match, but her colleagues had left much to be desired with their substandard and often bigoted view of the world. Most of the time he'd found it intolerable – the exceptions being Maria and Rob, who at least were willing to remind him of his foibles without making exceptions for theirs.

In fairness, he'd only really seen Leah in a subordinate role behind the reception counter. It said nothing for her personality or prospective charms; he need only give her the opportunity to show herself. And she seemed more than keen to do so.

After the meal, Leah urged him into a nearby nightclub where he paid outrageous prices at the bar for drinks. He refused to dance and sat at a corner table while she gyrated and twirled in front of him.

The repetitious thump of the music and spin of red disco lights began to disturb Sam. It made everyone look as if they were covered in blood.

Leah was swathed in the red glow as she glided closer towards him, her hands moving slowly over her breasts and down to her pelvis.

An unwanted memory invaded his thoughts: speeding through the darkened streets of Sydney following the stream of lights and sirens. And the scene that awaited him...

He got up, pushed past Leah and went into the men's room where he splashed cold water on his face and swore at his enervation. It took him a few minutes to pull himself together.

Come on, buddy. You're getting laid tonight.

'You okay?' Leah asked when he returned.

He downed his drink. 'Yeah. Let's go.'

They got a taxi to her house. 'It looks like Archie and Anne have already gone to bed,' she said.

'They won't mind you bringing me in?'

'What they don't know won't hurt them.' She giggled, dropping her keys. Sam retrieved them, took over the door.

'Besides, you're not just anyone,' Leah continued, hanging onto his arm while he tried to find the right key for the lock. 'You're Dr Samuel Tyler – master and commander, man of my dreams.'

He knew the comment ought to worry him, but there was only one thing on his mind.

'My room's at the end of the house,' she whispered as they went inside.

He followed her down a dimly lit hall. There were a few pictures on one side of the wall: a wedding, some glamour shots of a round-faced woman with curly hair, an amateur attempt at a painted landscape, another of a homestead.

Leah opened the last door on the right and flicked a switch on the wall that turned on a bedside lamp. The room was cramped, the bed too big for the space. Plush toys were gathered on the pillows and atop a cupboard, while there was a whole corner unit dedicated to dolls.

Sam baulked, stayed in the doorway. Maybe this wasn't such a good idea.

She started to peel off her clothes.

He came into the room, closed the door behind him; threw aside his jacket, stepped out of his shoes, dropped his trousers and pulled his shirt over his head. Impatient with Leah's attempt at a slow striptease, he hurried her along, removing her white laced camisole, and then fumbled with the clip at the back of her bra.

They fell onto the bed, hands everywhere, legs and feet pushing down the quilt cover, kicking away the plush toys.

'Kill the light,' he told her, the eyes of a hundred dolls on him.

She swung her hand to the side, feeling for the bedside lamp, but only managed to knock it over. It fell to the floor, dulled the room, turned everything to shadows.

Sam slipped his boxers off while he kissed her. He was ready for her, wondered if he would last if she insisted on foreplay. As if sensing his eagerness she opened to him.

He ignored her moans and inflated gasps. She arched and writhed, twisting her legs around him like a boa constrictor.

After it was done, he moved off her and rolled onto his back. She nestled against his shoulder, her fringe itching at his nose. He speculated at what in all decency would be an acceptable time to get up and leave. Not too long. He didn't want to risk falling asleep.

'How many children do you want?' Leah asked, stroking his chest.

'What?'

'Children. I'm thinking two. But I want boys. Girls are too much trouble. Unless *you* want a girl. I suppose I'd have to think about it then.'

'You've got to be kidding me.' He shifted away from her, started to sit up.

She reached for him but he pushed her hands aside.

'What's wrong?' she asked.

'Wrong? We've had sex once and you're talking babies. What is this all about?'

She sat up next to him, hugging her chest. 'Time isn't standing still for either of us, Sam. I'm twenty-seven, I don't want to be one of those old mums.'

He was off the bed and grabbing up his clothes in the muted light, furious.

'Come on, you *must* have thought about it,' she insisted. 'A son to carry on your name.'

'You don't know shit about any of it,' he snapped. 'The stupidity of this. For fuck sake, I was mad to come here.'

She scrabbled after him. 'Well, we don't have to talk about it now.'

'You honestly think I want something more with you?'

He zipped his trousers, threw his shirt on, shoved his socks, keys and wallet into his jacket pockets, stepped back into his shoes.

Leah began to cry. 'Stop. Don't go.' She grabbed a dressing gown from the back of the door and slipped it over her shoulders. 'Sam, I'm *really* sorry.'

'Not half as sorry as I'll be if you turn up pregnant. Is that what it is, you're trying to trap me? Have the boss doctor's baby and get a big lump of regular child support for the next eighteen years?'

'*No.*'

He left the silly, childish bedroom, muttering contempt at his folly. Almost immediately he was knocked sideways, crashing into the wall of the hallway.

'What the hell are you doing with my sister?' The shout was followed by several quick strikes to Sam's face.

He reacted by shoulder charging Leah's brother and the two men fell heavily onto the other wall, bringing down a picture frame. The glass smashed into shards on the timber floor.

'Archie, stop it,' Leah screamed.

Sam pulled the man up by his t-shirt and shoved him backwards before letting go. 'I was leaving anyway.'

He went out onto the street and could still hear Leah screaming until her brother told her to shut up and get inside.

A door slammed somewhere behind him. He spat blood and his right cheekbone burned with pain. He searched his pockets for his mobile phone, couldn't find it. Groaning at the realisation it must have fallen out in Leah's bedroom, he looked back at the house, but eventually decided it would be unwise to go knocking on the door to ask for it.

With no mobile phone and no chance of a taxi, he had a long walk ahead of him. Befitting punishment, he thought. But the battle had only just begun. It wasn't the walk or the physical stress on his body – it was the replay of memory that was damning, rolling through his mind like a tsunami. The fight with Sophie – four years ago, the last words they ever said to each other.

'You foul bitch, going behind my back. How could you Sophie?'

She held out an envelope to him, tears streaming down her cheeks. 'This is a future you can't run away from.'

'We have no future. You destroyed that when you cheated me.'

The memory seared Sam's mind as he trudged through the night – replayed over and over with all its torment. He was beleaguered with scene variations. In most of them he took the envelope and opened it. How different life might have been if he'd only done so – the strangeness of that fantasy, almost as though there were alternate versions of his life. But he was damned inside *this* reality, where he'd slapped Sophie's hand aside, the envelope fluttering to the floor as he'd turned his back on her.

It was after two in the morning when he reached the house. In the dark, he found the armchair, a hellish headache pounding through his temples. He removed his shoes, ripping blisters that he hadn't known were there, and swore in frustration.

He got up and shuffled to the bathroom cabinet. The pills were almost out again. Probably a good thing, he decided – nowhere near enough for an overdose. He didn't need to look in the mirror to know he was going to have a shiner, but there it was anyway as he closed the cabinet and caught his reflection – the discolouration under his right eye, red and deepening.

Squeezing his eyes shut, he winced at the pain, but worse was the agony of his heart. For the entire walk home he'd tried to push away the memory of Sophie's voice. But now, it was the only thing he wanted to hear.

He went to the spiral staircase and bounded to the top. His ear pressed against the plaster barricade, he waited – *he willed* – to hear something.

'Sophie.'

But there was nothing. Not even the sound of the ocean reached him. It was as though the air had been sucked out of the world.

He thumped the barricade and sank down onto the top step. Moments later he hurried into the spare room, turned the key sitting in the lock of the last drawer in his desk, and rummaged around in the paperwork until he came up with what he was looking for. Trembling, he stared at the envelope then turned it over. His thumb slipped under the corner of the flap, but it had sealed with time. He threw it back into the drawer and slammed it shut.

Burying his face in his hands, he cried in rasping sobs.

SEVEN

The air was thick with difficulty on Monday at work. Leah dabbed at her eyes and made a show of misery with quivering lips and unsteady breaths, before handing Sam the morning's files. On top she carefully placed his mobile phone.

She sniffed. 'Please, can we talk?'

Without replying, Sam pocketed his phone and took the files into his office. He threw the papers down on the desk and went over to the window, eyes unseeing on the bustle of the city street below.

His office door opened and slammed behind him. He didn't turn around, didn't need to as Richard's voice boomed across the room. 'What's going on? Leah's bawling and says you won't talk to her.'

Sam turned from the window, faced his colleague.

'Oh, Jesus,' Richard said, coming over. 'Is that a black eye?'

'What's left of it. And before you ask, Leah didn't do it.'

'So, what happened? Who hit you?'

Sam sighed and shook his head. 'It was my own stupid fault. Let's leave it at that.'

He walked back to his desk and opened his laptop, wondering how he might raise the subject of a prescription with Richard. He looked at the senior partner, but could only bring himself to mention the brand of antidepressant medication, adding, 'Do you have some sample packs?'

'Don't know,' Richard said. 'Why, who'd you have them in mind for?'

Sam thought better of it, shook his head. 'Doesn't matter.'

Taking a file from the outbox tray, he headed for the door, but Richard put a hand on his shoulder as he went to pass. 'Hey, you okay? I mean, I know I was fired up before. But I didn't know. Maybe you want to talk about it?'

'I'm fine. Really.'

Sam went out to reception, dropped the file onto Leah's counter and, ignoring her sniffs, asked for the storeroom keys. She took them from a hook under the counter and held them out to him. He snatched them, avoiding the linger of her fingers. Pausing outside the storeroom door, he looked back and thought he heard Richard talking to Leah. Quickly, he darted off to Richard's office. He didn't know where his colleague normally left his keys. There was one key in particular that Sam wanted.

He went behind Richard's desk and started opening drawers. Pens, paper clips, elastic bands, loose change. No keys. He looked around for a hook or something obvious, but there wasn't anything. Richard's desk was strewn with papers and folders. Sam lifted the nearest folder and found a wad of keys underneath.

Bingo.

He went back to the storeroom and let himself in, flicking on a light in the windowless room. The place smelt like a museum. There were two central compactor units for archive filing, and cabinets and cupboards against the other walls.

Sam closed the door and locked it. Richard was the only one with a key to the corner drug safe. After finding the right one from the wad, Sam opened the safe. There were a few bottles and packets, some with patients' names on them. He moved around the items, looked at the labels, and removed some of the other packaging until he found a bottle with his brand of medication. He stared at the label and the name: Marjory Steiner. One of Diane's patients she'd inherited from Glenn. Sam had no more time to think about it, opened the bottle and shook out ten of the pills. Ten won't be missed, he told himself. It wasn't enough, but it was all he could risk.

He found a small plastic sheath and dropped the pills into it, sealed it and shoved it into his pocket. He took some stationery items before he left, whatever his hand fell on; sticky notes and a packet of staples – and then headed out, locking the storeroom door behind him.

Richard was back in his office, squinting at some papers he held with an extended arm.

'Lose your glasses again?' Sam said, as he came to stand at the front of the desk.

'They're in the car. I'm going out soon – don't see the point in running out to get them.' He looked up at Sam. 'Everything okay?'

'Um, yeah,' Sam said. He began to talk about a patient. It was nothing, just trivia. As he did, he idly lifted a folder and managed to slip the keys under it.

*

Later that night Sam attempted to quell his guilt with a bottle of wine. He sat in the dark listening for the ocean. And he thought about Alice Lacey, about seeing her on the beach that time, seemingly absorbed in solitude. He allowed his imagination to play out a small scene. In it, Alice turned her face towards him as he stepped across the sand. When she smiled it was for him alone. He saw himself smiling back and lifting his hand to wave. It hardly counted as a fantasy, not that he would ever think of Alice in that way. But there was something about her smile.

A creaking noise overhead caught his attention. He stared up at the ceiling.

'All houses creak,' he finally muttered, attempting to dismiss the notion that it sounded like someone walking around up there.

It didn't work.

He put his wine glass on the side table next to the armchair, and then crept barefooted up the metal staircase to the barricade at the top. And there he listened, his ear pressed to the plasterboard.

It became quiet. He waited.

There was something odd. Sam couldn't quite tell what it was, but it was as if… someone was on the other side of the panel, also pressed against it. He could almost sense them, fancied he could follow the movements of their hands, mirroring his. And then a whispery voice, seeming to drift closer, then moving away. He listened to the flux, trying to make sense of it, until a serpent-like hiss sent him reeling backwards, and he almost slipped the rest of the way down the stairs.

*

Sam did everything he could to avoid Leah throughout the remainder of the week. He overlapped his patients or sat in with his colleagues for ambiguous meetings. The rest of the time he kept his head in paperwork.

At every turn Leah seemed to be waiting for him, following him down the hall, into the lift, the meal room, trying to engage him in a discussion about the state of their affair. He refused to be baited. Talking about it in any form was not going to be conducive to their working relationship. It was already in tatters, and the only way to rectify it was to disengage. But as the days moved on, the situation seemed to deteriorate.

On Friday, Alice Lacey didn't show up for her appointment. Leah was wringing her hands at the reception counter.

'Have you tried to call her?' Sam asked.

'No. I was waiting to see if she was just running late, like she did before.'

He checked his watch. 'We're well past that. Perhaps you could call her now.'

Leah's bottom lip began to tremble, confusing Sam. 'What's the matter?' he whispered, aware there were several people in the waiting area.

She shook her head, then picked up the reception phone and pressed the numbers. A few seconds later she hung up. 'It went to voicemail,' she said shakily.

'You should have left a message.'

'And say what?'

Sam made a noise through his teeth. 'Call her back.'

'Fine then.' She took up the phone and repeated the action, this time leaving an unfriendly message that Alice should contact the office and explain herself.

Sam was appalled but he didn't comment. This wasn't the time or place to talk about her attitude. He was about to return to his office when Leah cried out, 'Sam, please, we can't go on like this.'

Sam was stunned, glanced briefly at the two people in the waiting area off to the side.

'Leah, keep your voice down,' he said as discreetly as possible. It made no difference.

'Why won't you talk to me?' she cried. 'I've been trying all week and you keep pushing me aside. Don't you care about me, Sam?'

'Later, we'll talk later.'

'I want to talk *now*.'

The commotion had Cranston peering through a small opening of his office door and brought Richard all the way out to reception – his mouth opening and closing like a fish out of water, as though trying to decide what to say, but coming up with nothing.

'You can't keep ignoring me,' Leah went on. 'Sam! It's just not fair.'

Diane appeared from the hallway, her spectacles in her hand. 'Keep the noise down. I'm trying to work in here.'

Leah rushed into the ladies toilets on the other side of the waiting area, past the two clients who watched the scene as if they were privy to a live soap-opera performance.

Diane groaned. 'Good grief, I suppose I have to be the one to go after her.' She looked between her colleagues as though she might be wrong. But when nobody else moved, she followed after the secretary whose continued cries pealed out from behind the swinging door.

Sam ignored Richard's accusing frown and returned to his office. But his colleague was quickly behind him, slamming the door with such force that the wall shuddered and one of the pictures, an inspirational print of an eagle in flight, tilted.

'You mind telling me what the hell that was all about?' Richard said.

Sam turned and rubbed his temple with the heel of his hand. 'Everything's all right. Leah's just a bit worked up, I suppose.'

'You suppose? The girl is a mess. I don't know what happened between the two of you, but there's no place for it during business hours.'

'I didn't know she was going to erupt out there. I've been trying to keep out of her way, let the dust settle—'

'It's not dust, Sam. It's a major sandstorm and you need to solve it.'

'There's nothing to solve. She just needs to get a grip.'

Richard's hands flopped about as he turned back and forth, emphasising his frustration.

'You can't leave things as they are,' he said. 'Her heart is breaking.'

Sam eyed his colleague suspiciously. 'What's your interest? You seem unusually involved.'

Richard grunted and waved off the comment. 'Nothing. Nothing,' he said, but seconds later kicked at the floor, folded his arms, and released them. 'Well, if you must know, Leah's father and I go way back. He was a good man. In his last days, I promised to look out for his family.'

'Explains why you gave Leah the job.'

'She's qualified.'

'Not the most qualified if I remember rightly.' Sam sighed, moving over to the window, absently flicking the venetians. There was a three-car pile-up on the street below. People were wandering around inspecting the damage.

'You shouldn't have pushed me into it,' he said, still watching the scene. 'You should have left well enough alone.'

'Are you saying it's my fault that things soured with you and Leah?'

'I'm saying I would have liked some more time to think about whether or not I wanted to take her out again.' He turned to face his colleague. 'And you might have mentioned the fact you were her father's friend instead of pretending to be mine.'

'That's not fair.' Richard pointed a warning finger at Sam. 'This wasn't for Leah's sake. And nobody made you do it.'

'Do my reports on Monday morning,' Sam muttered.

'You can be an ungrateful bastard at times.' Richard tugged at his jacket sleeve and adjusted the cuff before thumping over to the door. 'Sort it out and do it today because I don't want to see a repeat performance of what occurred out there. Talk to her, and I mean properly, not one of your self-important spiels. This is a place of business, and I hold you fully responsible.'

*

Sam hastily headed out at lunchtime, narrowly avoiding Leah coming back from Richard's office. She called to him as he stepped into the lift, and he caught a brief glimpse of her forlorn expression as the door closed. He knew he ought to have that talk with her, for Richard's sake, but he had to get it straight in his head first. The trouble was he didn't know where to start. It would have been easier from the psychiatrist's chair, objectively, with a notepad on his knee.

He sat at a corner table at Rochester's Restaurant down on the Quay. It was far enough away from the office to prevent Leah tracking him down. Ferries came and went, dredging the sea floor in a wash of dirty foam. Street performers and an endless flow of pedestrians took up the walkway. Two police officers were talking to a man near the entrance of one of the ferry terminals.

Sam lifted his menu, his thoughts drifting to Alice. He could only speculate at what might have caused her to cancel her appointment today. Yet at the same time he wondered why he was bothered about it. Facts were that patients cancelled appointments and there didn't have to be a reason.

The waitress brought over his wine and then fussed a little too long, straightening his knife and fork and putting his serviette across his lap. As soon as she finished he put the serviette back on the table.

'Tyler, you old fart.'

Sam looked up and nearly tipped over the water glass in a rush to get to his feet to shake hands with a tall, skinny man with a Beatles haircut. A striking redhead was with him.

'Ben Travers, still as ugly as ever I see.'

'At least I've got a personality.'

Both men laughed and slapped each other on the shoulders. The woman was introduced as Veronica and she left them to talk, moving out into the sunshine.

'I tried looking you up after Sophie's funeral,' Ben said. 'But I was told you closed off your practice.'

'I took off for a bit,' Sam said.

Ben nodded. 'Understandable. Sophie was a great girl. I bet you miss her like hell.'

An awkward silence fell over them until Ben added, 'So, going by the poxy suit, I'd say you're practising again.'

'Not privately. I'm in with another practice here in Sydney.'

'That's handy. I'll have to call in on you next time my head falls off. You can put it back on straight for me. Listen, I've got a gig later at Hunters Nite Club. You should come.' Ben leant in closer, adding mischievously, 'You remember those big night outs we used to have? Man, did we play up.'

Sam smiled. 'So, you've still got the band together.'

'Different drummer, different bass player, but I'm still the lead singer. Can't beat quality, mate.'

'I gather you're doing well.'

'The pay is terrible. If only you'd let me plagiarise your essays.'

Sam got the details of where to meet. Maybe it would do him some good to get out – the right sort of distraction.

*

Leah was still lingering after five. She'd asked Sam several times if he needed anything. Finally, she approached his desk and he was forced to look up from his papers.

'Sam, can we talk? I mean, Richard said you were going to. I don't want to leave things as they are. It's uncomfortable. You know, about last week, and then the Alice Lacey thing today.' She didn't wait for his invitation to sit, taking up the chair on the other side of the desk, adding, 'I have to get this off my chest.'

He dropped his pen onto the papers in front of him. There was no point in delaying it any further. Let her have her say, get it over and done with.

'About what you said on Friday night,' she started. 'I would *never* try to trap you with a pregnancy. I just wanted you to know that – I respect you too much. Besides, I'm a bit old-fashioned. I'd want a ring on my finger before starting a family.'

Sam felt a nerve in his mouth twitch.

'And about Alice Lacey,' she continued. 'I thought you didn't like her and that you'd actually be pleased she didn't turn up. It sort of threw me when you insisted I call her, like there was some urgency to it... and that somehow it was more important than you talking to me or how I might have been feeling—'

The comment irritated him. He didn't let her finish. 'Anything to do with patients – anything at all – don't go making assumptions. These are people's lives. You can't manipulate situations to what suits you. You answer the phones and make the appointments and you leave the psychiatry up to the doctors.'

'I'm sorry. It won't happen again.' She stared at him, her eyelashes petrified in mascara.

He knew he ought to apologise too. But it wasn't easy. He wasn't used to admitting fault. He'd protected himself from it for years through detachment and solitude. Giving up any part of that now was like giving up his power. And he hated being wrong.

He coughed nervously. 'I'm... sorry too.' Was that the best he could do? 'Let's not dwell on what happened.'

'Sam, I wanted to ask you – would you come to my place for dinner next Friday night?' She jumped ahead of his response. 'I mean, it would really help if you came. My brother has been at me ever since... well, last week.' She glanced down at her lap, fiddled with something there. 'He was furious with me.'

Her comment piqued Sam's curiosity. 'Furious with *you*?'

'I explained everything to Archie. He didn't know you were my boss. He feels bad that he hit you.'

Sam almost smiled at the irony of it, that it should have made a difference to Leah's brother that it was her boss and not some random guy in the bedroom with her. The punch Sam had received was understandable considering the circumstances, never mind who he was.

'If you come for dinner,' she went on, 'then Archie will see that everything is all right between us and that I'm not about to get fired. He was convinced I'd be out of a job – and I'm supposed to be helping them with the mortgage.'

'You're not going to lose your job.'

'Please, Sam. No strings attached. Let's just clear the air on this once and for all. You don't know how awful I feel about this mess. I'll be inviting Richard and Laura too. I've been meaning to do this for a while anyway. Archie gets a bit... I don't know...' She screwed up her nose. '*Protective* is the wrong word. But he... well, he thinks of himself as the head of the family since our dad died. And it would mean a lot if you came and he could see that you're decent and last week had been a misunderstanding.'

Sam didn't know why, but he felt a bit sorry for Leah. Already, from what he'd seen, he suspected an undercurrent of dissonance at home. He thought about it. Perhaps having dinner with her family wouldn't be so bad if there were going to be others. And maybe he needed to show his face after last week.

'Okay. Next Friday night.'

She shimmered and brightened, and her hands came up under her chin as though she might clap them.

As soon as she left, he locked up and headed out. Shoving his hands into his trouser pockets, he walked slowly along the footpath. The city streets were packed with end-of-week revellers.

He didn't fit into this world anymore and he wondered if he cared. Maybe he did, just a little. But he wasn't sure what it would take to bring him back. Perhaps he should be asking himself what was lacking in his dreary existence. Someone to talk to at the end of a long day? Well, that had its pitfalls. Most of the time he didn't feel like talking. But maybe someone who understood that, who didn't push – content to just sit in the quiet and listen for the ocean with him. Leah didn't fit that bill. Probably no woman did. His experience was that women liked to talk and they expected a response.

He stopped outside the club where Ben's band was playing. The red neon sign overhead sizzled and hissed like an insect zapper, giving a bawdy impression. Every time the door opened to let patrons in or out, Sam caught the music. The familiarity of it spiked his memory: slow dancing with Sophie, no matter the beat.

'You coming in or what?' the flat-faced doorman said after a while.

Sam shrugged. But then he figured he may as well get it over and done with. He paid the entry fee and went inside.

Veronica, the redhead from the restaurant, greeted him like an old friend and got him a drink. Ben was up on stage singing with the band. He pointed to Sam, who returned the gesture with a raised glass. After a while, Veronica took his hand and led him to a booth.

When a slower, quieter song started, Sam said, 'Have you and Ben been together long?'

She laughed in an easy, likeable way. 'God, no. We're not a couple. Ben's my cousin.'

'Sorry.' Sam smiled, glancing down at his drink.

'Sorry that he's my cousin? Or that we're not a couple?'

'Um, just sorry for asking the question, I suppose.'

'I help manage Ben's gigs. That's the only reason we seem to hang around each other so much.' She leant forward, her vibrant hair framing her face like a fiery halo. 'But I can assure you, most wholeheartedly, I am... unattached.'

Ben came over during the breaks and by now Sam had switched to orange juice. It was watered down and left an odd taste on his tongue. There was too much talk about Sophie, and Sam felt uncomfortable. He kept his responses brief. Being reminded of the good times was as excruciating as the not so good. Even the funny stories bothered him.

Veronica seemed to sense the intrusion and steered her cousin often. After Ben went back to the band, she eased in closer to Sam. 'I should apologise for him, he's just pumped with adrenaline, not thinking straight. Always happens when he performs.'

Sam pushed aside the rest of his orange juice. 'Probably explains why some bands jump around and smash their guitars.'

'He means well. I know he's glad you came tonight.'

'Well, we go way back.'

She paused and touched his fingers lingering on the tabletop. 'I'm sorry about your wife. It must be a terrible thing to lose someone so close.' Sam didn't want to hear this. And he dreaded what might be the next question: how did she die?

But it never came.

'My place isn't too far from here,' Veronica said. 'Would you mind walking with me?'

He could hardly refuse.

*

There was a bohemian flavour to the little flat above the shop; orange and green curtains in the doorways, large floor cushions stacked one on the other, scarves draped across the walls like works of art. And there was an exotic fragrance of spices and incense.

Veronica threw her bag aside and went to a sideboard where she lit a large green candle. 'Make yourself at home,' she said.

'I won't stay.'

She turned to him. 'You got a hungry cat waiting for you?'

'Maybe a possum or two in the roof.'

'Then there's no rush. What can I get you to drink?'

'Um, water will be fine.'

She headed over to the small kitchenette and poured two glasses, then turned around and prompted him to sit by nodding at the floor.

He removed his tie as he contemplated the nearest stack of cushions. Awkwardly, he sat.

She laughed at him before she kicked down the stack next to him, crossed one foot over the other and eased herself onto the spread like a dancer taking a graceful curtsey. And all while still holding the two glasses of water. She handed one to Sam.

It was all he could do to keep balance.

He studied his glass and saw there was a piece of lemon floating in the water. He poked at it with his finger. 'Is this supposed to be here?'

'Detoxifies the liver.'

'I might need the entire lemon tree.'

She regarded him for a moment. 'You're a bit of a shy one, aren't you.'

'Shy?' He tried not to laugh. 'Try boring and dull.'

'You just need a bit of encouragement, that's all.'

The water tasted nice. He wondered where he should place the glass. 'I don't want to make any sudden movements,' he confessed.

'Stay right there,' she said laughing.

She got up, taking his glass and hers, dropping them both onto the nearby sink, and then went into another room.

He managed to get up and wandered to the doorway, pulled back one of the drapes and looked inside. Veronica was folding the quilt back from the bed. Noises from the passing traffic below carried through the half-opened window.

He backed away and quietly let himself out.

Sam collected his car from the parking station, set the climate control and turned on the seat warmer. The streets were still lively when he drove out, the weekend crowd heading in all directions. He hated that he didn't have the same social energy anymore. It made him feel like a different person. Or maybe he was just getting too old.

It was after midnight when he drove into Alice's street. When he found the house number he stopped outside and wondered why he was even there. It was a duplex, the double storey on the right, rendered and painted blue.

There didn't look to be any lights on, hardly surprising given the time, although he recalled her propensity to stay up as late as possible to avoid sleep and therefore the terrifying nightmares. Maybe she was in there now, sitting in the dark, feeling afraid.

Slowly, he drove the rest of the way home. As he neared his driveway, a brief flash of light from the extension window caught his attention. He stopped the car and craned his neck to look up through the windscreen.

He waited, but the light didn't come again.

EIGHT

On Monday Sam went through the latest pharmaceutical top-up, but it didn't include his type of antidepressant. He'd been calling an old rep, but she was on long service leave, and the replacement that finally came was pushing another brand.

There were no more bottles left in the drug safe to skim. But his colleagues might still have some old samples. He couldn't ask them. He'd already made half an attempt with Cranston, but Diane had interrupted them and ended up in the discussion, and Sam felt he'd pushed the matter enough times that he risked suspicion. It would require raiding their personal supplies, but they locked their drawers and cabinets each evening, so there was no chance he could go searching after they left for the day. His best bet would be during the lunch breaks, but it took until Thursday before he could coordinate it.

Diane and Cranston were getting ready to leave the office together, complaining and bickering about where to eat for lunch.

'You wanna come, good sort?' Diane called to Sam when she saw him through the open door to his office.

'I've got sandwiches,' he told her.

'How very domesticated of you.' She held her hand up in a wave.

Once they were in the lift, Sam flashed a nervous smile at Leah as he passed her in reception, regretting the gesture when she sat up straight and displayed a neat row of white teeth. In the hallway, he looked back once before going into Cranston's office, closing the door quietly behind him.

His colleague's office was bland – the pale furnishings adding to the swathe of neutral colour. There was an odd antiseptic odour, like the place had been wiped down with disinfectant.

Sam quietly opened drawers in the desk before moving to the long bureau under the window. The small safe at the back of the cupboard was a likely candidate. But it was locked. He closed everything up and cautiously returned to the hallway, going into Diane's office across the hall where he repeated his search.

There were noises out in reception. It sounded like Richard and Leah talking. Sam paused, crouched in front of the low cabinet, and listened for a moment. There was movement in the hallway and he heard what sounded like Richard's door close. He drew in a deep breath and returned to his search. The sliding door of the cabinet was locked. He went to get up but realised there was a key sitting in the lock on the other end. He moved over and twisted it.

There were a lot of medication samples carelessly strewn about in the cabinet and he sifted through these now. Not his brand. He told himself that all he needed were a couple more samples and he would be able to wean himself off them. That had been the in-tention with Glenn – the process had started just before he'd died. Sam had lost confidence after that, brought the dosage back up, increased it during difficult moments, and there'd been plenty of those lately.

The office door swung open behind him and he jerked his head around to see Leah standing there.

'Sam? What are you doing?'

He threw the items back into the cupboard, shut the door and straightened up. 'Um, I was just looking for something.' He ran a nervous hand over his hair and tried to think, noticing a flicker of consternation in Leah's eyes. He countered his guilt by saying, 'What are you doing creeping up on me anyway?'

She hesitated, but then, 'Oh, there's someone here to see you. She's in the waiting room.'

He was glad for the reprieve and didn't bother asking who it was. But if he'd known, he would never have walked out.

Sophie had always bore a striking resemblance to her mother, but in that first instance when Sam saw Delia Wilde standing at the reception counter, his heart crashed. The dark hair, parted in the centre like her daughter always wore it – and the same eyes, soft and brown, except less sympathetic than Sophie's.

'Delia,' he said, unable to hide the shock in his voice.

'Well, look at you, big shot working in the city again,' she said stiffly. 'Expensive suit, swish office. Last I heard you were in Queensland drinking yourself into an early grave. What happened, spend all the proceeds from the sale of your house on booze?'

He didn't know how she'd tracked him down, and he didn't care. It was in his favour that she thought he'd sold the house.

'What do you want?' he said coldly.

She stepped forward. 'You and I need to talk.'

'I'm working.'

'That's all right – I can stand here and say what I want to say. I don't mind an audience.'

Leah had drifted to Sam's side and he became aware of her now. He ushered his former mother-in-law into his office. Without waiting for an invitation, Delia Wilde went for the central armchairs. She sat in *his* usual chair.

Eventually, he moved forward to sit opposite her. It felt awkward, and he realised that the patient's chair was significantly lower.

'Let's get this over with,' he said.

Delia smoothed her skirt. 'It's gone on too long and you owe me answers.'

Sam didn't respond. He couldn't. The kind of answers she might want – well, that was anyone's guess. Too much like her daughter, the questions weren't likely to be easy.

'I have nothing left of Sophie,' she went on. 'You saw to that, taking her ashes. I don't know what you did with them, but you at least owe me the location you spread them so I can visit—'

'You can't visit,' he cut her off. 'I mean, it's not the sort of place you can just walk to.'

He thought of his failed attempt not too many weeks ago, the steep hike through the national park, the dangerous cliff edge... the disappointment at realising he couldn't remember having spread her ashes there or anywhere.

'Sam, how am I supposed to grieve for her? Four years on and I have no place to go to. Even if you'd shared her ashes with me, it would have been something.'

'*Half* of her. Do you know how macabre that is?'

'What's the difference with what you did? You threw her away. *Scattered* her.'

Sam realised the irony himself. 'It's what she would have wanted.'

'What she wanted? How about what she *needed* while you were still able to give her that?'

'Don't do this.'

'Afraid of the truth are you?'

'I'm warning you.'

'Warning me of what?' She thrust herself forward in the chair, her chin jutting defiantly. 'I'm not scared of you. You're nobody. You're nothing better than a monkey in a suit. It's all right for you – *your* life goes on.'

'I miss Sophie just as much as you do.'

'Don't tell me how I feel. She was your wife, but you can get another one of those. I can't replace my daughter. I can only mourn her. Or try to—' Sophie's mother faltered and began to cry.

Sam hadn't expected that. He rubbed the side of his neck, fighting back the sting of his own tears, the burning in his throat. He didn't want to be reminded of this – none of it.

'Please, tell me,' Delia finally managed. 'Where is she?'

He relented, but his voice gave away his anguish. 'The Royal National Park... near the top of the escarpment... there's an unofficial lookout known as The Leap.' He stood, unwilling to continue the conversation.

Delia didn't linger, neither did she acknowledge or thank him for the information. Sam closed the door behind her after she left, and slammed the wall with his fist.

Memories rushed him and he tried to push them away – of Sophie laughing, singing, running up and down the spiral staircase; of Sophie crying, shouting, telling him to go to hell.

Goddammit, he needed his pills. He wasn't going to be able to wean himself off them, not yet, he had to face that. The pills he'd skimmed from Marjory Steiner's prescription were out. He couldn't go to Richard about it. He couldn't go to anyone. They'd all quiz him before they started writing up scripts. Then there'd be follow-up and treatment plans. He'd lose his place in their estimation, of his reputation as the imperturbable psychiatrist, of his superiority in the practice and in the field. They would know him; see his weakness ahead of anything else. Hell, not only would his status be damaged, but they mightn't let him practise...

Okay, don't panic.

Stiff fingers ran up the side of his face and into his hair. He'd think of something – he would.

*

On Friday morning Leah greeted Sam with the first patient file and reminded him about dinner with her family. He knew he couldn't get out of it. The only reassurance was Richard and Laura would be there too.

In the afternoon, as he saw one of his patients out, Leah told him with a grimace, 'Alice Lacey hasn't turned up for her appointment again.'

'Was this her standard booking?'

'Friday, yes. I never got to reschedule anything else with her. She hasn't been answering her phone.'

Sam took Alice's file with him into his office and closed the door. After thinking about it for a moment he decided to call her. There was no answer on her home phone or mobile. There was no longer a prompt for voicemail.

He tapped on her file thoughtfully. Alice didn't take medication. She was a rare breed.

And now he had another idea.

He pulled across his laptop and opened a file, hesitated, but then typed. After he printed off the document, he called Leah into the office and asked her to get him a takeaway coffee from the café downstairs. She walked over to take the fifty he held out, and as she went to leave he feigned an afterthought. 'Oh, and you may as well collect this while you're out.' He took the page he'd printed and signed the bottom, then handed it to her. 'Take payment out of the fifty.'

After the last patient for the day, Sam tried Alice's numbers again, but was unsuccessful. He stood and went to the window. An old banner for the Chinese New Year flapped from an awning across the road, furling and unfurling in the corner where the tie had failed. Traffic and pedestrians weaved and flowed, reminding him that life went on regardless. He wondered about Alice missing her second appointment. She was on weekly visits, and sometimes that kind of intensive therapy could be overwhelming. He was probably worrying unnecessarily.

He returned to his desk and flipped open her file. Glenn's neat handwriting and impeccable organisation brought the major is-sues into focus. Sam ticked through Alice's symptoms and took note of Glenn's comments. Alice's last shift had been on a car crew in Coffs Harbour. Everything had been normal; she'd at-tended several jobs with her partner and they'd returned to the station for a meal break. But then she disappeared and nobody could find her. Eventually, she was discovered cowering next to the cistern in the ladies toilet. She had gone from functional to inoperative in a matter of minutes.

Sam closed the file. Maybe he *should* worry.

'Don't forget my place at seven,' Leah reminded him, putting her head around the door at the end of the day.

He was still thinking about Alice.

'Sam, did you hear me?'

'Yes. Seven.'

'You seem far away.'

'Hmm.'

Leah was closing the door when Sam suddenly remembered. He called her back in. 'Did you pick up that prescription?' He cleared his throat nervously. 'For Alice Lacey?'

'Yes. I locked them in the drug safe.'

'The safe? No, I want them in here.'

'I just thought with Alice not coming in today that—'

Abruptly he stood, sending his chair rolling backwards into the wall. 'I didn't ask you to be presumptuous. Those pills... the medication... I need them now.' He knew he sounded fraught. He settled himself. 'I'm – ah – going to do a home visit with Alice this afternoon and I need to take them with me.'

'Oh. Sorry. Richard is still here. I'll get the safe key from him.'

Leah eventually returned with the packet containing the prescription drugs and left for the day. Sam felt no relief. He removed the packaging and stared at the bottle of pills bearing Alice's name, noticing that his hands trembled.

'He who has himself for a physician has a fool for a patient,' he muttered.

The quote never had more meaning than it did now.

He'd just committed fraud.

Shoving the bottle of antidepressants into the inner pocket of his jacket, Sam locked up. He had no alternative but to drive to Alice's house.

*

At first he sat in the car trying to see if the place looked any different from last week. There was no lawn at the front apart from the verge, but it looked like whoever mowed one side of the duplex probably did the other side as well. He got out of the car and checked the letterbox. There was only one junk-mail leaflet.

He knocked at her door and waited. He knocked again and then came in closer. 'Alice, it's Dr Tyler.'

He tried looking in the window but the venetian blinds were closed tight. Stepping back onto the common driveway, he stared up at the second floor. There were two front-facing windows with the curtains pulled across, as if she'd packed up and gone on holiday. Maybe that's what she'd done.

He exhaled heavily and wondered what he should do next. He went to the other duplex and knocked. An elderly woman with a towel around her head opened the door as far as the chain would allow.

'Hello,' Sam said. 'I'm sorry to disturb you, but I'm trying to get in contact with your neighbour, Alice.'

The woman didn't say anything, just stared at him.

'Alice,' he repeated. 'Have you seen her? Or maybe she's gone away?'

There was still no response.

'Do you speak English?' he finally asked, beginning to feel frustrated.

The woman closed the door. Sam waited in case she was going to take the chain off. But thirty seconds later he was still staring at the pine, getting a feeling that an eye was observing him from the other side of the peephole.

'Goddammit.'

The image of Minh Luong dangling one leg over the side of a balcony came to mind. The thought troubled him. He went around to Alice's side gate and reached over, feeling for the latch. To his surprise he found it and could open it.

A path led around to the back of the house. There was a small courtyard: a triangular patch of grass with a garden bed that was mostly weeds, and a long, paved area that led to a pull-out clothes-line attached to the fence at the far end. A limp grey towel looked as if it had been there for a while – rained on more than once.

He almost stumbled on a dislodged paver. The whole path needed lifting and resetting. Tree roots from the neighbouring jacaranda were the likely culprits, he decided. As soon as he looked up again, he saw her.

'Alice.'

Barefoot and wearing what looked like pyjama pants and a grey hooded top, she was seated on the edge of a raised section of concrete bricks near the back sliding door, hugging her knees to her chest. There were shadows under her eyes and her cheeks appeared hollowed, as if she hadn't eaten properly in a while. She was a prime candidate for an extra in a zombie movie, Sam thought.

'You're a long way from home, Dr Tyler,' she said in a faint and scratchy voice, as though it were the first time she'd spoken in weeks.

'Actually, I live in this suburb.'

'I took you for a North Shore boy.'

He ignored her comment. 'I was worried about you, Alice.'

She shrugged. 'I'm still breathing.'

Surprisingly, he didn't feel pity for her, although he was certainly glad he hadn't found her dead with her service pistol in her hand. 'Do you mind if we go inside? I'd like to talk to you.'

She put her chin on her knees. 'I'd rather stay out here.'

He took a few steps closer. 'Come on, let's go in.'

She sighed and reluctantly got up, sliding open the glass door. Sam followed her inside. It was dark and dingy and smelt like a cheap pub. The source of the odour was revealed when Alice flicked on a light. The kitchen counter was littered with wine bottles. He picked one up. It was empty – McLaren Vale cabernet sauvignon. Well, at least her depression afforded her good taste.

She turned to face him. He held up the empty bottle and raised his eyebrows.

'It's a free country,' she said.

'Self-pity doesn't become you, Alice.'

'It's not me I feel sorry for.' She started to clear away the bottles.

'Then why didn't you answer the door just now? Why were you hiding out the back ignoring me?'

She snatched away the bottle he was holding and glowered. 'I thought you were meant to be the sympathetic sort.'

'What do you suppose I'm here for then?'

She turned away, fingered an opened newspaper on the bench before folding it and shoving it into a plastic garbage bag with the bottles, but then she stopped and looked back at him. 'I wasn't going to do myself in if that's what you thought.'

'Then maybe you should tell me what this is all about.'

Her bottom lip quivered and she bit down on it. She dropped the plastic bag and the bottles clanged against the tiled floor.

'Alice, what it is?'

'Garth Conroy, my colleague from up north... disappeared just over two weeks ago. Last week I got a call from Coffs Station asking me if I'd seen or heard from him...' She began to cry. 'Days ago now, a body was found in an overturned car in a gully on the side of the road.' She inhaled sharply. 'It was Garth. They think he must have fallen asleep at the wheel.' She crumpled to the floor, sobbing. 'He was with me... *at Bellingen...*'

'Oh, Jesus,' Sam muttered, moving to crouch beside her. 'I'm sorry. I really am.'

He sat her at the kitchen counter and then went through her cupboards trying to find the makings for a cup of tea. Eventually, he came across a jar of teabags and something he hoped was sugar. While the jug was boiling he rinsed two mugs under the hot water tap. The carton of milk from the fridge passed the sniff test. He poured the hot water, asked her if she took sugar, and then handed her one of the mugs.

He stood on the other side of the counter and in silence they sipped their tea.

After a while she looked down and brushed her hand across her top. 'Just so you know – I haven't been wearing the same thing all week.'

'I didn't come here to judge you.'

'I used to be a clean and tidy person. I just don't see the point anymore.'

'What about the beach?'

She looked at him as if he'd said something foreign.

'It's practically on your doorstep,' he added. 'When was the last time you were there?'

She shrugged.

'We can go there now,' he said. 'I'll come with you.'

'Is this like... therapy?'

'Of course.'

He waited while she went upstairs to change her clothes. Without the intention of intruding on her privacy, he looked around the lounge room. On a cluttered buffet there were several framed photographs. Notably, one of two little boys aged about nine and ten – Alice's nephews, most likely. There was a loose snapshot of Alice with a group of other police in overalls. They looked as though they'd participated in some sort of outdoor exercise. Most were covered in mud. There was a formal photo of Alice in uniform, probably taken when she was still at the academy. He picked it up and noticed that the metal frame had come apart in the corner. He pinched it together and let his fingers trace her image. She was young and fresh faced. The horrors of her work hadn't touched her life. There was still innocence and vitality in her eyes. Her smile was unaffected.

He put the photo back as Alice came down the stairs.

When they stepped out the front door she squinted even though the light was falling. It took only minutes to walk to the beach. Sam steered their course along The Esplanade, deciding that the exercise would do her good. It probably wouldn't hurt him either.

The kiosk at South Cronulla Surf Club was open and Sam, wondering about the last time Alice had eaten properly, bought a large bag of hot chips and two pieces of battered fish. They sat on the sand in front of the club and shared the food straight from the paper wrapping. Sam was acutely aware that this was not a social event. But his role as Alice's therapist dictated a certain amount of improvisation. Rarely did he go beyond the sanctified walls of his office. Otherwise, there was the risk of familiarity, where the line between doctor and patient would start to blur. Sam ensured he was never guilty of that. But maybe he'd taken one step further into this than he'd anticipated. Still, there was something important he needed to talk to her about, and she would have been less receptive inside the hovel prison of her home.

The sunset threw hues of lilac across the horizon and coloured the low shifting clouds. A group of surfers were tempting fate near the rocky inlet. Sam watched them, wondering how long they would risk it before darkness, or something else, devoured them.

Alice sighed. 'Oh, I missed coming here so much. Thank you... for getting me out the front door.' She kicked off her sandals, dug her toes into the sand and breathed in the salty air as if it were being served to her on a platter.

Sam fingered the pill bottle in his jacket pocket. He'd only come because he'd more or less been obliged to. But now he was glad he had, breaking into the cycle of her depression.

She looked at him. 'I missed your sessions too. You probably don't believe that.'

'Well, you didn't show up,' he said half in jest, watching the breeze catch in the ends of her hair. 'Or answer your phone. Or return my messages. Or open your front door.'

She smiled a little guiltily before scrunching the papers from the meal into a tight wad.

'Alice,' Sam began carefully. 'When is Garth's funeral?'

She turned her sights back to the sea, but he could see the small shudder of uneasiness that ran through her shoulders. 'Next Wednesday.'

'Up in Coffs?'

'Camden. That's where his family are from.'

'That's not far.'

'I can't go.' Her quiet voice was almost lost to the rush of incoming surf.

He got to his feet. 'Come on,' he said. 'Let's walk.'

They moved back onto the boardwalk, slowly retracing their steps, but then stopped at the thick rail overlooking the rock pool. The waves were breaking in spectacular fashion over the far corner of the pool as a lone swimmer in a bathing cap took calm strokes.

'It's important you go to the funeral,' Sam said.

'I'm not going. And you'll be wasting your breath if you think you can talk me into it.'

'At least tell me the reason you feel this way.'

She shifted restlessly next to him, eventually saying, 'Death and misery. I've had enough of it.'

Sam turned his attention back to the swimmer just as they performed an excruciatingly slow tumble turn before coming up smoothly to head in the other direction. 'The funeral is your chance to say goodbye to Garth.'

She shivered and hugged her arms. 'I can say goodbye to him just by looking out there at the ocean. I don't need to stand by his grave and say it.'

'What makes the ocean more suitable for your goodbye? What is it that you see when you look out there?'

'Renewal, redemption,' she said unhesitatingly. 'Why, what do you see?'

Not having expected the question, he almost laughed. 'Lots of blue water. And several foolish surfers.'

'You think I should go to the funeral.'

'I think you're making excuses about why you shouldn't go.'

'I can't see the difference in standing here or standing staring at a grave.'

'Believe me, there's a difference.'

She started walking again, headed down the steps that led to the rock pool. He followed her. In the falling light he misplaced his footing and stepped into a crevice of water between rocks. Alice turned back and stifled a smile.

He pulled his shoes off, tipped out the water. Italian leather, probably ruined. He stuffed his socks into them.

They headed back as the first of the emerging stars glimmered high above the horizon.

Sam's back pocket was buzzing. He'd forgotten his mobile phone was there. Gripping his shoes in one hand, he retrieved the phone and answered. It was Leah. Had he forgotten she was making him dinner?

He nearly swore. It had totally slipped his mind.

Alice whispered, 'Do you need to be somewhere?'

He shook his head vigorously. 'Um, I got caught up,' he told Leah. Alice moved away as though sensing his need for privacy. Watching as she strolled ahead, he added quietly, 'I'm still with Alice. Sorry. Look, don't wait for me. All of you start. If I know Richard, his stomach will be grumbling louder than his mouth.'

'Richard and Laura aren't here,' Leah said. 'I didn't get a chance to ask them.'

Sam briefly moved the phone away and mouthed a profanity. There went his buffer. He took a deep breath and calmed himself. 'Okay. I'll be there as soon as I can.'

He caught up to Alice and started to walk her home.

'I feel awful I've delayed you,' she told him on the way. 'Your wife cooked you a nice dinner, I bet. And here you were eating fish and chips on the beach with me.'

He was less concerned that he'd already eaten ahead of Leah's dinner, and more with Alice's assumption he had a wife.

'I'm not married,' he said. 'It's just a casual work gathering. Nothing important.'

She didn't seem moved by the information, and he wondered if that was what he'd expected.

As they reached her door he produced a business card from his wallet. 'Do you have a pen?' he asked.

She opened the door and he waited on her front porch while she went inside. He wrote on the back of the card with the pen she handed him seconds later.

'My details are on this.' He gave her the card. 'Here, I've written my personal mobile number. Call me anytime if you need to talk. I mean it – anytime.'

*

Leah smiled with relief when Sam finally arrived at her house. He'd gone home to change his shoes and trousers on the way. It was awkward, shaking hands with her brother, the same hand that had struck him two weeks ago. He recognised Leah's sister-in-law, Anne, as the woman in the hallway picture. She smiled giddily and greeted him as though he were royalty. All that was missing was the curtsey. He was disturbed by the undertone, wondered what Leah had told them.

He forced himself to eat the baked dinner. It was a leathery mixture of reheated vegetables and lamb swimming in thin, tasteless gravy. The television in the next room blared, dissolving the need for much conversation. Sam had no idea what he would talk to these people about anyway.

Later, while Leah and her sister-in-law were in the kitchen cleaning up, Archie handed him a beer and led the way into the lounge room. Sam wasn't a beer drinker as a rule, but he cracked the can and took a large sip out of politeness.

'So, you and my sister...' Archie put dirty feet up on the coffee table and stared ahead at the television. 'All I can say is, I hope you know what you're getting yourself in for, mate.'

Sam considered putting Archie straight on the matter – that he was not involved with his sister and two weeks ago had just been a drunken mistake. But he was pretty sure it would only be worth another black eye. So he said nothing, merely smiled with thin lips.

Leah and Anne were twittering and giggling in the kitchen. Sam felt the burden of what this meal had really been about. When the women eventually joined them in the lounge room, Leah sat on the armrest of Sam's chair, leaning on him, playing with the ends of his hair. He finished his beer and stood up.

'You off already?' Archie said.

'I've got a few things on this weekend. Need to make an early start. Thanks for the beer.' He turned to Anne. 'And the lovely dinner. Nice to meet you both.'

Leah walked outside with him, trying to take his hand. 'Sam?'

He opened his car door and turned to face her. Her features were pinched; she looked ready to cry.

'A show-your-face dinner – right?' he reminded her. 'I hope it helped your brother realise that everything is fine for you at work.'

'Please, don't say it's over.'

'Leah...'

'You can't just sleep with me and then *dump* me.'

Damn, why did he ever let it get that far? 'It was one night,' he said as gently as he could. 'We agreed.'

'We didn't agree to our feelings. To *my* feelings.'

He didn't know how to respond to that.

'What am I supposed to do now?' she cried, slapping fingers at her tears. 'Go back to work and pretend you and I never happened?'

'If we're going to keep on working together, then that's what we have to do.'

'You're being unreasonable.'

'I'm not trying to be. I thought we were clear on the subject.'

'Clear for you, or your version of it. Well, go to hell then!'

He got in the car and for a brief moment thought Leah might launch herself across the bonnet. She was dangerously close as he pulled out of the driveway.

'That's an end to that,' he muttered, and promised himself he would never act so foolishly again.

NINE

Sam was late. Every chair in the hospital meeting room was taken. Professor Wesley Jensen, visiting from Martinson University, had pulled quite a crowd. The professor didn't look up, despite the disturbance and the door clattering shut, and continued talking. Someone handed Sam several pages stapled together, and he found a place to stand against a wall next to a few other people who had also missed out on a chair.

Richard scowled at him over half-moon spectacles from the seated area. Sam shrugged but inwardly cursed himself – he despised tardiness, especially his own.

The listed topic was ethics. Sam tensed, thinking about what he'd done with the prescription, when the man to his right jabbed him in the ribs. 'Don't know why they make such a big deal out of it,' he said. 'You put men and women in the same room, there's always a biology taking place.'

'What?' Sam said, realising he hadn't been paying attention. Someone shushed him from nearby.

'The pendulum swings both ways,' came the professor's voice from the front of the room. 'Intense emotional incidents of countertransference are not uncommon. Therapeutically managing these feelings is one of the challenges facing therapists, but the difficulty lies in first identifying it, acknowledging it, and then addressing it. There's no doubt that an emotive response towards a patient can be disconcerting and significantly demanding, especially for the less-experienced psychotherapist. A patient who chronically annoys you...' There was a spattering of subdued laughter. 'Or finding yourself overly fascinated... I'm preaching to the converted, I know. But it's a reminder not to let emotions cloud our judgement or work ethic. This is where peer review becomes invaluable...'

As the professor cited case studies, Sam wondered now if he'd taken things a bit too far with Alice on Friday night. Going to her house had been within acceptable limits, but he had to remain alert to the fact she was separated from family and friends. He couldn't risk her becoming reliant upon him.

'There is nothing immoral in liking a patient,' Professor Jenkins went on to say. 'Even enjoying banter or humour during sessions. But it has to be balanced and not contradict the fundamentals that therapy is designed to examine.'

The tension grew in Sam's neck and shoulders. He rolled his head from side to side, felt the crackle of sinews. Someone shuffled past him and knocked the papers from his hands, and then stepped on them. They came up with the imprint of a shoe.

At the end of the meeting, Richard approached him. 'Hey, heard you did a home visit with the cop last Friday,' he said loudly, slapping a hard hand on the younger man's shoulder.

'Do you mind?' Sam said uneasily, looking around the crowded room.

Richard frowned. 'What's up? You seem jittery.'

'I'd be less so if you'd keep your voice down.'

'Keep my voice down?'

Sam felt as if people were staring at him. 'I'll discuss it with you back at the office.'

'Discuss what?'

Sam screwed up his trampled papers, tossed them in a nearby bin and left.

When Richard caught up with him in the office later that afternoon, Sam had settled. 'I'm sorry about before,' he said. 'I didn't mean to snap.'

Richard waved off the apology as he sat. 'You've got a lot on your mind. I understand.'

'No, I was rude. I was twitchy over you mentioning the home visit in front of that crowd, which in hindsight was ridiculous.'

'Ah, the ethics lecture. There's nothing untoward about a home visit. Anyway, how did it go with Alice? I take it she wasn't hanging from a light fitting.'

Sam frowned. 'Subtlety isn't your strong point, is it? But no, although she wasn't in great shape. She'd found out one of her colleagues had died and she was self-medicating with alcohol. Severe depression, quite a bit of personal and household neglect.' Sam explained the circumstances of Garth Conroy's death and Alice's refusal to go to the funeral.

Richard became pensive. 'You know, it might be a good idea if you accompanied Alice to the funeral. A bit of field work. Exposure therapy.'

'Therapy for whom? Police funerals aren't my scene.'

'Well, it's not for you, is it? It's for your patient. It's important for Alice to go – clearly, she's not going to get there under her own steam. As her treating doctor, you can make your observations, explore it later in session.'

'I don't think that's appropriate.'

'Of course it is. And valid too. You want to help her, don't you?'

Sam could see the potential value, but he had no intention of going to a police funeral. He frowned and shook his head. 'She's not keen. I don't want to push her. I'm still building trust.'

'I'm sure she trusts you. You were there for her, broke into that cycle of depression by going to her house.'

'It's not something I intend to do every time she doesn't turn up for a session.'

'But you're glad you went. Don't deny it.'

Sam shrugged and nodded at the same time.

Richard raised his eyebrows and chuckled lightly. 'There you go. See, I knew what I was doing bringing you and Alice together. Oh, that reminds me...' He reached inside his jacket and produced a wide envelope which he tossed across the desk to Sam. 'Here's something Laura thought you might like.'

Warily, Sam picked up the envelope. Inside were two tickets for the theatre production of *Phantom of the Opera*. It was at the Capitol in a couple of weeks' time.

'This is from Laura?'

'Don't worry, she doesn't want to take you on a date or any-thing. We've got another commitment that night. Take Leah, clear the air between you two.'

Sam dropped the tickets and the envelope they came in back onto the other end of the desk. 'I'm not going on any more dates with Leah. That's what this is all about, not Laura being generous with some spare tickets. You're still trying to play cupid.'

'I'm trying to get you moving again. The cleaner will be vacu-uming cobwebs off you next, the way you moon around here with your psychiatrist's face on. Come on, make things right between you and her.'

'The cleaner and I get along just fine.'

'So, you're a comedian now. Well, I suppose it makes sense you and the cleaner are on such good acquaintance. You spend a lot of quality time together.'

'She works hard, doesn't bother me with chit-chat, unlike some.' He stared in a less than friendly way at his colleague. 'Stop interfering.'

Leah knocked and came in without waiting for a response. She ignored Sam and kept her attention on Richard. 'There's a woman in reception asking to see you. She doesn't have an appointment but she says you know her. Elizabeth Banner?'

Richard grunted. 'Does she have a referral?'

'No. She just wants to talk to you.'

'She needs to make an appointment.'

Leah closed the door behind her. 'I tried telling her that. She's rather insistent. She says she can't afford an appointment and needs to see you in person to discuss it.'

'Sounds like a sting,' Sam said.

'Well, I'm not going out there on my own.' Richard pointed to Leah and Sam in turn. 'You two are coming with me as witnesses. If this woman is who I think she is, then I'll be standing on the other side of the room with my hands in my pockets. I want you to make a note of that – for later – at the tribunal.'

Leah gasped but Sam laughed. He followed as far as the door, looked out and saw an attractive middle-aged woman in a ban-dage dress attempt to take both of Richard's hands into hers.

In a seductive voice she explained that she could no longer afford her sessions and was hoping to come to some other sort of arrangement. Richard was consummate in handling the matter, not surprisingly.

'Gift of the gab,' Sam muttered to himself.

He returned to his desk and thought about Richard's suggestion to take Alice to the funeral. But a *police* funeral...

It had been hard enough when Glenn died. He missed his old colleague; the regular chats about everyday things, no doubt Glenn's way of keeping him on track. No notes were ever taken, or if they were they weren't kept on the premises. And he'd prescribed for Sam – quietly, privately.

Without Glenn, Sam had taken desperate measures to keep medicating. He was ashamed of himself. Last night he'd dropped the empty plastic sheath he'd used for the stolen pills into the bathroom bin and set the new bottle, bearing Alice Lacey's name, on the cabinet shelf. He thought about that now – how he'd stared at the bottle for ages, the all-consuming guilt. It was hard to believe it had come to this – pills that weren't really his, but they weren't hers either. And yet he'd used Alice. Her resolve was his failure.

He owed her.

He took out his mobile. He could hear his breath: short, almost laboured as he scrolled through the list of contacts until he came to her name.

Steadying himself, he made the call.

*

The police guard stretched both sides of the long driveway in front of the cemetery chapel. Mourners drifted around the perimeter, holding sacred the avenue of blue uniforms, as the Mercedes carrying the flower-laden coffin passed by every salute. An unseen drummer pounded a lonely beat. The guard turned to attention and began a slow and sombre march towards the graveyard.

Sam stood with Alice well away from the crowd on the other side of the avenue, beneath a tall tree in autumnal tones of crimson and gold. It was the first time he'd seen her dressed in black. He wouldn't say it was becoming. The only thing it suited was her depression. She'd hardly spoken, hiding behind her sunglasses even in the chapel during the service. He constantly steered his attention to her, making mental notes of what he could use in the follow-up sessions. But it wasn't easy. He tried hard not to think of Sophie's funeral.

Garth Conroy's fiancée waited on the top steps outside the chapel with a small child on her hip. An elderly couple, presumably his parents, stepped well away to the side of her. Sam had identified the uneasiness between them during the service.

He turned to Alice. 'Are you ready to speak to the family?'

She didn't move, and he couldn't tell where her sight fell. 'I'll never be ready,' she said. 'Maybe I want to skip that part and just go home.'

'It will mean a great deal to them. Think of it that way. They need your support at this time.'

She folded her arms tightly across her chest. 'My support – that's a joke. I have nothing to offer them.'

'You worked with Garth. You were with him during the train crash—'

'I was with myself,' she cut him off, 'quivering and crying and being useless. He carried the weight of my incompetence that day, my cowardice.'

'This isn't about blame, Alice. I'll come with you when you speak to them. And then we can leave if you like.'

She chewed for a moment on her bottom lip. 'You'll stay beside me?'

'If that's what you'd prefer.'

Once the procession had gone, they crossed over to the other side of the avenue and waited at the bottom of the chapel stairs. Garth Conroy's fiancée, still carrying her child, stepped down and came straight for them.

Alice trembled beside Sam and muttered something indiscernible.

The young woman stopped in front of them and stared at Alice before reaching for her hand. 'Oh Ali, I'm so glad you came.'

Both women began to cry.

Up until this point, Sam had been in control of his emotions, but now he was starting to unravel. His necktie felt like a garrotte, choking him with thoughts that Sophie should have been the one grieving for *him*, not the other way around. His breathing sharpened. He could no longer face it. At first he turned away, but moments later he found himself walking, breaking his promise to stay by Alice's side. Digging his finger into the knot at his neck, he returned to the sanctity of the overhanging branches of the large tree. With his back to the scene, he ripped his tie off and shoved it into his jacket pocket.

He pushed hard against the memory of Sophie's funeral, but it was rolling out in his mind like a newsreel: the coffin, front and centre in the church, covered in a massive display of blue and white flowers, her police hat positioned in the middle; a framed photograph of her in uniform on the altar, surrounded by more flowers and candles; discordant music reverberating around the chipped pale walls and stained-glass depictions of suffering; a wayward pigeon fluttering in the rafters.

He gritted his teeth. Several leaves floated onto him, stirred by the shift in wind. He picked one from his shoulder, burnt orange and perfectly formed. He concentrated on it, slowed his breathing, tried to refocus.

'Doctor Tyler, I'm sorry, but I need to stay a bit longer. Will that be all right?'

Sam crushed the leaf in his hand, slipped his sunglasses over his eyes and turned around.

Alice held knotted fingers to her chin. 'Emily's feeling ostracised by Garth's family. She thinks everyone's blaming her for what happened to him. Apparently, he was driving home after visiting her and his son when the accident happened. She wants me to stay with her for the burial.'

'As long as you feel up to it.'

She shrugged. 'I'm not keen on the idea, but I couldn't really say no. And of course, you'll be with me too, so...'

He hadn't banked on that, to stay with her during the interment. But he'd already deserted his post once today.

*

There were no more than twenty people waiting at the plot. The police guard had, thankfully, retired. Emily held on tightly to Alice's arm. The child was no longer with her. Sam felt out of place in what was clearly a private ceremony. He stood back like a secret service agent, his hands linked in front of his body, his sunglasses firmly in place despite the blanketing cloud cover.

The minister recited the final prayers and quoted words Sam had hoped never to hear again, 'Earth to earth, ashes to ashes, dust to dust...' The rest was drowned out in a heavy blood rush that made it seem as if Sam's heart had taken up residence in his head. Silver microdots flickered in his vision as his blood pressure climbed. He regretted having removed his tie because now his throat threatened to give up his anguish. He yearned for the restraint, a discomfort to concentrate on ahead of something much worse – a complete loss of control. He drove the fingernails of one hand into his fist.

As the coffin was slowly lowered, Emily began a heart-wrenching wail, her knees almost completely folding. Alice struggled to support her. Others around them also joined in on this song of woe, clutching one another, as the lone drummer made his presence felt once more with a strident beat.

Sam had to get out of here. But he couldn't leave Alice. She was still preoccupied with Emily. Her colleague's fiancée wasn't going to be able to stand much longer and nobody else was attempting to come to her aid.

Reluctantly, Sam stepped in and took Emily's other arm. Her breathing was quick and shallow, and she was at risk of hyperventilating. Sam moved the three of them away from the scene, settling Emily on a bench further down the long row of graves. Alice sat beside her while Sam took a step back.

Emily expressed her gratitude.

'This is Sam Tyler,' Alice said. She hesitated before adding, 'He's a... friend of mine. He drove me here today.'

Emily held out her hand and Sam stepped forward and took it. 'I'm sorry for your loss,' he said.

'There's a wake at Garth's parents' place. I was wondering...'
Emily turned to Alice. 'Well, would you both come with me?'

'Do you think going to the wake is a good idea?' Alice said. 'The
way Garth's parents have been with you... maybe you should just
go back to your sister's—'

'They're not going to push me away,' Emily said firmly. 'I owe
it to Danny. He's not even two and his father is gone now. Garth's
parents blame me for his death, I just know it, but Danny is their
flesh and blood. I won't let them turn their back on us. For Garth's
sake, I can't allow that.' She started to cry again.

'Where's Danny now?'

'Clare has him. She'll bring him across.'

Sam drove Alice and Emily to a property just outside of
Camden. He suggested he wait in the car, but the two women
looked at him with frightened eyes.

How did I get tied up in this mess?

Once inside the house, he found himself a discreet corner of the
lounge room next to a tall potted palm. Someone handed him a
drink. It might have been brandy. He knew he shouldn't, but he
swallowed it in quick gulps. The heady liquid did nothing to ease
the tension in his muscles.

It took him a while to realise that the mantel next to him was
set up as something of a shrine: several candles of varying size and
shades burned around a framed photo of Senior Constable Garth
Conroy. It occurred to Sam that he couldn't remember if there had
been photos or candles at Sophie's wake. It had been held at her
mother's house. But he hadn't been there long enough to notice.
He'd felt out of place, as if he didn't belong. People had tried to
approach him, to commiserate, but all he'd seen was the blame in
their eyes. He'd not lasted more than half an hour before urging his
sister and brother-in-law to take him home. He felt no different today, standing in this house of strangers.

He left the confines of the lounge room and went outside onto
the back lawn where there were fewer people. The evening was settling in early due to heavy cloud, accentuating the morbid mood.
The Conroys were there, making a tearful fuss of their grandchild.
Emily was off to the side watching.

Alice joined Sam minutes later and he was relieved to hear she was ready to go.

*

During the ride home in the car, Alice kept her face turned away from Sam, staring out the side window. He only caught glimpses of her reflection, but her tears were not lost on him. He knew he should talk to her, but right now he wasn't in the mood to play doctor.

When he pulled the car up at her house, she made no move to get out. Instead, she continued to stare out the window.

'Are you okay?' he asked.

She nodded and barely glanced at him to say, 'Thank you.' She opened the car door, but hesitated. Staring at her house again, she added, 'Ironic, I'm the cop. I'm not allowed to be scared.'

He said nothing, didn't quiz her, didn't offer to walk her inside. He wanted her to go. Her pain was irrepressible – it seemed to transcend the air between them, desecrating the energy.

Finally, she got out of the car and he drove off, not looking back.

The Cape Cod was shrouded in darkness by the time Sam drove into his street. He felt as if he were being watched from behind the hooded eyes of the upstairs windows. He shook off the feeling by heading straight for the pill bottle in the bathroom cabinet. Alice Lacey's name on the label disturbed him. A black felt-tip pen solved that problem seconds later.

Returning to the lounge room, he removed his jacket, then undid the first few buttons of his shirt. He was treading water, biding time until the moment his life should be snuffed out. His existence seemed pointless, but so did anyone else's for that matter. What was the purpose anyway? You were born, you died, and everything in the middle was struggle and pain. A minister once told him that life was about suffering, like Christ had suffered. One of his more philosophical patients had said that bad things only happened to those whom the gods favoured, to teach lessons that helped a soul to grow. It annoyed Sam how people tended to lean towards the God theory all the time. If there was no satisfactory answer, no rhyme or reason to this harsh world, then the problem got deferred to some almighty being who quite conveniently didn't even need to show up. Glenn Whittaker had been more succinct: he'd said that people thought too much about their mortality.

One thing was certain, Sam knew – it wasn't something he could control. Nobody could. Maybe Glenn had been right: it didn't warrant thought.

The microwave finished the recommended cycle but Sam's frozen meal was icy cold in the centre. He ate around the edges and threw the remainder into the bin. Then he poured himself a large glass of merlot and took it over to the front window in the lounge room, winding out the lever to let in the breeze.

The distant thrum of the ocean smashing against the rocky coast was like nature's own orchestra. It was the one certainty in his life, a focus, a soothing distraction. He rubbed the back of his neck with his free hand and then took a large sip of the wine. The strain started to ease.

The funeral had taken a toll, but he'd mostly handled it. It had been important for him to go, just as much as it had been for Alice, he realised now. The images, the memories that had resurfaced, they were inevitable but also essential. In order to face his demons, he had to first release them from their prison at the back of his mind.

I can get through this.

The flickering streetlamp across the road caught his attention. He'd rung the council about it enough times—

Glass shattered onto the timber floor at his feet; red wine splattering and spraying like a cut artery.

The policewoman standing beneath the faulty light was staring right up at him. Her dark hair severely parted in the centre and pulled back... like she always wore it... her ghostly presence flashing in time with the fractious electrical current.

He hit the floor and rolled away as if someone had taken a pot shot at him. He felt on fire. The room seemed to dip and spiral until he put his back to the wall, drawing in steadying breaths. 'It's not Sophie,' he told himself. 'There's nobody there.'

Carefully, he edged his way back to the window, peered out from the side. The apparition was gone. But there was something – a flash of movement.

Seconds later he stumbled out onto the porch and ran down the steps. He tripped over the garden hose but was quickly to his feet again. He went to the very spot he had seen her, and turned back and forth – the light pinching and pulsing overhead. But there were only shadows. His breath was sharp and painful, as though the air was abrasive.

He turned and looked up at the house, at the window where he'd been standing just minutes ago, the honey-warm glow behind the slatted blinds. And then above it, at the ominous and soulless appendage, like a vulture clawed to its prey – where there was nothing... except regret.

TEN

Patient expresses demoralisation and overwhelming feelings of failure and hopelessness. She has taken to spending lengthy amounts of time in an upper area of the home that remains incomplete. Her appetite is poor and her concentration, particularly at work, is reduced. She is still unable to properly express her concerns to her husband, and claims that any attempts to talk to him have resulted in arguments.

I brought into focus one of her recent diary entries. She read through the notes and on the second or third reading, seemed to reconcile an aspect of her behaviour she had not considered before.

My birthday. Thirty-four. It sounds so damned old. Sam didn't say anything at first and I thought he'd forgotten. But after I made him breakfast he tossed a badly wrapped package across the kitchen counter to me. It was a makeup purse with a cheap lip gloss inside. I felt like throwing it at him, but instead I played along. I gasped and told him it was exactly what I'd wanted and how did he know? I was trying to make my point, but he merely smiled and went back to his toast.

Of course, it got the better of me, and eventually I shouted at him that he was a useless prick. I used much worse language as well, and even cried in temper. It was so infuriating.

'Sophie, stop it,' he complained. He tried to say more but I threw a wet dishrag at him and stormed out of the kitchen. He followed, trying to haul me back, saying words that I was too angry to listen to.

I went upstairs to the extension, shouting back that he had no intention of getting it finished and that we'd be living with incomplete rooms forever. As I went in I stopped cold. In the centre of the room was a massive display of thirty-four rainbow roses. I know because I counted them.

The card, in Sam's handwriting, read simply, 'You colour my world.'

Plan: continue in-house therapy and discussion of selected diary notes.

G. Whittaker

'What are you doing in here?'

Leah snapped shut the file she was holding.

'Sam.' She stood up, then shoved the file into an archive box on the desk in front of her. 'After Diane took Glenn's office, Richard said I could organise the old files in here before transferring them into the storeroom compactors.'

'Well, I'm sure he didn't mean for you to sit and read them.'

'No, I wasn't. I was just...' She swallowed. 'Did you want me for something?'

'I saw the light on.' He took a sip of his takeaway coffee, then flicked his head towards the other end of the hall. 'Has the meeting started yet?'

Leah checked her watch. 'Half an hour ago.'

Good, Sam thought, part of his ploy to spend as little time as possible listening to his colleague's preliminary machinations.

He went to go but thought of something. 'While you're here, I'm missing some paperwork from Alice Lacey's file. It might have got separated in the rush when Glenn's patients were divvied up.'

'What sort of papers?'

'The initial psych report from Coffs Harbour and some other police reports. Also, a list of the most significant jobs in Alice's career. Glenn's marked them up on a checklist, so I know they exist.'

'I'll keep a lookout for them.'

She seemed demure, quiet for a change. Sam wondered about it. 'Today, if you don't mind.'

'I'll do it now.'

Richard scowled as Sam came into the meeting room a moment later. 'Nice of you to finally join us.'

From the other side of the table, Diane sat back in her chair holding her pen like a cigarette. Cranston rummaged through papers, muttering something about a less than infallible filing system. Sam hardly ever brought anything with him. He could discuss patients off the top of his head if need be. He continued to sip on his coffee.

'I was just saying to the others,' Richard went on, smugness easing across his lips. 'You'll never guess who was in my office this morning.'

'Jonas Monroe,' Sam said.

'Jonas Monroe,' Richard savoured the name until he realised the discrepancy. 'What? How did you know?'

'Saw him in the lift.'

Richard sighed, but quickly recovered. 'Didn't think you followed football.'

'His controversial lifestyle is usually front-page news. Hard to miss.'

'He's here on a court order,' Diane said. 'Richard's his get-out-of-jail-free card.'

'Good publicity for the practice though,' Richard added.

Diane tapped at the low stack of files in front of her. 'Only if I get some work out of it.'

'With a bit of luck we'll get the contract for the whole team. That's what I wanted to talk to you all about today – lifting our profile. There's a big opportunity here.'

Sam preferred to be counted out of the matter; he had enough clientele without taking on anything close to a whole football team. He sat back and let them witter on, turning his attention to the rain smashing against the long window. It seemed to lend a depressing, almost dangerous feel to the air.

His thoughts eventually trailed back to the apparition of Sophie last night. There were a few possibilities, although one stuck out above the others – that he was losing his mind. Sam didn't really believe it. It had been nothing more than a mild aberration brought on by a combination of trauma, tiredness, the police funeral, and Alice's palpable depression during the drive home. Those things had no doubt contributed to his agitation. And not forgetting his chemical reliance; he really needed to work on that, haul back the levels of medication and get himself straight.

Diane flicked his ear on her way out of the meeting room, dragging him back to his senses. He looked down to see the paper cup crushed inside his hand.

Sam headed out and as he crossed reception, caught sight of Ben's vibrant-haired cousin standing beyond the glass panel, pressing the button for the lift. She turned and saw him in the same moment.

'Veronica,' Sam said, surprised.

Her lips thinned as she came over to him, glancing briefly at Leah who was poised at the reception counter glowering.

'It was nothing important,' the tall redhead said. 'Just returning something you left behind in my flat. I thought to donate it to charity, but it appears to be personalised.'

He opened his arm towards his office door. 'Come in, please.'

Veronica hesitated, but then went ahead. Sam closed the door behind them and offered her a seat, taking up the opposite armchair. She removed his tie from her handbag, dropped it on the table between them.

'Your secretary refused to take it. I think she presumed it was a gift.'

'Thank you,' he said. Truth was, he knew he'd left it behind. 'And look, I'm really sorry about running out on you that night.'

'There was no need to make your escape the minute my back was turned. I don't know what you thought was supposed to happen.'

'It wasn't anything you did, I promise. I'm just... inept.' He picked up the tie, his initials embroidered on the end of the fine grey material. 'You could have put a match to this.'

She regarded him for a moment. There seemed something sympathetic in her eyes. 'I might have done just that... if not for...' She glanced at her hands. 'Well, you've been out of the game for a while I expect. It can't be easy.'

He inwardly cringed at her meaning and realised she mightn't be so charitable if she knew about him and Leah.

'I'm overseeing Ben's gig this weekend,' she went on. 'Maybe you'd like to come along. We're at The Thirsty Camel tomorrow night... if that interests you.'

Sam nodded. He knew the venue. It was a trendy nightclub in The Rocks. 'Sure. I mean, great.'

They exchanged phone numbers. Then he walked her to the door where she turned, touched his arm, and said, 'You're a nice man, but I think you're being hard on yourself. Maybe it's time to come in from the cold.'

'Tomorrow night,' he said.

'Until then...'

He waited until she was safely deposited in the lift, ignored Leah's pinched expression, and closed the office door.

*

The next morning, Sam was relieved to be out of the office for a few hours, away from Leah's scrutiny. He attended the university for a lecturing gig; spent time with the faculty over examination papers and the marking criteria; and visited Minh Luong who was still in hospital. When Sam arrived at the office, Leah was ready to pounce.

'I was wondering if we could talk,' she said, as he came out of the lift.

'Is it about work?'

'Well, no. But it's important.' She put her hand on his arm, halted him momentarily. 'Please. I've got to tell you how I feel, so that you'll understand and maybe we can—'

He cut her off. 'It makes no difference. Nothing is going to change between us.'

'Won't you hear me out?'

'Not now. I'm working. And so are you.'

'This afternoon?'

'Leah, you can't—' He noticed his first patient was already in the waiting room. He cleared his throat. 'Gordon, come through.'

Once the stocky man was inside the office, Sam turned back to Leah. 'You've got to cut this out,' he told her with quiet urgency. 'This is not the time or place.'

'It's never the time or place for you,' she said, not bothering to adjust her volume. 'You won't take my calls, you ignore emails. Maybe I should make an appointment? Or dye my hair red. Would that help?'

He huffed, couldn't find a suitable answer. Maintaining eye contact was difficult, especially as she seemed to gloat at his discomfiture. Finally, he managed, 'Don't disturb me before five o'clock.'

Alice was his last patient for the day. She was wearing a floral dress and a high-cut denim jacket. Her hair fell over one shoulder. The dark roots were getting longer. Sam still wasn't sure if this was an attempt at style.

'I'm sorry I'm late again,' she said. 'I just can't get organised, and the bus system is so unreliable and confusing. Some of the services have been cancelled because of this weather.'

Sam leant forward slightly, one elbow on the armrest, his other casually across his knee. 'Town Hall Railway Station is about five minutes from here. St James, perhaps another minute.'

'I don't do trains.'

'It might be worth a try, save you the hardship of buses and all those changes you have to make just to get in here.'

She rolled her eyes. 'Can we not talk about trains?'

He sat back. 'Okay, let's talk about Garth's funeral.'

'Not that either. I went and that was enough. I paid my respects and supported Emily. But that's it – I don't want to pull the whole experience apart.'

'It wasn't my intention to dissect it moment by moment,' Sam said. 'It's more about how you handled your emotions. Those insights are important.'

'Isn't it enough that I handled it? I didn't throw myself on the coffin screaming or begging Garth's forgiveness.'

'Why would you need Garth's forgiveness?'

She shot him a dark look. 'Nice try, Doctor. You don't get me that easily.'

'I'm not trying to trick you, Alice. But you do need to trust me. At some stage we're going to have to talk about things that you find uncomfortable.'

Her sigh was resigned. 'Why can't I just keep them all inside?'

'Because they have a way of coming out, regardless, and usually when you least expect it. It's already happened to you before in Coffs Harbour, when you went AWOL on duty and they found you hugging the cistern of the ladies toilet.' He paused, noting her uneasiness at the memory, his intention to make the point. 'It's better if we can face them in session under a controlled environment. You're safe here, Alice. There's nothing to fear.'

She didn't respond.

He took up her file, remembering too late that he hadn't chased Leah about the missing paperwork. It wasn't urgent. But it would have been good to see a sample of Alice's most challenging jobs, get an idea of the sorts of things she'd had to face in her fourteen years of service. It was particular to police, the nature of their psychological injuries – it wasn't just the job, but every traumatic event they had ever experienced, starting from childhood, piling one on the other. And she, like her colleagues, became proficient in suppression, pushing away the feelings, locking them deep within in order to cope; until finally something gave – that one job or one trigger that set it all loose in a chaotic mash of emotion. He needed to coax it out of Alice, get her to release those pent-up anxieties, not be afraid of them.

'Tell me about Garth. What was he like to work with?'

She shrugged. 'He was a good cop. Reliable. Knowledgeable.'

'Is that all?'

'I don't know what you mean.'

He paused, studying her. She was fidgeting, staring at her lap, at the armrest of the chair, at something on the end of her sleeve.

'How did you feel about him?' he said quietly.

This time her eyes flashed to his. It was brief, but it was enough: a wild sense that her innermost secrets were at risk of being revealed.

'Feel? I liked him if that's what you mean.' Her bottom lip began to tremble, her guard failing. She mouthed a profanity, looked away, half turned in the chair.

'It's all right,' Sam said.

She started to cry. 'No, it's not all right... it's not.'

He moved the tissue box towards her on the table. She took one automatically but did nothing with it. He waited for her breathing to settle.

'Are you ready to tell me about it?'

'I think you already know.'

'About you and Garth?'

Her lip trembled again. 'I feel... bad about it. At the funeral... I thought maybe Emily...' She wiped her eyes with the tissue.

'That Emily had known?' He paused. 'Had you seen Garth in recent times?'

'Not since coming to Sydney. But it was... well, we weren't really... I mean, he would have... but I...' She sighed, adding resignedly, 'I don't know what I mean. I don't know anything anymore.'

He made no comment and waited until she was ready to say more.

'To be honest, I was surprised during the service when the minister said Emily was his fiancée. Garth told me he didn't want to marry her, even with the child. They never even lived together.' She looked at Sam, her green eyes making him think of an impenetrable jungle: complex, perilous, beguiling. 'What's the point of this? These questions?'

'It helps me to understand you better, how you process things, manage your emotions.'

'I've never told anybody. I'm not used to confessions.' She paled, sank further in the chair. 'The last time I saw Garth we had a fight.'

Sam nodded his sympathy.

'Things had ended between us,' she went on. 'I decided to move, to leave Coffs, leave it all behind.'

'And that included Garth?'

'That's how he saw it. He said I was running away from him. But I wasn't. Not really. Even though he didn't live with Emily, he had a son, he still had that responsibility whether he liked it or not. I couldn't get in the way of that, of his relationship with Danny. I had to leave. And Garth had to stay. That's all there was to it.'

Sam put his notepad aside. He hadn't written anything on it anyway. 'Why was that up to you? Garth's child was his responsibility, not yours.'

She clenched her fists. 'It wasn't going to work out. How were we supposed to look at each other again? I didn't know how to love him anymore. It was gone. If he touched me I freaked out. All I could see was Bellingen, images of that day, overturned carriages and Garth trying to help people, trying to organise them, calling for backup. And I was... frozen, useless. And he never held it against me, never said anything about it. But it was there, it was always going to come between us.'

Sam allowed a longer pause than usual before prompting her to go on.

'I don't know why he had to keep arguing the point. Coming over and ringing me and just... wouldn't let it go. And begging... God, I couldn't handle it. I had to get away.'

'When was the last time you saw him?'

'The day I moved from Coffs. The removalist truck was in my driveway and Garth came in just as the last of the stuff was being loaded.' She put her hands to her face. 'The last time I saw him... the very last time... the angry and hurtful things I said...'

He went to speak, to bring an end to her distress, but she was already on her feet.

'Stop asking me about him, stop asking me these things. He's gone and I won't ever get the chance to say how sorry... how *very sorry*—'

'We're going to leave it,' Sam said calmly. 'It's all right. Just take a seat.'

She sat automatically, her face in her hands. But now it seemed the banks had broken and there was no end to her tears. It was like their first session all over again. Only this time it wasn't impatience Sam felt, nor annoyance or ways to be rid of her.

'Alice,' he said softly after a while, but it wasn't to draw her attention back to the session or to recapture her composure. It was because he felt for her, for all the bad things she'd seen – bad things like Sophie had seen; for the wrong turns she'd taken in life; for the disastrous end to the relationship with her colleague; the hurt and the sadness and the loneliness.

Leah opened the door and then knocked on the panel. 'It's ten past five, Sam. Oh...' She stared over at Alice like she was some sort of anomaly.

Sam got to his feet and went straight over to the secretary. 'What do you think you're doing?' he said in a harsh whisper, moving her out of the doorway and back into reception.

She blinked black, petrified lashes at him. 'I thought she'd gone. I didn't realise the session was still going.'

'You didn't realise? What did you think?'

'I was in the ladies room. I made a presumption...' She bit onto her lower lip and Sam noticed the smear of recently applied red lipstick. 'You said not to disturb you before five, and I—'

He felt like having it out with Leah but he couldn't leave Alice alone any longer. 'I'll talk to you later,' he said irritably.

'So, should I stay?'

'No. Go home.'

'Will you call me? Maybe we could catch up.'

He found himself nodding, but it was only to appease her, to make her leave.

The interruption seemed to have broken Alice's crying. She looked up as he came back in, her bottom lip still trembling.

'I'm sorry about that,' he told her as he sat down.

She sniffed and took another tissue. 'It's okay,' she said. 'I suppose it was all a waste. The session. Disastrous, really.'

'On the contrary, it was progress.'

Sam could tell she was fighting off more tears. She clutched at the tissue – the whites of her knuckles exposed. The session was ended. It would be unethical to go on.

He waited until she'd composed herself, asked her how she was feeling, and when she'd assured him enough times that she was all right, he stood and walked her out. It was a relief that Leah hadn't lingered. He went ahead and pushed the button for the lift.

'Goodnight, Alice,' he said.

'Goodnight, and thank you,' she returned quietly.

The lift opened and he watched as she stepped inside; her eyes downturned until just before the door closed. He felt a jolt of something near his chest, a kind of ache or longing, the intensity of those green eyes forged into his senses. He remained and listened to the descent of the lift, the strain of cables and pulleys, the clunking of the mechanics. It stopped seconds later and he imagined Alice stepping out at ground level.

He returned to his office and fished around in the drawer, found the bottle of whisky, and downed a large glass. It was harsh, scorched his throat. Then he looked at Alice's file again, flicked through the papers, but he couldn't concentrate. Maybe it was time to reduce her visits to once a fortnight. Ease off. Yes, that would be best. They'd been spending too much time in each other's company lately. Three times in one week: the home visit, the funeral, and to-day's rather heavy session.

His thoughts drifted to Veronica. He'd been playing around with it in his mind all day, whether or not to meet her again. It wouldn't harm either of them if he didn't show. But after the week he'd had, the last thing he felt like doing was returning to that house of haunted dreams.

ELEVEN

Sam grabbed his coat and headed out of the building. The weather hadn't improved. The streets were awash with mini flash floods that overshot the drains and gutters and were made into fountains by car tyres, splashing over the footpath and soaking the ends of his trousers. He pulled up his collar, shrugged his hands into his pockets and, keeping as well as he could under the awnings, headed to The Thirsty Camel.

The club decor was themed as desert and oasis. In one area were soft amber chairs with big tasselled cushions, and there was a canopy over the dance floor like the inside of a Bedouin tent. On the other side, at the bar, were lush potted palms around tall stools with metal tables. The patrons looked like professional types – straight from their offices. The end of another working week, united in binge-drinking.

Veronica smiled when she saw him. She took his coat and huddled him into a semi-circular booth, pouring two glasses of champagne from a bottle.

'I assume you won't be driving tonight,' she said.

'I guess I'll have to rely on public transport.'

'Good thing my flat is only one stop away then.'

He smiled and raised his glass to hers, clinking lightly. Moments later he thought he was seeing things when Alice Lacey walked in.

What's she doing here?

He sat forward and watched her go straight to the bar.

She pulled up a stool at the far end and immediately was attended to by one of the barmen. He poured her a large white wine and shared a joke with her. She took her wine in both hands and drained almost half of it in a matter of seconds.

Well, it wasn't his problem, Sam decided. She was a free agent.

Ben came over to chat and Sam found it hard to concentrate on the conversation while he was so aware of Alice. He watched her discreetly.

She finished her wine and the bartender poured her another. She seemed to be making short work of that one as well.

Veronica must have followed his line of sight. 'Someone you know?' she said.

'In a way,' he replied, turning his attention back to the flaming redhead.

The band members had set up and Ben went over to join them. The music started; a minor hit from years ago. A few people got up to dance.

After a while, Veronica held up the empty bottle. 'We're all out. How about another?'

'I'll get it,' Sam said.

Alice was still at the bar when he went over although she didn't seem to notice him. Her head bowed, she teetered a little on the edge of her stool. The bartender topped up her drink without asking, then came over to serve Sam.

'She's had enough, hasn't she?' Sam said with a flick of his head towards Alice.

The bartender winked at him. 'Not yet, mate. But she's nearly there.'

Sam didn't like the connotation. He placed his order and paid, keeping watch on Alice. A tall bearded man approached her and asked if he could buy her a drink. She didn't respond to the interloper, turned away from him. When he persisted, she took her glass and got off the stool, although she stumbled, spilling her drink.

The man went to steady her but she pushed his hands aside. 'Don't touch me,' she said. She put her glass on the counter. It fell over. A female bartender stood it up, asked if she wanted her to call a taxi.

'I'm not going anywhere,' Alice said. 'Get me another drink. White wine.'

The female bartender got a fresh glass and began to pour another wine.

'Hey,' Sam said, leaning over the bar. 'She's had enough. Right? Enough.'

'What's it to you?' Alice said angrily, turning towards him. But then a shadow of recognition fell across her features. 'Oh my God. Sam.'

His cover was blown. There was no point in pretending. 'What do you think you're doing?' he asked.

'I'll give you a clue.' She blew out a sharp breath, dug in her shoulder bag, slapped a twenty on the counter, took up the glass of wine and told the bartender to keep the change.

Veronica came over. 'Is everything okay?'

Sam grabbed the champagne bottle and the two glasses. 'Yeah, it's fine,' he said through gritted teeth. They returned to their booth near the dance floor.

'What was that all about?' Veronica asked as she sidled up to him on the padded bench seat.

'Nothing. It was nothing.'

In between pouring the champagne, he managed several glances at Alice and noticed she was back on the stool, the first barman in attendance to her as before. The bearded man lingered nearby, being egged on by several other men who rubbed his shoulders like he was about to go in for another round in the boxing ring.

And Sam didn't like any of it – didn't like it at all.

*

Ben came to the table with a tray of Sambuca shots. 'Get 'em down. They're on the house. The band drinks for free during the breaks.'

'I'm not part of the band,' Sam said.

'I told them you're my adviser.'

Veronica counted to three and they all threw back the shots except for Sam. He wrapped his hand around the glass and kept it aside.

Although he'd told himself he didn't need to keep watch on Alice, his eyes darted towards the bar often. But the club gradually filled and it became harder to see her. It was probably better that way, he decided. Alice's private life was absolutely no business of his and she'd made that perfectly clear to him. He was kicking himself for having got involved in the first place.

But eventually it got the better of him and while Veronica became occupied in discussion with the club manager, Sam got up and wandered back over to the bar. There were many people crowded around it, vying for service. Alice was nowhere in sight. He lingered in the area, looking around for her. Finally, he asked the barman who pointed to the front door.

'You just missed her, mate.'

Sam went back to the table and told Veronica, 'Something's come up. I've got to go.'

She frowned her concern. 'Is everything all right?'

'Just a work thing. I'm really sorry.'

'Of course. If you must.'

'I'll give you a call.'

He grabbed his coat and hurried out.

Rain spiked at his face as he stood at the kerb, looking left and right down the street. He couldn't tell which direction Alice might have gone. It seemed stupid now, rushing out. Alice was an adult. Still, he couldn't help but wonder if she'd left with anyone.

He figured he may as well go home. But as he turned he caught sight of Alice standing with her back against the brickwork of the club, the awning giving little protection from the weather.

Relieved, he went over. 'Are you all right?' he asked.

'Why wouldn't I be?' she slurred.

'You've had a bit to drink.'

'I still know how to call a taxi.'

'Oh, right.' He looked into the night, at the thin rain that appeared like steely blades under the streetlights, issuing a sense of hazard.

'At last,' Alice said as a yellow taxi pulled up. She started a jagged line towards the kerb.

Three women spilt from the club and hurried ahead of her, squealing at being caught in the rain. They piled into the back of the taxi.

'Hey, get outta there,' Alice called, but the doors slammed shut and the taxi drove off. 'That was mine. Those bitches stole my ride.'

She fumbled in her bag, took out her phone, grumbling about losing the taxi.

Sam took out his own phone and booked an Uber. It would be here in less than a minute.

The club doors swung open as several young men were thrown out by security. One of the males vomited on the footpath. Alice reeled backwards, dropping her phone. Sam retrieved it and moved her away from the scrabble of hands and legs and bodies.

Heading down the street, he spotted a set of headlights that he presumed was the Uber. He stepped out onto the road, his arm raised. It pulled swiftly into the kerb. Sam opened the back door, then turned and took Alice by the arm. She felt like a wilted flower. Her breathing was short and rapid.

He sat her on the backseat but her head was starting to loll.

The driver turned around, his eyebrows knotted together. 'Hey, don't be sick in here, love.'

'Just give her a minute, will you,' Sam said through the opened door.

'Mate, if she spews, that's me out of business for the rest of the night.'

'She's not going to spew.' He tried to nudge Alice across but she wouldn't budge. He closed the door and raced around to the other side and got in. She slunk towards him and put her head on his shoulder as they took off. Seconds later he could tell she was asleep.

*

The ride home was longer due to the weather, forcing several detours. Heavy downpours washed over the windows, reducing visibility, turning the city lights into unfocused streaks of colour.

The driver wanted to engage in useless conversation. Sam obliged with the occasional bland reply. He gave directions and, as they turned into Alice's street, he tried to wake her. She half sat up – was disoriented – put her head back on his shoulder.

'Can you wait? I won't be long,' he said to the driver.

'Wait for what?'

'To take me the rest of the way.'

'But this is the address you booked.'

'No, I booked *my* address. It's a few minutes from here. I've just got to get her inside.'

The driver huffed. 'Don't be too long. I've had enough of this weather.'

Sam helped Alice to her door. She could hardly stand. He asked her for the keys and she shoved her bag at him before sinking down onto the front porch step. Reluctantly, he opened her bag and found a wad of keys. After a few tries, he got the door open, leant in and flicked a switch that turned on the light over the stairs.

Alice was asleep again, her head resting on a terracotta pot that was filled only with dirt. When she didn't respond to his requests to stand, he carefully pulled her by one arm, but her knees were powerless and she mumbled something about being left to sleep where she was.

'You can't stay out here,' he said, but she wasn't budging.

He crouched down, put his arms around her waist and got her to her feet. She staggered inside with him as far as the first sofa, which she fell into, curling into the fetal position. He went back for her shoulder bag. Remembering he still had her phone, he removed it from his pocket and put it in the bag.

He didn't linger. He'd done enough – more than enough.

Just as he came outside, he saw red taillights disappearing over the crest. He swore several times.

TWELVE

Sam cut through the open-air mall, past the Friday-night crowd that were taking advantage of the break in the weather to rush between venues. He looked up. There were no stars. Had he expected to see any? The rain started again.

The long incline of his street was before him. There was no foot-path and the grass was soggy, so he stuck to the bitumen.

The revving of an engine caused him to look back. Headlights from a stationary car sprang on. The engine revved again much louder, and the wild spin of tyres blew out shadowy fumes that caught in the streetlights as the car roared towards him.

Sam stepped off the roadway and onto the grass verge, but the car changed trajectories, heading straight for him. He didn't have time to think, only to react. In his haste, he stumbled and fell – the right wheel of the car clipping the kerb just inches from where Sam had landed. Then it sped off, disappearing into the darkness, leav-ing behind a spinning hubcap that clattered to a halt seconds later.

Sam didn't move. The water laden grass seeped through his clothing, chilling his skin.

Eventually, he got to his feet and brushed the muck from his trouser legs, amazed he was still in one piece.

'What the fuck was that all about?' he muttered.

He got moving, limping with a strained muscle in his right thigh.

Still shaken by the close call, he lumbered up the front steps of his house and felt for the keys in his pocket. As he did so he saw a white item jutting out from between the diamond shaped grill of the security door. It was a note. As he pulled the paper away, it broke apart, sodden from the wild weather.

Inside, he tried to piece it together, to see anything of the words that had been written there, but he couldn't make it out. But maybe he didn't need them. Maybe he already understood those elusive words.

He went into the bathroom and hesitated over the bottle of pills before taking one. Then he stripped off, saw the mud and grass stains on his clothes, checked his body for injury – there was redness along his thigh, mud under his nails and his elbow was sore. He ran the shower and washed himself as if it was urgent.

After he'd dried off he returned to the note and put it under a stronger light. Carefully he pulled at it, opening it out, trying not to destroy it any further, and scanned for clues. His head started to throb. There were words, two that he was sure of: CUT OFF.

Cut off what? he asked himself, tossing the wet paper aside.

Take your pick of body parts, came the answer.

*

Sam couldn't sleep, his thoughts in a tailspin.

He staggered from the bedroom in the dark wearing his boxer shorts, and went to the front window. He opened it and thought he could hear the gentle lull of softer surf. Slowly, he began to relax. After a few minutes he became lucid enough to wonder about the sodden note that had been left on his front door. Was it coincidence that someone had also tried to run him down?

His mind turned back to a time just after Sophie died. Lots of upset cops back then, lamenting and mourning their fellow officer's passing. There had been many cards and messages of sympathy and support, even from strangers, cops from different states of Australia, some from overseas. But there had also been the hang-up calls, or the ones with obscenities shouted down the line, all apparently untraceable. Patrol cars with lingering spotlights on the front of his house had burdened his sleep for weeks, but claimed they were only watching out for him. But he knew how they'd all felt,

Sophie's colleagues. His behaviour the night of her death – word had certainly got around. They'd never forgiven him.

So, four years on, was it possible someone could reignite a grudge? Stupid question – McGuire was the top contender.

Slimy piece of filth, Sam thought. McGuire had made his feelings known at Minh's suicide attempt. If he could find the motivation to get Sam's car towed during a critical incident, then he probably had as many resources as he needed to find an opportunity and drive the message of hatred home.

It would be pointless running to the cops with his sopping note. They wouldn't want to help him.

They protect their own.

*

Hauling himself out of the chair as first light eased into the room, Sam remembered it was his birthday. Thirty-nine. He'd tried to ignore it as just another day in the calendar. But suddenly he felt that he ought to care about it, especially with a body that didn't seem to heal as fast as it used to.

He showered again to warm his muscles. His clothes from last night were still on the bathroom floor, the grass and mud stains dried into the material. They were ruined.

As he offloaded the trousers into the garage bin, he noticed the canvas covering his motorbike against the far wall. He hadn't thought about his Harley for years. Sophie had loathed it – called it the suicide machine. But maybe he needed to prove to himself that he wasn't an old man yet.

Dressed in jeans, boots, and his old leather jacket that smelt of rust and oil, he added fuel from a jerry can to the bike, put his helmet on and then his gloves. He sat on it and faced it towards the open tilt door, but the engine didn't even come close to kicking over.

It was a risk, but he was going to try to clutch-start the bike.

He rolled it to the top edge of the driveway and looked down the steep roadway before him. Engaging the second gear and with the ignition on, he pitched the bike and leant forward. It was ominous, the silence as the machine gradually picked up speed. He waited for sufficient momentum and then released the clutch.

Fail!

He tried again, picking up more speed now. The engine didn't even sound interested.

'Shit.'

He wondered what it was going to be like ploughing through the grove of melaleucas dead ahead. That was provided he wasn't cleaned up by traffic. Either way, it was going to be a painful experience.

Another go; the engine finally caught just before he ran out of roadway, and then it was a hard left, chugging like it had the hiccups. Slow revs brought it back to life. He rode to the service station, filled the tank and checked the tyres.

Sam had forgotten the solace of the open road: nobody to bother him, no calls, no interferences, no responsibilities. He pushed the speed limit on the highway once he was clear of the suburbs, really leant into it. By the turnoff to Helensburgh and the coastal road, he had the hang of it. Machine and man were one again.

A small vibration in the front wheel wasn't particularly troubling, but he thought he ought to check it out. Maybe it was the tyre. Sitting idle for years wouldn't have done it any good.

He pulled over at the first opportunity and parked before realising he was at Bald Hill lookout. Set on the edge of the escarpment, he'd passed it too many times to count, but had never stopped before now. It was famous as a take-off point for hang-gliders, their colours in the sky nearly constant on the weekends.

He forgot about checking the tyre. Instead, he removed his helmet and walked onto the grass. The Pacific dominated from this height, rolling in slow motion as if it were really made from one piece of velvet. A haze rose from the horizon, blurring the line between water and sky. It was beautiful.

'Sophie!'

Sam's head jerked in the direction of the voice. A man was chasing after a small child along the grass verge. 'Gotcha now,' the man said as he caught up with the giggling girl, lifting her into the air.

Sam pressed the area on his chest with the palm of his hand in an attempt to calm his racing heart. But his imagination took over, and with it came an old memory. *His* Sophie was walking towards him now. He trembled at how real this seemed. She was clear in his mind: her long hair pulled into the severe style she wore even on days off; high-cut shorts and a tight t-shirt accentuating her sexy curves. She had been so beautiful.

'I hate that horrible suicide machine. You've got to get responsible, Sam, if we're to start a family.'

He saw himself, as though the ghost of the memory had stepped outside of his body. It met with Sophie's image, stood over her.

'How is selling my motorbike getting responsible?'

'Because we won't be able to afford it with a baby.'

'Maybe it's the baby we can't afford.'

Sam squeezed his eyes closed, cut off the image, drew himself back. He returned to the bike and kicked the tyre. He wasn't going to bother with it.

He decided to weave his way home through the national park. He was coming up to the sharp bend at Dead Man's Creek when a van driving in the opposite direction breached the centre line. Sam automatically swerved, but the bike fishtailed and he completely lost control, machine and body parting company. He landed in a thicket of ferns between two large gum trees.

At first he was too shocked to move. There seemed to be a strange silence, as though time had stood still. He stared up through the canopy of leaves and branches above him, at the gentle blueness of the sky beyond – and watched in almost dull fascination as though the simplicity of this moment was all he required. He didn't want to move; he didn't want to ever have to care about anything again, or to think beyond the colour blue.

The illusion was fractured by the hysterical screaming of a woman as others rushed over to him. He tried to sit up.

'Mate, don't move.' A grey-haired man with desperately worried eyes put a hand on Sam's shoulder. 'We've called an ambulance.'

He ignored the advice and sat up and thought about removing his helmet, but changed his mind.

'You were lucky,' the same man said. 'You couldn't have landed anywhere better. If you'd hit a tree, you'd be a goner.'

Dread rushed Sam veins. Two close calls in less than twenty-four hours. What were the odds of that? Someone had tried to run him down last night, and this time he was successfully run off the road. Only luck had saved him.

'Oh God, I didn't mean it,' another man said rapidly. 'The corner came up on me. I couldn't do anything about it. Are you all right, mate? I'm really sorry. The cops are going to give it to me. I've only got a few points left on my licence.'

'I've got to go.' Sam pushed aside well-meaning hands.

'You're in shock,' someone else said. 'You should wait for the police.'

'I don't need the police. It's all right.'

He got up and hobbled over to his bike and a couple of young guys helped him stand it up. It was scraped severely down one side from where it had lost paint on its slide across the bitumen. Gingerly, he swung his leg over the seat, and was relieved when it started.

Against protests from the onlookers that he should remain, Sam left them all behind, slowly riding back to the house, trying to reconcile the matter in his head. It didn't take him long to realise he was being paranoid. Nobody could have known he was going to take his bike out. Even if he'd been followed, the van he'd almost collided with had been coming in the opposite direction. And the driver would never have stopped to apologise if it had been anything other than an accident.

When Sam got inside he saw the red flashing light of his answering machine. Four out of the five messages were from Leah. He deleted them without listening to the entirety of them, but he'd caught enough in her first words: whining about not being able to contact him, something about him promising to talk to her over the weekend. The last message on the machine was from Richard asking him to call.

He dialled Richard's home number. Laura answered and Sam tried to be gracious when she attempted to exchange pleasantries. Then she put her husband on. Richard was suspiciously jovial.

'You may as well get to the reason you wanted to talk to me,' Sam said.

Richard coughed. 'The – ah – conference in the mountains. You were going to think on it and give me an answer.'

Sam realised his arm was aching from being dragged along the road when the bike went down. It fuelled his temper. 'No, *you* said I should think on it. But I've already given my answer. I'm not going.'

'Come on, Sam. Someone has to go and you're the best one for it.'

'I'm not the only one who can deliver a speech.'

'It's not that. I can't rely on the others. They'd stuff it up. It's the image of the practice that's important. You're exemplary. You and Glenn, you've held the business together, kept our professional rating strong. Do you want me to beg? I will, you know.'

'You can beg, you can send me bouquets, and you can kiss my arse if you want. But it still won't make a difference. I'm not doing it. Got that?'

'What's the matter with you, you grumpy bastard? You could at least be reasonable.'

'I fell off my Harley.' He didn't mention the near miss from last night.

Richard paused. 'You fell off? Are you okay?'

Sam heaved a sigh. 'A few bruises...'

'And a fractured pride, I bet.' His colleague tried for something of a laugh.

'I've got to go.'

Sam hung up and headed for his stash of pills, changed his mind and took out a bottle of wine from the buffet. But before he opened it, he went out to the garage, covered the Harley with rough hands and tied it down.

'Blasted piece of junk.'

THIRTEEN

A breakthrough with the use of diary notes, enabling the patient to examine her feelings and hone her thoughts in relation to perceived dilemmas within her marriage. She feels somewhat hopeful now and that her previous notions of failure may have been exaggerated. This is intensified with the high pressure of her work. Therapy has focused on identification and separation of the two factions. Patient is insightful and has proffered her own strategies.

Sam and I still make love. That's the strange thing. Maybe the intensity of our former youth has waned a bit, but there is still beauty, there is still something precious and almost indefinable in our embrace. He strokes my hair and my skin, his lips warm and heavy on mine. And I take from him and I give to him and I love him. I never question this. I am never reminded at how ruined I have believed this marriage to be. Those thoughts are impossible when I am wrapped inside his arms.

Plan: reduce meetings to monthly.

G. Whittaker

On Monday morning Sam called Leah into his office. She took the chair he offered at the side of his desk, smoothed the sheeny fabric of her skirt, and folded her hands expectantly on her lap. Her expression soured as soon as Sam began to speak.

'Last Friday you barged into this office during a confidential session with a patient. Not only that, but your intrusion interrupted a crucial stage in the therapy.'

Leah frowned and went to speak but Sam pointed at her.

'You are a secretary. You sit out in reception and handle paperwork, answer calls and make appointments. I don't know what else you do here and I don't care. But if you ever pull a stunt like that again, you'll be looking for another job – I'll make sure of it.'

Leah sucked in a short, shocked breath.

'That's it,' he added, a little less harshly when he noticed her trembling lower lip. 'You can go.'

She didn't hesitate, and rushed from the office.

Richard was in Leah's vacated chair five minutes later. 'Poor girl's crying her heart out in the ladies room.'

'What were you doing in the ladies room?' Sam replied without humour.

'Come on, matey. There's no room for lovers' spats here in the office. We can't have our receptionist in tears every Monday morning just because the weekend fell flat for some reason.'

Sam slammed down his pen. 'What on earth has she been telling you?'

'Actually, I couldn't make much sense out of her. Something about her life being over – and your name mentioned several times. To be honest, I'm not very good with crying women. I never know what to say.'

'She did the wrong thing last Friday during a therapy session with Alice Lacey. Try asking her about that.'

Richard sniffed, settled back. 'So, you want me to talk to her? I mean, a good sit-down chat?'

'I've already handled it.'

'Maybe not delicately...'

'I said I've handled it.' Sam tossed his papers aside, stood and walked to the other end of the room, his hands going to the back of his neck, feeling something tight there. He started to pace. 'She's here to perform a function, not barge in when I've got a patient in the chair. Every bloody day she's either crying or wanting to talk or staring at me like her world is about to end. Then she goes running to you and you play along for some reason.'

Richard had swivelled around and was watching him. 'Okay, settle down. Geez, I was only trying to help.'

'Help what? Do I look like I need help?'

'Come on, Sam. What's really the issue here?'

'The issue is she ought to know her place. And you – you ought to mind your own business and stop jumping to her defence every time she opens her mouth. I don't care if you made some deathbed promise to her father.'

'That's not the case.' Richard stood abruptly, sending his chair backwards. His cheeks had exploded in colour, accentuating his frizzled hair. 'You're screwing with my staff. That makes it my business.'

'I'm not screwing her. No matter what she tells you. We're not a couple and we're not going to be a couple. What passed between us was brief and it's most certainly over.'

'I'm supposed to rest easy on that, am I?'

'You can do whatever the hell you want with it.' Sam stomped his way back to his desk. 'Now, if you're done.'

'Oh, I'm done.' Richard slammed the door on the way out, but was back two seconds later. 'By the way, Leah's lost her necklace, wants to take a look in here.'

'Why would it be in here?' Sam snapped.

'How the hell would I know?'

'Why are you always doing her bidding? Has she got something on you?'

'It's a small thing called *caring* about people. Not that you'd know.' He went out slamming the door for a second time.

*

Leah kept a low profile over the next few days, knocking gently on Sam's door and always waiting for permission to enter. The air between them remained dense but Sam was grateful for the reprieve, as short as it might be. Leah cold-shouldering him was better than her hovering and offering doe eyes. And at last she seemed to be concentrating on her duties.

Diane Briggs was in Sam's office between sessions on Friday, complaining about her dwindling clients.

'Either they don't like my methods or I'm curing them.' She put her heel up on the desk and scratched at her ankle. 'Bugger, I think the dog's got fleas. They go for the lower part of your legs first, don't they? Cluster bites, I think that's it. Nah, but this is only one.' She looked at him. 'What do you reckon?'

'I think there are drops for that now, under the fur at the back of the neck,' Sam said.

'I meant about my clients. Like, what's your secret? I know it can't just be your good looks, although that probably gets them in the door. But you must have some sort of... I don't know... magic tricks up your sleeve to be able to keep them coming back. I mean, I got a good load of Glenn's patients, but they've nearly all whittled away. Then someone came and saw me for the first time a few weeks ago, and here I was thinking *this is promising* – but it turned out they requested *you* first, or their GP did, but your books were full. And on top of that, they were asking about the likelihood of an opening so they could transfer to you in the future.'

He didn't know how to respond. He offered her a thin sideways smile and shrugged.

'Hmm.' She watched him pensively for a moment, then nodded. 'Might be the fact you say very little, don't give anything up of yourself.'

Sam had only ever sat in on one of Diane's sessions as an observer. She'd overplayed her part, no doubt to impress him, with wide sympathetic eyes and a dull tone. And she'd definitely talked too much.

'Well, it's not about us, it's about the patient,' Sam said.

'Yeah, but you're like that all the time. Even at Christmas parties you find a corner and you stand in it. People have to come up to you to talk.'

She bounced up straight in her chair, like a puppeteer had suddenly pulled her strings. Then she fished in her pocket, pulled out a gold item, held it aloft. 'Hey, this is something that will interest you. Found it jammed in the compactor this morning.'

Sam frowned. But then he realised what it was. 'I think Leah's been looking for that.'

'I know, she's been ranting around the place all week. But I think I know why she was so frantic. Take a look inside the locket.'

Diane tossed the chain across the desk. Sam picked it up. The clasp at the side of the heart-shaped locket was broken, dropping open. He muttered an expletive. Framed inside the heart was a photo – of *him*.

Leah tapped on the door. Sam closed his hand around the chain and locket, called for her to enter.

'Sorry to interrupt, Doctor, but Alice Lacey has been waiting for a while now.'

'We won't be a sec, Lee,' Diane said, not making any move to leave.

Sam was staring at the secretary, wondering what he should think about his photo being inside her locket, whether he should say anything to her. It wasn't necessarily the crime of the century. Disturbing – yes, but maybe he wanted to think about it some more. Maybe he wanted to shove it under Richard's nose first to make his point about how unstable their secretary was.

Leah hovered, but then she backed out, clicking the door closed. Sam opened his hand, looked at the locket photo again.

'A bit creepy if you ask me,' Diane said. 'You want to watch your back with that one. She's got *Fatal Attraction* written all over her.'

He nodded. For once he had the feeling Diane was right. He walked her out, although she paused in the doorway. 'Oh and I'm glad you're going to do the conference. I hate those blasted things. Sitting through all those boring talks, listening to psychiatrists prattle on. I swear half of them have been dipped in Formaldehyde – there's a few scarily well-preserved dinosaurs amongst them.'

'I'm not doing the conference,' Sam told her.

'But Richard said—'

'What Richard says and the reality of it are very different things.'

Diane's nostrils flared. 'Is he losing the plot? I mean, he doesn't seem himself lately. He's vague. It reminds me of Glenn.'

'I don't recall Glenn ever being vague.'

'But you know what I mean, quiet, not himself, the calm before the storm.' She leant in, keeping her voice low. 'Glenn never complained of chest pains, and you'd think that would have been the obvious thing before a heart attack. My aunt, God rest her soul, whinged for weeks about indigestion, burped once, and fell into her soup. But Glenn, there was nothing pointing towards a heart attack other than him kind of fading out.' She seemed to think about that for a moment and shuddered.

Sam thought how Richard had kept his distance since their falling out over Leah. Maybe it was just their colleague's low profile that Diane had noticed. 'I wouldn't worry about Richard,' he said. 'He's probably got a lot on his mind right now.'

She sighed. 'Yeah, maybe. Oh well, thanks for the heads-up about the conference. I'll keep *my head* down until he finds some other sucker, namely Cranston.'

Sam forced a smile and then invited Alice into the office. He hadn't seen her since the previous Friday night when he'd deposited her onto her sofa. It felt a little awkward now. He made a point of formality with her, commenting on the improved weather, and then gave her the news that she would be moving to fortnightly sessions after today. She tilted her head slightly as though this was a mild curiosity. He wondered if he'd expected a different reaction.

'I owe you an apology,' she said while still standing. 'About what happened last week.'

'It's not necessary, Alice.'

'It is. I was rude to you at the club, and I had no right to be.' She sat and crossed her legs. 'And I called you by your first name. I had no right to do that.'

Sam took up his chair opposite. 'On the contrary, it was appropriate. About using my first name.'

'I drank too much, I know that, and I probably shouldn't have been there.' She shrugged and rolled her eyes. 'I *definitely* shouldn't have been there. God knows how I made it home all right, but I did. There must be a homing device in my brain, activated when drunk and disorderly or whatever.'

Sam frowned. 'You don't remember how you got home?'

'No. But apparently I rang a taxi. I checked my mobile phone the next morning.'

He didn't know if he should remind her that she'd missed that taxi, and he'd taken her home in an Uber, her head on his shoulder as she'd slept. But she'd be embarrassed. Frankly, the memory of it mortified *him*. And if Alice couldn't remember it, then there was no point in giving her the details. Unless she was lying to save them both the humiliation.

He had to ask. 'How much do you remember?'

'Um, I remember leaving this office. I meant to go home but the bus never arrived, cancelled I suppose courtesy of the weather. I don't know... I was a bit low. I started to walk, thinking about a taxi, but everyone else must have had the same idea. Do you know how hard it is to hail a taxi in the pouring rain?'

He didn't answer, just clicked his pen on and off.

'Maybe I was depressed about Garth, talking about him... anyway, I just walked into the club. It was there and I felt like a drink. That's about it, apart from seeing you at the bar.' She turned worried eyes to him. 'Having blackouts like that, not remembering getting home, it's scary.'

'What do you suppose the solution is to that?' he said, moving back into doctor mode.

'Obvious, isn't it? Don't drink when I'm depressed.' She stifled a scoff. 'Which means, don't drink at all.'

The office phone rang. Sam forced a congenial expression. 'Excuse me a moment.'

He got up and walked to the front of the desk, reached across and took up the receiver. It was Leah. She was full of apology for disturbing the session, but Mr Davis, the insurance investigator, was on the line and needed an urgent meeting.

Sam let out a bored breath and turned his diary towards him, opening the page to the date. 'I've got a full schedule today. He's going to have to wait until after my last session.'

'Tonight?'

'I can't put him in any other time, not if he wants to see me before the weekend.'

Leah was muttering something as he ended the call.

He went to close the diary and realised the theatre tickets were sitting on the page. He'd forgotten all about them. They were for tonight. Bloody Richard.

Sam went back to the armchair and took up his notepad again.

'I've noticed on a few occasions now, at the funeral and during last week's session, you've used words that equate to feelings of guilt and perhaps shame over your behaviour at the Bellingen crash site.' He watched as Alice began to chew on her lower lip, her gaze seemingly unable to rest in one place. 'I'd like to explore this further with you.'

She took a deep breath as though in preparation. But then she shook her head.

'What's the matter?' he asked.

She widened her eyes as though it couldn't be more obvious. 'The matter? It's my fault there's eleven people dead and twenty-four injured from that train crash. And you want me to talk about it?'

Sam remained calm. 'Why is it your fault? Were you driving the train?'

'Of course not.'

'Did you do something to the railway tracks that caused the derailment and overturn of the carriages?'

'You know I don't mean that.'

'Well, how is it your fault?'

'Because I made mistakes that day. I didn't do enough.'

'Just to be clear, you weren't driving the train?'

'You're being ridiculous...' she muttered.

'So, the train crash *wasn't* your fault.' He sighed. 'Look, I'm not meaning to torment you over this, but your memory of the event is likely distorted by some pretty powerful emotions, the same ones you push away, bury inside your mind because they're too painful to face. But you're taking the entire blame, all of it onto your shoulders, and most unfairly. I'm just trying to point out that you didn't cause the train to crash. You were *not* responsible for it.'

There was a gradual slump in her shoulders, eyes moistening, as her confidence dissolved.

'Alice, when we talk about this, it's to clarify each moment, and we can work through those very issues where you feel you ought to have done better. But this is not a blame game. Your judgement is clouded by your emotions. By pushing these things away, burying them, you're not allowing yourself to fully process the experience. I don't pretend for a moment that it's going to be easy. It's going to be confronting, talking about the actual event. But ultimately, it's going to help you learn how to face these emotions, to manage them. I'm on your side. I'll see you through this. Step by step.' He nodded his encouragement.

She looked down at her lap, jerking a charm on her bracelet until Sam thought it might snap off.

He allowed the pause. This was not a process to be rushed or forced. The digital clock on the bench behind her ticked over. He waited, poised with the notepad across his knee.

Another minute passed.

He moved slightly in his chair, caught her attention. He explained the process: he would be asking her minor details about the lead-up to her and her colleagues attending the crash scene. By painstakingly picking through these features, it would hone her memory, keeping it on course to the facts rather than the negative impulses that gave into recalling only the most disturbing of images and emotions.

She answered, setting up the scene. This was the easy part: shift start time, day of the week and weather. She almost laughed when she recalled what she'd eaten for breakfast the morning of that Coffs Harbour shift.

'An egg roll with tomato sauce from the bakery. The egg was overcooked. How do I remember that?' she said more to herself, shaking her head.

He didn't explain the complexities of trauma and memory. For now, she was talking, and that was good.

'After we got the urgent call over the radio, we made a frantic drive into the countryside. Garth seemed to know where to go, but he was frustrated as all the gates to the paddocks were locked. So, we had to leave the police truck and go in on foot.'

'What was the terrain like?'

'Difficult. You ever try stomping through the bush loaded to the hilt with police gear? Baton, gun, handcuffs, portable radio. Tools of the trade.'

Sam thought of Sophie and how she often complained about the things police had to carry on them at all times.

'And then, of course, I was worried about snakes and spiders and falling into holes, breaking bones.' She drew in a long breath. 'As if that really mattered...'

'So, you arrive at the scene,' he said, getting her back on course.

'Yes,' she whispered.

'This is where I want you to tell your story, Alice.'

'How much do I tell?'

'As much as you want. Or as little. You decide.'

'Oh, God.' She looked around the room as though her words were going to be cast like a dangerous spell and she was finding the appropriate target for them to land. She was sitting up high in her chair, gripping the armrests as though preparing to stand. 'I don't know what to say.'

'What was the first thing you saw? Take your time. Just picture the scene.'

She took several steadying breaths. 'The first thing I saw... was smoke. A fire had started from underneath one of the derailed carriages. I don't know how, maybe it was the dry grass. And it had spread rapidly in and around the carriage'– her voice raised in pitch, becoming tremulous – 'and there were people inside... *trapped...*'

'Bring it back,' he said calmly. 'You see the smoke. What was that like?'

'Black. Sooty. Kind of billowing. It seemed to dull the sky, put a haze over everything. And the smell was rancid... I looked at the ground... just in front of me there was...' She stopped talking, as though she was lost in that thought now, moving through the memory.

'Tell me what you saw on the ground.'

'A... body. A woman's body.'

Sam felt a jerk in his stomach but his mind pushed against the sensation. He scribbled on the notepad, nothing in particular.

'She was just... lying there... in the grass. That's when I froze, couldn't move.'

He listened as her breathing changed. Her demeanour: she'd come forward in her chair.

'And where was Garth?'

'He ran into the scene, into the carnage... of smoke and fire and people crying out... I hadn't heard them until that moment, but they seemed to be everywhere, wandering around, confused, some of them with burns, others with injuries... Garth was shouting into the portable radio, calling for backup, and trying to help them, organise them. And he was yelling at me, giving me some sort of instruction. But I was... useless, unable to do anything... unable to move past the woman on the ground.'

Sam fidgeted, leant to the side as though a tight muscle dictated release. Alice had barely begun her story, yet he was dreading where this was going. It didn't make sense for him to feel this way. He already knew the details of the train crash – news reports and witness accounts had dominated the television channels for months after it happened. There was also a brief report in Alice's file from her commander in Coffs, based on an approval for commendation for Alice and her colleagues who'd attended the Bellingen scene. It had all been in her file, everything that had happened that day. And he'd heard plenty of unpleasant stories over the years – some of the most graphic descriptions.

He cleared his throat excessively, shifted in his chair, clicked his pen, turned over a page of the notepad, coughed some more.

Alice seemed oblivious to his discomposure. 'I was trying to work out how this body was so far from the crash site. Had this woman dragged herself there? Did someone else drag her there? Had she been thrown from the impact? It didn't make sense.'

Shit. Sam's mind was traversing back in time – following the swirling red-and-blue lights through residential streets...

'And life is so fragile,' Alice continued. 'It stuns me at how someone can be a living, thinking, breathing person, with hopes and ambitions... and then in a flash... it can all be over.

'Staring down at her, all I could think was that here was someone's daughter, sister – that somewhere were people who loved her. And that they didn't know she wouldn't be coming home to them...' Alice paused, her fingers moving to her lips. Then she clasped her hands together, almost in prayer. 'She was so young, no more than twenty, her face virtually unscathed...'

Sophie's face; her beautiful face...

'But down her body, oh, she had terrible, terrible injuries... and I was afraid—'

'We'll stop there, Alice,' Sam said as evenly as he could.

She looked at him, her brow pinching together. But for the moment he didn't quite see her. His mind flashed the strongest image yet: *Sophie – lying on the grass – a hole in her chest. And blood – blood everywhere!*

He put his notepad aside and abruptly left the room. In the reception area, he paused briefly at Leah's desk and noticed the confusion in the secretary's eyes as she scanned him from over the top of the computer. She didn't say anything. He made his legs move again and found himself at the water cooler. His hands were shaking violently and he stared at them, fingers splayed. He fisted them to make them stop.

'Could you take a cup of water in for Alice?' Sam asked Leah, thankful his back was to her. 'I'll be a few minutes.'

He stepped to the right of the cooler and through the swinging door into the men's toilets. Thrusting himself forward to the sink, he twisted the tap to full. The water gurgled and repeated into the drainpipe, spraying back onto his crisp blue shirt and matching silk tie with the handsewn initials. He tried to put his face under the running water, but the sink wasn't deep enough and he whacked his cheekbone on the chrome tap. He used his quivering hands to wet his face, the cold reviving to his feverish skin but not his brain. Frustrated, he kicked the tiled wall and then slammed the electric hand dryer several times in quick succession. It protested in a loud thrust of air that shrouded his cry. He would have put his head through it if he thought it would stop the pictures – of Sophie... lying there... *dead eyes... dead eyes.*

He caught his reflection in the water-splattered mirror, the droplets distorting and blurring his features. He willed himself to find control. There were no tears, just the fire behind his eyes. But the pain was good – it was good because it burned at the image that lay there, like setting fire to a photograph, curling from the outside in.

Come on, get it together.

Breathe. Breathe.

*

The door to Sam's office had been left open and Leah was sitting on the armrest of his chair talking to Alice. They both looked at him as he walked in. He'd discarded his jacket and tie, and rolled his shirt sleeves back, holding a paper cup of water, his hand barely steady.

'Thanks, Leah,' he said, noticing the empty cup in front of Alice on the small table. How long had he been gone? He glanced at the clock. *Jesus.*

'Sorry about all that,' he told both women. 'Something... I ate.' He put the palm of his other hand to his stomach as though to confirm the problem, and felt stupid about it right away.

Leah got up from the armrest and halted just in front of him. 'You have a bit of a mark,' she said, touching her own cheek, 'just there.'

Automatically, he put his hand to his face and felt the small sting from where he'd hit his cheekbone on the tap. 'Just a scratch,' he said indifferently.

He stepped around her, avoiding further scrutiny, returning to his chair. He couldn't bring himself to look at Alice. Not yet. Instead, he put his cup on the table and picked up his notes, staring at the pages.

It was a long time after the door clicked shut that he heard Alice's quiet voice.

'Doctor?'

He looked at her. If he'd been worried that she might have noticed something odd about his sudden departure, then it wasn't in her eyes. If anything, she looked lost, confused – like she'd been victim to a failed trust exercise, falling backwards into what should have been waiting hands, except there'd been none because he'd walked away.

He forced a smile that was meant to be encouraging, and felt the corner of his mouth quiver. Putting the notepad aside, he took up the water, gulped the rest of it and then crushed the paper cup in his hand.

'You did amazingly well,' he told her, clearing his throat. 'But, I think that might be enough for today.'

As Alice slowly nodded, Sam thought of the bottle in the bottom drawer of his desk, of the pills at home in his bathroom cabinet.

'So, we'll pick up the story next time?' she asked.

'Yes.'

'I could have gone on. I thought you said... well, it wasn't as...' She seemed unsure now.

'It's a process, Alice. Not to be rushed.' His tone wasn't as controlled as he'd expected. He swallowed hard.

She started to say something else but he concluded the session by standing. He walked her out to reception where he told Leah to make fortnightly appointments from now on.

FOURTEEN

The next patient was in the waiting room. Sam made an excuse and returned to his office, closing the door. He was unravelling again. Leaning forward on his desk, he asked himself how this could have possibly happened, losing control, having to walk out of a session. Why had he faltered? The trigger had been Alice's description of the woman's body. He'd related it to Sophie, seeing her image in his mind's eye. Her face unscathed.

Her lovely face that he would never see again, never touch, never kiss...

The image threatened to return. He took out the whisky bottle and removed the lid, but hesitated. This wasn't going to be the answer. He was still working. There was another patient to go.

'I can't do it,' he told himself and put the bottle down. As he did he saw the diary in front of him, still opened on his desk, and stared at the theatre tickets. A distraction, that's what he needed. No, more than that – a woman to hold. Long hair to bury his face into. He could pretend...

He took out his mobile phone and brought up the number he wanted, then pressed the call button. 'Veronica,' he said. 'Sam Tyler. Look, sorry about last week, rushing off. I was wondering if perhaps I might make it up to you. Are you doing anything tonight?'

After the call, he went back to reception and asked the next patient to go through. Then he turned to Leah. 'Would you do me a favour?'

The high-pitched ping of the lift drew his attention and he was surprised to see that Alice was only just leaving. He watched her step inside. They smiled politely at each other as the door drew smoothly closed.

'Sam, you wanted me to do something for you?' Leah brought him back to the moment.

'Yes. Sorry. Could you collect my suit from the dry cleaners down the road? I don't know where the docket is, but it's under my name.'

'Your suit?'

'I won't have time to go home and get changed,' he said, looking back at the dull silver door of the lift, still trying to settle his mind, wondering if he'd ever be able to face another exposure therapy session with Alice again. He should probably send her to a psychologist.

'Sam?'

'Yeah. I've got that meeting with the insurance rep.' He looked more intently at the secretary. 'Is that okay? You don't mind?'

'Of course not.' She had a smile bigger than the Cheshire cat.

*

The last patient for the day went into overtime. There had been a kind of settling drone as Andy Hammond relayed very ordinary events in his life. When Sam came out of the office his suit was hanging on a hook next to Leah's chair in reception. The secretary had already left for the day. He took the suit from the hook and pulled off the plastic sheath.

Richard came out of the tearoom carrying a steaming mug. 'You still here?'

'No, I went hours ago.'

It was the first time they'd spoken since the argument over Leah earlier in the week. Richard half laughed at Sam's comment, then halted as if he wasn't sure it was meant to be funny.

'You won't believe this,' the older man said, 'but I actually fell asleep at my desk.'

'I'd believe it.'

'Don't tell Laura. She's been paranoid ever since Glenn carked it in here. She'll be packing me off to the quacks who'll stick needles in me and do invasive tests no man my age should have to suffer.'

Sam noticed his colleague's face appeared ruddier than usual. 'Are you all right?'

Richard grimaced. 'I don't know. Could have been the dodgy kebab I ate at lunch. Or maybe I'm just getting old – you know, everything starting to seize up.' He nodded at the suit Sam held. 'What's with the bag of fruit?'

'Going to the theatre on those tickets you gave me.'

'Tickets?'

'*Phantom of the Opera*. It was your idea.'

'Oh yeah, I forgot about those.' Richard tapped his foot as though he was thinking of something.

'I'm getting changed here and I'll walk down.' Sam looked around. 'Actually, my late appointment should have arrived by now.'

'Mad Dog Davis, the insurance gumshoe? He's in my office. Bastard woke me up. You were busy. I tell you, it's lucky they don't give that man a gun. He thinks everyone's a fraud.' Richard held up the mug. 'Don't worry, he's only getting the cheap instant stuff. I'll take care of him. We're almost done anyway. You go get yourself ready.'

Sam nodded, thought about saying something more to Richard – an apology perhaps, but he was too proud to muster it.

*

Sam managed to get to the Capitol Theatre just ahead of Veronica. She looked lovely in a pale, knee-length dress with sheer three-quarter sleeves. Heels gave her extra height. Her hair was drawn over to one side, held in place with a diamanté clip. She carried a purse in the same colour as her dress.

She walked over to him, smiling warmly, and leant in to kiss each cheek in turn.

'You're a sight for sore eyes,' he told her closely.

'Oh, bad day?'

'Negated by your presence.' He returned her smile. 'Thank you for coming. And I'm really sorry about last week, having to go when I did.'

'Let's put it behind us, shall we?'

'Are you sure you can forgive me?'

Her lips lingered over his before offering the softest kiss. 'Forgiven,' she whispered.

As soon as the theatre doors were opened they went in and found their seats – left of centre and five rows from the front.

Sam made a point of admiration to the architectural features of the iconic theatre. He discussed some of these with Veronica, remarking that the theatre had started out as a fruit and vegetable market.

She made an intelligent and interested companion. It kept his mind occupied – kept it away from the turmoil that had been conjured during Alice's session. He needed to maintain the momentum, find his way back to the calm and stoical manner that preserved his sanity.

The lights went down and the show started.

It wasn't long before Sam was bothered. Tremors started in his hands as the muscles in his neck tightened. The young woman on stage, in the role of Christine, could have been Sophie with her long dark hair. The menace of the phantom: haunting and cruelly manipulative, held the character in perpetual misery.

Sam fought to regain his composure. It felt as if it was slipping away again. Veronica leant against him and he concentrated on her; on her perfume, the way her fingers mingled with his.

When the intermission lights came up, she excused herself, and Sam waited in the foyer. He checked his mobile phone and was surprised to see several missed calls. They appeared to have been made from his office.

That was strange. He began to play back the messages. Leah's voice bordered on hysterical, asking him where he was. He couldn't understand most of what she was saying – it hardly made sense.

Veronica found him. 'Is everything okay?'

He continued to look at his phone. 'I'm not sure.' He brought up Leah's number; it went straight to voicemail. 'I think there might be a problem at the office.'

'What sort of problem?'

'I have no idea. My secretary's hysterical about something...' But then it dawned on him. Richard would have been the last to leave tonight. He'd stayed behind to take care of the insurance rep for Sam. He'd looked flushed, complained about falling asleep... And now Diane's words came rushing back at him, from their conversation earlier today about Richard being vague, not himself – like Glenn.

Glenn who'd died at his desk from a massive heart attack!

'I've got to go.'

Veronica's poise seemed to shatter. Her brow puckered and her lips thinned. 'Go?'

'I'm so sorry,' he offered uselessly. He'd already abandoned her twice before, and he was about to do it again.

'Will you come back?'

'I don't know. I'll... call you. *Sorry.*'

He left her, running all the way, dodging people and traffic, darting across roads against pedestrian stop signs, not bothering with the lift once he reached the building – taking the stairs two at a time. Almost out of breath, he punched in the entry code on the panel next to the door and went straight for Richard's office. It was in darkness so he flicked on the light. Chairs were pushed in, papers on the desk piled neatly to the side.

Sam was confused, but then remembered that the calls had come from *his* office. He started to hurry down the hall but his stride slowed as he saw the splash of pale yellow light spilling across the carpet from the partially opened door. His stomach felt knotted.

He paused at the threshold, and then silently stepped inside.

*

The dark-haired woman was in Sam's usual armchair, leaning forward on an awkward angle, facing away from him. At first he thought she was wearing a wedding dress – the ends of the pale crinoline gathered near her feet; the low scoop of neckline revealed by her high-piled hair. She held a glass of something... he noticed the bottle of Walker Blue on the small table next to her.

Her limp-wristed hold on the glass had already spilt part of the contents onto the rug.

Leah turned in the chair, startled in a way, as though having just realised she was being watched. Her expression was a mixture of surprise and bewilderment, but then her stare hardened as Sam stepped the rest of the way into the room. Closer, he could see she had been crying. Apart from the ruddiness of her complexion, the trails of black mascara down her cheeks were macabrely Gothic.

He went to speak but realised he had no idea what to say. He was trying to piece the scene together, make sense of it. Leah, sitting in his office dressed like the jilted bride from a Charles Dickens novel.

'Well, if it isn't the man of the moment,' she said, slurring her words. 'Mr Wonderful. Mr Professional. Man of my lousy useless dreams.'

'Leah, what are you doing in here?'

'What am I doing? As if you don't know. I'm mourning you – us – our demise. *Demise* – is that a big enough word for you? Did I pass the intelligence test? Might you deem me suitable to be seen in public with you? Oh, too late for that. You've replaced me with another. It's that redhead, isn't it? She's the one you took to the theatre tonight, on *my* ticket.'

'The theatre?' He didn't understand.

'You were supposed to take *me*.'

It struck him now, although he must have been an imbecile to have only just realised. 'Oh Leah,' he muttered wearily, removing his tie and sinking onto the armrest of the opposite chair. 'There's been a misunderstanding.'

She jerked around to face him. 'I didn't misunderstand anything. You were given strict instructions from Richard to take me. All along – it was supposed to be me. You even said so yourself – that first time we went out. You said you ought to take me to the theatre. That's why Richard got the tickets. He was trying to help – thought you'd feel better going somewhere fancy.'

She was still ranting while Sam attempted to sift through the information, trying to think back to the moment Richard had handed him the tickets. 'He only suggested I take you.'

Leah seemed unaware he'd even spoken. She was mimicking him about the suit, how he'd asked her to collect it for him, how he'd said he was going to get changed at work.

'*You* put the tickets in my diary.' He was still piecing it together. It would explain how the tickets appeared on the page, and why Richard had seemed confused when he'd mentioned it to him tonight.

'I rushed home and got changed and I came back here. Because that's what you said, you'd get dressed in your suit and we'd go from here. But you were gone. So I went to the theatre, and I couldn't find you. I walked around. And then I thought you must have gone to your seat, but the doorman wouldn't let me in without a ticket. And he said I had to leave. And I came back to call you, but you didn't answer. Because you were too busy with *her*!'

A shadow seemed to fall across Sam as he thought of the locket sitting in the top drawer of his desk – his photo inside; she'd become transfixed with him, some ideal knocking around inside her warped imagination. He'd not been paying proper attention to this, to Leah's state of mind. And yet it had been there all along; her behaviour these past weeks, the hysteria. Diane's warning after finding the locket. *Fatal Attraction*, his colleague had told him. *You want to watch your back with that one.*

'Leah, I'm sorry, I really am.'

She stood and pulled frantically at the front of her dress as though a spider had crawled down her cleavage. One of the thin straps snapped.

'All of this was for nothing,' she screamed. 'All of it wasted.'

Sam went to her now and very carefully took hold of her flailing arms. He tried to steer her back to the armchair. She resisted, pulling from his grip, and then slapped him hard across the face.

His fingers automatically went to the area, the burning heat on his cheek, convinced she'd cut him with the sharp edge of the bluestone ring she was wearing.

She began to sob and threw herself at him, and he caught her. When she looked to him for a kiss, he pulled her closer so that her chin was on his shoulder.

FIFTEEN

Sam drove. From the passenger's seat, Leah's hysteria had turned to quiet tears. She was partially side on, watching him, her head resting against the back of the seat. He was angry with himself, he had to be. He should have seen Richard's plan, realised that he was being set up all along over the tickets. Richard's insistence, his interference, his continued interest in the union.

'Oh, Sam,' Leah whimpered beside him. 'I don't know how we ended up like this. And *I hit you.*' She said the last part in a horrified tone, as though only just realising what she'd done.

He didn't speak. All he wanted was to get her home and be done with it for tonight. Be done with it forever.

'I've been trying so hard to make you happy, Sam. I *want to* take care of you. If you could only know how much I... *love you.*'

He drove into her street and stopped the car outside her house, the engine still running.

She made no move to get out. 'Sam, we can't leave things like this.' She reached out for him with fingers that twinkled as if performing a children's lullaby. 'Say something. Tell me what I've got to do to make you love me.'

Sam had had enough. He'd never asked for this, to be tricked, played. Having to do penance for it no longer seemed sane. He moved her silly fingers aside.

She got angry again, sat upright. 'You're always pushing me away.'

'You're drunk. Go and sleep it off.' His patience was beyond thin.

'Why are you doing this to me? Don't you want to save our relationship?'

'Leah, we aren't a couple. Now please—'

'Is this how you treated Sophie?' she blurted out. 'You just shoved her aside like she wasn't important? Any wonder your marriage was on the rocks. Any wonder she was so unhappy. Having to put up with your whims, your cruelty.'

A rush of heat invaded Sam's body. 'What the hell are you talking about?'

'Never being there for her – always finding reasons to go out and not come home. She thought you might be having an affair. Well, she might have been right, like I was tonight – you being with another woman.'

Sam snapped. He reached across and shook Leah by her upper arm. 'Don't you dare. Don't you ever speak about... *my wife.*' His voice cracked on the last words. It was too raw, too close to the surface. He'd fought all night to get rid of the pictures in his head – the last image of Sophie, the one that was fused to his retinas at night; that invaded his soul and stomped through his mind. Sophie with blood in her hair. And her eyes. Her *dead eyes.*

'Well, we were fools, Sophie and I, for even thinking you could care for us.'

His hands gripped the side of his head as if he could squeeze that image away. 'Don't. I can't take it.'

Leah touched her lips as though she'd just remembered something. 'Oh, Sam. I didn't mean it. I didn't.'

'*Get out.*'

'Please, don't make me go. I'm sorry. I shouldn't have said that about Sophie. I know how much it hurts you. Richard said you can't help it, that you have a complicated grief. I should have remembered that. But you made me so angry.'

Sam was out of the car and he thundered around to the passenger-side door. Leah screamed and pleaded when he reefed her from the seat, stumbling over the hem of her dress. Her brother was suddenly there asking what the hell was going on.

Archie took a hold of Leah's arm and she swung at her brother, demanding he let her go.

'Calm down,' Archie shouted at her. Then he glared at Sam. 'What did you do to her this time?'

'She needs to be locked up,' Sam threw back.

Leah bit her brother and he yelled, let her go. She flung herself at Sam again, begging his forgiveness.

Neighbouring porch lights came on. Someone shouted to keep the noise down.

Sam disengaged Leah's grip and she fell to her knees on the damp grass where she began to wail.

'Hey.' Archie stepped up to Sam, but he seemed to be lost for anything else to say, staring back at his sister.

Sam slammed the passenger door of the car shut and went around the other side, got in and tore away from the kerb, making a loud wheel-spin, fishtailing like one of the local hoons. He swore as he sped through the streets, beating the steering wheel and thrashing about with his elbows and feet like a man possessed.

When the car screeched to a halt in Richard's driveway, three suburbs across Sydney, his temper was no less, and it was made dangerously known when he pounded on the carved front door of the house. The lights were still on inside and it was Laura who answered in her dressing gown.

'Sam.' She smiled falteringly. 'This is a surprise. What brings you—?'

He stepped around her and went inside. '*Where* is he?'

Richard was coming out from the kitchen wrapped in a long brown robe with a mug in his hand. 'What's going on?'

Sam punched Richard in the face. The older man staggered backwards and hit the wall, the contents of the mug he still firmly held going everywhere. Laura made a short, alarmed scream. Richard stayed half-fallen against the wall as Sam, fist still clenched, shouted, 'You had *no* right.'

'Jesus, what did I do?'

Sam was leaning over him, ready to strike again. 'You've been talking to Leah about *Sophie*. Telling her things, about me, about my *grief*—'

'You've got it wrong,' Richard said shocked, still holding his mug out as though he was a beggar in the street asking for alms. 'I never said anything of the sort.'

'She's just the *bloody* secretary.' Sam sprayed his words in fury as he grabbed the frightened man by the lapels of his robe. 'My private life has nothing to do with her. With anybody. Not even you, you stupid old fool. Do you understand that?'

'I hear you, mate. I hear you. But you've got to believe me. Whatever Leah said about Sophie, she didn't get it from me.'

'She was in my office tonight dressed up like she was getting married and drinking my whisky. I thought it was you, that something had happened and you were *dead on your desk*.' Sam realised he wasn't making much sense, but he was so angry that the words spilt out with no control over their order. 'You interfering old bastard. You set me up with those tickets.'

'I don't understand.'

'The tickets, you fool. For the theatre. You gave them to Leah, didn't you?'

Richard nodded. 'You said you didn't want them. I thought she may as well use them, take a friend or something.' His face screwed up in consternation. 'But you agreed to go with her. You told me this afternoon. I saw you with your suit. You said you were going to walk to the theatre.'

'I didn't take Leah. The tickets were on my desk in the diary. I thought you must have put them there to remind me.'

'I don't know about it. I gave them to Leah, that's all I did, I swear.'

There was blood tricking from Richard's nose. Sam released his hold. With shoulders slumped he half turned and noticed Laura clutching her dressing gown at her throat. She was trembling. He looked back at the tortured posture of his friend against the wall: knees bent and neck twisted.

Mouthing a profanity, Sam squeezed his eyes closed for a moment. Eventually he put his hand out to Richard who flinched at first – then realising the gesture took hold and was hauled to a proper standing position.

'I can't work with Leah anymore,' Sam said. 'I can't bear to look at her face. It's either her or me.'

'Why don't you sit down, let's talk about it, mate. You want a coffee? Something stronger? We'll sort it out, work through it—'

Sam couldn't bear to linger in any way, in any form of discussion. He had to get out. He didn't know what else to do as the pictures continued to flash through his mind – so frightening, so terrible, of Sophie...

He shielded his eyes as though he had the sun in them. There were hands on his shoulders but he jerked away and left the house.

*

Sam didn't have a hangover. It was too painful. His brain must have exploded and seeped out through his ears. He was lying on his side, his left cheek nestled against something sticky.

Through burning, bloodshot eyes he saw the result of his depression strewn across the lounge-room floor, not far from where he'd fallen into alcoholic oblivion: empty and part-empty wine bottles, a shot glass with a black Sambuca tide mark. His mobile phone was in pieces and he had no memory of how it got that way. He could see down the barrel of the pill bottle. He lifted his head just enough to see pills scattered in all directions across the floor. He was naked apart from his trousers low around his hips, fly undone. One black sock was halfway on his foot. He couldn't see the other sock. For all he knew he'd eaten it along with countless pills.

He groaned, tried to sit up. The room spun. He sat it out, held onto his head as if it were about to roll from his shoulders.

Finally, he half staggered, half crawled, to the toilet. It stung when he peed. He must have thrown up in the early hours – made it to the bathroom but not the toilet bowl. His toes dipped in coagulated muck were testament to that. The place smelt like the septic tanks of a brewery – only worse.

He went back to the lounge room. On hands and knees he started to gather the pills one by one. He was finding a lot of them. His watch was under one of the chairs. It read five o'clock. He'd been out of it for most of the day.

Slowly, he collected the empty wine bottles but only made it as far as the kitchen sink, dropping them into the stainless-steel bowl before laying down on the tiled floor with a wet dishcloth over his eyes.

There was a knock at his front door. He couldn't summon the will to answer it. That, and the fact he just didn't care.

The evening brought a different sound that he couldn't ignore. Footsteps overhead. With his eyes closed, he seemed to be able to hear every creak, nuance and vibration in the unfinished extension.

Nobody could be up there – he was certain of it. There was no access. Windows that had never been used were locked. And empty rooms – there was nothing of any interest or value. An intruder would have nothing to steal. The toilet wasn't even plumbed.

What did he care anyway?

'All squatters welcome,' he called out. 'Make yourself right at home.'

He forced himself to sit up. But the movement interrupted his stomach. He barely made it to the bathroom – slipped in his sticky vomit, banging his head on the edge of the sink on the way down. Somehow he got to his knees and retched into the cistern. From there he forced himself into the shower, feeling so weak and wretched that he was under the water before he remembered to take his trousers off. And then he slumped against the tiles and sat hugging his knees to his chest until the water ran cold.

*

Alice moved gracefully down the spiral staircase and stood before Sam, the moonlight streaming in from the front window, silhouetting her slender curves through a delicate sheath of pale fabric. He couldn't see her face but he could smell the wildflowers that seemed woven in her hair, could sense her smile – a smile that he knew was for him. It was wrong, but he could bear it no longer and he closed the gap between them, reaching for her. She melted willingly into his arms, the fullness of her lips inviting. And he bent his head to taste, a surge of excitement rushing to his loins. He'd forgotten that kind of turn on, the intensity and throbbing demand that seemed to spill into his veins. He could not remember ever having wanted someone so badly...

An air horn blasted from close by, followed by the shouts of hooligans. Sam jolted awake at the sound – at first pissed off that his dream had been interrupted. But then he realised it had been about one of his patients. He blamed the lapse on the toxic mix of chemicals in his system.

Just after his morning coffee, and glad it was still the weekend, he stood at the front of his house and looked up at the two windows of the extension. It was a long way up, higher than the average second storey due to the drop-away slope of the land. He wasn't even sure a ladder would reach. At the base was a rockery that serviced mostly weeds.

He went around to the back of the house where there was another window. It wasn't as high as the front windows, but it still didn't seem possible for anyone to bother climbing up there for the sake of sitting in empty rooms. Everything seemed intact, undisturbed. The noises he'd been hearing didn't make any sense.

But then he spied something.

It was the neighbours' large gum tree with heavy looking branches that hung over onto Sam's side, one in particular that tipped the bottom edge of the window. Even now, in the morning easterly breeze that lifted from the ocean, the end of the branch moved, rubbing against the glass.

Maybe that was it. He should probably get someone up there to take a proper look.

He took a slow walk from the headlands to Wanda Beach. His stomach was still tender. The oil refinery in the distance at Kurnell loomed jagged and twisted like a scene from a post-apocalyptic movie. He stepped towards it, finding no difficulty in believing he could be the last man on the planet. He wished it, unsure he could face anyone again. Especially Veronica. His phone beyond repair, her number was irretrievable.

Richard was sombre on the home phone that night. 'Look, I spoke to Leah. She does seem a bit... unstable. So, I've given her some extra leave until I work this thing out. Laura's going to take over in the office for now.'

'What's to work out?'

'Well, it's a bit my fault, pushing you two together. I got carried away. It's not really Leah's fault, not that part of it.'

Sam grunted, felt he was being smoothed over for Leah's eventual return to the office. She ought to be fired. Too bad who her father was to Richard.

'And I don't know where she got it into her head to start on about Sophie,' Richard said. 'I've never talked to her about your past, not like that.'

'Like what then?'

'Like nothing. Okay? Why on earth would I talk about you?'

'She mentioned complicated grief.'

'She did? Where did she get that from?'

'You tell me.'

'Maybe she's been doing extracurricular activities, refining her psychiatry skills.'

'That's not even remotely funny, Richard.'

'Sorry. I wasn't cracking a joke. Darn stupid sarcasm, that's my problem.'

Sam realised it was pointless to be pushing this with Richard. Whether or not his colleague had said anything to the secretary, it didn't excuse Sam thumping him in his own home in front of his wife. He apologised for that now.

Richard dismissed it.

Sam rubbed his brow with the thick of his fingers. 'I think I need a couple of days off.'

'Whatever you want, mate.'

'Might go into the bush for a night – the Turrets in the national park.'

'I've heard of it.'

'Just need to zone out for a while. I'll be back Thursday.'

'Laura can sort your appointments.'

Sam took a deep breath. 'Get Laura to reschedule all of the next week's appointments too. I'll... um... do the conference in the mountains.'

It was the least he could do.

SIXTEEN

Sam spent the day gathering his camping gear: a reasonable sized backpack with a foam roll and sleeping bag that tied underneath, a square piece of tarp, canned food and water. The sleeping bag smelt like mildew but it was dry. Nevertheless, he hung it unzipped in the sunlight.

Later that night a current-affairs television program was interviewing a survivor of the Bellingen train crash that Alice had attended. The one-year anniversary of the event was this coming Friday. Sam wasn't going to see her now until he was back from the conference. But he'd call her on Friday, see how she was faring.

After a larger than normal breakfast on Tuesday morning, he drove to Waterfall. It was the most southern suburb of Sydney. After parking in the railway station's car park, he took out his pack and headed along the track to the region known as the Turrets. He still hadn't replaced his mobile phone, but it was pointless in the bush as it wasn't easy to get a signal. Besides, he didn't want to talk to anyone. He needed distance from the madness of the world – a chance to think – or preferably, not to think.

Nearly two hours later he made his camp in a small clearing. He found an old scrubby lean-to made from skinny branches interwoven with strips of shrub and tied off with twine or something similar. He adapted it along with his piece of blue tarp to form a simple shelter. After stowing his backpack there he set off to find Uloola Falls, a short distance away. He stood at the very top and listened to the rush of water spilling down the rocks, then he climbed across to a ledge and took in the view.

Beyond the falls was dense bushland. The sun's rays splintered through the patchy cloud, warming the air with an intoxicating aroma of eucalyptus. The falling water made a background murmur to the bird medleys being played out intermittently from every quarter.

Sam couldn't be sure how long he'd stayed in that place. It seemed that he'd fallen under some hypnotic spell of nature. But it felt good. For a time, at least, he hadn't thought about anything.

He returned to his campsite. After clearing away some dry leaves and sticks, he rolled out his bed. The lean-to with the tarp made the perfect shelter and the surrounding patch of spindly scrub gave him privacy. He gathered some kindling to start a fire and then a few heavier pieces of wood that he had to venture further into the bush to find. As the daylight faded, the clouds changed to soft amber and mauve. When it had all but disappeared, he lit the fire. He kept it small and contained and fed it constantly, staring into the flickering flames, listening to it crackle and spit. His dinner was a tin of Irish stew, warmed atop the glowing embers.

The moon lifted from the horizon and stars formed into constellations, trembling between slow moving cloud. A cool breeze filtered through the branches and danced lightly with the remainder of flame at his fireplace. Sam waited until it was close to out, then he dumped dirt on the rest, took his torch and headed down the track to the Turrets.

The two monoliths rose from the bushland in rocky peaks as though they were the breasts of Mother Nature herself. Sam climbed onto one of them and settled at the very top where he took in the skyline of Sydney. It was amazing, so close and yet far enough away for it to be meaningful. He felt he was able to observe his life from a distance, the glow of the city where he spent his days now set against a black milieu of bush and sky. Leaning back on his elbows, he looked up at the stars and tried to see into forever.

*

The following morning was overcast. Breakfast was a tin of spaghetti, cold this time because he didn't want to light another fire. He was still hungry but decided to ration the rest of his food throughout the day. He was in no hurry to go home.

He cleaned up the site, packed everything and then returned to the falls. A small tent was pitched in the camping ground, but otherwise the place was deserted. He lingered at the edge for a while, wondering if he could find the same tranquillity as he had the day before. A misty spray lifted from the rapidly falling water, refreshing his skin. While he stood there soaking it up, he decided he would head out to Karloo Pools. From memory it was about a five-kilometre walk generally north.

Slinging his backpack, he set off. After half an hour the trail began to peter out but was still discernible. A minute later Sam stopped cold. A snake was curled up in the centre of the track. It was massive. It could have been a diamond python – not dangerous. But it looked more like a brown snake – deadly. Both types were common to the region. Sam didn't want to get close enough to find out what kind of snake it was. He decided to make a detour and stepped off to the right into the bush. A few twigs from low-hanging branches scratched at his hair and the side of his face. He dropped his head lower, using his forearm as a shield. In order to go around the snake, he had to shuffle through a multitude of fern and thick scrub. It was ironic that he was avoiding a snake on a clear path, and yet where he trod now was probably laden with far more deadly creatures or even potentially noxious plants.

His foot caught in a vine and he half fell and then stumbled down the rest of the slope, eventually slamming against a large tree that was seeping some sort of sticky substance. It was on his hand and he wiped it against his jeans. It was still bothering him as he walked on, but a minute later he stopped again. The bush seemed to have closed in, no sign of any track.

He looked around, trying to get his bearings. There was nothing familiar – he couldn't even be sure which direction he had just come from. But even with the fall he didn't think he would have gone too far from the track.

He pushed his way through the bushland gaining height. But it was taking too long. There was still nothing of a track or any familiar landmarks. Overhead, the canopy of trees seemed to have closed in tighter, blocking out most of the sky.

The terrain became difficult and he had to change direction many times in order to avoid sheer outcrops or fallen trees. Finally, after several hours, Sam had to admit that he was making no progress. He sat down on a log and took off his backpack, drank some water and tried to work it out. It had been so long since he'd been to this part of the national park and, without a map, he needed to rely on his memory. But that wasn't proving helpful. It was so easy to become disoriented in the bush.

Something slithering in the scrub nearby got him to his feet.

The light was fading early due to the thick cloud. Sam knew he wasn't going to be able to walk out of this tonight. He moved around to find somewhere suitable to bed down, and it took him a while, but eventually he was able to clear an area next to some large rocks. The scrub was too dense to risk lighting a fire. That particular worry became void when it started to rain. It wasn't going to be suitable to stay where he was.

He moved around the rocks and started to climb upwards. Just on dark he found a small recess in the rock face that offered reasonable protection, and took the piece of tarp from his backpack, pushing it into the crevice overhead to help waterproof it. Staying as dry as possible was important. He dug in his pack to see what other supplies he had.

There was a small bag of peanuts, the rest of his bread and two more tins of stew. He had a spare pair of socks and a fleecy top he'd worn the previous night in his sleeping bag. He put the top on but decided to save the socks.

He had enough bottled water, but he put the plastic cup out in the rain anyway. He ate another of the Irish stews cold from the tin. He didn't bother getting in the sleeping bag, but unzipped it completely and wrapped it around himself.

The rain intensified and Sam barely slept. There were strange noises in the night, cracking and possibly trees giving up their wasted branches; animal hoots and squeals.

The weather was no better at first light. Finding his way out of a quagmire was becoming less realistic. The weather meant there would be few, if any, bushwalkers – nobody to call out to, no human sounds to follow. He was forced to wait out another long downpour.

With nothing stimulating to look at, Sam was alone with his thoughts. He didn't like it. He was here to forget – not remember. Images of Sophie came forward in his mind and he steered them away, chose the better times. Being in the national park reminded him of the hikes they used to take. Sophie had been fearless – some would have said reckless. She always bounded ahead of him, leading the way, calling back that he was becoming a slow old man. But as exuberant and athletic as she was, she was also the gentlest and sweetest lover. How she could soothe his rattled nerves with a soft stroke of her fingers, and barely there kisses just to tease him and make him want her more. She could be a savage beast when she was angry, but by the stars she was an angel for everything else. He tried to smile at those memories now, but he was fooling himself. His head hurt and he hadn't brought his pills; they weren't the sort you went cold turkey on.

The bush seemed to crackle and shift, as if it had become haunted and unknown creatures moved carelessly over fallen timbers and through the creeper vines. He was the intruder; he belonged in the city in an expensive suit and a silk tie with his initials embroidered on the end – not here in nature.

And nature stunk. Wet, rotting vegetation. He couldn't remember why he'd wanted to come now, why he hadn't found himself a resort-style hotel with a decent bar and room service. Why the park? Solitude could be found just about anywhere. He didn't know why he'd done this to himself.

He came out of his small cave to relieve himself. Then he hurriedly returned and went through his backpack. He ate the peanuts. They felt slippery on his tongue and tasted stale.

His stomach ached for a decent meal.

'*Why didn't you pack something better for yourself?*'

'Because I was in a hurry.'

'*Ah, the big escape. But what do all boy scouts say? Be prepared!*'

'I was never in the scouts.'

'*Oh Samuel. This is a dreadful way for things to end.*'

She emerged slowly from behind a eucalyptus tree, her dark head and then her face. She stood quite still in her uniform, said nothing; seemed to be eying him with pity.

He squeezed his eyes shut, but the image wouldn't go. Hallucination brought on by stress… and swift withdrawal from his medication. It was only going to get worse.

Keep moving, he told himself.

Despite the rain and poor light, he packed up everything. Wrapping the tarp around his body and over the backpack, he set off. There was no plan to this and it was stupid. He should have stayed put, stayed in the shallow cave. But he couldn't bear to sit wallowing in memories either. Good or bad, they served nothing but to torture him.

He trudged through the rough landscape for several hours but by the time he reached the river he was too exhausted to go on.

His third night in the bush, two more than expected – he positioned his torch and ate his last tin of Irish stew along with the rest of the bread. The rain slowed but he was still shivering. He spread his tarp over the long fronds of a tree fern, making something of a shelter and used the foam roll to sit on. He took off his boots and changed his socks and t-shirt; put the fleecy top back on. His jeans were wet and he had to take them off. Then he got into his sleeping bag and zipped it up high to his neck.

The water trickled through the leaves and tapped at the tarp over his head. It was all he could hear, the steady tap-tap-tap, growing louder by the nanosecond.

His body craved the drugs and he began to shake.

*

Sam was drowning. Wave after wave slammed into him, took him under, twisted and contorted his body through the violent undercurrents. He wouldn't surrender to it even though all hope was gone. He surfaced to the night sky, to the swelling clouds of black and grey that matched the sea, and shouted, 'Help me.' Another wave collapsed over his head.

Hands were on him, pulling him from the water, dragging him over the side and onto the timber deck of a boat.

And he heard her voice, somehow over the raging storm, but he couldn't see her. '*Samuel,*' she cried. '*You're not out of the woods yet.*'

Sam emerged from the delirium. It was still dark and raining harder. He lay in his twisted position inside his sleeping bag on the bed roll. He was numb, empty, as if the world had chewed him up and spat him out.

He tried to sit but the movement caused his stomach to give up its meagre contents, burning his throat like acid. The tarp, laden with rain, dribbled from one corner over his shoulder.

You deserve to die out here.

SEVENTEEN

The morning sun was trying hard to make an appearance.

Slowly, Sam sat up, taking several confused minutes to reconcile his thoughts with his surroundings. With arms shaking, he managed to pull on his wet jeans and pack up the rest of his stuff. There was a timber sign, a marker indicating the track. He headed for it. Three painstaking hours later he came out at Karloo Pools, his original destination. The place was deserted and he stopped to rest. His stomach was tender but there was nothing in it to throw up, not even bile. Carefully, he sipped some water, the only thing he had left in his backpack. When he set off again he knew his way. He decided to head for nearby Heathcote Railway Station and catch the train back to Waterfall where he'd left his car. The thought of the train stirred his memory. The anniversary of the Bellingen train disaster. He wondered how Alice was faring.

The trail seemed to go on forever and the humid conditions sapped at his already depleted energy. Just after midday he finally came out at the rear of the railway station. Several police vehicles were in the adjacent car park. A squad of about five officers in blue overalls were leaning over a map spread across the bonnet of one of the vehicles.

Sam's less than favourite detective sergeant was there, in his trademark bad suit. They saw each other at the same time. McGuire sneered and said to the nearest officer, 'Hold it, that's him.' He walked over to Sam. 'What time you call this?'

'Sorry, I wasn't expecting a welcoming party.'

'Not my idea. But I heard you went missing, decided to come down in case they needed someone to ID the body. But here you are in one piece. Used up another one of your nine lives, I see.'

The other officer got on the handheld police radio. 'Rescue Sixteen, looks like the missing person has just shown up at Heathcote. He appears to have walked himself out of the bush.'

The radio operator's voice came sharply from the speaker, 'Copy that Rescue Sixteen. Do you require an ambulance to your location?'

Detective Sergeant McGuire looked at Sam and raised his eyebrows. 'Need any leeches removed from your bum, Doc?'

'What's your problem, McGuire? Disappointed I'm not in a body bag?'

The detective lost his sneer. 'You got yourself lost in the bush, Tyler, just remember that. Wasting police time and resources. We've got a shitload more cops out at Waterfall where they found your car, a large team getting ready to go in to look for you. So, don't get smart.'

'Then don't let me hold you up,' Sam snapped. 'Go and ruin someone else's day.'

A high-speed train rushed noisily through the station just behind Sam. Silver microdots flashed in his vision, his balance faltering and he staggered slightly to his left, his backpack falling heavily from his shoulders. McGuire was suddenly at his side, placed a hand on his arm and steadied him.

Sam pulled away, staggered again.

'Get your arse over here,' McGuire said after the train had gone, picking up Sam's backpack and heading towards a parked car a few metres away.

Sam hesitated. He knew he had to get home, take his pills. Reluctantly, he followed. A minute later they were on the road, McGuire driving painfully slowly.

'Where're we going?' Sam asked.

'Get you some medical attention. You look like crap, Doc.'

'I don't need it. Take me to my car.'

'Forget the car. One of the boys can bring it around later.'

Sam shot the detective a hard stare. 'We're out of sight of your colleagues now – you can boot my backside to the kerb. Nobody will believe me if I complain.'

'You got a death wish or something?' Mac huffed.

Heat coursed up Sam's neck as he thought of the sodden note on his door a few weeks ago with the illegible words, the spinning hubcap from his close shave with the car the same night. 'Let's not pretend anything. You blame me for what happened to Sophie.'

The detective heaved his bulky frame in the driver's seat. Clearly the case of a cop who'd let himself go, Sam thought.

'How about we leave those accolades for the bastard who pulled the trigger.' He huffed again. 'And maybe that lazy good-for- nothing Maria.'

'Maria?' Sam said.

'The trouble with you, Doc, is that you didn't know what you had. Shit, if Sophie had been my wife...'

'Yeah, well she wasn't.'

'Delivering paperwork,' McGuire went on. 'Of all the things to get killed over. You know, I still think about it, drive down that street and look up at the house and wonder how it could have been any different.'

Sam turned his head and stared out the side window. 'Next you'll be telling me you lay flowers.'

'Don't you? The house is still empty.'

Sam hadn't been anywhere near the street since Sophie's death. He was surprised to learn that the house was the same. Somehow he'd imagined it demolished or rejuvenated, the tragedy of the past wiped over with the complexities of other peoples' lives. Why did McGuire have to tell him this? He'd been better off not knowing.

'Just drive me home,' he said, his throat constricting with a surge of grief that wanted to break free. 'I need sleep.'

*

Richard settled on Sam's lounge, put his foot on the small leather pouf and looked around. 'You know, this is one hell of a big room. You ought to think about furnishing it properly though.'

'What's wrong with it?' Sam had turned his armchair around to face Richard.

'Well, it's a bit like your office,' Richard said. 'Clinical. You need a home you can relax in, that doesn't remind you of work. And what's with the spiral stairway to heaven? Is it art, a metaphor?' He didn't seem to require an answer. Grunting, he sat up straight and tossed a folder into place where his foot had been. 'Anyway, here they are. Glenn's notes for the conference lecture. Might need a bit of tweaking. Hotel is booked – it's a nice suite. Details all in there. Laura moved your appointments over.'

Sam nodded.

'So, you get much sleep after your big Bear Grylls adventure in the bush?'

'Up until the point you pounded on my front door.'

'Well, I wanted to see for myself that you were all right. Told the clients yesterday and today you were caught up with something important. Didn't want to worry them. Wasn't sure how I was going to explain two dead psychiatrists in a matter of months.'

'Nice to know you care.'

'Seriously though, I was worried. Diane was freaking out because she thought she might have to go to the conference in your place. I caught Cranston eying off your office.' Richard shook his head. 'I really should think about getting some quality shrinks into the practice. Since Glenn, you're all that's left.'

'I wish you'd stop comparing me to Glenn. He was one of a kind, you know that.' He lifted his tea mug and drank. It was nice to have something warm in his belly.

'Since when did you get all organic?' Richard looked into his own mug. 'Don't you have anything decent like fifteen-year-old Scotch? I thought I gave you some for Christmas, imported, boxed in a nest of shredded fibre. Ring any bells?' He sighed. 'Probably the last thing you feel like. So, what was it like out there? Were you forced to cut your arm off with a pen knife? Drink your own urine?'

Sam didn't want to laugh in case it hurt. 'There's nothing to tell,' he said. 'Still got everything I went in with.'

His colleague grunted disappointedly, put his mug down on the table. 'Your good-sort cop was in the office today looking for you.'

'Alice Lacey?'

'Apparently she'd been ringing since yesterday and Laura kept telling her you were busy. Didn't want to frighten her by saying you were MIA somewhere in bushland. Same thing this morning, kept calling, and then she just turned up, said she'd wait to see you between patients. I had to come out and tell her you weren't in. Looked a bit confused, poor thing.'

'Shit,' Sam said. 'It's the first anniversary of the Bellingen train crash. I meant to ring her.'

Richard waved off the notion. 'No. Leave it. She'll be right. Don't go dredging it up.'

Sam wasn't sure that was a good idea. He didn't want Alice to think he'd been avoiding her.

'Hey, here's something you might enjoy,' Richard said, this time with a flicker of mischief in his eyes. 'And let me tell you, you'll be glad you got yourself lost in the bush on this one. Remember that Liz Taylor wannabe who came fishing around for a free appointment?'

'Elizabeth Banner?'

'Well, she was back, in a fur coat and a tiara, no less. But good ol' Cranston, always on the lookout for patients, and in this case didn't know the backstory, took her into his office to discuss her plight. Except he got more than he bargained for.'

Sam began to smile.

'The old darling dropped her kit, just let the fur coat slide off her shoulders and she was starkers except for that glittering tiara perched on her head. Said she could no longer afford her sessions and was offering herself to him. Imagine that, desperate enough to want to have sex with Cranston. You should have heard him yell.' Richard finally gave up to laughter, slapping his leg. He regained his composure enough to add, 'We all came running. And there was Cranston trying to hide behind his chair with Liz posed like a statue in the middle of the room with nothing left to the imagination.'

Sam was laughing loudly before he even realised. There was nothing painful about it. In fact, it felt good. It felt *really* good.

Richard's car was parked in the driveway and Sam walked him out. It was just coming on dusk. The chilled air was still, not even a hint of breeze. The older man opened his car door, but then paused, growing sombre. He regarded Sam for a moment before reaching across the front seat for a blue folder.

'In the clean-up of Glenn's files… well, I was debating whether or not to give this to you.' Almost reluctantly, he handed the folder over.

Sam had already caught sight of Sophie's name neatly printed at the top. 'So, why are you?'

'I think Leah might have been through it. It could explain where she was getting her information about you and Sophie. I thought you should know.'

Sam nodded. He tried not to show his unease at the fact there was a file holding very personal details about his marriage, probably his failings as a husband, and just how far Richard had been through it and what he must think of him now.

'What are you going to do with Leah?' he eventually asked.

'I really don't know.' Richard pointed briefly at the folder Sam held. 'It's too speculative to fire her. And as for the debacle the other night over those tickets, well, that was my fault. I should never have got involved. Not even sure why I did now. Maybe I thought I was helping, nudging you forward while there seemed to be a bit of momentum in your otherwise dreary existence.' He held up his hand as though anticipating Sam's censure over the jibe. 'I couldn't have been more wrong. Laura found out and wanted to crack the other side of my skull – told me I was an old fool.'

'I thought you said the tickets were her idea.'

'I asked her to get them – you know, she does that charity thing with the main theatres. Anyway…'

'Where's Leah now?'

'I told her to take a holiday.'

It wasn't really satisfactory, but Sam was too tired to argue. He watched as Richard drove away, then went inside and dropped the folder on one of the lower rungs of the spiral staircase. He stared at it for a moment. 'Dammit, Sophie,' he muttered. 'Was I really that big a bastard?'

Returning to his chair, he switched on the television and channel surfed. Eventually, he found a foreign movie on SBS. He

watched the dark scenery of windswept countryside, and charac-
ters who seemed to be searching for something. He didn't care for
the subtitles. It made the perfect background until sleep finally re-
captured him.

EIGHTEEN

Early Saturday afternoon on the beach was cold and miserable. A lone surfer was the only fool risking the conditions.

Sam wandered close to the shoreline, allowing the rhythmic rush of freezing water to reach his ankles. He pushed his hands further into the pockets of his fleecy windcheater.

There was an odd feeling about this day; he couldn't quite put his finger on it, but it was as though this was the last time he would walk these sands, smell the salt air, feel the faint rays of muted sunshine on his skin. A condemned man – maybe that was the best description for it.

He saw a figure ahead, jeans rolled up, standing knee deep in the water. It took him a few seconds more to realise the figure was Alice. He stopped and watched her, wondering what she was doing. She took a few steps further out to sea, but then shuffled back with the next pounding wave.

He moved closer. 'Hello,' he called, and then louder, 'Alice.'

She didn't change course. He stepped further in. His feet had become used to the cold during the walk, probably slightly numbed, but the chilling water on his legs shot up the rest of his body almost painfully.

'Alice!'

She turned now at the sound of his voice, seemed shocked to see him there. She wiped vigorously at her cheeks and looked away, but he'd already seen she was upset. He said her name a few more times, but she didn't respond other than to bow her head. Oblivious now to the series of waves heading her way, the first one hit her and she stumbled, the second unbalancing her. Sam had already waded in, didn't quite catch her in time, although he managed to grab her so that she was not completely submerged. She gripped his arm, held on as he pulled her to her feet, then fell against him. He wrapped his arms around her body to steady her as another waved crashed into them. As soon as he walked her out of the water, he let her go.

'What do you think you're doing?' he said incredulously.

'As if you care,' she cried, her hands fisted as though she wanted to pound him.

'Of course I care. I wouldn't have gone in to drag you out otherwise.' He watched as she shivered violently. 'What's going on, Alice?'

'I just wanted to feel the cold.'

'You didn't need to get wet for that.'

He tilted her elbow and led her further up the sand. Closer to the weedy dunes she came to an abrupt stop.

'We should get you home,' he said. 'You're soaking.'

'No, I don't want to. I can't face that house anymore. It's haunted!'

She sat heavily, pushed her fingers into the sand. Sam watched the long patterns she made. But then he saw something. He crouched down, grabbed her left hand and turned it over to reveal the inside of her wrist. She tried pulling away from him but he held her in place to get a proper look. There were several lines, seemingly cuts, on her skin.

'What have you done, Alice?'

She snatched her hand back and held it close to her chest as though it needed protecting. She got to her feet and headed back to the shoreline.

He was quickly after her. 'Hey, talk to me. How did you get those marks on your wrist?'

'Do you really need to ask?' She wouldn't look at him.

He felt wretched, useless. 'Bellingen. I didn't forget,' he said.

'You didn't take my calls.'

'My phone was broken. I had to replace it this morning.'

'It doesn't matter now anyway.'

'Of course it matters.'

She sighed, rubbed her arms for a moment, and then muttered something that was lost in the thrash of surf.

'What?' he said.

'A butter knife.' She looked up at him. 'My wrist. I cut it with a butter knife.'

He knew better than to react. It took effort to push down his anger. Not at Alice, but himself, for getting lost in the fucking bush when he should have been here for her.

He took back her hand, gently now, and examined the cuts. They weren't deep and there was no sign of infection. He didn't suppose too much damage could be done with a mostly blunt piece of cutlery. But it was the fact she'd done it at all. Things were escalating. Next time she might go for a sharper knife.

'I'm sorry I wasn't here for you,' he said. 'It wasn't intentional. I got... well, I took a few days off to go into the bush and... bloody stupid of me—'

He realised she was crying and that his words were wasted in the squall of gulls anyway. And it wasn't about him, or his self-justifying excuses. That was the last thing Alice needed.

More than anything he wanted to console her – put his arms about her. Would that be so bad given the circumstances?

He already knew the answer to that. He had to treat this as a session.

The noisy seabirds lifted after a minute. Now it was just the waves Sam had to compete with.

'The first anniversary is often the most difficult.' That wasn't right. That made it sound like it would get easier every year.

He forced calm and rephrased his words. 'There will always be reminders – triggers – but it's about learning strategies to deal with those emotions. They're going to come up, but you'll get better at handling them.' It was only part of the answer. The rest relied a great deal on support. And Alice had none.

'You're going away,' she said. 'My next session has been cancelled.'

'I've got a conference in the Blue Mountains,' he replied regretfully. This really wasn't a time for him to leave again. 'But I'll give you a call while I'm away. And I want you to call me too, Alice. If you need to talk, any time. It's the same number as before. Okay?'

She wiped away more tears. 'Did your phone really break?'

'Yes.' He took out his new phone. 'Look, see? Brand spanking new. And I even put a shatter proof cover on it.' He wasn't sure she was convinced. 'Alice. I'll be able to answer the phone next time. You can count on me.'

Finally, he convinced her to go home. He saw her to the door, waited while she went in. And then he walked off. But his heart was heavy, like someone had backed up a truck and tipped cement into it.

*

Glenn Whittaker's handwritten lecture notes were ordered and concise. He had the penmanship from an era now lost to word processors and digitalised notes. There was none of the lazy cut-and-paste attitude of transferring information from one document to another. Not Glenn – this was pure heart-and-soul research.

Sam put his feet up on the coffee table at home, sipped his wine and read through Glenn's prepared speech for the conference.

Policy of the police department, according to Glenn's notes, was that when an officer was off work with stress, there should be no contact with that officer by other serving members. The philosophy was that the injured officer should not be reminded of the trauma associated with their job, and so a total blackout was put in place. There might be a monthly contact from a senior officer, more often someone from a desk job required to call up long-term sick officers, tick their name off a list, and basically make sure they were still breathing. But the warm support of colleagues, the sense of family through shared experiences – those ties were disconnected – and Glenn was scathing that the system designed to protect these officers in their recovery cut off their very source of psychological nutrition.

Sam thought about Alice. Her colleagues were all in Coffs Harbour, seven hours drive away. Nobody called her, but they would have been warned off. And the ones who shared her disposition of being away from work, had their own issues.

There was another problem: suicide. The statistics were frighteningly high. And not just concerning those diagnosed with PTSD, but officers who tried to function inside the job, who'd not been diagnosed, probably never even received a day of counselling. In Glenn's opinion, all officers carried this burden to some extent. With all they saw, how could they not? They learnt to mask it, to push it down; not lose face with colleagues; not give cause for family to worry. They became expert at suppression. The tragic events police officers faced required they move aside from normal human response. They had to hold back the tears, the grief, save it up until later. Save it up until the end of the shift – wait for the sergeant to finish bawling them out over something else, some neglect, some failure with paperwork or unfinished jobs; wait until they got home – snap at their spouse, if they had one; crack open a beer or bottle of wine, and then tried to forget. And back at it the next day, the next shift – this never-ending cycle of cruelty, trauma and grief – with no room for expression. Eventually, something had to give.

The cuts on Alice's wrist...

It wasn't really a suicide attempt, Sam told himself, but he couldn't ignore the significance of her action. These things often started out that way, a bit like a trial run. She'd made the marks with the knife on her skin to distract herself. But the ultimate distraction was never to have to think about any of those bad things again, to eliminate the pictures in her head, to never have to feel the guilt or the shame. To not have to think at all. Perhaps that was why she'd opted for the freezing water today at the beach – a discomfort that detracted from the emotional turmoil that she had no control over. Each time she was moving into more dangerous territory.

It was getting dark, so he got up and turned on a few lights. Then he wandered to the staircase. The blue file with the name *S. Wilde* was still on the third rung. He wondered how he'd been able to ignore it since he'd dropped it there last night, as though it had disappeared into some void, reappearing only when he'd looked down. He didn't need to open the file to know that Sophie's conversations with Glenn would not have centred on the difficulties of her work – that may have been part of them, or maybe they had started out that way – but it would have been their shitty marriage that took the starring role. How could it not? Dealing with scumbags on the street had probably seemed an easier option than dealing with *him*.

He finished the bottle of wine and moved to the side cabinet to open another. His hand shook as he poured and he spilt it over the side of the glass.

'Fuck it.'

He went to the kitchen for a cloth, but by the time he'd returned, the stain had leeched into the pale timber of the cabinet. In temper, he tossed the cloth – it splattered diluted wine onto a rung of the staircase and dribbled through the metal grate onto the blue folder below. He swore again and hurried to retrieve the file, but fumbled with it, papers falling out onto the floor at his feet. Bending down, he started to gather them.

He stopped, his hand holding one of the loose-leaf pages. Glenn's handwriting.

Unmanageable crying at the start of session.
The patient indicates feelings of loneliness and abandonment...

Sam's mobile phone was ringing. He left the file and the fallen papers, pulled the phone from his pocket and answered.

'Hello?' There was no response. 'Hello,' he said again, firmer now.

'Dr Tyler, it's Alice Lacey.'

This was a surprise. His angst melted. 'Alice, is everything all right?'

He heard her sniff. Then her voice quivered, 'I'm sorry, so sorry. But I'm... I just needed to talk. And you said any time. And I... well, I wasn't sure you'd answer.'

'Well, I'm here. So go ahead.' He looked at his watch. It was almost seven. He moved back to his armchair, reached forward to the coffee table, turned over one of the lecture pages to the blank side and took up his pen.

'I'm scared,' she said, not waiting for a further prompt.

'What are you scared about?'

'Of being on my own. Of... dying alone.'

'You're not going to die, Alice.'

'One day I will. We all will.'

Instinctively, he wanted to tell her she wouldn't be alone, but there was no qualification for such a comment. It was a blind promise. Strange that he still wanted to make it.

'Don't fret for the future,' he said instead. 'It's not here yet.'

She hummed a thoughtful sound, reminding him too much of Sophie. Her breath seemed almost intimate. He imagined her lying back on the lounge, or maybe the bed, her hair across the pillow, her arm crooked with the phone to her ear.

He cleared his throat, realised he was rapidly clicking his pen.

'I wish you weren't leaving for your conference,' she said.

He had to stop himself from saying, 'me too.' He was her doctor, after all, not her boyfriend. 'I'll be back before you know it.'

'I've been thinking about those poor people from the train... a year ago... feels like it's only just happened. It's so clear in my mind, every little detail...'

'Try not to dwell on those memories.'

'But I can't get rid of the images. I close my eyes, and I still see them... those people... their injuries... the bodies... I want it to stop. I don't know how to make it stop.'

'You need to distract yourself.' Shit, wrong wording. She'd already sliced her wrist trying to distract herself, followed by a dip into the freezing surf. 'A book, some music...' He thought fast. 'Maybe a holiday. A trip to Perth to visit your family—'

'I can't see them. Things are not good between us.'

'Well, it's my recommendation you get away – away from the house.'

'I'm not confident.'

'A change of scenery will help.'

'I wish I could, Doctor. I really do.'

'What about Coffs? Is there a friend or colleague there you could visit?'

'No.'

'Then go to Perth, Alice. Make peace with your family.'

The truth was he knew just how vulnerable she was. She was emotionally trapped behind the walls of her house, at risk of spiralling further down, wallowing in self-pity and wine. If she were with family, they could keep her safe.

'My father doesn't want to see me,' she said. 'We had words on the phone tonight. He told me... well, to get over it. To pull myself together, that I was an embarrassment. And to stop calling, that I was upsetting my mother.'

He heard himself tsk. 'Families don't always know how to handle this sort of thing. They react more out of fear, in not knowing what they should do or say.'

'They still haven't forgiven me for divorcing Henry. My mother says I should have tried harder, been more like Elaine.'

'Is that your brother's wife?'

'Yes.'

'Maybe your brother feels differently. Have you spoken to him?'

'Luke is far too busy these days. He's made no move to get in contact with me. I don't know what I'd say to him anyway.'

They were both silent now, and he listened to her breathing again – the small tremors behind her tears – and he tried to think of a solution. He knew he should say something to her, all this back-and-forth sighing and breathing wasn't getting them anywhere.

His sight fell on Sophie's blue folder and the spilt papers still on the floor. He looked away, but he became too conscious of it. Holding the phone to his ear with one hand, he went over and picked up the folder with the other, tried to shove the papers back in. But then he paused over the page he'd held before, caught sight of words that caused his stomach to grip like it had a vice attached.

... feelings of loneliness and abandonment...

Alice had said she was afraid of dying alone. But that's exactly what had happened to Sophie.

It was impossible to know if the idea came to him at that moment or not. Maybe it was fairer to say it had been festering in the back of his mind for a while.

'Well, you could come to the mountains,' he said. 'I've got a suite. I won't be using it apart from putting my head down at night. But the rest of the time—'

'Your conference?'

'Yes. I mean, it'll only go to waste.' He hesitated. 'You could have one of the bedrooms.'

She seemed to be lost for words. And now he was wondering what the hell had just possessed him to make the offer. It was insane.

But maybe it made sense too. Leaving Alice behind while she was in such a fragile state held far more consequence than taking her with him. He would be clear of her for most of the time, involved with the conference day and night. But he'd still be able to keep a bit of an eye on her. And he still felt bad for being stuck in the bush – that maybe, somewhere deep inside himself, he'd done it on purpose just so he didn't have to attend to her on the anniversary of her most significant trauma.

'Are you allowed to do this?' she asked.

His laugh was short and nervous as he suddenly pictured himself standing before the frowning faces of the psychiatric board, being struck off in dramatic fashion and shown the door.

'There's nothing untoward. You'll hardly see me. Think about it if you like. I'm not leaving until Monday morning.'

There was a long pause before she sighed. 'A change of scenery. Well, you're the doctor.'

For the longest time after the call, Sam stared at the phone – finally putting it down as though it weren't safe in his hands.

The enormity of what he'd done didn't escape him. He was about to go away to a psychiatric conference with his traumatised, vulnerable patient. But what else was he supposed to do? He couldn't abandon her.

He gulped his wine, then wiped his mouth with the back of his wrist.

It would be fine, he assured himself... so long as nobody found out.

NINETEEN

Alice was waiting for him at the front of her house on Monday morning, an oversized backpack on the ground next to her feet. She wore jeans topped with a smart leather jacket, and black boots that might have been police issue.

Sam parked the BMW and turned the engine off. She came over, dragging her backpack as he got out and opened the boot. Without saying anything, he put her gear in the boot next to his, and for a moment glanced discreetly around to ensure nobody was watching them.

They drove in silence for a while. Sam tried hard not to think about what he was doing. It was just work, he reminded himself. Well, it was outside the parameters of conventional therapy, but it was the modern world and you didn't get results unless you were willing to take chances. He'd been reading up on the work of Belgian psychiatrist, Andre d'Anethan, who was sometimes criticised for his avant-garde approach to therapy. The Belgian claimed that the treatment of patients had become too contained and restrictive, and that doctors were more concerned with possible lawsuits than risking a more creative, even experimental, approach that could have positive benefits.

Of course, taking a patient on holiday probably didn't fall into the creative range the Belgian had in mind.

He glanced across at Alice. 'We shouldn't... I mean, it would be prudent to not say anything about... any of this.'

'I know,' she said. 'I won't tell.'

'And... call me Sam. It'll be easier.'

They made Katoomba just before midday. The precipitous town was stuck somewhere in the seventies with a definite hippie culture, but quirked with the modern features of internet cafes, Thai eateries, health food stores, and an out-of-place red double-decker sightseeing tour bus. The place was popular with backpackers and other trendies, a hot spot for antique and art collectors. Sophie had always loved coming here.

He briefly looked at Alice only to discover her staring right back at him. She shifted awkwardly in her seat and refocused her attention out the side window.

After parking on the gravel driveway of the High Point Hotel at the end of town, they got out of the car, leaving their bags for now, and went inside. Together they collected the key from the desk and were directed to the suite. Sam felt strangely nervous as he opened the door. Alice, beside him, seemed calm, but he wasn't game enough to look her in the eye.

The suite was a large room with a king-sized bed beside an eye-catching picture window. There was a flat-screen TV on the wall opposite, a small sofa underneath it, a round table with two chairs near the balcony door, and a wardrobe with fogyish features. The second bed, a single, was around the corner in a small alcove and adjacent to the one and only bathroom.

Shit.

He heard movement behind him and turned in time to see Alice go onto the balcony. He swore under his breath, then joined her at the railing.

The hotel was on the very edge of the Jamison Valley and there was a panoramic view of the Great Dividing Range. A stream of air scented with eucalyptus filled Sam's senses as he watched the sunshine glide across Alice's face.

'There's obviously been a mistake,' he said. 'With the room. I'll sort it out.'

She nodded but didn't look at him.

*

He headed downstairs. Nobody was at the reception counter and he stood for several minutes ringing the bell. The concierge finally turned up and raised his thick black mono-brow when Sam made a request for a second room.

Tapping rapidly on the computer keyboard, the concierge said, 'Dr Tyler, we're fully booked, so I can't offer you a second room.' He eyed Sam sceptically. 'Your suite has two beds.'

'I need another separate room.' He didn't think he should have to explain his situation.

'Well, I could check with other hotels, that would be your only chance, but there are several other events in Katoomba all week…'

Sam rubbed his forehead, wondered what he might do.

'You're booked for five nights,' the concierge added. 'There might be a cancellation in that time.'

'If you could let me know,' Sam said, but he wasn't happy. 'And please chase up with the other hotels.'

'Certainly.'

Sam retrieved the bags from the boot and took them up to the room.

Alice was sitting on the sofa, her feet pressed together, fidgeting with her bracelet. They didn't speak. He put the bags down and went back to the BMW to get his suit carrier. When he returned to the room, she hadn't moved – her backpack untouched where Sam had left it.

'I'm sorting out the room,' he said. 'But this is yours. So, make yourself comfortable.'

'I've caused you a hassle.'

'No. It will be sorted. But for now—' He checked his watch. 'I – ah – have to get down to the conference centre. Registration is from midday. I'll be gone for some time.'

'That's what you're here for,' she stammered.

'The lookout isn't far,' he said. 'Don't know if you want to check it out. The Three Sisters. Pretty famous.' He felt ridiculous.

She nodded. But he wondered if she'd even still be in Katoomba by the time he got back.

He drove to the conference centre – a large complex nestled in a grove of stringy paperbarks only minutes from the hotel. The car park was full. Someone waved him around to an area behind the main building where he parked.

He signed in at the door, picked up his name tag and a program. Then he went inside. There was quite a crowd, the same lot he was going to have to deliver his speech to. He was used to lecturing at the university, but it was going to be a different dynamic with his peers. It had been some years since he'd faced any of them. He stuck to the edges of the room, moved slowly amongst the groups.

Frank Warner, a well-dressed man of average height and grizzled sideburns that touched the corners of his mouth, stepped up to the podium and demanded attention. He gave a dull account of the program for the week. There were dining suggestions and other social events. A formal dinner tomorrow night was also set down and everyone was expected to attend.

Alcoholic and soft beverages were being offered on trays by a series of passing waiters dressed in penguin suits. Sam had forgotten the pretentiousness of these conferences.

He took a glass of red wine. One wouldn't hurt.

'Sam Tyler. Good heavens, I thought it must have been a misprint on the program when I saw your name. But here you are in the flesh.'

A tall, attractive woman in her late forties with blonde hair and eyes the colour of sapphires was standing directly in front of Sam. He felt ill. Gemma Scott was the last person he'd expected to see.

'Gemma,' he said, his tone cutting through her name like it was poison.

She faltered slightly at his reaction. 'It's been a while, I know.'

'Four years,' he muttered.

'Four years, indeed.'

He couldn't look at her, couldn't bear it. He put down his glass on the nearest table and left the building.

*

The hotel concierge offered Sam a bland smile of greeting and said his name. If he was piqued at receiving no response, he didn't show it.

Sam charged up the stairs and into the hotel room, but then stopped in the middle as if he couldn't remember why he was there. He moved again, grabbed his bag, and pulled out clothes, dropping them and other items onto the floor, until finally he came up with the bottle of pills. And now he stared at it – Alice's typewritten name still legible beneath the black marker. Where was she? He couldn't see her bag.

He closed his fingers tightly around the bottle neck and took some slow, steadying breaths, then headed for the bathroom.

Unintentionally, he caught his reflection as he swallowed a pill; saw the red streaks of tension in his eyes, the dark hollows like camouflaged war paint underneath.

Gemma Scott – the memory of that wretched night four years ago: *clawing at each other's clothes like they were on fire; the impenitent sex.*

He stripped off and stepped into the shower, turning the water pressure to maximum, upping the heat until it threatened to scald his skin. Then he thumped the tiled wall with the heel of his hand.

'*Damn* you, Tyler. *Damn* you to all eternity.'

*

After changing into jeans and a long-sleeved t-shirt, Sam sunk onto the sofa, his thoughts scattered. He shouldn't have come here. How was he supposed to see this through?

Alice walked in carrying a plastic shopping bag. She jerked backwards when she saw him. 'Oh, I wasn't expecting you back so soon.'

'Sorry,' he said, just as surprised to see her. 'I thought you'd...' He sensed her discomfort and knew he was the cause of it. He shouldn't be here, not when he'd promised her sanctuary and privacy.

'I'm – well, my room isn't ready,' he continued, wondering what he was going to do if another room didn't become available. 'And I just took a shower. Hope that's okay.'

She frowned. 'Why wouldn't it be?' She eyed the mess of his clothes on the floor as if they somehow created a barrier.

He came forward and scooped them up, shoving them back into his bag. Pocketing his wallet, he grabbed his jacket. 'There's a thing...' he said. 'A drink... some of the guys from the conference.'

There was no drink, but Sam couldn't think of what else to do. He couldn't really hang around in the room with her.

The mountain air was blisteringly cold. He started walking. Minutes later he reached the lookout. Undulating folds in the landscape and the encasing ranges carved into pale orange and mauve, the colours shifting in intensity according to the sunlight. To the far left, the jagged monolithic Three Sisters seemed fragile against the ridge, as if they had to cling to each other or else fall to their fate in the deep valley below.

He wandered there for ages, blending in with tourists, watched as the afternoon light began to fade. Closer to dark, he walked into town and the first bar he could find, tucked himself into a private corner and ordered a Jim Beam.

'Ah, my young protégé. You slumming it down the low end of town too?'

Sam looked up from his drink at a scruffy, dishevelled man who'd pulled up a chair opposite him. But then he smiled. 'Professor Edgar Camberwell.' The two men shook hands across the table.

'Please, you know how much I hate formalities. We're equals, after all. Just call me "Professor."'

Sam gave proper homage to the joke with a quiet laugh.

'So, what's this then?' the older man said. 'Since when did you go for the cheap seats? I hear you're doing well in the city these days. A high flyer. You should be out with all the other high flyers, competing for superiority over who has the best water views, the biggest yacht.'

Sam held up his glass. 'Flying under the radar tonight.'

Edgar grumbled and then called over the waiter who seemed reluctant to take his order.

'He's okay,' Sam said to the waiter, putting money on the tray. Then to Edgar with a smile, 'Still being mistaken for a homeless person, I see.'

'Mate, it doesn't matter what I do. And this is a new suit.' The older man tugged at the lapel of his pale-blue jacket. 'Permanent press and all. It's just the way I wear it.' Then he rubbed the grey patch of bristle on his chin. 'And the fact I'm not much use with a razor.'

They both laughed, but Sam's was more awkward. He knew Edgar too well, that his old mentor had an uncanny knack of seeing inside a person. Sam's invisibility cloak didn't stand a chance.

'Now see, I'm trying to work out something about you, Tyler…'

Here it comes, Sam thought.

'You've come a long way, granted, being at this conference for one. But I see in the program you're also giving a talk. And I think that's progress for you. Yet, here you are tucked away in a corner of a bar looking like a man who's had a fight with the missus, except you and I know better than that.'

Sam didn't give anything away, shrugged as though it was a lightly amusing observation. 'Just wanted a quiet drink.'

'A quiet drink is sitting in your hotel room with the mini bar and the flat screen, not in this place.'

'Needed an atmosphere.'

The older man regarded him, shook his head. 'Word of advice?'

'Don't remember asking for any.'

'Stop fighting it. It's going to catch up to you sooner or later. These things always do. You're better off getting a head start on it than letting it take your feet out from under you.'

Sam concentrated on the amber liquid in his glass. 'The "it" you're referring to?' – not sure why he'd asked the question.

'Fear, of course. Gets in the way of everything we do. But' – the professor tapped his spindly fingers on the table between them, as though calling on Sam's attention – 'there are times when you've just got to face certain things… and certain people.' He paused. 'Saw you at the registration earlier today.'

'You're talking in circles.'

'Spirals, I prefer.' Edgar nodded. 'Gemma Scott. Beautiful woman.'

There was no point in denying it. Edgar knew the story; he'd been on Sam's doorstep days after Sophie's death.

'Was I that obvious?'

The old man grunted.

'Great,' Sam muttered.

'It's not her fault, you know.'

'Never said it was.'

'You can't expect people to react to the way you're feeling inside. You carry this with you, it's your burden. But—'

'I know what you're saying,' Sam interrupted sharply, not wanting to be psychoanalysed any further. It was true: none of it was Gemma's fault. He was the one who'd called her up after the fight with Sophie four years ago. He was the one who'd made it clear where he wanted that night to go, had fallen into bed with the sexy woman while his wife was being gunned down.

It fell uncomfortably quiet. The professor was still regarding him, but as soon as the waiter brought across his drink, he raised his glass to Sam. No words followed. After a few seconds Sam raised his also. The two men drained their glasses and then ordered another round.

*

It was late when Sam returned to the hotel. His first stop was at reception where the night manager informed him there had been no cancellations. He found himself eyeing off a sofa through the open door into a sitting room. But one look at the manager, who was half leaning over the counter to watch him, brought that idea to a halt.

Alice was in the bathroom when he let himself into the room, her overnight bag sitting on the end of the single bed. He picked it up and took it over to the large bed around the corner.

At the same time, Alice emerged from the bathroom. She was wearing grey flannelette pyjama pants and a pink, long-sleeved t-shirt. Her hair was damp on the ends.

'Sorry,' he said. 'I'm still waiting on another room.'

'I'm sure we'll manage as it is.' She looked at the single bed. 'Where's my bag?'

'Oh, I moved it. I'll take the single.'

'I was going to sleep there.'

'No, it will do me. You take the big bed.'

'Sam, this is your conference, your hotel room. I shouldn't even be here.'

She sighed heavily. Even from this distance, he thought he felt the subtle movement of her breath on his face. And he detected wildflower. It reminded him too sharply of the dream he'd had of her.

He bounced himself backwards onto the single and adjusted the pillows behind his head. 'This is good,' he said. 'So, I'll hear no more about it.'

TWENTY

Sam was late for the first day of the conference. He burst into the auditorium and it was as if he'd just disrupted a memorial service; the solemn air of approximately one hundred and twenty participants, all seeming to turn in their seats to frown upon his noise and tardiness.

Frank Warner, speaking from the podium, stalled mid sentence, drawing attention to Sam as he searched for a spare seat at the back of the venue.

'There's a few spaces left up here.' Frank waved Sam forward.

Someone coughed.

It felt like everyone was watching him as he reluctantly moved forward down the centre aisle.

'Good one, Tyler,' someone else said as he went.

A few others sniggered, but Frank called for quiet as Sam found a spare seat in the front row. 'I'll just quickly run over the housekeeping again' – he glared at Sam – 'for those who may have missed it.'

Like a steward on a plane, he indicated the location of the nearest exits, the toilets, and asked that all mobile phones and pagers be switched off or silent and not responded to until the breaks.

The first lecture began. Sam wasn't paying attention. He was thinking about Alice, about their first night in the hotel.

From his single bed, he'd been acutely aware of her presence. He'd listened to her move about, caught glimpses of her as she came into view when preparing the king bed, pulling down the quilt; the rustle of sheets as she'd got in, the swishing sound of her hands smoothing out the fabric.

There'd been something comforting in her presence and the gentle sounds. It had lulled him into sleep. But he'd woken in the early hours – thought for a moment he could hear her crying. Creeping from his bed, he'd put his head just around the corner, barely making out Alice's form beneath the coverlet. Another small sound, talking, too soft for him to make out the words. Then her breathing changed, quickening like she was afraid of something. He moved a little closer, waited for her to settle. And even for a while after that...

He'd forgotten to set the alarm, had overslept. And then there'd been the awkwardness of being in the same room, of moving about and around each other, trying to keep out of the other's way.

The conference dragged on. The speakers, one by one, droned in monotone voices. Sam didn't know how he was going to get through the rest of the week listening to it.

Lunch was catered: a variety of sandwiches, fish pieces, spring rolls, salads, crumbed vegetables, and pastries. He felt awkward standing around on his own, like the new kid in school. Years ago, he'd have been eager to join in on drink fests and pub crawls. Nobody would have thought to leave him out. But now, he almost feared being approached. It was the quiet life he sought these days.

After the food, he poured himself black coffee, more to have something to do with his hands. He poked at a floating speck with the plastic spoon, wondering at the wisdom of communal beverages.

Gemma Scott approached him. He'd been discreetly aware of her all morning, keeping watch of where she sat or stood, so he could avoid her. There was no escaping her now.

'I recommend the bottled water,' she said with a smile, holding one up.

'Very wise,' he replied, abandoning the coffee, looking around for the possibility of escape.

Gemma stepped in closer. 'I come in peace, Sam Tyler.'

He didn't respond and yet she seemed to be waiting. Her smile dropped and she sighed. 'I've offended you, I can see that. It wasn't my intention. I thought maybe... Oh, Sam, there's so much I want to say—'

He cut her off abruptly. 'Not here. Don't talk about... *that.*'

'No, I wasn't going to...'

She touched his arm, her fingers crimping his sleeve. He wanted to pull away from her, leave the room and never have to lay eyes on her again. But that would only make it worse. The trauma of that night four years ago – that he had been with Gemma in a hotel room while his wife lay dead on someone's front lawn – it would distort to this moment, add another dimension to his agony, his guilt. Edgar Camberwell's words came to mind about having to face people at some point, about this not being Gemma's fault. Sam knew his old professor was right. It wasn't going to be easy, but he had to start somewhere.

'Look, I didn't mean to be so rude to you yesterday. I just hadn't expected to see you.'

She nodded and he saw tears well in her sapphire eyes. 'It's my fault,' she said. 'I took it for granted that somehow things would be... okay between us. We were always such good friends. And it's not as if... well, we never parted on bad terms.'

'No, we didn't.' He didn't want to be talking about this, not even indirectly.

'I could always go out and come back in, and we could try again.' Her smile was feeble and he realised this was probably hard for her too. 'I'd like another chance to get it right,' she added.

He forced his own smile, although it was strained and brief. He took the hand still on his jacket sleeve and turned it into a gentle handshake. 'Gemma Scott,' he said. 'How very nice to see you again.'

She looked relieved. 'Sam Tyler, the pleasure is all mine.'

*

The old heritage-listed building at the high end of Katoomba was the venue for the formal dinner. Although they'd made no arrangements,

Gemma appeared to be waiting for Sam at the top of the front steps – stunning in a sleek black dress that came off one shoulder and fell in scalloped folds from thigh to ankle. Her hair was pinned high into ringlets. A small glittery bag was strung over her wrist. As Sam moved slowly up the stairs towards her, she made no secret of her approval.

'Thank heavens for formalwear hire shops,' he told her, fidgeting self-consciously with his tie and then his jacket sleeve.

Gemma smiled sweetly and hooked her arm into his and they walked in together.

The piano bar was reminiscent of an era past. Tall windows with heavy curtains looped open to one side, contrasting with the pale walls. There were gold-painted pillars, urns with cherubs next to long sofas, and an impressive lantern clutched by a bronze statue of a Greek maiden. A wide corner bar held shining glasses and bottles of champagne on silver trays.

The white-haired pianist was positioned next to a curving stair-case, and played a moving piece about "coming home" with enough flourishes to put Liberace to shame. Gemma was still hold-ing onto Sam and she rubbed his arm. 'Fancy a dance?'

'What, here?' He looked around at the gathering group of psychiatrists, most of them pressed up near the bar.

'Come on, Sam, use your imagination,' Gemma said.

She lifted his arm and twirled herself underneath. Then she laughed. Sam got the message although he made no move to gratify her desire to dance. If she were blighted by his refusal, she didn't show it, twirling some more beneath his limp arm, and laughing and smiling as though she'd expected this kind of reaction from him. She finished by touching his cheek lightly with the back of her long fingers, then elegantly applauded the pianist.

The adjoining function room was made up with rows of long tables and chairs. After preliminary drinks from the piano bar, Gemma led Sam over to seats closest to the sizeable window. The setting sun offered a kaleidoscope of ever-changing colours across the escarpment. People turned to the scene often as though it were part of the entertainment, a backdrop to the mellow music from a quartet.

'Penny for your thoughts?' Gemma's words brought him back to the moment.

He didn't want to converse with her, not this small talk. He'd never meant his olive branch to be taken beyond the perimeter of colleague. For now, he forced congeniality.

'I think you'll find since we've converted to decimal currency and dropped the ones and twos, the cost for thoughts has increased to at least a dollar.'

She laughed in a relaxed way. 'Okay, a dollar for those elusive thoughts of yours. Or perhaps, for you, I'll even spare several.'

Now he was sorry he'd said as much. He smiled and shook his head. Looking into his drink, he told himself that anyone in this room with even a hint of his mind right now would have him drawn and quartered. It was Alice who traced his thoughts. The truth was he hadn't wanted to leave her tonight. She'd been quiet, but relaxed, and that had suited him. Curled on the big bed with a book, she'd invoked a non-obtrusive calmness, looking up only once as he went to leave.

'You'll be all right?' he'd asked.

'I manage every night of the week on my own.'

'Stupid question, wasn't it?'

'It's fine, Sam. Have a nice time.'

The conference dinner consisted of four courses and plenty of alcohol. Sam was restricting his intake. He needed to keep his wits about him.

After several useless speeches with poor attempts at humour, Frank Warner stepped aside for the quartet to resume. Cheese boards and port were brought out and placed on the tables.

Sam got up and wandered into a conversation where Edgar was holding the floor. The old guy drew him in before making him the object of a funny story from years ago. Sam took it with the good humour it deserved, although managed to follow up with his own Edgar story that had the group roaring with laughter. He didn't know he still had it in him.

Eventually, he left the room, moving through several corridors until he emerged into an open courtyard with a centre fountain that didn't appear to be operating. He stared into the murky pond and noticed several bloated goldfish tip the surface with expanding lips as though desperate for air.

'So this is where you got to.'

Sam offered Gemma a cursory glance, resenting the intrusion. 'I was going to head off,' he said.

'Where are you staying?'

'High Point.'

'I'm across the road from you at Lily's Boutique Hotel. Come on, they've organised transport for us.'

He followed her to the front of the building and they climbed into one of several minibuses parked in the driveway. Gemma sat beside Sam in the back, leaning against him. 'How's the view from your hotel room?'

'It's very nice,' he replied.

'My room overlooks a car park. Not very exciting.'

The bus let people off along the way, and it was just four left for High Point and Lily's. The two hotels were on the opposite side of a very narrow one-way street close to the lookout. Sam and Gemma stood in the centre of the road after the bus departed. The others bade them goodnight before moving on, one with a wink.

It happened quite suddenly, while Sam was thinking of the right thing to say, that Gemma stepped up to him, cupped her hand at the side of his face, and kissed him on the mouth. He didn't reject her. He allowed the kiss; perhaps he even encouraged it to a point. Surprisingly, the trauma of that old memory didn't arise. He hadn't expected that. The kiss was lovely, held promise.

His hand pressed gently into the small of her back, and she responded by draping her other arm around his neck, slowly moving her body against his. It would be easy, Sam thought, to simply walk the short distance to *her* hotel room, perhaps spend the rest of the week with her. That would solve the dilemma of sharing with Alice.

He knew as he was telling himself this, exactly what he was going to do. The kiss ended and Gemma was close to breathless. She was also a touch emotional.

'Sam, I've wanted to call you for a long time now.'

He tried to quieten her words, but she went on ardently. 'I knew you'd left your practice. But then about a year ago someone said you were working with Richard Madden in Sydney. There were so many times I wanted to pick up the phone. I'm sorry I didn't. But I didn't know how you felt.'

'It's okay,' he whispered, trying to disengage her embrace in a diplomatic way.

'You don't know how glad I was when I saw your name in the conference program,' she said, seemingly unaware of the dissociation. 'And then when you walked into the hall yesterday...' She smiled up at him, her tears flowing freely, but changed now, no longer sad.

He took both her hands in his and it was then she faltered. Perhaps it was the psychiatric observer in her that told her his meaning because her smile began to melt and was replaced with a mask he'd seen before – of poise and grace. And dignity. But her disappointment was not completely hidden.

'I suppose I'm a bit more tired than I thought,' she said. 'Maybe you can show me your view another time.'

He half smiled but refrained from nodding. 'I'm nervous about the speech. I've got to brush up on my notes.'

She seemed relieved by the change of subject. 'Well, that explains your mood. I can't say I envy you. They've asked me three conferences in a row to speak, and I keep saying no. I'd fall to pieces in front of all those people.'

He laughed briefly. 'You might have to pick all of me up after mine.'

At first he was glad when she returned a smile, but then he noticed the flicker at the corner of her mouth. 'Nothing would give me greater pleasure,' she said softly. She kissed his cheek this time. 'Goodnight, Sam. We'll talk tomorrow.'

She left him then. He waited a few seconds, watching her go. She drifted like a sylph on a breeze, turning back briefly to raise her hand in farewell.

Sam walked in the opposite direction to his hotel.

*

Alice was asleep when Sam came into the room. She'd left the bathroom light on for him with the door slightly ajar. He stood for a moment next to her bed, wondering if she might be pretending sleep out of politeness. She was on her side, curled into a ball – one arm over the sheet, her hair almost in ringlets, like she'd washed it and let it dry on the pillow. Her breathing was slow, gentle.

He wondered what she'd done today, whether she'd gone walking or visited art galleries and antique shops. He'd not asked her that in the brief time when he'd come in to change for the dinner.

There was a pamphlet on the bedside table. He picked it up and smiled. It was for the chocolate factory.

He went around the corner to his bed and stripped off to his boxers. Then he turned the light out in the bathroom and got under the covers.

*

Sam yelled, grabbing at his chest. He didn't know where he was. In the dark, he could see the outline of furniture, but it was all wrong – shadows of things, objects, some he didn't know, things not where they should be. He went to get out of bed, but there was a wall. He started to panic.

'Let me out.'

His breathing was short and rapid as a grating surge of dread rippled through his core.

Hands were on him, and then came her voice – calm, soothing. 'It's okay, Sam. I'm here.'

No. She was dead. Four years ago, lying on the grass covered in blood.

He jerked back from her unearthly touch, felt her hands slip away; a spectre of comfort that only ever belonged in his imagination. But then he remembered: *Alice.* They were together in a hotel room. Doctor and patient. His nightmares…

Why did it have to happen now?

'Are you all right?' Alice whispered, and he could see that she'd stepped away from the bed, hugging her shoulders.

He didn't answer. Instead, he got up and moved past her into the bathroom and locked the door behind him. Silently, he fell against a wall of cold tiles and allowed his weight to take him down. Fisted hands to his temple, the sharp sting of tears broke the surface. He contained his sobs, choked on them, as the agony of grief polluted his soul.

After a while there was a light knock on the door. 'Sam?'

He wiped his mouth with the back of his hand. 'I'll be out in a sec,' he managed as blandly as he could.

But now he wasn't sure he could face her. Hell, he didn't know how he was even going to look at himself again. His body shuddered with the wretchedness of the situation.

I should never have brought her here.

TWENTY-ONE

The morning rays of sunlight streaked across the valley and warmed Sam as he leant over the balcony rail. Alice had been gone when he woke, so he'd not had a chance to speak to her about quitting the conference as soon as his speech was done. She didn't appear to be down in the courtyard where they served breakfast. Her stuff was still in the room, so maybe she'd gone for a walk.

It would have to wait.

He grabbed his suit jacket and notes and headed out to take the courtesy bus to the conference centre.

Sam was the first speaker of the day. Already, he wanted it to be over. There were the usual hecklers in the crowd as he came up to the podium. He wasn't in the mood. He threw back some of the banter, made light of it, but was ashamedly lost for words moments later when someone made a bawdy suggestion about him and Gemma Scott.

'How about we get our minds out of the gutter, and get on with it?' he finally managed after sorting uncomfortably through his papers. He tapped the microphone and an ear-splitting squeal shot through the speakers.

'I saw you and Ms Scott *in* the gutter, mate. Last night outside the hotel.'

Laughter broke out amongst a few in the audience. The flush in Sam's face showed his embarrassment. That became the subject for further taunts and he felt awful about it, more for Gemma's sake than his. He saw her now, mid row and close to the exit. She stood and left the auditorium. Maybe she'd expected him to defend her honour better than just standing up front, poking the microphone.

Sam cleared his throat.

'Glenn Whittaker's great interest in the treatment of post-traumatic stress disorder focused almost exclusively on police officers. He had a large following. His research, in particular his compassion and understanding of the problems and issues facing officers in their day-to-day struggle on the streets, gave cause for several of his papers being published in psychiatric magazines both here and internationally, and his opinion was often sought by the medical profession. The talk I'm delivering today is on behalf of Glenn. It's *his* research, *his* words. And I'm honoured to be paying homage to him by presenting a small portion of his work.'

The crowd had been successfully subdued. Glenn Whittaker was now a champion in the field. Death tended to do that – enhance a reputation. Sam used the momentum to put distance between himself and the earlier jokes.

He saw Gemma at the first break, standing with others in a tight circle. She didn't appear to be participating in the conversation. He thought about approaching her but when she looked across and noticed him, her eyes narrowed and she turned away.

When the next round of lectures started, Sam found a seat near the back of the room. One lecture ran into the next. He was too distracted to pay attention to all the in-jokes.

A round of applause was followed by the lunch announcement. Sam walked outside to the wide steps of the conference centre, rubbing the back of his neck. There was no rush to leave, not now that Alice had likely gone for a bush walk – he'd seen the brochures scattered on the sofa before he left the hotel room that morning.

Edgar Camberwell joined him and stared out across the valley. 'An excellent speech and very brave of you. I imagine that particular subject was a hard one to deliver.'

'It wasn't my speech,' Sam said flatly. 'All I had to do was read what was already written.'

Edgar made a sound through his teeth. 'Don't sell yourself short. There was plenty of adlib. Glenn Whittaker was a champion, I'll admit, but he was no speechmaker.'

'I'm just glad it's over.' Sam looked at his old professor. The dignified profile of the older man induced an odd need to confess about Alice – perhaps not directly though. 'I've started taking on police,' he said cautiously. 'Just one at the moment. Richard's been at me to take more but... I don't think he understands the challenges.'

'Police require a bit of special handling.'

'Exactly.'

'It's a process, Sam. Truth be told, we're still learning about this PTSD business. Glenn's approach was unique – going into police stations, building trust, and quite sincerely too, I would imagine. But there was nothing empirical in his methods. I'm not even sure it was useful. Kind, maybe.' Edgar faced Sam. 'You're not thinking of taking over where Glenn left off?'

'No. But I am interested in exploring a more... innovative form of treatment.' He stopped. What was he saying? Nothing that he'd meant to. Bringing a patient away and sharing a hotel room with her was hardly *innovative*. He chewed on the inside corner of his lower lip. 'Maybe it's not so much to do with the therapy. But instead, *caring* about patients.'

The old professor slapped a bony hand on Sam's shoulder. 'What did I tell you years ago? Never get sentimental. Leave the innovations to the trailblazers – namely, the psychiatrists who can't get clientele. They've got nothing better to do with their time other than write books and manifestos, or get funding for research that amounts to nothing. Just remember, caring becomes worry, and worry will keep you awake at night.'

A thunderous rumble drew the attention of the two men. The air quivered ahead of a blue-and-white helicopter that lifted dramatically from deep within the valley, as though released from a secret underground hangar. It roared into view, shifting and pivoting like a dark monster picking out its prey. And there were plenty to choose from as people came running outside to see what the commotion was about.

'PolAir – the police helicopter,' Sam said, although his voice was drowned out in the rush of noise.

As the chopper swung around and followed the edge of the cliff, sirens could be heard – at first distant, growing louder by the second.

'Down at Echo Point.' Edgar pointed in the direction. 'Someone must have gone over the cliff.'

TWENTY-TWO

Sam rushed into the hotel room and called Alice's name. After checking the bathroom and then outside over the balcony to the garden courtyard below, he grabbed up the brochures from the sofa. He didn't know which trek Alice had gone on – or even if she'd gone on one at all. There was little phone reception but he tried Alice's mobile number anyway. It wouldn't connect.

He could still hear the thrum of the helicopter.

Sam headed down to the reception desk. The desk clerk ignored him at first, typing something on the computer.

'Do you know what's happened?' Sam asked him urgently. 'Down at Echo Point?'

'Just a moment please...' The clerk typed some more and then looked at Sam. 'Oh, Dr Tyler, good news, we've had a cancellation. An extra room has become available.'

'No, I don't care about that. Something's going on. There are helicopters and sirens. An emergency of some sort.'

'Maybe someone fell over the cliff. Happens from time to time.'

Sam's heart began to pound. 'The woman I'm staying with, did you see her this morning? Did she say where she was going?'

'Um, sorry. I'm not sure...'

Amid the curious questions and remarks from the people milling into reception, Sam took off. He missed the bottom step on his way out of the building and skidded into a couple coming the other way.

The startled pair reproached him and the man shoved him aside. Sam recovered and kept running.

People were streaming towards the lookout and Sam was quickly caught up in the throng. He got as far as the information centre before being shuffled back by police and officers from fire and rescue. People were asking what was going on.

He heard several replies:

'Stranded bushwalkers.'

'Someone's gone over.'

'Jumper.'

'You can't get through,' the man next to him said as Sam attempted to go under the police tape as it was being erected.

'I've got someone down there.'

'Mate, my daughter's on a hiking trip with the school. So don't give me that. They'll only turn you back.'

'I've got to try.'

He didn't get far before a fireman in overalls with a "rescue" insignia manhandled him backwards with a few others who'd followed Sam's lead. Sam stumbled, almost fell from being shoved.

'Bloody rubbernecks. Move on,' the fireman shouted.

'You don't understand. I know someone down there. She went on a walk.' He pointed over the fireman's shoulder to the gaping hole of the valley.

'And what do you expect to do about it? Levitate down there?'

'I expect you to let me through.' His request was irrational, he knew it. He added, 'I'm a doctor. I might be able to help.'

The rescue guy's attitude shifted. He put a hand on Sam's shoulder and eased him more considerately back behind the line. 'Look, my job is to keep the gawkers back. I can't let anyone in.'

'What's happened?' Sam asked, but the fireman had moved along the line, some other reprobate taking his attention.

A contingent of police officers arrived and began shouting instructions to the onlookers, telling them to move away. They started to press people back from the taped area. When the helicopter swung into view, Sam guessed they were making room for a landing. Had they picked someone up from the valley?

He tried Alice's mobile again. Still no signal.

'This can't be happening.'

He couldn't be certain of anything; whether Alice had gone on a walk, or even if she would have been in this area. There were lots of trails, lots of organised walking tours. The possibility remained that she was in the town centre somewhere, antique browsing, in one of the art galleries, or taking a red-bus tour of lesser known waterfalls and lookouts.

More police arrived. More cars and sirens. Sam didn't want to leave. But he didn't want to miss Alice in case she'd returned to the hotel. He decided to go back and check.

He hurried into the suite. She wasn't there. He returned to reception, asked as many staff as he could find about Alice. Nobody had seen her. Back in the room again, he sifted through the brochures. They were all for organised walking groups. Using the hotel phone, he started ringing the numbers. The first two companies didn't have her name. The third did. Alice had booked for a walk that started at eight that morning. She'd turned up, her name was ticked off and she'd signed the disclaimer form. The guy on the phone assured Sam that she was in good hands. He'd heard that a female tourist had fallen from a rock ledge just down from the Three Sisters lookout, and that several others were possibly stranded.

'I can promise you it wasn't anyone from our company's group. They should be back in about an hour.'

Sam got the details of where the group would emerge from the track and headed down there, although it was in the area blocked off by police. Freestanding barricades had been set up with the police on one side. Sam was jostled in the crowd of onlookers as he tried to get an advantageous position. He squeezed in at the front. By now there were rescue vehicles with lights blazing, and a group of six or seven in climbing gear were organising themselves at the top of the trail leading to the Three Sisters.

All he could do was wait.

The designated hour came and went. And then another half hour. No sign of Alice.

Media and reporters were setting up cameras. A female correspondent in a tight skirt and undersized jacket was arguing with a police officer who refused to give her access past the barricades. The solidly built officer asked her politely yet firmly to move away. The television presenter hurled insults and abuse at him, but to no avail. Minutes later she was appropriately sombre as she reported to the camera that some sort of tragedy had taken place in the mountains, the details sketchy, but it seemed several people had fallen from the cliff. Sam felt a wrench in his gut at her words, although assured himself that it was little more than speculative commentary.

Some people were coming up from behind the cordoned area. The police further along moved aside the barricades to let them through; a group of about seven, some with backpacks – they'd obviously come up from one of the tracks. Alice wasn't with them. Regardless, Sam rushed over as they came through and went to the leader.

'There was a woman. Alice. She went walking today.' He was quite aware of his desperate tone. 'Did you see her? Was she with you?'

'Don't even know what's going on, mate,' the man said.

'Someone fell from the cliff.'

'Not from my group.'

Stragglers continued to appear from the tracks intermittently – Alice not amongst them. It was wearing on Sam, the time stretching out, drawing the day with it. The wintry chill of late afternoon drifted in with the fading light.

It was taking too long. Did he get the location wrong? Or maybe something really had happened to her. The tour operator he'd spoken to might have been downplaying the drama. He'd been unable to say exactly what had taken place, yet seemed well assured it had nothing to do with his company. Deniability – that had probably been his strategy.

Sam swore under his breath. He felt ill. He knew he was dehydrated. His heart was in overdrive, taxing his energy. He wanted to leave and he wanted to stay. Alice might be back at the hotel, having returned by a different route. Or, she might be down there in the valley, caught up in whatever tragedy was unfolding.

He looked at his phone as if there might miraculously be a signal.

Some of the onlookers were starting to move away. The helicopter hadn't been seen in a while although Sam could still hear it further down the valley.

Two more groups of walkers arrived. No sign of Alice. Sam paced up and down the barricades. His eyes were stinging and he had the headache from hell.

God, if anything had happened to her, it would be his fault. He'd brought her here. He'd done this. So much for protecting her, taking care of her. He may as well have thrown her under a bus for all the good it had done.

He turned away from the scene, from the gouged landscape that brought no joy, no longer any awe.

And he saw her.

She was with a small group that came from a pathway at the furthest end of the northern perimeter. Wearing khaki shorts, a black t-shirt and a small backpack, she was walking slowly.

Sam pushed past a number of people to go to her – knocked over a freestanding barricade. 'Alice!'

She stopped on hearing her name and looked around. She smiled faintly when she saw him – part surprise, part confusion.

He couldn't help it – he grabbed her up in his arms. And he was ridiculous and incoherent.

Alice allowed his hug but then pulled back a bit to study him with the deepest consternation. 'Sam, what's happened?'

He couldn't answer at first and simply held onto her.

'Sam. What is it? What's going on here?'

'I thought you were gone,' he finally managed, unable to look at her properly, ashamed of his tears. 'God, I'm such a fool,' he added under his breath.

'You thought I was gone?' She glanced around at the gathering of people and emergency services and media. 'Did you think something had happened to me?'

'Someone went over the cliff – there was talk of a woman.'

'Oh no! They actually fell?'

'When I found out you were walking on one of the trails, I panicked.'

She reached up and gently stroked his wet cheek.

He responded by pulling her closer to him, and he held her like he never wanted to let her go again. She was warm-bodied from the walk, and she felt wonderful beneath his hands. 'I thought I'd never see you again.' His voice was barely above a whisper.

Alice let her backpack drop from her shoulders and she swung her arms about his neck. 'It's all right,' she said. 'I'm here. Nothing bad happened to me.'

He cupped her face. She was soft and she was real. Flesh and blood and beating heart.

His mouth took hers with a passion that he'd long forgotten he possessed. For the fact she was in his arms, that she was safe. For *not* being lost to him.

Two ambulances came through the area at high speed, lights and sirens whirring in manic crescendo. At the same time the chopper made an appearance, soared low over the car park, whipping up dust and litter.

Alice pulled back and Sam found himself confronted with the swirling red-and-blue lights of a police vehicle. He staggered, but then regained his footing as he realised he had to get Alice out of here. He picked up her bag and guided her away from the madness.

Back at the hotel, Alice hovered in the doorway of their room and stared out towards the balcony. Sam went ahead and closed off the window, pulled the curtains.

If he didn't act quickly she would close down. Her condition did not respond well in this sort of situation. A flashback to the train crash may have been triggered through the madness of the emergency services vehicles and the marauding chopper.

He would guide her through this moment. He would steer her thoughts, console and comfort her.

'Come in and sit down,' he said, not sounding at all calm.

She didn't move.

He felt a rush of anxiety and moved to reach for her, intending to bring her the rest of the way into the room – but she pulled back, whipping her arm away from his touch.

'What are you doing?' she said warily.

'I'm trying to help you. It's bedlam out there.' God he could still hear the sirens. What was the point of that now? 'They should turn the bloody things off.'

Alice bit on her lower lip, staring at him as though he must have lost his mind.

'The sirens,' he explained. 'Trigger-happy emergency workers. They seem to love the sound of themselves in any form.'

She took a deep breath and held up both her hands, stepping back.

'Alice?'

'I can't do this. Just... leave me alone.'

She turned and began to walk swiftly away.

He followed her down the stairs, out the front door of the hotel, trying to convince her to come back to the room. But the chopper drowned out most of his words. He stared up at the beast and swore, wishing the wretched thing to hell.

When he looked back, Alice was standing to the side of the cherub fountain at the front of the building. Sam made no move to approach her – simply waited and watched for a while. Eventually she sat on a bench seat near a grove of ferns, her head bowed as though in silent prayer.

Reluctantly, he returned inside. He stood in the middle of his hotel room; he didn't know what to do with himself. He drew long breaths, trying to work out why Alice had chosen to retreat.

Because you fucking kissed her, you loser!

'Jesus.' He rubbed his hand at the back of his neck.

Unwell and reliant on him, he'd just exacerbated Alice's vulnerability. During a critical moment, he'd kissed her. And then he'd tried to become her doctor again. It would have confounded her. Dammit, it confounded *him*.

Defeated, he pulled off his tie and sat on the end of the bed, wondering how it had come to this. He'd never taken this path before. Always detached to the point of rudeness, he'd become the cool and calm doctor, formal to his colleagues, unremitting in his privacy. It had saved him because his emotions could be buried, the bad memories repressed inside his psychiatric work. But he'd lost it – these last few days. His mask, the impenetrable shell of constraint had been shattered.

How could he put this back together? He leant forward, elbows on his knees, and held his head.

But logic failed him.

TWENTY-THREE

Someone was standing in front of him.

Sam looked up from his hands. It was Alice. He hadn't heard her come in.

'Are you all right now?' she asked quietly.

'What?'

Her fingers played feather-soft on his cheek, stroking the area under his eyes, tenderly removing his tears. Her touch infiltrated his soul as though she had the power to heal all hurts. His heart surrendered. He could forget. For now – he could forget all the bad things.

She reached down and took his hand, and he stood as though silently commanded to do so; and she led him into the bathroom, closing the door behind them. Still no words, she turned on the shower, then faced him again, and without hesitation began to remove her clothes.

Every aspect of her, every nuance and sweet curve of her body was not lost on his senses. It took him a few seconds more to snap out of this stupor – and with less grace than she had done – he kicked off his shoes, removed his shirt, trousers and everything else, and followed her under the steaming cascade.

She wasted no time in drawing his body to hers and he trembled at the feel of her skin against his. The water rushed over them, between them, blurring his vision as though he were standing in torrential rain; but it was more than that. It was cleansing; the bad things of the past were all being washed away, forgotten. He was sure of his tears now, but they were lost to the running water.

Taking both his hands, Alice guided him away from the direct force of the cascade and into the corner of the cubicle. Shimmering droplets sprayed and glistened on their skin – and she stood up on tiptoe to kiss his mouth. Her lips touching his were gentle, barely there, like the breath of a butterfly.

His arms moved slowly around her. Her breasts were soft against his chest. Her hair was darkened from the water and he moved it from her forehead, pressing it away from her face. And he kissed her, lingering now as she pushed her fingers into his hair and then behind his neck, encouraging his mouth.

He wanted to stay locked away in this tiny space with her, where there was no time, no roles to play – where illness and regret and sadness had no place, because none of those things existed.

He couldn't remember her shutting the water off, but it stopped and after a few seconds they stepped out. She pulled on a white towelling robe that had been hanging on a hook at the back of the bathroom door, and tied it in one loop at the waist. He watched her, mesmerised by her graceful, fluid movements. She cupped a white towel around his face, moved it down from his neck to his shoulders and then his chest, where he took it over and wrapped it around his hips, hooking the corner into the top edge. Then he followed her into the next room.

They lay on the king bed together, facing each other at first, but then she manoeuvred her body over his and he rolled onto his back taking her with him. She sat up into a straddle, and he lifted his shoulders from the bed to kiss her. She allowed the kiss, but then settled him back to the pillow.

He undid the tie at the waist of her gown, and she let the garment drop from her shoulders. His fingers traced the sweet silken sheen of her skin, reaching up to her breasts – dark nipples firm and defined. A surge of desire rushed his veins. He wrapped tight arms around her and in one movement changed their position, rolling her to her back.

He discarded his towel.

There was a raw edge to their lovemaking; intoxicating, vibrant, at times possessive – alternating from frenetic to gentle rhythmic streams. He could tell she was close to climaxing and he wanted nothing more than to give her that, but when her breath sharpened and her back arched in wanton need, his body rebelled to meet his own pleasure.

*

Seated on the edge of the bed, Sam stared out through the glass balcony doors, watched the stars slowly pinpoint into oblivion as the morning light lifted from the valley. He wasn't welcoming the new day. He almost feared it. Everything had changed.

Alice slept soundly, curled on her side, one arm above the sheet, the fingers of her other hand looped in her hair.

Quietly, he got up, then grabbed some fresh clothes from his bag before going into the bathroom and locking the door. He took his pills from their hiding place in the shaving bag; avoided his reflection as he swallowed two. Then he ran the shower and got under it cold. The alpine chill was not punishment enough and it didn't clear his mind. He turned the water off and stood shivering in the cubicle, pressing his fingers to his forehead, desperately wanting to work out this mess.

By the time he returned, Alice was awake and half sitting up in the bed. She gathered the sheet closer around her breasts. Sam was more than aware of her nakedness, her form defined beneath the thin fabric.

He shoved his hands into his pockets – released them again. Finally, he sat opposite her on the sofa. On the table next to him, he picked up his conference folder, randomly flicked through some notes.

'I didn't bring you here for this,' he said stiffly, without looking up. 'It was never my intention.'

He heard a faint rustle.

'Then what did you bring me for?'

Now he looked up at her. Shadows seemed to fall across her features, the dark roots of her hair having lengthened since the time he'd first met her. 'I... well,' he started unsteadily, 'you needed a break...'

'I did? From what?'

His eyes narrowed. Was she testing him?

'Are you really going to sit there and...' She lifted one hand and let it drop back to the sheet. 'I'm sorry,' she went on. 'It's just that I seem to be the one asking the questions. So perhaps I should be writing this down.'

Realising her meaning, he tossed aside the papers he held. 'I wasn't implying that...' He ran a hand hard over his head. 'I don't need to tell you that what happened between us last night was completely wrong.'

'Oh, well done. What a fascinating claim. I suppose you're going to tell me next that it was all unexpected. The last thing on your mind.'

He let out an incensed breath. 'Well, what do you think!?'

'I think you're angry with me. That it's all my fault.'

'Don't tell me what's in my mind.'

'Why not? I might know it better than you.'

He huffed but wasn't sure for the moment. Mostly because he didn't think he understood himself right now. But she certainly didn't either. She was the patient. She was the one in need.

'It's not about blame,' he finally said. He drew in a deep breath, realised he had trouble filling his lungs. He had to find his words. When he did, they came out slightly jagged. 'I take... full responsibility... for what happened—'

She fell back against the pillow. 'Oh spare me!'

'Why won't you let me finish?'

'Because I already know what you're going to say. It wasn't planned. It was unfortunate. Your judgement was clouded. Oh dear, it was such a dreadful mistake.' Her arms stiffened beside her. 'Which is all well and good after the event. But doesn't mean a damned thing. I'm lying here in your hotel room, in the bed we shared last night.'

'I didn't mean for this to happen.'

'Yes you did.'

He wanted to be outraged; stopped himself from getting up to leave. This wasn't something he could run away from, although he yearned for the frigid mountain air on his face. To stand in front of the Three Sisters and just figure things out.

'You promised me my own room,' she continued, bitter tears forming in her eyes. 'A suite you said. You won't see me, you said. Yet you gave me a key and told me to put whatever onto your tab. In case you didn't notice, your toothbrush is right alongside mine in the bathroom. I've seen you in your jocks and you got a good look at me in my p-jays and fluffy socks. So how did you not know we were going to end up here?'

'I've been trying to tell you!'

She held up both her hands before letting them drop heavily onto the sheet either side of her body, accentuating her form, like she was really a mermaid, or a siren who'd lured him to his fate.

He found himself wanting to blame her. She had led him to the bed yesterday.

But that was wrong. He'd wanted to go with her. He'd wanted nothing more than the comfort of her warm, supple body.

His jacket felt confining and he stood and ripped it off. Why the hell had he even put it on? He went to the window and looked out. The morning was tree-whipped, flutters of leaves, several clinging to the balcony rail, shivering like they were lost.

There was a logic to this, and he needed to convey that to Alice. First, he needed to find it. Step back in time, like he did with all his patients. Draw up the moment when he first made the decision to invite her. It had been when he was looking through Sophie's folder at home – the one Glenn had kept.

'I used to be married,' he started, forcing a calm tone; his doctor's voice coming through. 'To a police officer. And I remember how hard it was for... my wife. She didn't always say anything. But most of the time she didn't need to. I could tell if it had been a bad shift.' He hadn't always given Sophie the right sort of support, he knew that now. He'd been too impatient. Too selfish. 'And I wanted to help you. I couldn't leave you in Sydney as things were.'

'As they were?'

He turned to face her. She was sitting up again. 'Alice, you were up to your waist in the surf.'

'I wasn't trying to kill myself.' She came a little forward, her tone incredulous. 'I just wanted to feel the cold. Feel something other than this sickness of my mind.'

'You cut yourself.'

'With a blunt knife,' she came back at him, part of the sheet moving to reveal a dark nipple that she quickly recovered. 'God, if I'd really meant it I'd swallow whatever crap medication you and other doctors have been trying to put on me since this all started.'

He thought of the bottle of pills he had in his shaving bag. *Her pills.* How close he'd come himself to making that fatal plunge, perhaps even closer than Alice—

He wouldn't let himself think about it. He shook his head. 'That's how these things start. You want to block out the pain, replace it with something, but it can escalate from there.'

'If you really believed that, then you should never have brought me to this place with its cliffs and plenty of time on my own.'

He realised he had no answer for her.

She went on. 'You're a nice man. And… dare I say a good doctor. But you need to go a lot deeper than all this superficial stuff. You wanted me here, and that's why I came. *For you.*'

'For me? Don't be ridiculous.'

'I saw you, Sam.' She pointed to the door without looking at it, her voice unsteady as she fought off tears. 'Yesterday, you were panicked. I don't know what the hell you might have been through in your life, but I wasn't the one in need. I wasn't—'

'I'm quitting the conference,' he jumped in. 'I have my CPD points and if I need any more I can do a quiz or two online—' He didn't know why he was saying this to her, what good it was supposed to do. And he had nowhere else to go with it. What was to come from this moment? He honestly didn't know. He paced towards the balcony door but stopped short of going out.

He heard a noise and turned around to see Alice scrunched over on her side, trembling and sobbing into the pillow.

Oh Jesus.

He went to her, sat on the edge of the bed, and tried to pull her around to face him. She resisted and he left her for a moment. But his heart felt her pain. This was worse than anything else – bringing distress to her life through his need to justify his actions.

There was no justification to this. She was right – he knew all along where this could go. Maybe he even knew there would be no adjoining rooms. No fancy suite to speak of. Why would Laura have booked such accommodation for him? A single man who was attending a conference and needed only a bed at night and a bathroom. He could have slept in his car or bunked in with Edgar. He hadn't made any move towards that because deep down he'd wanted her company. He hadn't wanted to be alone anymore.

And because Alice had reminded him of Sophie.

What he would give to be able to go back in time and take care of his wife. He'd never taken her to a conference. They were always opportunities for him to play up. But Sophie could have done with the break. And now his days were dreary reminders for all he'd lost.

'Alice,' he said softly. But he had no follow-up to it.

He leant in behind her and sensed the traces of his essence still beneath the covers. He'd washed her away, sprayed his body with fragrance, and clothed himself with the starched trousers and shirt of his profession. His silk tie was lying over the back of the single seater next to the bed – initials delicately embroidered at the lowest point. He felt ridiculous and wondered what on earth he'd been try-ing to prove by paying stupid money for something so impractical. As if any of it could make a difference. He was as naked as her, as vulnerable and afraid.

He moved his hand and kissed her shoulder, then her cheek, and didn't mind that it was slick with grief. Kicking off his shoes, he eased his legs onto the bed, wrapped an arm around her, his face in her hair, scented in lovemaking and eucalyptus and perhaps even the mountain air. And in that moment he didn't want to be any-where else.

'I want you in my life, Alice.'

Tears still streaming, she rolled around to face him. 'Sam...'

'Let's tell the whole fucking world.' He realised the impractical-ity of his words, wondering how he could even utter them.

'But… you can't say that,' she stammered. 'We can't…'

'We'll do as we damned-well please.' He tried to smile. The truth was he had no idea how this was supposed to play out.

But one thing was clear. They were on the same sinking ship.

TWENTY-FOUR

The telephone in the hotel room was ringing. Sam wished it into oblivion. He hugged Alice tighter when she stirred in the bed beside him.

'Sam,' she said sleepily. 'The phone...'

'Ignore it.'

'It might be important.'

He lifted his head and saw the bedside clock read a minute to midnight. He grunted his frustration, released Alice, and fumbled in the dark for the receiver. 'Hello,' he grumbled.

It was the concierge. He sounded tired. 'Dr Tyler, there's a gentleman here to see you – Dr Richard Madden.'

That got his attention. He quickly sat up, swinging his legs over the side of the bed. 'Richard Madden? He's here?'

'Yes, sir. Shall I send him up?'

'Um, no. No. I'll be down shortly.'

As he hung up he felt Alice move on the bed behind him. 'What is it?' she questioned tensely.

Without looking at her he said, 'I think we might have a problem.'

He turned on the bedside lamp, then got up and dressed in his jeans and t-shirt. Alice was sitting up in bed watching him. He picked up the room key and headed downstairs.

The concierge directed him to a small closed-off bar. Richard was standing against the furthest wall. He looked like a hit man –

one hand inside his jacket as though about to pull a gun. The concierge left them, shutting the door noiselessly.

'Your mobile phone is switched off,' Richard said tautly.

Sam kept his distance. 'There's no signal up here.'

The senior partner glanced around the small room. 'Bar's closed. Could do with a drink. How's your minibar stocked?'

Sam hesitated. This wasn't a social visit and there was no point in pretending otherwise. Richard hadn't driven two hours in the night to have a drink with him. He hadn't shaken his hand, patted his back or even opened with a joke.

'Maybe you should just get whatever it is off your chest.'

Richard grunted. Then his face darkened, and for a few seconds he looked like a man at war with an inner demon that was trying to escape; his mouth twisting and contorting until he finally blew. 'Are you out of your mind? Alice Lacey – *your patient* – here with you in your hotel room. Not only that, but during a psychiatric convention.'

'Calm down.'

'Calm down?' Richard started to bounce on the balls of his feet. 'Oh, that's it, that's the solution, let's all calm down, shall we?'

Panic rushed through Sam's veins, gored at his conscience. He wished he could push it away, but his mind dredged up his and Alice's indulgent day of room service. And intimacy. So what was he supposed to say to Richard? *It's not what it looks like? There's been a misunderstanding?* Or was he to completely lie? *What's got into you? Alice Lacey isn't here.* Could he deny it? He wanted to. But maybe he'd missed the boat with his initial reaction to calm down.

In the end, all he managed was, 'How did you find out?'

Richard stopped bouncing and sneered. 'A little thing called the nightly news.' He paused as though for dramatic effect, then added satirically, 'Those people who fell from the cliff – it was on all the channels. Media captured you and Alice so beautifully. Quite a touching scene – pushing your way through the crowd to run to her. Like a big romantic love story. Is that how you see it, Sam? You think you're in love with your patient?'

Sam had watched the news with Alice. They'd not studied it, but were aware that there had been one reasonably clear shot, although distant, of Alice coming up from the track; and then, briefly, the back of Sam as he'd breached the barrier to go to her. But you had to know the players to be able to make anything of it; the camera panning away to take in the hovering helicopter, the rescue squad, then to the accounts of eyewitnesses, the statement from the police spokesperson. There'd been nothing damning in it.

'I don't buy it,' Sam said, more to himself.

'I'm taking Alice home. Now.'

Sam eyed his colleague disdainfully. 'What is she, your runaway teenage daughter? She's a grown woman for Christ's sake.'

'You're having sex with your patient, and my reputation is *on the line*. My business, everything I've worked for. I'm not going to let you ruin that for me. These things, they fester like a sore that's been picked at. From here on in, it's about containment and control.'

'This is not your concern. This is my personal, private life. And Alice can do as she pleases.'

'If she had her head screwed on straight, sure. If you met her at a club or a party, then I couldn't care less. But you didn't. She's your patient, which you seem to have lost sight of. You dragged her here under false pretences.'

'That's not true.'

'Then why is she upstairs in your room right now?'

Sam could feel perspiration bead and dribble down his back. 'It wasn't like that. She was unwell – morbidly depressed – and I couldn't leave her in Sydney.' He could hear how pathetic he sounded.

'There were plenty of other options at your disposal. You could have phoned her – every day if need to be. Or got the mental-health nurse to make a home visit. Or even me – I could have taken her in for some counsel until you got back.'

'I'm not trying to make excuses for how things turned out. But I promise you it wasn't planned.'

Richard feigned surprise, his eyebrows shooting up towards the folds of his forehead. 'What a relief. For a moment I thought I might be out of line. You know, you had one job, to give your lecture on behalf of the firm and Glenn. By God, there was a good doctor. May he rest in peace.' He rapidly crossed himself. 'And this is how you choose to honour his memory.'

Sam lost the last shred of his composure. 'I didn't want to bloody come here anyway. You forced that on me.'

'Oh, so it's my fault.'

'It didn't help.'

'No, of course not. That's the mountain air for you though. It's like shredded grass – makes you horny.'

'Why didn't you wait until morning? Call the hotel and speak to me properly?' Sam snapped. He could feel the heat of his temper rising with every passing second. 'Instead of this drama where you get to show yourself off and—'

'I've no intention to leave her for one more minute alone with you!'

'So, you've got some big brave plan, have you? What is it? You going to airlift Alice out in some urgent evacuation? Take her in for deprogramming?'

'Don't turn this around and make out I'm the bad guy. Who knows what unspeakable damage you've caused her in all of this.'

Sam crossed his arms, and just as quickly let them fall. 'She won't go with you, and you can't force her.'

'She'll come. She'll see reason. And if she cares about you, which I suppose she must think she does, then she'll understand that it's not just for her benefit.'

'Leave me out of your concern, Richard.'

'I'm sorry, did I not make myself clear? This isn't for you. Not one part of it.' He paced a few steps until he was almost against the bar, seemed to realise the futility of it and turned back. 'What is it about Alice anyway? Does she remind you of Sophie? Yeah, I guess she would. Damaged cop. Jeez. And there's Leah, all this time, right in front of you. But you don't want her, do you. The poor girl has been beside herself, crying her heart out.'

'Leah?' Sam snapped to attention. 'What's she got to do with this?'

It was plain Richard regretted his words. He rolled his top lip under and made a grunting sound. 'Nothing. I'm just saying.'

Sam didn't believe him. His mouth became dry. 'You may as well tell me.'

Richard was studying him. 'If you must know, Leah picked it up.'

'What do you mean, picked it up?'

'The news report.'

Sam waited. 'Well?' he prompted.

Richard slunk into a chair, buried his head into his hands. 'Isn't that enough?'

'I saw the news. It doesn't show anything.'

'Is does when you take a closer look. And I did my own research. Discovered Alice wasn't at home. Her neighbour told me she'd got in a fancy car with some tall bloke days ago.'

Sam's stomach tightened. He wanted to tell Richard about Leah's locket being in the compactor. That she was obsessed with him. But how would that help? Regardless of Leah's derangement, it didn't change the fact that he'd been sharing a bed with his patient.

'How do things stand with Leah then?' he asked quietly instead.

Richard dropped his hands and looked at Sam. 'Yeah, she's all sunshine and rainbows.' He blew out a disgusted breath. 'How do you think things are?'

An awkward silence fell over them. Then Richard continued, a little calmer, 'Look, it might be okay. With Leah. After she made me look at the news playback on the internet, I made up a story. Weak as piss. I said Alice was up in the mountains as a case study. For the conference. Because your talk was about police and she'd agreed to… actually I don't know what else I said because I was shitting bricks.'

'She wouldn't have believed you.'

'I don't know. I played it right down. Had to take her for lunch, didn't I, pretend the world was really a pleasant place. Told her all my best jokes. She seemed all right.'

Sam leant against the back of the door and tried to steady himself with slow breaths. A strong powdery odour, like overworked carpet shampoo, irritated his senses. He shifted footing, stood up straighter. 'Go home, Richard,' he said wearily.

'I came here to get Alice.'

'You can't take her tonight. It wouldn't do her any good. Let me work it out.'

'There's nothing to work out. You know what has to happen.' Richard stood and started to leave, but stopped just next to Sam at the door. The older man was grave, his features pinched. 'You end this with Alice *now*, and I just might forgive you.'

As soon as Richard was gone, Sam slumped into the nearest chair. He felt ill, as if Richard had left his demon behind and now it was stalking the corridors of Sam's soul, seeking out the intricacies of his shame. Well, it didn't have far to look. The enormity of what he'd done took centre stage in his mind. He couldn't escape it. His secret was out. He'd failed. He'd failed Alice and he'd failed himself. Worse, he'd potentially sabotaged the most important thing in his life: his work.

It was a long time before he slowly wandered upstairs. Alice was perched on the bed, her eyes never greener, like emeralds, and wide with anguish. 'What is it?' she said. 'What did Richard want?'

'He knows you're here.'

'And?'

Sam shook his head and went into the bathroom, locked the door and leant over the sink. Then he took his pills from the shaver bag and stared at the bottle. Christ, what was happening to him? He threw the bottle into the basin – it clattered and bounced around the porcelain like a roulette ball. In the same way, Sam had gambled with his health, with his life. And he'd dragged Alice along for the ride.

Damn it.

He said nothing to her when he finally emerged from the bathroom. He stripped down to his boxers and got into bed, pulled the sheet up and turned away.

TWENTY-FIVE

The morning sun flooded the room as Sam opened his eyes. Alice was standing at the foot of the bed dressed in the same clothes as when they'd arrived, watching him with cold, regretful eyes.

He sat up alarmed. 'What are you doing?'

'Take a guess.' She lifted her backpack from the floor, set it on the sofa, and unzipped a side pocket.

'You're leaving?'

'I'm getting the train back to Sydney.'

Sam was out of the bed and at her side. 'No.' He went to take the bag from her, but she shouldered him away.

'You know this is the only answer,' she said. 'You just couldn't say it to me last night. But I got the message loud and clear, watching you curl into the fetal position and cling to the edge of the mattress like a condemned man.'

Sam glanced back at the bed with regret, remembering that he'd been trying to work out a solution. But he'd been exhausted. 'Look, I didn't mean to fall asleep. I was trying to formulate a plan. It's just not happening the way I would have liked—'

'And how was that?' she asked ironically, staring up at him. 'Was there supposed to be some better way to explain what you and I were doing? Face facts – this was never going to turn into anything meaningful.' She left the backpack on the sofa and headed into the bathroom.

Sam was close behind her. 'It was always going to be complex. It was never going to be a matter of just coming clean with everyone – not right away.'

She turned and glared at him. 'Not ever, Sam. Not ever. You're a psychiatrist. You can't have a relationship with a patient or even a former patient. It can't work. I don't know what I was thinking to listen to you yesterday, with your ideas that we could do whatever we pleased, that somehow you were going to find a magical cure to this. There is no cure. That's why you couldn't say anything to me last night. There isn't an answer because there isn't a way.'

He knew it – damn he knew it. But somehow it seemed too important, him and Alice. He couldn't allow her to disappear from his life.

'I don't accept that,' he said, trying to keep his voice steady. 'There is always an answer to everything life throws at us.'

She closed her eyes for a moment and shook her head. 'We had our fun, let's leave it at that.' She stepped away from him, to the shower cubicle where she took items from the shelf and put them into a toiletry bag.

'Alice, you're here because I care about you.' He grabbed her hand, turned it over to reveal the faint cut marks on her wrist. 'You weren't coping. How could I walk away from that?'

She made a small, incredulous laugh. 'Are we really going back to that argument again?' She took her hand back and began to gather her makeup from the top of the vanity unit. 'Anyway, we already agreed what this was about. Why pretend—?'

He saw it at the same time she put her hand on it. The pill bottle.

'Wait, that's mine,' he said.

She moved aside and studied the bottle. 'But I can see my name on it. It's been crossed out or—' He grabbed her wrist, took the bottle from her. 'What have you been doing, Sam, crushing antidepressants into my coffee?'

He didn't say anything, just bowed his head while he tried to figure out an excuse.

'Oh, I get it.' She punched his shoulder. 'I'm your supplier.'

'Of course you're not.' He put the bottle into his shaver bag, zipped it up. 'They're legitimate. A little while back I had an issue and... Glenn Whittaker prescribed antidepressants for me. I just couldn't get them after he died.'

'Then they're not legitimate. Is that the real reason you invited me here? You're using me to get drugs?'

'Medication.'

'Oh *sorry*. Let's get the terminology right, shall we? Makes all the difference.'

'Look, it's not what you think. I mean, it is, but I didn't use you... you weren't taking anything and... I'm weaning myself off them anyway. They're not addictive.'

'If they're not addictive,' she shouted, 'why do you have to wean yourself off them?'

'It would make me sick to stop them cold, what's known as discontinuation syndrome.' He'd experienced it first-hand in the bush. 'I can't write out my own prescriptions. I'm not allowed. These particular... drugs, there is a register for them. Doctor and patient are noted, recorded. I didn't want to see another doctor. It was only meant to get me through—'

'You sound like a junkie full of excuses.' She shook her head, the line between her eyes deepening. 'It's ironic, isn't it? You're the psychiatrist and I'm the patient. Yet you're the one swallowing pills.' She headed out the bathroom door, put the toiletry bag in the backpack, and slung it over her shoulder.

Sam was beside her, his tone desperate. 'It's not like that. Four years ago, after my wife...' In his panic he struggled to get the words out. 'I wasn't coping. Okay? I'm human, like everyone else. And I was treated for depression – and these pills were to help me.'

'You've been doing this for four years?' she said aghast. 'Why the hell are you treating people like me then?' She squeezed her eyes closed, like it was all too much to comprehend. A frustrated guttural sound followed. 'You know what, I don't give a shit. You're a liar. All this time, you knew what you were doing.'

Tears spilt down her cheeks. They were angry tears, disappointed and discouraged. He'd let her down, hurt her. And he'd never meant to. She put the back of her fist to her mouth as though stifling a sob. Her eyes sprung open but she didn't look at him.

'I just wanted to do something nice for you,' he implored. 'Inviting you here – there was never an agenda. And it wasn't because of the pills either. I would have seen Richard or someone else about them in time. It was easier, that's all – cowardly, I'll admit, to take advantage of the fact you weren't taking anything. I thought I could avoid the scrutiny.'

She started to leave. He tried to block her path but she shoved him, went to the door.

'Alice, wait.'

She kept walking and he was after her down the stairs. It wasn't until they reached the foyer that he realised he was only wearing boxer shorts.

The concierge held the door for Alice, staring at Sam as if he'd lost his mind. 'Sir, we have a dress code—'

'This won't take a minute,' he told the concierge. And he put his hand out to Alice again. 'Come back inside, and we'll talk about it.'

'I've had enough of your talk,' she cried. She shrugged away from him. Sam tried to follow her but another member of the hotel staff stepped in front of him.

'I have to insist, Dr Tyler. You need to return to your room and put clothes on.'

Without touching him, the two staff members directed Sam backwards. Over their shoulders he saw Alice get into the hotel courtesy bus that was parked on the gravel driveway out front. He had to stop her leaving, from getting on the train.

He rushed back to his room, except he'd left without his key and the door had locked behind him. As he bolted back to reception, he saw the courtesy bus pulling away, and he shouted at the staff member to give him access. When he finally got into his room, he pulled on jeans and a t-shirt, socks and boots – grabbed his car keys and rushed for the door. But as he reefed it open, Gemma Scott was standing there, her hand lifted as though she'd been about to knock.

She looked startled; her sapphire eyes surrounded in thick black eyeliner that made her look like Cleopatra. 'Sam, what's wrong?'

'I'm in a hurry. I've got to go.' He stepped around her but she was close on his heels.

'Sam, wait.'

He headed for his BMW in the corner of the car park. A four-wheel-drive had parked him in. 'Jesus,' he shouted angrily, looking around for a possible owner of the offending vehicle.

'Are you going to talk to me?' Gemma asked. When he didn't answer, she added, 'Where are you going in such a hurry anyway?'

'The railway station,' he said, suddenly interested in her presence. 'Where's your car?'

She frowned, but led the way to the other hotel car park just across the road and her silver Mercedes.

*

Sam wished he'd volunteered to drive. Gemma was going too slow, stopping at give-way signs, over-anticipating for pedestrians at crossings. And she wanted to talk. All Sam was interested in was stopping Alice from getting on the train.

'I was worried about you,' Gemma said. 'You didn't come to the conference yesterday, and I wondered if it was because of me. I behaved childishly, getting up and walking out on your lecture.'

He didn't care for this. He didn't want to know.

'It wasn't until later,' she went on, 'that I thought how foolish I'd been. For so many things too. Sam, I hadn't stopped to consider just how hard all of it must have been for you, standing up on stage, listening to those silly jibes. You'd think psychiatrists would know better. But then I also realised they couldn't possibly have known about you and me back then, about that night we spent together.'

'I'd rather you leave the subject alone.'

'You're wrong. We need to talk about it. So many things have been left unsaid.'

He huffed, shook his head.

'If you can't say it, then I will.' She paused, glanced cautious eyes across at him. 'Sophie dying – it had nothing to do with you and me, what we did. Granted our timing wasn't great—'

He half turned in the seat to face her. 'Our timing?' he said incredulously. 'You mean there was a better moment for me to be unfaithful to my wife?'

215

'I mean that we cared for each other, Sam. And by the time we did something about it...' She sighed. 'I accept my part in it. And it's not something I'm proud of. But if Sophie hadn't died that night, things might have... well, who knows how things might have turned out for you and me.'

He was shaking his head again. But then he became alarmed. 'Where are you going? You just passed the entry to the station.'

'Round the back. It's easier to park.'

'No, you should have dropped me off at the front.' He could see a train had just pulled into the station platform.

Gemma finally seemed to understand his urgency, and picked up speed. As they came into the railway car park, Sam was opening his passenger door.

'I don't think you're going to make that train,' Gemma said, slamming on the brakes.

He was out of the car and running. The train doors were closing just as he reached the platform. A station guard tried to stop him jumping the barrier and chased after him, shouting. Sam ran alongside the departing train and managed only to bang on the nearest carriage door calling Alice's name, trying to catch a glimpse of her in the flick pass of windows that followed.

He watched as the train cleared the platform and was on its way. He swore, turned back and kicked the nearest garbage bin, scattering several pigeons.

The portly station guard finally caught up to him and was shouting something about the requirement to swipe a valid rail pass.

'I don't want to catch a train,' Sam shouted back. 'I was trying to stop someone from getting on it. Okay?'

Gemma came running up to him, awkward in her high heels. 'Who were you trying to stop?' she said when she reached him, almost out of breath.

He couldn't answer. He looked away, not sure if he was ashamed or afraid. Something caught his attention. At the end of the platform, someone was sitting on the ground, their legs partly protruding from behind a bench seat.

Sam's heart began to pound. 'Alice.'

He ran to her and crouched on the rough concrete. She was crying and shaking.

'Alice, it's me,' he said gently, putting his hands on her shoulders, trying to get her attention.

She lifted her head and took in her surroundings as though only just realising where she was. Then she looked at Sam and gasped. 'I couldn't get on the train. I tried. But I just couldn't do it.'

He should have remembered her aversion to trains. 'Of course you couldn't.' He scooped her into his arms and kissed her wet cheeks. 'I'm here,' he soothed. 'Everything is all right. I won't let anything happen to you.'

*

Gemma drove them back to the hotel. Alice clung to Sam on the backseat of the Mercedes, burying her face into his chest as though she could no longer bear to look at the world. He could tell Gemma's stunned curiosity from the flash of her eyes in the rear-vision mirror, but was relieved his colleague wasn't asking any questions. This was not something he wanted to explain. She dropped them off at the hotel, left the engine running as Sam offered his quiet gratitude... and silent apology.

In their room, Sam helped Alice to the bed, and he closed off everything. Then he lay beside her. There were no words as he encouraged her into his arms.

A strip of sunlight breached the gap in the curtains and struck the centre of the bed like a flaming sword. There remained no solution to the situation – doctor and patient in a relationship. But Sam couldn't think about that now. Now, it was about Alice and what she needed. There had been enough loss in both their lives.

He kissed the top of her head, and felt the heat of despair scorch the back of his throat.

TWENTY-SIX

Alice seemed to be moving in slow motion, taking in the first room as if it were sacrosanct, looking around at the plain walls, running her fingers across the light-wood buffet, and then the back of the antique armchair. Sam had rushed in ahead of her – picked up discarded clothes and tossed them down the hall, before gathering books, magazines and endless papers that he dumped in a pile on the kitchen counter. The furnishings throughout the entire house were minimal, the walls devoid of artwork or decoration. They'd all been cleared out after Sophie died, when Sam had decided that the bare essentials were all he could stand in a house of painful memories. But now Alice treated everything with graceful reverence.

He waited. It took her just a few minutes to move to the front window where she peered through the slats of the venetian blinds.

He moved in beside her to pull up the blinds and open the window. The sound of the surf drifted on an easterly breeze.

'Don't you wish you could bottle it?' Alice said and took a deep satisfying breath; Sam smiled broadly at her pleasure. 'And with such a view too.'

'What view?' But now he looked in the same direction and was astounded that the scene had opened and the magnificence of the shimmering ocean was no longer impinged by a mass of trees. 'Far out, when did that happen? I didn't have this view last Monday. Actually, I've never had it.' And now he was staggered at how beautiful it was. He looked at Alice again. Two beautiful sights together – he could only marvel at them.

She moved away from the window to the spiral staircase, placing her hand on the rail and looked up. 'A staircase to nowhere?'

'It just looks that way. There used to be an opening to the upstairs, but I blocked it off years ago.'

'Why on earth would you do that?' She started to step up. 'What's up there?'

'Just two big empty rooms and a bathroom that's not plumbed. It was my wife's design. Her dream. But, after she died, I just couldn't face it.'

Alice gasped and turned to him. 'She died?'

'Yeah. It was a few years ago.'

She came down from the stairs. 'I'm so sorry. All this time, I assumed you were divorced.'

'Well, it's not my favourite subject.'

'No, of course not. I didn't mean to intrude.'

'You're not intruding. It's totally ridiculous, I know, to have a staircase with no purpose. I was going to get it removed altogether, but I suppose if I eventually sell the place, then I might need to open up those rooms.' He huffed and shook his head lightly. 'It makes no sense now. My wife dies and I take it out on the house.'

'That's grief for you.' She took his hand. 'Anyway, you don't have to explain.'

He brought her fingers to his lips and kissed them. 'Come and I'll show you the rest of the house.'

His bedroom contained an unmade double bed with a bottom sheet, two flat pillows placed one on the other, and a coverless quilt. There was a single bedside table in pine with an alarm clock, a lamp and a psychiatry textbook.

Alice picked up the weighty book in both hands. 'A bit of light reading before bed then.'

'Your boyfriend has been leading a dull life.'

She turned to him. 'My *boyfriend*,' she repeated, smiling. 'I like the sound of that.'

He laughed. 'Well, I can hardly say *doctor*, can I.'

'*Doctor* still has a nice ring,' she said impishly.

He took the book and dropped it back on the side table before drawing her into his arms, playing along with her mischief. 'Oh, I see how it is.'

Afterwards, as they lay in each other's arms, she said, 'How worried are you about this – about what we're doing?'

'I'd be lying if I said I wasn't concerned.' He stroked her cheek with the back of his fingers. 'Being together, I know it *can* be done, Alice. It just depends how discreet Richard and Leah are going to be.'

She pulled away slightly and lifted onto one elbow to face him. 'I thought you said your boss had told Leah a story about why we were in Katoomba at the same time.'

'I doubt it will stick. Leah's not that gullible. At some stage she'll come poking around.'

He hadn't ventured to explain about the lovesick secretary, only that she had been the one who'd identified them on the news report.

They'd both gone over the playback again. At first glance, it wasn't anything too damning. But played over and over, it was easier to make something of it. And with the right sort of inquiry, it wouldn't be hard to lay the facts before the Board of Psychiatrists that he and Alice had shared a hotel room.

'Sam, I'm damaged goods. Even if we can get over the hurdle of your work, what are the chances we can really make a success of this? We might be fooling ourselves. There's no guarantee we even have a future together. And it's not worth it if you end up losing your job over something that was doomed right from the start.'

He gently cupped her face in both his hands. 'Hey, enough of the worry.' He kissed her. 'Let me take care of everything. It's going to be all right. I'll make sure of it.'

She returned his kiss, lengthening it, and he welcomed her by rolling onto his back, pulling her on top of his body. He was ready for her again. It didn't take much. She was so sexy and soft – so wonderful.

*

It was dark by the time Sam rode his Harley to Richard's house. He still wasn't sure what he was going to say to the senior partner. But he didn't have the luxury of time on his side to work it out any further.

Richard was livid when he saw Sam standing on his doorstep. 'You were supposed to be back here yesterday.'

'I had things to do.'

'Where's Alice?'

'She's at my place.'

Richard looked like his head was going to explode. His skin turned blood red and if it had been at all possible, Sam wouldn't have been surprised if a burst of steam had come out of the older man's ears.

Sam took a deep breath, his helmet tucked under his arm – and he stepped inside when Richard indicated with a dramatic sweep of his arm to do so. Neither man sat but stood in the centre of the lounge room.

'I won't beat around the bush,' Sam said. 'Alice and I are together, and that's not going to change.'

At first, Richard was lost for words. He raised his hands as though to draw on the strength from a greater source, and then let his arms drop to his sides. He looked Sam squarely in the eyes and mustered a calmness that the younger man found unnerving.

'This is countertransference, Sam. You know as well as I do how common this is in therapy. It's nothing more than an emotional entanglement. I don't know how you did it, but you did. You got yourself tied up in a knot over this cop. You, of all doctors. Damn, I should have listened when you said you didn't want to take her on.'

'It's got nothing to do with her being a police officer. My feelings for Alice are real.'

'Real?' Richard said astounded. 'You're looking at Alice as though she's Sophie.'

'Don't be ridiculous. They're nothing alike.'

'They *are* the same. Now, at least. But that's you're doing. Same job, same age, same experiences. You're the common denominator, linking them even closer.' He threw his arms open wide. 'Why am I even spelling this out for you? It's basic stuff.'

Sam became increasingly frustrated. 'Don't start preaching to me now, Richard. You were the one who argued with me that Alice *was not* Sophie, that they weren't the same. You stuck your finger in my face and told me to get over it, to move on and stop making comparisons because there were *none* to make.'

Richard took a harder tone. 'Don't you see, you've *turned* Alice into Sophie.'

'That doesn't make sense.'

'The guilt you feel over what happened to your wife, you're trying to make it up through your patient. And she's leaning on you too. Maybe you're the husband or the father figure she never had. Her parents are off whoop-whoop somewhere, they don't have time for her. And here you are, her only form of contact, the strong male role model she's been looking for, who understands her, who listens, guides her, *cares* about her welfare.'

'I thought you said I was lacking when it came to caring about people.'

'Are you serious? You've taken this well beyond all decency. If you were having feelings for her, you should have opted out, come and seen me. Or you could have explored it in therapy, anything other than taking her to a hotel and sleeping with her.' Richard paused. His features distorted as he seemed to have a new, horrifying thought. 'You didn't have sex with her in the office, did you?'

'No, of course not. There was nothing between us in all that time before the conference.' He let out a harsh breath. 'I didn't set out to do this, Richard. It was the anniversary of the Bellingen disaster and she had nobody – not even her colleagues.' He thought of how he'd found her waist high in frigid waters, and the cuts she'd made on her wrist. He was sure that had been the impetus for his decision to take her with him.

'So you were worried about her.'

'Yes,' he said defensively. 'She was bordering on self-harm—'

'So are half your other patients. Are you going to fuck them too?'

Sam's lips thinned at the insult. 'Men and women get together. They fall in love. And it can't always be helped. Sure, this sort of thing is frowned upon, a doctor-and-patient relationship, I know. But it's not impossible.'

'Frowned upon? The Board of Psychiatrists won't be pulling faces at you, Sam. They'll crucify you.'

'Richard, you know me. I don't give in to emotions, certainly not with any of my patients. I hold back, I don't mingle or involve myself with them. That's why this is different.'

'Why can't you see it? You've effectively transmuted your guilt over Sophie into the care of your patient. And you're trying to justify it.'

'You can diagnose it if you want, put a title to it, but it doesn't change how I feel about Alice. I'm not giving her up. She's going to see another psychiatrist. I've drawn up the preliminary reports. A transfer at this stage isn't going to alert anyone.' Sam paused and attempted to settle his breathing. 'She's not going to say anything, Richard.'

'Why would she? You've got her all tied up in your web of misery, dragging her along in your wake. She'd follow you to the ends of the earth and jump off if you asked her to.'

'I can't see the problem other than what you're making it into with your hysterics. If you want to help someone, then maybe you should take a look at Leah.'

'Don't flip this around.'

'She's been unstable for months. Diane found her locket in the compactor at work and—'

Richard grabbed the front of Sam's jacket lapels and pushed him backwards. Sam dropped his helmet. 'So bloody what?' Richard shouted. 'I already had this out with Diane. Stupid, petty grievances. *You're* the problem here, not Leah. You think you've done nothing wrong, that you're in control, but you're not. This manic grief you carry is like an unexploded mortar in your head. And when it blows you'll not only take down yourself, but you'll destroy Alice.'

'Look, I only came here tonight as a courtesy.'

'A courtesy to what?'

'To tell you how things are.'

'I'll tell you how they are. You're out. I'm done with you. Find yourself another place to work.'

'Stop it!' It was then Sam realised Laura was in the room. 'Both of you, just stop. I can't take it anymore.'

Sam held his arms out to indicate he wasn't going to retaliate. Richard let go, then stumbled backwards, falling into the armchair, grabbing both sides of his head. And he began to groan like a man in agony.

Laura went to him, but he brushed her aside. She turned to Sam. 'What have you done to him?'

Sam felt a wrench in his gut. Richard and Laura had been so good to him and he'd never meant to cause either of them distress.

'He'll be all right,' he finally managed, a lump forming in his throat. Unhappily, he shook his head. It shouldn't end like this. He picked up the motorbike helmet from the floor, then turned back to Richard, but realised there was nothing else to say.

TWENTY-SEVEN

First thing Monday morning, Sam went into the practice. Laura stood abruptly from behind the reception counter.

'Oh, Richard won't be in until later,' she said.

'I'm not here to see Richard. I've just come to get my things.'

She sucked in her breath and muttered with uncertainty, 'I – ah – don't really think...'

'Won't take me long.' He wasn't going to stand around to work out the points with Laura. Richard obviously hadn't anticipated Sam coming in, otherwise he might have given his wife better instruction.

Sam took up the flat-pack boxes he'd brought with him and went into his office. He erected the first box, taped the bottom, and started to pack. There were journals and psychiatry books – he'd only take the useful ones. There were still some patient files in the locked section of his bureau, the ones he'd been working on in recent times. He'd have to go into the storeroom to get the others.

He went to the drawers, opened them and pulled things out. He didn't have time to go through everything properly; he imagined Laura was already on the phone to Richard. His hand drew out the framed photo of Sophie and he halted, staring at the back of it, at the thick piece of cardboard that would act as a stand if he'd ever dared to use it.

He turned the frame over. Was it easier to look at her face now?

Maybe the burning in the back of his throat wasn't there. His eyes didn't hurt. But then he looked at his hand – it wasn't steady. Quickly, he packed the frame and erected the next box.

Laura stiffened when he brought out the first box. Sam placed it on the floor next to the elevator, pressed the button and went back to his office for another box he'd filled. The elevator door smoothly opened as he returned. He put the box he was carrying on the floor against the door frame to stop it from closing, then he went back to his office to get another two boxes of items. When they were all in the elevator, he dragged in the first box that had been jamming the closing mechanism.

Ben was waiting for him in the downstairs lobby. He helped Sam bring out the boxes and put them into a van parked in a loading zone at the front of the building.

'I've got to go and get some more,' Sam said.

Ben nodded. 'I might have to drive around the block a few times.'

Sam returned to the office. He approached Laura at the reception counter and told her, 'I need the keys to the storeroom.'

'Sam, I wish you'd wait until Richard was here.'

He didn't say anything, just reached over the counter and took the keys off the hook, then headed down the hallway. All his current patient files were in two cabinets on the right side of the room. He grabbed an armful, then returned with them to his office where he placed them in a box he'd already made up and left on his desk. Then he went back to the storeroom for the rest. On his next return, Diane called to him from the open door of her office. He went in. She was at her desk with several folders in front of her. She lifted one and held it out to him.

'What's this?' Sam asked as he took it.

'It was in with some patient files I inherited from Glenn. Alice Lacey. She's one of yours, right?'

Across the front of the folder in red ink was *A. L. Confidential.* Sam opened it. There was a report at the front headed: David Penry, Clinical Psychologist, Coffs Harbour. Sam quickly flicked through the rest of the file and saw three handwritten pages stapled together and marked "serious jobs list". The first item noted was the

Bellingen train crash. He glanced at other jobs: an armed hold-up at the Westpac Bank, a suicide at the Old Mill Factory, three drownings on the same day at Diggers Beach.

'I've been looking for this.'

'I have no idea how it got separated from the main file or why Glenn marked it so vaguely. But that's Glenn for you.' She sighed. 'God I miss the old bugger.'

Sam closed the file. 'Yeah, he was one of a kind.'

She sat forward. 'Anyway, what are you doing stalking about the place?' She looked him over. 'I don't think I've ever seen you in jeans before.'

'You wouldn't have heard. I've been fired. I'm just here to collect my things.'

She laughed but just as suddenly stopped. 'Shit. Who did you murder?'

There was no point in watering it down, Sam realised. He needed to come clean about his relationship with Alice. She'd find out anyway, so she may as well hear it from him.

Diane, for once in her life, was lost for words. But after a few awkward seconds she said, 'Why would you do that? You know it can't work. And certainly not mid therapy.'

He didn't know how to respond to that, or to the downturn of her mouth. For some reason he hated the idea that he'd disappointed her.

She blew out a breath, then came around from behind her desk and kissed his cheek. 'You stupid bastard,' she said. 'But to be honest, I'd have probably fucked you too.'

He returned to his office and glumly packed the last of his things.

'What the hell are you doing here?' It was Richard. He shut the door loudly behind him.

Sam looked up briefly. 'What does it look like I'm doing?'

Richard came across and grabbed at the box on the desk. 'You can't take them. They belong here, to the practice.'

'They're the files of my current patients. You can't stop me taking established patients.' He'd secured a new office a few blocks away, nothing fancy, but it was all he could manage at short notice.

'What if they don't want to go with you? What if they want to stay here?' Richard challenged.

'That's their option.'

'They won't want you once they find out what you've done. Or once the psychiatric board finds out, it will all be over anyway.'

Sam eyed his former colleague cautiously. 'Maybe nobody will find out.'

Richard returned with raised eyebrows. 'And maybe they will.'

'Well, I'll cross that bridge when I come to it.'

Sam moved over to the sideboard and opened the bottom sliding drawer. He fished around for anything else he might need. When he turned back, Richard was going through the files that had already been packed.

'You can't have this one.' Richard held up the file marked: *Alice Lacey*. He glared at Sam. 'She's no longer your patient, so you're not entitled to her paperwork.'

There was nothing Sam could do. It was true, Alice wasn't his patient anymore. He had no right to take her file. Her new psychiatrist would have to send for it. There would be some difficult questions, but Sam was going to have to work that out with Alice later. For now, he nodded, put the rest of his things into the last box, picked it up and headed out.

*

A flurry of seagulls lifted from the sand as though they'd been ejected, and scrabbled onto the breeze in no particular pattern. Up ahead on the weedy sand dunes, Sam could see Alice. She was seated on the highest peak, and when she noticed him she raised her hand in a wave, and smiled.

She's smiling just for me. He almost laughed at the paradox of an old fantasy he'd had about a moment just like this. She stood as he neared and he quickly closed the gap. He couldn't wait to hold her, drawing her in for a kiss that was both sweet and poignant. She was so lovely.

Holding hands, they started to walk along the edge of the shore.

'How did it go at the office?' she asked him after a while.

'As you'd expect.' Sam wasn't sure he wanted to go into detail about it: Richard's gruffness that was really a shield against the disappointment and lingering threat of disrepute that might still fall on the practice. 'I'm hoping nothing more is said about you and me, that there won't be an investigation, and I can go on working.'

'Maybe Richard won't say anything.'

'Maybe.'

They walked in silence, Sam slipping his arm about Alice, pulling her in closely. She seemed to fit into the side of him, like a missing piece of a jigsaw puzzle that now made him complete. He didn't care what the textbooks said – he knew what he felt for Alice; it wasn't some warp in the therapeutic alliance between doctor and patient. Of course, it didn't mean the world was suddenly perfect and all their issues had faded away. When Sam had driven Alice home last night, she'd sat shivering in the car, staring out at her house like the devil was in there walking around. And he still had a pill problem, although he'd promised Alice he'd properly wean himself off them.

One thing at a time.

But that he dared to be happy, or at least to acknowledge something of a shift in him? He'd been so far down, lost inside a torturous, elongated bereavement that he'd worn beneath his psychiatrist's suit. It felt liberating to be out of it. He wasn't going to mess this up. He'd been given another chance, a reprieve.

They walked home to his place. It was still an ugly house, Sam decided, as they came up to the t-intersection. But maybe it wasn't as ferocious as he'd once imagined. It didn't look as though it was going to eat him. It was just a house, after all.

I should sell it and we could make a fresh start.

Alice halted and jerked backwards from Sam. He turned to look at her. Her hands went to her cheeks as she stared up behind him at the house.

'What is it?' he asked.

'There's someone on your roof.' She pointed and he spun back, but he didn't see anything. 'I swear there was someone there.'

He reached for her hand but she pointed again and this time he saw it too. A glimpse, someone around the back end, crawling over the tiles like Spiderman. 'What the hell...?' He hurried on, Alice close behind him. When he got to the house, he saw a truck and a number of people standing around. One of them was his neighbour, Brad, who approached him now.

'Sorry, Sam, but the guys had to get on your roof. We knocked first but you weren't home.'

'What's going on?'

'Finally getting the old tree removed. Got council approval. It's got a fungus disease – that big branch would have come down on your roof in time. I put the details in that note I left you.'

Sam stared at him. 'What note?'

'I left a note some weeks ago on your front door. You don't have a letterbox. About cutting off the branch.'

The note. The one that had been left on Sam's door, sodden, that he thought might have been a threat. 'Shit. It got wet,' Sam said, almost stupidly. 'I couldn't read it properly.' He shook his head. The words had been *cut off the tree branch*. Not, *cut off your head*, as he'd imagined.

'Sorry, mate,' Brad said. 'I came over a few times, but you're a hard man to catch. It's fine them being up there?'

'Yeah, of course.' Sam started to laugh. Brad and Alice stared at him, but the sheer relief he felt was as if a weight had been lifted. It was as though the sun had come out, the dark cloud that had been hanging over him, poisoning his mood, was now gone. There had been no threat. Nobody wanted him dead. Which meant it could only have been a hoon that night on the street when the car had charged towards him; and nothing more sinister than his over-worked imagination.

'Sam, what is it? Is something wrong?' Alice asked, her forest-green eyes filled with concern.

He pulled her in for a hug, still laughing. 'It couldn't be better.'

TWENTY-EIGHT

The corner alcove of the oddly shaped office was filled with pot plants. Sam wasn't sure if they were a good addition or not. He'd never had an office with more than one token plant. It was his new landlord's idea. 'At no extra cost,' Carlos had assured him.

Sam had spent the last three days setting up. The room was in desperate need of painting. Rendered walls were flaking, revealing dull grey and tarnished patches. The floorboards were wide and raw – if there had ever been a polish on them it was long gone, and there was a draught that seemed to seep between the boards. The square window at the end of the room had no covering and the sun streamed through, seeming to light up every dust particle that hung in the air. The ceiling was ultra-high, almost as though there had once been another floor above. And a light fitting hung from the centre on the longest cord Sam had ever seen. It made him feel like he was a mad professor in a laboratory. Well, maybe that wasn't too far from the truth. The whole thing, all of it, felt off key, out of whack. It was a big comedown from the luxury fittings of his old office.

The rental included a slightly rustic, but stable wooden desk, and Sam had invested in two high-backed chairs, one on each side for doctor and patient. There was an old sofa he'd thrown a sheet over, but it was a bit creepy, so he'd pushed it under the window with the plan to do away with it as soon as he could.

He'd brought in his laptop and printer from home and set these up on a wheeled stand for now.

The new filing cabinets had only arrived late yesterday and Sam brought over a box with the files he'd taken from the old practice, ready to put them away. He took out the first few and sorted them alphabetically, but the next one he pulled out was the blue folder marked: *A. L. Confidential*. Richard had missed it when he'd gone through the box. Alice's missing papers. That was weird, he thought again, having them marked in such a way.

He should take this home, he decided. Maybe he and Alice could go over the notes together. He mightn't be her doctor anymore, but that didn't mean he couldn't go on caring for her. For the moment, his eyes scanned the front page of the job list that she had written out for Glenn.

There was a knock against the open door of the office. 'Wow, this is different.'

Sam looked up from the papers. A young woman with a hippie sense of fashion was smiling at him from the doorway. It was his first patient in this new set-up.

'Hello, Faith. I'm sorry it's a bit disorganised here at the moment. Come on in.' He put Alice's file aside, and then went across the room to close the door.

Faith sat and Sam took up the other seat at the desk.

'Not quite the same as the old place,' he said. 'It's still a bit of a mess.'

'No, I like it,' the young woman said, twisting in her chair to look around. 'It has good energy.' She turned back and pointed at Sam. 'Groovy t-shirt.'

Sam realised he hadn't thought about his attire. He was dressed casually, but only because he'd been moving stuff around. And yet, there was something pleasantly quirky about it, humbling even.

He started with a rehearsed speech that he planned to give all his patients, about them being free to return to the old practice if they liked.

Faith huffed. 'I'm not going anywhere.'

Late in the afternoon Sam sat back and surveyed his new office and thought about the sessions that day. He'd seen five of his current patients, and all of them wanted to stay with him. He would have liked to have been pleased about it, but there was a nagging doubt that this could last.

Alice crossed his mind. He liked to think about her. He'd tried not to allow it before this, not let it interfere with his work. It felt okay to think about her now, not like before when she was still his patient.

No matter what happened, he decided, whether his career was about to do a nosedive or not, at least he had Alice. And that meant there was something good in his life.

*

Alice was wrapped about him, her legs entwined with his under the covers, and he'd only just stopped kissing her.

'You should move in here with me,' Sam said.

'What?'

'Move in here.'

Alice pushed against his shoulders, made him move back, as though she needed to study his face. 'It's too soon,' she said.

'Too soon for what?'

'For goodness sake, Sam.' She wriggled out from beneath him, and they settled together on the same pillow, facing each other. 'I've only been in Sydney a short time. And this...' she lifted a hand and waved it briefly in a musical way, 'is all new. Moving in together should be the last thing on our minds.'

'So, you'd choose Freddy Krueger over me.' He laughed softly at her puckered brow. 'Come on, we're not kids.'

'You think it's as serious as that?'

'You're in my bed. What could be more serious?' When she didn't answer, he kissed her lips lightly. 'This is not fleeting, Alice. I want you, for always.'

'You're my doctor.'

'Former doctor.'

'We need to keep a low profile for a while. Anything else will just enrage your old boss and inflame the situation.'

Of course, she was right – although he'd enjoyed that small moment of abandoned rationality.

She traced his cheek with the back of her fingers. 'When did you know?' she said faintly.

'Know?'

'How you felt about me.'

'I think it was the first time I ever saw you on the beach, off in the distance, sitting on the sand. You seemed so lost, sad.' He sighed. 'I wanted to wrap you up and take care of you. Maybe I didn't exactly understand my feelings back then. But they couldn't be any clearer now.'

She smiled.

'So, it's your turn,' he prompted. 'Was there a defining moment for you?'

'When you pulled me out of the ocean,' she said unhesitatingly. 'I was asking God to help me, praying for an answer, a reason to go on... or some meaning to my life, at least. And you were there.'

Sam huffed. He would have preferred to tell Alice it wasn't God who'd helped her that day, and even if one existed, he was hardly the answer to anyone's prayer. Still, he went with it. 'That's not reason enough for you to move in with me? Something as profound as that – a sign, I'd say.'

Her lips thinned. 'Stop nagging. You know it's too risky, and besides I'm only a matter of streets away from you.'

He let out a long, resigned breath. 'I've always been curious about why you picked Sydney.'

She made a soft humming sound. 'I thought I'd be better off in a city. You know, better health care, more choices, more places to hide.'

'Still, it's an odd choice. Sydney and Coffs are worlds apart. There's nothing much here for you.'

She shook her head and nestled into his shoulder. 'There may not be people here I know, not really. But I think that was part of the appeal. It's easier to be anonymous in a city. Back in Coffs, it feels like everyone knows your business, who you are, what you've done. I needed to get away. Mind you, Broken Hill looked good for a while.' She laughed lightly. 'But the trouble with country towns is that if you're not a local, then you stand out, you never belong. The city is far more forgiving.'

He could see her point. Perhaps that was why he stayed in Sydney. Less scrutiny. He was just another face in the crowd.

'It's strange,' she went on. 'I found my place here at Cronulla, nice and close to the beach. And I thought it was perfect. But less so when you think that the cop shooting I went to wasn't all that far away. Of course, I didn't realise at first, not knowing the area all that well—'

'Cop shooting?' he cut her off.

'Yeah, you know the one.'

'In Coffs—?'

'No, here in Sydney.'

'But you never worked in Sydney.'

'I had to come down one time on a prisoner escort. It was Garth Conroy and me. We had this nutter who was scared of flying, and he was due in court in Sydney the next day. So we drove him...'

Sam didn't want to hear this – his least favourite subject. For a while it seemed that every time there was a police shooting, people looked to him, as if he'd become some sort of expert on the subject. A few times he'd been requested to talk to a victim's family, in his capacity as psychiatrist, and someone who fully understood the pain of that type of tragedy and loss. But he never did. In Sydney alone, just last year, there'd been four officers gunned down, two of them fatally. A local newspaper had contacted him over one of them, asked him to comment. He might have to make a rule with Alice, he realised now: no talk of cop jobs in the bedroom. Or maybe at all.

'Don't go on,' he said.

She was still talking. '... six hours of driving. We were buggered. We'd dropped the prisoner off at the cells and were heading for our hotel for the night when the call came through on the police radio. Signal one, officer down. Of course, it doesn't matter where you are, you hear something like that, you just go. Garth knew the area. We got there so fast. Second or third car off – I can't remember. But we were too late. She was down, shotgun—'

'I said *stop*.' He pushed Alice from him and sat up, but felt bad for being so rough. He reached for her but she shoved his hands aside. 'I didn't mean it,' he said. 'It's just that... my wife, she was shot on duty.' Saying the words, he felt as if his heart had been ripped out.

'Shit,' Alice said, shocked. 'Oh, Sam. Why didn't you tell me?'

'I never talk about it,' he murmured.

They became quiet. The air felt still, like they were in a vacuum, hermetically sealed from the outside world. The clock ticking beneath the lamp on the bedside table seemed to be making the most of the silence.

'She?' he found himself saying. 'The shot officer was female?'

'We don't have to talk about it.'

'You said not far from here. When was it?'

She hesitated. 'A few years ago.'

'When!?'

She jolted at the thunderous tone of his voice, pulled the sheet up to her neck. 'I don't remember exactly.'

'You started this. So think about it. *When* did this shooting happen?'

He didn't wait for her answer. He got up, pulled on his jeans, t-shirt and shoes, like he was going somewhere. But then he stopped, faced the wall, leant his forehead against it.

'Sam...'

He could hear rustling. When he turned around, Alice was out of the bed, her naked form shivering, her hands clenched under her chin.

'Sam,' she said again. 'What is it? What—?'

A wave of nausea seemed to swamp him.

Gingerly, she came across the room, stood in front of him, her eyes wide, her lips dry and pale. 'What was your wife's name?'

Bile reached his throat. He swallowed hard, tasting the foul acid.

Alice's breath was rapid as her fingers touched her cheeks. She said something but the words got lost, lifted like vapour, dissolved into the walls and the ceiling.

The ceiling. He looked up and could almost hear Sophie now, walking around, going through the rooms. She'd come and tell him soon how beautiful it was, how she could smell the ocean, how they'd be sleeping under the stars. And the room at the back... for the baby.

Samuel, it's time we started a family.

Their baby who would *never* be born.

He glared at Alice. Her eyes no longer reminded him of deep-green valleys, of forests or emeralds. They were the eyes of someone who had seen death, who had touched it, smelt it, held it in her hands. It had got under her skin, through every layer of muscle and bone, infected her veins, penetrated her soul. And she could never be the same, could never mean the same to him.

'This can't be happening.' He was hyperventilating.

The room seemed to tilt as Alice breathed the words, 'Oh my God. My God. You're... you're Sophie Wilde's husband, aren't you?'

TWENTY-NINE

Sam was on the floor. He could feel Alice's hands on him. She was crying. He was crying. He didn't want her to touch him. Not those hands.

'Get away.'

She wouldn't go. 'Sam, please—'

'You knew. All this time. You were in on it.'

'In on what?'

'You and McGuire. Bringing me down. *Screwing* up my career. *Laughing* at me.'

'No. I don't know what you mean.'

He grabbed her shoulders and pulled them both to their feet. 'You kept it from me. Sophie – that you were there the night she died. You came in on this to torment me, get me back for what I did.' He had another horrible idea. 'Or was it Richard? You conspired with him. He put you up to this. What was it, revenge?'

'Sam, no, I didn't know,' she cried. 'Stop, you're hurting me.' But he held tight. She broke his grip with some police move, but faltered backwards, landing on the bed.

'Then why didn't you tell me?' he yelled. 'Why did you keep this secret?'

'There's no secret.'

'You kept it from me – the police shooting. I was your fucking doctor and you never told me about it.'

'I told Dr Whittaker everything,' she said desperately. 'I even wrote it out for him, all the bad jobs. *You know this*, surely you would know.'

The list of bad jobs. The most significant of her fourteen years in the force. Alice's missing paperwork that Diane had handed to him when he'd gone to collect his stuff.

He began to panic. There wasn't enough air. 'No. I don't believe you. You're a liar.'

He rushed out across the hall into the spare room where he tipped out the box of folders and papers, things he brought home from the new office, until he came up with the blue folder marked: *A. L. Confidential.* He grabbed a handful of the papers inside.

'It's *not* true,' he was telling himself.

But he had the notes. They were in his hands. Alice's most significant jobs. His eyes were speed-reading over the handwritten words. Drowning, robbery, suicide, another drowning, assaults, violent messy stuff. And on the second page, more misery, more sadness, one tragedy laid over onto the next. Fourteen years of it. A never-ending war zone.

He crumpled to the floor when he came across the entry on the bottom of the second page: *Police murder/suicide. Senior Constable Sophie Wilde at Bakerton Street, Caringbah. Response vehicle. Two deceased.*

Sam screwed the papers in his fists as his head fell forward. It had been here all along. 'No. No.'

Suddenly, Glenn's method, his reasoning for in-house therapy, came into sharp focus. His colleague had meant to contain the information, that Alice had been present at Sophie's murder, and he'd most likely separated the paperwork so nobody could make the connection. The files on all patients were accessible, discussed in meetings. In the few sessions Glenn had had with Alice, he'd probably been trying to formulate the best course of action. And he'd not told Richard, he'd not told anyone. He'd never got the chance.

Alice was in the doorway, her voice soft with compassion. 'I really didn't know. And I'm so sorry, Sam. I'm so sorry for you and for Sophie.'

He dropped the pages and stared up at Alice. She was dressed, clenching her hands together.

'Don't give me your sympathy,' he said. 'I can't stand it.'

'Sam, please...'

'Please what?' he shouted. 'Please can we do a rewind on the last few weeks? Can we go back to the part where I *hadn't* slept with you? Actually, take it all the way back to where Cranston Jones was supposed to be your doctor. *Not* me. It was never supposed to be me.'

He got to his feet. Outside, he ripped open the shed door. He threw things around in the dark until he came across what he was looking for – a long metal crowbar with a sharp spike on one end. He met Alice on the way back in. She seemed alarmed at the sight of the crowbar and backed herself against the wall.

Sam went for the spiral staircase and charged up to the top where he plunged the sharp end of the bar into the barricade. After several shouting thrusts he made something of a gash in the plasterboard, and fine particles started to rain down over him.

'What are you doing?' Alice screamed over the noise.

'She loved this, and I shut it off. *I shut her out of my life.*'

He dropped the metal bar and it clanged loudly down the first few steps before falling between the rungs and banging onto the timber floor below. He pulled at the plasterboard with his hands but was making little progress. His fingers started to bleed from the effort of clawing frantically at the material.

He let out a distressed yell, punched at the stubborn obstruction as more particle dust came down on him. It got in his eyes, his mouth, and he spat it away.

'*Sophie.*' He sunk helplessly onto the top step and buried his face into his hands. Images were flashing through his mind, rapid speed, back and forth; his brain tossing up every memory he had crushed over the years, forced away. They appeared now as fragments, out of order: the yelling, the crying, punching walls, blood and bullet holes, accusations, pills, booze, funerals, cliff tops, smashing surf, the letterbox splintering into a million pieces...

Samuel.

He raked fingers through his hair, felt snot dribble and mix with his tears. He wiped his nose with the back of his hand, stinging the cuts on his fingers. When he looked up he saw Alice standing at the base of the stairs, hugging her arms, shivering.

'Why are you still here?' he said.

'Sam, I'm worried. I don't understand what's going on.'

'Pretty plain, isn't it?'

'I think you're having a breakdown.'

'Oh, so you're a psychiatrist now.'

He wiped his nose again, sniffed. She was stone still, watching him with sad eyes. He couldn't bear to look at her. He got up, went to the sideboard and took out a bottle of Lark single malt.

With his back to her, he heard her say, 'Tell me why you agreed to treat me. If your wife—'

'In case you missed the action back in the bedroom just now, I had no flaming idea who you were.' He cracked the seal of the whisky, took a long swig and faced her. 'You couldn't have got it more wrong. I never wanted you. I did all in my power to get rid of you. Richard was the one who put you on my books. But that first day, the very first session I had with you... couldn't you tell?'

She seemed to think about it. 'I was upset. Dr Whittaker had died. And you were so kind to me...'

Sam returned to the stairs with the bottle, choosing one of the lower rungs. 'You know, you really are a bad omen.' Alice was still standing there and it bothered him that she was staring. 'Richard was right. I turned you into Sophie. I tried to make everything better through you just to salve my conscience.' He huffed, thinking how Richard had also warned that he was a walking timebomb. 'I couldn't have been more wrong.'

'What are you going to do?'

'As well as a bad memory – you've got eyes, haven't you?'

'Getting drunk won't help.'

'It's always worked before. Now bugger off, go home, and don't come back.'

Her bottom lip quivered.

He took a large swallow of the whisky. It was good and strong and heady; the vapours hitting his lungs. He suppressed a cough with the back of his hand.

She was still standing there.

'Don't you get it? It's over between you and me.'

'No, Sam, I'm not going to let you do this to yourself. I won't leave you.'

'You and Conroy – remember that debacle? How you couldn't be with him after the train crash. Every time I look at you, I'm only going to think of *her*, of Sophie, with a hole in her chest. Dead. Never alive. Always dead.' He groaned, pounded his head with his free hand trying to rid himself of the memory.

Slowly, Alice started to step towards him. 'Maybe... maybe we could talk about it. Like when I told you about Bellingen, putting it into perspective—'

He pointed a finger at her and she halted. 'You know where I was the night Sophie died? Fucking another woman. But you'd know that. Every cop knows what I did.'

She shook her head.

'I got a call from the police station,' he went on. 'One of her colleagues, saying Sophie had been involved in something, wouldn't say what. I thought maybe she'd crashed the police car, or there was some sort of siege – but not that she'd died. Actually, I don't know what I thought, not really. Probably too busy getting my story straight. I drove onto the scene that night.' He glared at Alice. 'You were there. You must have seen me.'

'I was guarding the crime scene in the house. The guy that—'

'At the funeral. Remember the hunched over bloke with the pathetic look on his face? Don't tell me you missed that.'

'I didn't go to the funeral. I was back in Coffs by then.' Tears streamed down her face. 'I'm as shocked as you are. You have to know that. But we can work through it. We might even be able to help each other.'

'Sleeping with my patient... where's the help in that? I'm no good for you, Alice. I'm toxic. Be smart and walk away before this gets any worse.'

'I already told you I'm not leaving.'

'You would if you knew the rest of it. If you knew that Sophie…'
He stopped, squeezed his eyes closed and let the tears bubble out.

Finally, he put the bottle aside, stood and came down the stairs.
Alice retreated – her eyes wider.

'What are you doing?' she said warily.

He picked up the fallen metal spike and bounded to the top of
the stairs and the barricade. Again and again he thrust the spike
end into the plasterboard, gouging, scraping, pulling at the loosened bits with his other hand.

Alice called up to him. 'Sam, stop it. This is madness.'

Ignoring her cries, he thrashed the bar continuously into the
wall. When he was done he threw the bar over the side of the rail
where it crashed onto the floor again. He stuck his head through the
hole he'd made in the plasterboard. It was dark and dank, like an
Egyptian tomb. He moved back out, picked up his whisky, dropped
it in the hole, and then squeezed his upper body through the jagged
opening, landing on dusty boards.

Sam stood up in the space, waited for his eyes to adjust. The
moonlight helped. He was in the main front room of the extension;
two tall windows to his left, a wide opening on the right into the
back room.

It was odd, he'd always imagined these rooms empty; and yet
there were boxes, other items he couldn't quite make out, maybe
pieces of furniture. Straight ahead, against the far wall, was a
chunky item. He squinted. It was a long sideboard or buffet with a
mirror backing. Teak, he remembered now, an old piece from the
sixties. It had once belonged to Sophie's aunt. He'd hauled it up
here, after the shooting, using a rope pulley system, single-handedly
manoeuvring it over the spiral railing.

Sam headed over to it but tripped on something, went down
heavily. It was a paint tin and it rolled away. The bottle of whisky
had slipped through his fingers. He groped around on the floor for
it, but couldn't find it in the dark.

He swore, then got up, pushing several boxes aside to reach the
buffet. There was something that had caught his attention just before he'd fallen – an oval-shaped item like an unexploded mortar
shell, silhouetted and central on the old teak.

'Jesus, no.'

Reverently, he lifted the item. His fingers traced over the smooth pewter surface of the urn, found the engraving. He couldn't read it in the dark but he knew it was her name there – Sophie Angela Wilde – and underneath, the date of her death.

Loose tears tasted like salt on his lips.

She was still here. There was no special place in the national park. He'd never taken her ashes there. He'd meant to. But he'd forgotten. Pushed into the recesses of his mind, he'd made a story where there had been none – a memory invented from guilt.

Sophie's mother had wanted the ashes. Delia Wilde, who had followed the inquest into her daughter's death through every trial and minute detail – who had threatened a legal injunction to make Sam hand over Sophie's ashes to her. But Sam wouldn't relinquish them, not even in part, and made up a story about scattering them according to Sophie's wishes. And he'd come to believe it. But the truth was he'd never been able to let her go.

Sam put the urn back in the centre of the sideboard. His fingers touched on other items there. He picked one up – a tea-light candle. Of course. He'd held his own ceremony up here. Alone. As soon as he'd been able, he'd collected Sophie's ashes. Away from the unforgiving stares of his mother-in-law and Sophie's colleagues that day of her funeral, he'd made his own altar, paid homage to Sophie *his* way. It was coming back to him now. He'd not stood out on a cliff top in the national park with the urn. That was why he could never find the place. It didn't exist. He'd stood at the front windows with the backdrop of blue sky and ocean, and with his head bowed had said a prayer. 'Panis Angelicus'. No, not said it, he'd played it on the CD player. It was a hymn.

He fished around now, almost frantically, for matches or a lighter. He opened a drawer in the sideboard, couldn't see what was in it; pulled things out – photos, papers, whatever they were, fluttered and rattled onto the floor. The next drawer was no different. Why hadn't he thought to bring up a torch? The third drawer along contained more papers, but then his hand settled on a small box.

He pushed his thumb against the end of the box and it slid open, spilling the contents. He'd opened it upside down but at least now he was sure it was matches. He felt around on the floor where they'd fallen and managed to grab a few, struck two together along the side of the box. They flared into life. Quickly, he lit the tea light he'd been holding before, and then the others next to it. There were more candles, pillars on stands. He lit three that were close together, using the flame from one of the tea-light candles.

Sophie's smiling face eased from the darkness. Framed in the centre of the candles was a close-up of Sophie on their wedding day. A gold-and-black bodice with intricate beadwork on the thin straps of her dress, her hair pulled sharply at the front but coiffed high, elegant, classy. She held long-stemmed flowers in deep purple and turquoise, with splashes of baby's breath, and tied with silver ribbon. She stared out from the frame with a life, a vibrancy that made it seem impossible that she should be gone, turned to ash...

Sam felt the burn of more acid-like tears. 'How did I do this? Forget you so easily?'

He turned and took in the room, the candlelight reminding him of what he had closed off four years ago. There had been no air flow up here in all that time. Thick and oppressive, it seemed to envelope him.

He went to the front windows. The first one was jammed tight, wouldn't budge. The second went up part of the way, stiffly. It was enough – a gentle breeze carried in the smell of the ocean.

Sophie's view. There wasn't much to see in the night – a few tankers in the blackened waters, lit up like Christmas trees.

He turned back – the dust he'd stirred up seemed to hang in the air, caught in the muted glow, resembling swarms of tiny flies. There had never been anyone up here – the noises, the sounds of someone walking around, nothing more than his distorted, chemically-driven imagination.

As the breeze bent the candlelight, a soft amber hue fell across Sophie's photo.

Samuel.

He returned to the buffet, reverently traced her image with his fingers. As his hand fell away, he touched another object. It was the small CD player he'd used in his private ceremony. He flipped open the top – it contained a disc. His hand trailed the cord at the back to the power outlet and he flicked it on.

His foot nudged the whisky bottle. He retrieved it and sank down onto the floor as the music started. Pavarotti, 'Panis Angelicus'. And even though he didn't want to, he began to remember. Memories he had forced away, had kept bound and subdued. Properly now, not fragmented. They rushed at him, carried in a tsunami of emotion – unstoppable, irrevocable.

There was no turning back.

THIRTY

Four years ago

The cork hit the ceiling and champagne hissed from the bottle in a foamy lather over Sam's fingers. He poured two glasses and handed one to Gemma, then got back on the bed beside her. He wasn't interested in her conversation. Instead, he stared at the hotel room's overstated furnishings: thin floor lamps with tulip shades, vague watercolours that a monkey or elephant could have painted, everything else appropriately crass in burgundy and white and silver trim.

His mobile phone started ringing.

Sophie, he thought and regret hit him hard. He shushed Gemma as he reached to the end of the bed for his trousers and retrieved the phone from the back pocket.

It wasn't Sophie. It was Maria, her colleague. 'Sam you better get down here. I've been listening to the police radio. I think Sophie's been involved in something serious.'

'What's happened?'

'I... don't know.'

Sam looked at the clock on the bedside table. It was almost midnight. 'Is she on patrol?'

'Yeah, one of the car crews.'

'I thought she was station officer tonight.'

He could sense Maria's hesitation.

'Maria?'

'Just get here as soon as you can.'

Hurriedly, he pulled on his clothes.

'What is it, Sam? What's happened?' Gemma asked.

He didn't know how to answer, shook his head.

It was cold and the rain had started again. Sam waited impatiently under the domed canopy at the front of the hotel while the valet fetched his car. By the time it was driven up he'd tried Sophie's mobile phone at least three times. On the final call he left a message. 'Yeah it's me. Listen, Maria said something's happened at work.' He paused, wondering if he should apologise for the fight earlier that day. Maybe she didn't want to speak to him.

'I – ah… just call me and let me know you're okay.'

He got in his car, the closeness making him aware that he smelt of sex and wine. Would she notice? Maybe he should head home for a shower first. Closer to the police station he made the decision and swung his car at the left turn towards Cronulla.

Two police vehicles rushed past him in a frenzy of lights and sirens. Sam watched as they punched through a red traffic signal. He could hear more sirens, distant but getting closer.

Something big had happened.

He thought of Maria's message and his heart rate quickened.

Please, God. Don't let this be about Sophie.

He slammed his foot on the accelerator, tore through the intersection, and followed the flashing lights. He kept with the police vehicles, more joining in, converging, weaving through the dark residential area. Maria's worried phone call played over and over in his head:

I think Sophie's been involved in something serious.

What had he been thinking? Meeting up with Gemma Scott as though he deserved it – retribution for the fight he'd had with Sophie earlier in the day, for what she'd done. Deceiving him; shoving that white envelope under his nose, demanding he look at it.

This is a future you can't run away from. That's what she'd told him.

There was a roadblock up ahead. It looked like every police officer working in Sydney tonight was here. Sam stopped his car in the middle of the road and got out. The area was cordoned off with police vehicles and checked tape. Red-and-blue lights swirled into the canopy of box gums that lined the street, bouncing off windows and houses, throwing blurred patterns across the wet ground. There were people out on their porches, some trapped within the confines of the cordon, wrapped against the drizzling weather.

Brian Heath was at the southern perimeter on the roadway, standing with half a dozen officers. Sam walked over.

'What's going on?' he said.

'Shit, what are you doing here?' Brian's face was ashen.

Sam scanned the faces of the other officers, some of them openly emotional. Reactively, he went under the tape and pushed his way through.

Brian grabbed him by the shoulders. 'You can't go in there.'

'Where's Sophie?' Sam yelled. 'Sophie.' He struggled and broke free of Brian's grip, made it a few more paces before several officers hauled him back. 'Let me go!'

'Calm down,' Brian shouted at him.

'I want to see Sophie.'

'You can't.'

The struggle continued, Sam lashing out until they put him on the ground.

Detective Sergeant McGuire was there. Sam could hear his voice. 'Mac,' Sam called out, 'why won't anyone tell me what's happened? Where's Sophie?'

'Let him up, boys,' Mac said.

They stood him upright, but kept a firm grip on his arms.

Mac came in close. He looked like he was in pain. But his voice was even. 'Sam, I'm not going to mince my words here. Sophie's dead. She's been shot.'

The throbbing light from a nearby police vehicle threw a shroud of red over Mac's face. The detective sergeant stepped aside and the scene opened.

Sam saw her then, ahead on the front lawn of the property; knew it was Sophie beneath the blue tarp awash with the bright spotlight as the rain flitted down. Mac told him in a calm and monotone voice what had happened, but all Sam could hear were the last words he ever said to his wife as she'd left for work.

Angry, hateful words.

Mac was trying to get his attention. 'What?' Sam said, still focused on the scene.

'We need you to make a formal identification. Can you do that?'

'Me?'

'You're her next of kin.'

He felt like he was sleepwalking as he was led over, that none of it was real. Someone lifted the tarp back about halfway. Under the spotlight, Sam tried hard not to look at the bloodied hole in his wife's chest, just concentrate on her face – her lovely face. Some of her dark hair had come loose from the bun and had blood on it. He could see a few of the wispy curls that she'd complained of so often, but which he'd stroked only a few nights before. Her soft brown eyes were black now – half opened. Dead eyes! The paperwork she had come to deliver to the residential address was still clenched in her hand. That had been all it was. Not an arrest. Just papers.

'Is this Sophie Wilde, your wife?'

Why were they asking him this? he wondered stupidly. Of course it was her. They all knew her. He looked to Mac in that moment and realised what was required of him.

'Yes, it's Sophie.'

The voice hadn't sounded like his. It held no emotion. It was like it came from a stranger. A pen was put in his hand and he signed his name on the paper attached to a clipboard that another officer held.

Detective Sergeant McGuire said, 'We can't move her, Sam. Crime scene are still doing their thing, and there's a dead body in the house too. Looks like the bloke topped himself after he shot her. We have to be sure of everything.'

Sam felt his knees go, and Mac and Brian grabbed for him, stopped him going down. His head titled back and he tasted the cold, bitter air of a now different world.

*

An officer drove Sam to the police station. Maria was crying and threw herself into his arms as he came in through the station doors. But he was numb. He didn't think it was possible to ever feel again.

His whole life, his reason for living, had just been ripped from him. He wanted to wake from this nightmare. He wanted to wake and hold Sophie in his arms and tell her never to return to that awful job again – and to make babies with him – a dozen of them.

They sat him in an office and gave him a mug of coffee. He didn't drink it. The commander came in and spoke to him, told him how sorry he was, how sorry all of them were, and was there anyone they could call to be with him tonight.

He didn't answer.

Glenn Whittaker turned up. He placed a gentle hand on Sam's shoulder. It was the first real sense of genuine compassion Sam felt. But he was unable to respond. Glenn went through the contacts in Sam's phone and passed on information to the commander. There was talk about sending a car crew to Sophie's mother's house to give the death message.

A couple of hours later Maria drove him home and she and Rob stayed with him, all of them sitting in the dark of the lounge room until first light. Maria cooked eggs and toast. None of it even came close to Sam's lips. He pushed his plate away.

They organised to take him to the morgue in the city. One last look at Sophie. He couldn't refuse, didn't know how. But at the last, he couldn't go in through those grey metal doors. Maria urged him, but Sam sat out with Rob in the waiting room at the morgue. Then they drove him home.

He went to the second-bottom rung of the spiral staircase and stared at Maria while she sobbed in Rob's arms on the sofa. And he realised, he would never get to hold Sophie again. Not even one last time.

Later, Mac and a few other detectives came to the house to speak to him. It was awkward – they needed to look around the place.

'What for?' Sam asked, confused.

'We've got to draw up a full picture of what happened,' Mac said. 'The gunman who killed Sophie is dead. We have to come at this from all angles.'

'What could you possibly find here?'

Mac looked worn out, like he hadn't slept in a week. 'I'm sorry, Sam. It's procedure. We need to eliminate any possible connection

Sophie may have had to the gunman, or that you may have had. And we need to understand Sophie's state of mind at the time – whether she made any mistakes last night; the possible factors that may have caused her guard to be down. I have to ask you questions.'

'What sort of questions?'

'Mate, this is a murder investigation—'

Sam cut him off angrily, 'What are you looking at me for? I didn't pull the trigger.'

Maria stood and came to Sam's side, took his hand.

'Nobody is saying you did,' Mac said. 'But you know I can't just close the book on this and walk away and write it off as a bit of bad luck. It's more complicated than that.'

'Sophie was shot by a lunatic and it wouldn't have mattered which police officer went to his door. It just happened to be Sophie. What's so complicated about that?'

Mac looked at Maria for a moment, and something twitched in his top lip. 'You might be right – could have been Maria.'

The brown-haired woman shivered and firmed her grip on Sam's hand.

But then the detective sergeant's attention was back on Sam. 'Let's take a seat.'

Without prompting, Mac and another detective headed for the dining-room table. Maria sat next to Sam on the other side. Rob watched from the corner of the room with the third officer.

The detective sergeant opened his notebook and pulled a pen from the breast pocket of his jacket. 'How did Sophie seem before she left for work last night?'

'Um – okay. A bit tired maybe.'

'How tired?'

'I don't know. Tired. It was the night shift.'

'Tell me about that.'

Sam glared at Mac. 'Tell you what?'

'Did you have a fight?'

'What?' Sam said, astounded.

'A fight. Jarrod, her partner on the car crew, said you had a blow-up with Sophie before she left for work last night.'

'That's ridiculous. How would he know? He wasn't here.'

'Come on, you know what cops are like. We tell each other PIN numbers, passwords, who's sleeping with who. No secrets on night shift.'

'Then why don't you ask him?' Sam offered sarcastically. 'He seems to know everything.'

'All he knows is you had a fight. Nothing more. Sophie didn't break it down for him.'

Sam knew he was screwed on this one. He let out a long, shuddering breath. 'Yes, we had a fight.' Then he glared at McGuire again. 'That's what married couples do from time to time.'

'I'm not here to criticise.'

'Doesn't feel that way.'

'So, how bad was the fight?'

'What does it matter?'

Mac was heating up. A vein pulsed in his forehead. 'It matters.'

'It's not going to bring Sophie back.'

'Nothing is. But this is a murder investigation.'

Sam was starting to shake. What good would it possibly to do to discuss the fight he'd had with Sophie? He didn't want to remember the final words he'd said to her, the last she'd ever hear from him. He didn't want to tell it either.

'Is there nothing sacred?'

'Just help me out here, Sam, and answer the question.'

'What happens in the privacy of my own home—'

Mac exploded in temper. He pushed his bulky weight back from the table and stood, sending his chair over. 'I've got two dead bodies and one of them is your wife. I've got a coroner's inquiry and mine and every other officer's arse is on the line. I have to know absolutely everything, and I'll decide what's irrelevant, not you, not anyone else.' He slammed his fist on the table. The tears in the big man's eyes were not lost on Sam. Rob moved forward like he was going to intervene, but the officer standing beside him held him back by the arm.

Everyone was upset, of course they were.

'So, I'll ask you again,' Mac boomed. 'How bad was that bloody fight?'

Sam bowed his head, ashamed. He swallowed hard. It felt like razor blades were jammed in his throat. 'It was bad.'

'Did you hit her?'

Sam looked up sharply. 'No, I didn't hit her. I've never laid a hand on her. How could you even ask that?'

Mac sat again after retrieving his chair and wrote something in his notebook. He seemed to be heaving in the air like it was thick and unmanageable. 'So, it was yelling?'

'Yes.' Sam left out the details of their argument. Sophie's deception; the shock of her confession; the white envelope she'd held out to him and how he knew exactly what was inside. Instead, he told Mac they'd disagreed over one of the new rooms in the extension. 'It's been stressful, all the building, paint colours... stupid really.'

'How did things end up?'

'She didn't want to go to work, complained she was too tired and upset, that she wanted to stay home and sort things out with me. But I was frustrated, angry. I suppose I... well, I don't know... I took her uniform from the wardrobe hanger, tossed it at her, told her to get out of my sight.'

Maria started to cry and let go of Sam, getting up and moving to the corner of the room to bury her face into Rob's shoulder.

'So, you bullied her out the door,' Mac said.

Inwardly, Sam flinched. 'I wouldn't call it that. And to be honest I didn't think she'd take any notice of me. She doesn't usually. I was surprised when she got dressed and left.'

'You want to tell me why your letterbox is in a million pieces out the front?'

'Sophie, when she tore out of the driveway in the car. I don't think she meant it.'

'Go on.'

He wouldn't tell Mac that as soon as Sophie left that night, he'd put his fist through the plasterboard in the hallway. The hollow was there – maybe they wouldn't notice it when they went through the house. 'There's nothing else. Sophie went to work.'

'And what did you do?'

Sam shook his head, looked away. Mac repeated the question.

'I went out.'

'Where?'

'This part is really irrelevant. I don't care what you say.'

'We'll find out whether you tell us or not, search your phone records, turn the whole city upside down if we have to, but we'll find out where you were.'

'What good will that do?'

'How many times do I have to tell you?' Mac said through gritted teeth, looking as though he was about to snap his pen. 'This is a murder investigation. And all of this is to save your skin, not have the finger pointed at you.'

Sam frowned. He didn't understand.

Mac spelt it out. 'You had a massive fight with your wife just hours before her death. So, I don't know...' He held up his hands. 'Maybe you set her up, got one of your twisted patients' in on the job as a hit man. Or maybe you lay in wait for her, knocked off the bloke that lived in the house that Sophie went to, and then stuck the gun in his hands to make it look like he killed her and then himself.'

'That's completely outrageous and you know it.' Sam was to his feet, ready to go around to the other side of the table and punch out the fat prick. But Rob and the other officer rushed forward and grabbed him, made him sit down.

Mac shouted, 'Of course it's outrageous. But I've got to tie this up nice and tight. So, tell me the fuck where you were all night so we can back it up.'

Sam was losing it. His head was swimming, as if the ocean was washing through his windows and doors, drowning him. Somehow he found the words. 'I met a friend.'

'What friend?'

'A colleague.'

'Doc, you're not helping yourself. Just tell me what you were doing and who you were doing it with.'

Sam didn't want to say anything else. But he was fighting a losing battle. 'Gemma Scott,' he finally managed. 'She's a psychiatrist. She was in Sydney on business.'

'Where did you meet her?'

Sam shook his head and looked down at his hands. What the hell did it matter? Were they just looking to humiliate him?

'The Grand Plaza Hotel.'

The room fell quiet and when Sam looked up, Mac was staring hard at him.

Sam felt himself sinking, going down. He started to bawl, but there were no tears, just the pathetic sounds of a dying animal.

*

Gemma Scott confirmed Sam's story, and the hotel manager produced the paid invoice for the room that included a bottle of *Jacques Selosse* champagne.

The findings for the inquest were copied and sent to Sam. He couldn't bring himself to read the report. Julia, his sister, did it for him. Whether he liked it or not, she made him listen to the details.

'You should read this,' she kept saying to him. 'There's a lot in it, you need to understand, come to terms with it.'

But he'd been scared. The fight with Sophie, bullying her out the door that night, the affair at the hotel with Gemma – how much of it was in that stinking report?

It hadn't been there when Julia read it out. Not much of it sank into his guilty head at the time, but he'd heard the words, processed them, packaged them and shoved them into the back of his mind. They emerged now in the musty extension, clear and defined.

Ramon Arthur Waddington was a forty-two-year-old unemployed man with a history of violence. A month before the tragedy, police removed three children from his care and returned them to their mother at an undisclosed location. Two days before the murder, Waddington was given the news that he was not the biological father of any one of those children. He made a threat, serious enough for police to apply to the court for a restraining order on behalf of his ex-partner.

Sophie Angela Wilde, a thirty-four-year-old senior constable with almost fifteen years' service, was delivering the paperwork to Waddington on that final night of her life. She had not taken the usual precautions. If she had, she would have waited for the radio operator to get back to her and would have heard the warnings associated with the address.

Nobody could account for her actions that night; why she'd gone on ahead, leaving her partner, Probationary Constable Jarrod Baxter, in the police vehicle waiting for radio response. Baxter had received the warning just as Sophie took her first step up to the porch.

It was confusing about what happened after that. Neighbours alerted police to the sound of gunshots. By the time a patrol car found Sophie's partner, he was several kilometres from the scene and still running.

THIRTY-ONE

Sam couldn't say when the music had stopped. He took in the room, the mess of objects and furniture he'd hauled up there. Any wonder he'd been unable to sell it – the place was like a mausoleum.

He swigged a mouthful of whisky, annoyed when most of it ran down the sides of his mouth. Expensive stuff wasted inside his misery.

He knew this feeling – he'd lived it for almost a year in Queensland after Julia and Paul had bundled him up and taken him there following Sophie's funeral. Julia had said the drink would kill him. But when they got holed up waiting for the cyclone, it was the fact Sam had no more booze that became the danger. He didn't leave a note, just got up from his chair on the veranda one day and walked a straight line down to the beach. No matter how many times he tried to go under the water, he just kept coming to the top like a cork.

He'd lain on the sand and stared at the sky, wondering if maybe the elusive cyclone would make an appearance and lift him into oblivion. But it never showed.

Well, so be it. But I'll do it my way. That's what he'd told himself before he'd got up and returned to the B & B, his clothes drenched with seawater, sand stuck in his hair. His brother-in-law had stared open-mouthed at him.

'Death doesn't want me yet,' Sam had explained. He'd gone into the house, packed his meagre belongings, and flown back to Sydney the next day.

And he'd managed. More than that, he'd reinvented himself. The psychiatrist: elite in his field, always above average.

'Fat lot of good,' he muttered now. He was a washed-out wreck. Three years of diligence and impeccable conduct – and he'd blown it all in a matter of a few short weeks. He'd committed fraud by self-prescribing, had sex with his patient, broken the code of ethical conduct.

'Oh, Sam,' her voice whispered.

He looked up from the whisky bottle and jerked backwards. In the corner of the room, her form faintly lit from the candle glow, Sophie stood in her police uniform.

'What are you doing?' he said, but it was more a question for himself, that his mind should conjure the image. But then it wasn't the first time he'd seen her like this – there had been that night after Conroy's funeral...

The apparition answered. 'The station got the call. When I heard it was you, I took the job, came to see that you're okay.'

Sam was confused. He started to get up, staggered, dropped the bottle and heard it roll away.

She stepped out of the shadows then, but came no closer.

'Maria.' He couldn't believe it. 'Why are you dressed like Sophie?'

Maria tilted her head curiously. 'I'm... I'm on duty.'

'Your hair...'

She automatically touched the top of her slicked head.

But he already understood. She looked so much like her. It was the uniform, he realised, but maybe... she was trying a bit.

'What are you doing here?' he asked.

'Concern for welfare. Some people are very worried about you.'

'People? What people? I'm in my own home getting drunk. Since when was that a crime?'

'You've not been acting rationally. Come downstairs, let's talk about it.'

'Talk about what?' he said angrily, taking a step towards her. 'That I made a hole in my wall with a crowbar? It's my fucking wall. I don't need anyone's permission.'

Maria had shuffled backwards. In the shadows again, he could see why he'd made the mistake of thinking she was Sophie. A shocking idea struck him – the apparition outside his home after the funeral of Garth Conroy. 'You've been stalking me. It was *you* outside my house – *weeks* ago. I saw you from the window.'

She chewed on her top lip.

'Don't deny it. I know it was you.'

'Not stalking,' she said, swallowing hard enough for him to hear. 'I was... worried.'

'So you got dressed up in police uniform and thought you'd hang out under the streetlamp outside my house. Makes sense,' he said sarcastically.

'No, it wasn't that. I was coming home from work and I thought I'd... well, after seeing you that time outside the supermarket...' She faltered, looked around the room briefly and then took another small step backwards.

'You thought what?'

She seemed to be having trouble making eye contact with him. 'I wanted to talk to you, Sam.'

'Then why didn't you? Why didn't you knock on the front door and speak to me?'

'I – I couldn't. I changed my mind.'

'Changed your mind?' he said, as though it should make more sense repeated. It didn't. 'So, you ran away. Left me wondering what the hell was going on. I thought I was seeing things, that it was Sophie...'

Maria flinched.

What is it? What isn't she saying?

He realised he was angrier than he ought to be with her but didn't know why. Maybe it was because she looked like a miscreant child who'd got caught dipping her fingers in the sugar bowl.

He threw his arms open and let them flop to his sides. 'Well then, why don't you tell me now what you couldn't say back then.'

She hesitated, glanced over at the hole in the barricade.

Sam stepped closer to her and this time he saw the fear in her eyes.

'I'd only wanted to say,' she began, trembling, '... how sorry I was... for what happened to Sophie.'

'We've been down that road. Four years ago. You were sorry then too.'

She swallowed. 'Anyway, why don't you come downstairs? Your boss and your friend are down there. They want to talk to you, make sure you're all right.'

Richard? What would he be doing here? They'd said all they were ever going to say to each other.

'I don't have a boss. I work for myself.' He shook his head and thought of Alice. She was the friend he supposed Maria had been referring to. What else could have been said about her? His girlfriend? Lover? His patient slash lover? He turned away. 'Tell them to get lost, leave me alone.'

Maria came up behind him and put a hand on his back. 'Come on, Sam, we'll have a cup of tea.'

The heat of anger still simmered in his veins. He jerked away from her touch and faced her.

'Since when did you become the *cop*.' It wasn't a question; it was a bitter accusation. 'Trying hard, aren't you? But you were never a police officer's left boot.'

It came back to him now, the way it had been. How Sophie would come in from work and complain to him about her friend. Lazy Maria, always shirking responsibilities, always working the switchboard, always in the station.

Maria was quivering and Sam didn't like it. He wanted to be wrong about where his thoughts were going. But not even alcohol could get in the way of his psychiatrist's logic. The conversation he'd remembered earlier, when McGuire and the other cops had come to the house to talk to him about the hours leading up to Sophie's death; McGuire had thrown Maria a dirty look when Sam had said it wouldn't have mattered who'd gone to the shooter's door that night. And then more recently, McGuire's comment in the car after Sam had emerged from his luckless trek in the national park; the inference that Maria had somehow played a part.

'How about you try again?' Sam said, a dangerous calm falling into his tone. 'Tell me the real reason you ran away from me that night, what it was that you changed your mind about saying. And don't give me the sorry routine again.'

Maria didn't answer, shook her head. He grabbed her by the shoulders and she cried out. It disgusted him that she didn't have any fight, any moves. Even Alice, naked, and with all her trauma and depression, could still break an arm lock. But Maria had nothing.

'James,' she shouted.

'What are you calling on your partner for? What do you think I'm going to do? All I want is for you to tell me the truth, Maria, because not a lot is making sense. You got something to say to me? Come on, spit it out.'

'Sam, let me go. I didn't do anything wrong.'

'It doesn't feel like it.'

'It was all looked into. They went through everything. I was cleared.'

'What are you talking about? Cleared of what?'

'The thing with the roster. Because it was changed. And Sophie had said it was okay.'

'What was okay?'

'To swap duties with me. Her final night at work, I wasn't feeling well and she said she'd take my place on the car crew.'

And there it was. In her panic, Maria had just confessed what had been nagging at Sam's conscience, tapping away for his attention.

'It should have been you that night,' he said, hardly able to believe it. '*You* changed the duties on the roster.' His grip tightened around her arm. 'Sophie shouldn't have been out there. She was confined to the station. She—' He stared hard at Maria. 'But you knew, didn't you? She would have told you about the...'

He couldn't say it, couldn't admit it. He'd only found out that night – the last night of Sophie's life – when they'd fought and shouted at each other and all because she'd gone behind his back, and finally she'd had to tell him, admit that she'd deceived him. And he'd been so angry, so bitter and uncompromising.

Maria's features darkened further. She seemed to shrink in front of him. 'Yes, I knew Sophie was pregnant and that she shouldn't be out on patrol.' It felt like a knife to Sam's heart, twisting and gouging. 'But... she wasn't showing and... it was still a secret. Besides, it was just the night shift and raining and I didn't think it would matter—'

He stifled an ironic laugh. 'Didn't matter? God Maria, her pregnancy didn't matter ahead of whatever triviality you'd decided was more important.' He huffed and ran a hand over his head. 'So, what was it? Did you have a runny nose, broken fingernail?'

'Sam don't, it's hard enough as it is.'

'Well heaven forbid that you should suffer.' He wanted to strike her. 'You sent Sophie out there, to her *death* because you were too fucking lazy to shift your arse off a chair. And my wife had to pay the price for that. You took it away from her, *everything* she could have had – too selfish to see past your own trifling needs.'

'I didn't know what would happen.'

'You didn't care. You had the hide to console me with your tears and pawing at my sleeve.' The words tasted sour in his mouth. 'At Sophie's funeral you held onto me, never left my side. But it was you all along. And you never spoke up – just pretended to be my friend.'

'I wasn't pretending anything. I loved Sophie too. And I feel bad and I have to live with it.'

'Yeah, you get to live, that's the whole point. You get to go home to your husband, plan for the future, have a pile of babies if you want!'

'James,' she cried out again. 'Get up here.'

A flashlight pierced the room. 'Step back,' a loud voice called. But Maria's partner came no further. He was jerking around in the small crawl hole Sam had made in the barricade. With all the equipment cops wore on their bodies it was no wonder he was struggling. The police officer went backwards – there was the loud sound of something dropping down the stairs, as though he might have let his whole gun belt off.

Well, at least he won't be able to shoot me.

'Let me go.' Maria started to struggle pathetically under Sam's grip.

He manoeuvred her over to the sideboard where the candles were set up next to the urn and the photograph of Sophie. Her serene smile eased from behind the glass in the yellow flickers of candlelight.

'She was beautiful and vibrant,' Sam said. '*My* wife. *Your* friend. And look, this is all that's left.' He lifted the lid off the urn with the one hand and set it aside, then forced Maria to look inside. 'This is it. This is all of Sophie, a pile of dust in a pewter jar.'

Maria was crying hard. 'What more do you want from me? I can't bring her back. And I can't change what happened.' She stopped struggling and turned her face away as if ashamed.

Sam didn't know what he was trying to say, to prove. Nothing was ever going to bring Sophie back. Everything was wasted.

'Oh, Maria,' he groaned softly. He wrapped arms around her.

Then he was off his feet, slammed sideways into the sideboard, and felt the heat of one of the candles on his skin.

'You're under arrest,' the oversized police officer announced as he grappled with Sam, hauling him up by his t-shirt.

'Get your filthy hands off me,' Sam shouted.

'You assaulted a police officer in the line of duty.'

'I was giving her a hug.'

The officer twisted Sam's arm behind him as Maria called out, 'James, it's all right. I wasn't assaulted. Let him go.'

'I saw him grab you.'

'It was a hug, like he said.'

'You were yelling.'

'I made a mistake.' Maria's face was ashen, even in the twitching candlelight.

Sam shook himself free from the officer's grip and brushed at his arm from where the candle had burned his skin. 'You heard her, a mistake. Now how about you both get out of here and leave me alone.'

'We'll go,' James said. 'But you'll have to come downstairs with us. We've got to write this job off and we can't leave you up here.'

'What difference does it make?'

'It means we can assess you better, make sure you don't need any other attention.'

'Like what?'

'You just made a hell of a gash in your wall.' James pointed over his shoulder, then glanced around the room. 'What is this place anyway?'

'Never mind,' Maria said quickly. 'Let's just take this downstairs.'

Sam caught her awkwardness as she blew out the candles. He felt the same and wished rid of her. It was too personal and she'd encroached on his misery for long enough.

Following Maria's torch light, they headed for the hole. Head first, she wriggled through easily.

'You next,' the other officer said to Sam.

'No, you go.'

'Let's not argue the point. I'm twice the size of you.'

Sam reached through the gash and took hold of the top step, levered himself out, but ended up falling the rest of the way down, slamming his shoulder.

Richard was there to help him up. Sam dusted himself off, looked around the room. 'Where's Alice?' he said.

'I sent her home. Laura's with her.'

James was grunting and puffing from above them, halfway through the hole, his forehead wet with effort, swearing with every strain. Richard went up the stairs to assist. If it weren't so serious, it could have been a comedy act.

Sam headed into the kitchen. Maria was leaning against a bench next to her partner's appointment belt, a notebook and pen in her hands. 'You okay?' she asked quietly.

Sam heaved a sigh. 'I suppose I will be.'

'I'm so sorry,' she breathed, barely audible.

He folded his arms and remained on the other side of the room. 'When your partner gets down here, I want you both to leave,' he said. 'I don't want to see you again.'

Maria nodded.

James came through and hitched his belt back on. He had white gyprock dust in his hair and on his eyebrows, looking like he'd been in a snowstorm. He glanced between Maria and Sam, seemed to understand.

'No further action here,' James said into the portable radio. 'We're back on, returning to the station.'

Richard saw the officers out and Sam heard their muted voices. He returned although came no further than the kitchen doorway.

He had a dark, heavy look in his eyes, like a man weighted with incredible burdens.

Sam felt ashamed. 'I'm so sorry about all of this. When you see Alice, will you tell her... I didn't mean it. Not any part of it.'

Richard stepped up, getting into Sam's face. 'I'm not passing on your messages. She's been through enough. Just keep away from her. You hear me? Because so help me, Tyler, I'll rip your spleen out through your ears if you go within a mile of her again.'

Sam rubbed at his brow, eventually nodding. 'Yeah, you've made yourself clear.'

Without another word Richard turned and left.

THIRTY-TWO

I rather fancy I can hear the whales singing tonight. Far off, out there somewhere in all that dark water. It's strange, that I get the most from this place at night, usually after a late shift. Maybe it's the peace and serenity of being up so high, that distancing from the rest of the crazy world. I wish Sam would come up here with me. I know it would help. To see what I see, to hear what I hear, feel all that I feel when the stars seem to be in reach and the breath of the ocean washes over me...

The effects of the whisky had worn off and Sam was beyond sleep. He was at his desk in the spare room with the green Bankers lamp focused over his hands. The blood had dried on his fingers from where he'd clawed his way into the extension. But his knuckles remained swollen and sore.

He'd only come in to try to salvage what he could from Alice's confidential file – the papers he'd screwed up and cried into. Carefully, he'd straightened them as best he could.

Sophie's file had been there too, sitting near the lamp as though waiting for him. He'd been unable to ignore it any longer, opened the cover. That's when he'd caught sight of those words about the whales. Some sort of diary requirement that Glenn Whittaker often got his patients to do.

Sam shuffled through the papers. They didn't appear to be in any order – not surprising considering the irreverent hands and eyes that had been through the file. He released a long and heavy breath. Sophie's thoughts... could he bear them? Just how much of a person's essence remained in their written words? The notion tempted him to find out. The yearning for her voice, her touch, to walk with her through these rooms once more...

Why am I the only one who loves the idea of the extension? I know I nagged Sam that we should build it, but I don't think he even cares. It's as though once it's done, he won't be coming with me up here to our new bedroom, that he'll just stay downstairs. I've been showing him paint colours for the walls and he said he'd leave it to me to decide. I thought to test him on it, so I told him I rather fancied a pale-pink colour. He was supposed to hate it, tell me I was crazy, and take an interest. But he merely nodded and replied that he knew nothing about these sorts of things. I threw the colour chart at him then and he was really annoyed. But at least he looked at me.

We had a terrible argument after that, but nothing to do with colours. I wish it had been about colours. I wish he was as interested and as passionate about this as me. Instead, it feels like he's on the edge of something. God, I wish I knew what it was. If I could get inside his head for just a moment, then I would know what to do, how to take better care of him.

*

Another fight with Sam. I don't even remember what it was about this time. We screamed abuse and hurled the most insulting profanities at each other. In the end that's what it became about – the one who could be the most wounding. He pointed his finger in my face. I hate it when he does that. It's intimidating. Worse than if he shows me his fist. He doesn't hit, but sometimes I think he could, like he mightn't be able to help himself.

And so I walked out on him. Packed a bag, got in my car, and went. Sam yelled after me that I'd be back, that I was too weak to stay away. I stayed long enough for him to call and ask if I'd please come home. I was at my mother's and she tried to snatch the phone away. She yelled her disgust at me in Greek. She forgets I barely understand a word. Another reason for her to be disappointed in me.

Sam remembered, although it might have been one of several occasions. Sophie often retreated to her mother's place after a big fight with him. And without fail he'd ring and ask for her forgiveness. When he went around to plead with Sophie one time, Delia threw a broom at him and the point of the handle got him on the cheekbone. He'd called his mother-in-law a nasty, spiteful bitch.

Sam put the page down and wiped his eyes. Delia had been right. It was about what Sophie needed that mattered. Instead, he'd only ever made it about himself.

He thought of the urn in the upstairs extension. Sophie's ashes belonged to her mother. At least that was one thing he could put right.

Sam's phone rang earlier this evening while he was in the shower. I looked at it, a private number, and I answered with, 'Sam's phone.' The person on the other end didn't say anything but I knew someone was there. So I told them to stop playing games and speak to me. And finally they did. It was a woman, refined voice. One of his snooty shrink friends as it turned out. I don't know why they all think they're a cut above the rest of us. But that's not what bothered me. What bothered me was that she'd not expected me to answer, and so it made it plain that it wasn't just an ordinary call, or a call about work or whatever shrinks talk about to each other. It was a call from a woman to my husband. As simple as that. As devious and sneaky as that. She asked if Sam was available. I told her he wasn't. I decided not to give her details of my husband being in the shower because that seemed information she should have no part of.

It might seem a silly thing to write out and examine. A phone call from a colleague. I get them myself from time to time. If only my mind wasn't so suspicious, delving deeply into everything. Sam says it's the cop in me, always on a case. In the grocery aisle while I'm comparing prices, he's standing over me asking what I'm trying to prove. But this felt different. Maybe because it was a woman calling. Dr Scott, she said. Apparently no first name. Maybe she thought announcing herself as a doctor made it less suspicious.

When Sam came out of the shower I still had the phone in my hand. He looked at it and then at my face. And it was there, without me saying a word, it was there in his eyes. He wrapped the towel firmer around his waist before taking the phone from me. And he stared at it like he'd never seen a mobile phone before. He turned his back, and his tone was cautious as he spoke to Dr Scott, standing in nothing but a damp towel, water dripping from his hair. It wasn't a long conversation and Sam seemed to be the one who ended it. 'I have to go,' he said into the phone. And then without explanation, he left the room.

'Damn it, Sophie.' Sam groaned and rubbed the side of his head, recalling the incident all too well. What a fool he'd been to suppose that just because she'd never confronted him about the call, he must have got away with it.

A loud thump from overhead lifted his sights. Less the ghosts haunting his soul, he realised now. More likely a possum in the rafters, or something loosened from his earlier escapade in the extension.

He went back to his reading.

It was the most awful shift the other night. A head-on in the national park near Bundeena. Three dead. Mangled cars and bodies. How does it happen? All that road and late at night when there's no other traffic. And yet two cars come together at that single, fractional moment.

You never get used to it. And I can't say if it's worse when a young person dies or an older person. I mean, they are all loved and someone is going to miss them no matter what.

We were reverent, me and my colleagues, the ambulance and rescue squad members, as the bodies were finally released from the vehicles and laid out on the roadway. Three young people: two from one car, and the driver from the other.

One of the deceased, Lauren Sharpe, was a local girl and afterwards it fell on me and my partner to deliver the death message. I rang the doorbell of her mother's house – a light behind the glass panel came on. A woman wrapping a thin gown around herself opened the door.

Here we were, two police officers in the dead of night with sombre expressions.

'It's Lauren, isn't it?' the woman said.

We removed our hats and followed her inside.

I told Sam all about it when I got home. He listened but didn't say anything, just held me while I wailed on and on. He kissed my cheeks, my fingers, the top of my head.

It was exactly what I needed.

*

I have cheated Sam in this marriage by going behind his back. But there was nothing else to be done. The truth is I can't live my life knowing what is right for us and pretending that he'll eventually come around, find the necessary enthusiasm, tell me he thinks it's time also. It's not in his nature or his vocabulary. He's stuck in the mindset that parents of children are mean and spiteful.

Sam's mother left home when he was very young. His sister told me that he cried every night for months. His father, needing to give his son some sort of answer, said his mother had gone on a long journey to do something that was very important but was too dangerous for small children. One day, Sam packed his suitcase and headed out. There was a frantic search, but eventually six-year-old Sam was found at the railway station. A guard had contacted the police and sat with him until his father came. Sam doesn't remember the event and in any case refuses to discuss it with me. At the time, he had said to his father that all long journeys started with a train trip, and if he hurried he could catch up with his mother.

The desire for a baby is stronger in a woman than a man. It has to be that way, or else there would be no world. Men take a more practical view. They look at finances and worry how they will be as fathers. They remember their own childhood and become afraid. Women worry too but are drawn in by the overwhelming need to nurture. It's inbuilt in us. And to deny it is to deny ourselves.

Every morning, for a while now, I have removed a contraceptive pill and washed it down the sinkhole. I know Sam checks. So I made it easy for him. No longer does he need to search in my drawer. I have placed the packet in the bathroom cabinet next to his razor. The deviousness of my behaviour appals me. And yet, I have no regrets.

Sam reached down and opened the bottom drawer in his desk. Inside were papers, old correspondence, passports and certificates, legal things. He didn't have to search for what he wanted. It was right there on the top. Slowly, he withdrew the envelope, softened by age, revealing the square shape of the item sealed within.

On the last night of her life, and after telling Sam he was going to be a father, Sophie had held out this envelope to him.

He had no time to think of this now. He had to see it and he had to suffer for it. The final part of his penance, although it would never be enough.

He tore the side of the envelope and let the black-and-white picture fall into his hand.

There was nothing obscure about the scanned image. The fetus lay back as though relaxing on a recliner, in profile – eye socket, nose, mouth, chin. Little legs curled up. A hand held out with stubby fingers as though in protest of the photo.

A small laugh escaped Sam's lips. He was deeply shocked by his reaction. Not of despair or loss. But of the miracle of Sophie's child. *Their* child. He examined the photo in every detail, of time and date, Sophie's name in the corner, a series of measurements and other numbers. The contours of that precious profile. He was in awe, unashamed.

They would have been a family. They would have got over this hurdle. If the roster had never been changed that fateful night, Sophie would have gone to work and sat at the station desk, and she'd have come home and somewhere in time, after the angst had melted and tempers doused in a good dose of reality, Sam would have looked at the photo. And Sophie would have been right. It would have made a difference because he'd have loved their child as he loved it now. As he loved Sophie. As he had *always* loved her.

For the first time he could accept that Sophie's death wasn't his fault. He'd fought with her, been a prick that final night before she'd stomped away from him, but he'd been afraid and angry and his pride had been savaged. He'd been more upset that she'd got one up on him, taken him completely by surprise. And he'd retaliated in the only way he knew how. By making his own deception. Running out to be with another woman.

But this would have made them, this precious child…

More noises from above.

Sam stood and went out into the hallway, staring up at the ceiling. Scraping, like something being dragged.

What the fuck was going on?

He knew it couldn't be in his head. It was a different sound, anyway, movements that seemed far more purposeful, corporeal.

Still looking up, he tucked the photo into the back pocket of his jeans and walked slowly to the spiral staircase. Pausing on the bottom step, he listened. There was a kind of rustling, like cellophane being scrunched. And there was a smell. He couldn't define it. Quietly, he went up the rest of the way, pulling on the balustrade. At the top he looked into the hole he'd made earlier in the evening. The smell was stronger and there was a faint light, flickering—

Shit. It was a fire!

He thrust his way into the extension, scuttled on hands and knees until he could get upright, cursing himself for not having checked all those candles and tea lights had been extinguished. And a further profanity for not bringing something with him to throw over the flames. But a second later he was brought to a halt as the scene opened up to an astonishing sight.

She was sitting on the floor, crossed-legged, her back to him. Her black hair neat with a coloured comb pulling up one side. In front of her was one of the tall candles Sam had lit earlier. And next to it a small flaming pile of papers. No, they were photos. Photos of Sophie. He could see his wife's image curling in from the applied heat.

Leah held the next photo by the corner over the candle flame. As it caught she dropped it on the pile with the others and took another from a crate beside her. Sam recognised it as the one Sophie had used to store their snapshots and albums.

He came around and stared down at Leah. 'What the hell are you doing here?'

She looked up at him. He could tell she might have taken something. Her eyes were vague, lids hooded.

'Richard told me tonight that I can't come back to the office... so, I came to ask you... no, actually *demand* you give me a job at your new practice, seeing as it was all your fault.' She hesitated, returning to the photo in her hand. 'Instead, I found this.'

'What are you talking about?'

'Don't you see? It wasn't you or me or anyone else. It was Sophie all along... coming between us. You know, I think she actually led me here, so I can help you forget her.' Leah dropped the next burning photo onto the pile. 'We can be together then. You won't be thinking about her all the time.'

Sam took a long steadying breath and slowly crouched next to the young woman, keeping watch of the precarious little fire. 'This is not the way,' he said carefully. 'We should talk about it.'

'Oh don't make me laugh,' she snapped. 'Take the time to talk to me? You're all self-absorbed. You didn't even hear me knock on your front door tonight. Too busy hunched over your precious work.'

Shit. She must have let herself in. Richard had been the last to leave. He wouldn't have locked the door.

'No, I didn't hear you knock,' Sam said. 'And I'm sorry about that. You're right, I haven't been fair with you. I should have listened. Things were... they were pretty intense for a while. But I'm here now, Leah. I'm ready to talk. So, how about we go downstairs...'

He reached for the next photo she'd picked up, but she slapped his hand away and jerked towards the burning pile. The movement fanned the flames and they lifted. He caught a pungent whiff of singed hair.

'Don't try to stop me,' she shrieked. 'It's for us that I'm doing this.'

'Okay.' He held up his hands. 'We'll talk right here. Just... stop burning the photos for a moment. Let's sort things out.'

'Sort what out? You're not exactly thinking straight right now,' she said, greedily bunching more photos from the crate onto her lap. He could see one with him and Sophie at a restaurant. Others were from the wedding album. 'By the looks of it, you haven't been doing much of a job of things,' she went on. 'There's a terrible mess down the bottom of your staircase. And this gaping hole in your wall.'

Sam thought of how he'd smashed his way in here. The violent act to salve his grief and guilt. Were they so different, him and Leah?

He had to do something, stop this madness. His mobile was in his bedroom. He'd have to go back down; maybe grab a woollen blanket from the linen press...

That's no good. He couldn't leave her up here with all this flammable stuff. The fire was sizzling and snapping, and it was close to her skirt. She could catch alight at any moment.

'Come downstairs,' he said, firmer now. 'I know you're upset with me. But this is too dangerous.'

She flashed indignant eyes to him. 'I'd never hurt you. God, Sam, I might get angry and make a scene, but there's a limit. Like that time when I could have run you over, but I didn't.'

Sam wasn't sure what he'd just heard. 'Run me over?'

'It was only meant to make a point. I'm not heartless, you know.'

'A point?'

'For ignoring me.'

Sam thought back to the night he'd deposited Alice on her living-room sofa. Walking up the hill towards home in the rain. The rev of an engine. Turning back and seeing headlights spring on.

'That was you? You drove a car at me?' He knew it was true. It had to be. Not his distorted imagination. Not paranoia. Of course it wasn't. It had been too contrived. A hoodlum would be racing around the streets, not sitting and waiting, not picking their mark with some random stranger.

Sam rocked back into a seated position, elbows on his knees, he gripped his head. 'Do you know how close you came? You could have killed me.'

'Don't be so dramatic.'

'Dramatic?' he shouted. 'If I hadn't jumped out of the way—'

'You're one to talk. You left me hanging all night after promising you'd call, that we were going to do something over that weekend. And I waited and waited. But then it got so late that I knew you had no intention. So I came over in my brother's car and sat off your house, trying to work out what I ought to do. But then I saw you walking right past me. You'd been out drinking, enjoying yourself, that's why you weren't in your car. You can't blame me for what happened next.'

Leah put another photo to the candle. It was a large wedding photo – Sam in his suit, arms linked with his beautiful Sophie.

'And now I'm going to fix things,' Leah said. 'Fix us. You won't take the time or the bother. It's up to me to wipe Sophie clean from our lives. She's caused enough damage and I won't let it go on any longer.'

This was too much for Sam. Her manic obsession with him. Sitting in his upstairs extension burning photos of his dead wife.

He grabbed her wrist and snuffed the candle with the fingers of his other hand. At least one flame was out. He pulled at the photo she'd just lit, at the same time getting to his feet and dragging her up with him. She thrashed violently, kicking her legs as she tried to bite him. They staggered about the room, bouncing off boxes and furniture.

'Give it back,' she screamed, punching at him when she realised she'd lost the photo.

'Enough. We're going downstairs.' Sam held onto her while he stamped the rest of the photo out beneath his shoes.

'Not before this is done.'

She let her weight go and he lost his grip. Scuffling along the floor, she headed back to the small pile of simmering photos.

Sam went after her and grabbed her around the waist. He overbalanced and fell on top of her. She pivoted, something in her hand; he saw it was his bottle of whisky. She smacked it into the side of his head. He'd flinched and ducked just enough that it didn't have the full impact, but it bloody hurt all the same.

The bottle left Leah's fingers and rolled away towards the fire. Sam watched as though it were happening in slow motion – the bottle spinning like in the beach game, the rest of the contents splashing out before it wobbled to a halt.

A bright flash brought the whole room up, engulfing the bottle and the crate of photos Leah had been going through. Like a chain reaction everything around it began to catch, boxes and memorabilia, and the items Sam had tipped onto the floor when he'd been looking for matches earlier in the night.

The southerly wind arrived in an instant, whipping through the small opening of the window, fuelling the flames, lifting burning papers and pieces of material, spreading them across the two rooms.

Sam got up, grabbed Leah and pushed her towards the hole in the barricade. 'Hurry!'

Another burst of flame, this time with a whoosh. He didn't bother to see what it was that had caught alight. There was enough flammable stuff in here, from papers to paint thinners. The whole place could go in seconds.

Leah baulked at the hole. 'No, Sam. I want to stay with you,' she screamed, clutching at him.

'I'll be right behind you. *Go on.*'

He had trouble prising her fingers from his neck. She braced her feet either side of the opening when he tried to force her into it. The flames were licking higher, from one object to the next. Sam could feel the heat expanding. They had to get out and fast.

'Leah, *go through*,' Sam shouted over the sound of splintering cracks and groaning beams, as if the whole extension were packing itself up and getting ready to follow them through the rough hole as well.

Sam turned Leah around and forced her upper body through, speeding the process by shoving her on the backside with his foot. Headfirst, she fell into the stairwell.

He went to go after her but then looked back. The urn with Sophie's ashes – it was still sitting on the sideboard.

Leah was calling to him. 'Sam, come on.'

I've got time, he told himself.

He darted off towards the urn. Holding his arms up to the flames, he negotiated the burning floorboards and boxes immediately in front of the sideboard, grabbed for the urn but was driven back by the heat. The fire had come up so fast. He circled around it, tried to find another way in, then impulsively jumped the flames.

He had the urn. The lid was gone so he hooked his fingers around the inner lip, then turned back. His path was blocked completely by a wall of fire. Orange flames licked up the walls into the rafters of the incomplete ceiling. Another splintering sound as the house seemed to lurch and growl.

Leah was screaming his name. He thought he saw her, just a glimpse on the other side of the wildly lashing fire, trying to climb back in through the hole.

'*Go back*,' he yelled.

There were other voices. He was pretty sure one of them was his neighbour, Brad. Thank God. Someone with sense enough to get Leah out of the house. He was getting his wish after all, to see the whole thing razed to dirt level. Except he wasn't going to see it – he was going with it!

The wind savaged through the partially open window again, made the flames bend. Sam didn't think, he jumped at what seemed the lowest dip in the blaze, then lunged for the hole in the barricade. His path was blocked when another wall of fire shot up in front of him, as though the house was going to keep him – *if I'm going down then you're coming with me*. He could feel the burning heat surround him; sharp, acrid, deadly. And the black soot of the rising smoke, creeping up on him like a giant hand, outstretched, ready to take him under.

It was the smoke that would get him first, he knew that.

He backed up. An explosion. Something in the back room flared fiercely. It was probably one of the paint tins. The house rumbled as if a freight train was going to come charging through the walls at any moment. He reacted without thinking, lifted the urn like a shield, charged through the flames and hit a window. It was the one that he'd been unable to open. He tried again, pointlessly. It was stuck just as hard. The second one was funnelling black smoke. He wouldn't get through the small gap.

He started coughing and wheezing. His eyes clamped shut from the febrile effects of the smoke. He went to his knees.

Smoke rises.

Getting as low as possible, he sucked in air, but it was hot, felt like it was searing his lungs. Another explosion and he was thrust onto his side, still gripping the urn with Sophie's ashes, something sharp digging into his ribs.

He couldn't open his eyes. A jackhammer wouldn't be able to shift his lids. He crawled, inches maybe, no idea of direction. Blistering heat touched his leg and he instinctively kicked whatever it was away.

He made a decision – madness or not, but he couldn't stay here waiting to burn to death. The heat was unbearable, every breath was agony.

Struggling to his feet, he felt around for the first window, coughing violently. Everything he tried to touch was on fire. Then he found what he wanted. The glass panel should be wide enough. There was no time to think about whether or not this was going to work. He gripped the urn with both hands, his fingers on the inside lip, and held it up near his face, ducking low as if he were going into a scrum. Forced to get the longest run up possible, he stepped back.

Just do it.

He ran at the window, hoping he was in line and not about to burst through a burning box or into the wall between the two windows, knock himself out. He charged ahead like a footballer about to ram into an opposing player.

The glass shattered as Sam's body hit it dead centre, and the air drafted violently around him. He rolled outside the window onto the sloping platform of roof tiles, immediately losing the urn as he groped blindly, trying to grab onto anything at all. He dug his toes in, flattened himself to stop from sliding. But the momentum was too great and he felt himself going over the edge.

As his legs swung free into the night air, one hand found the guttering, and he held on tight.

Sirens in the distance...

The air on his face was fresh. He could smell the smoke, but it was on an automatic draught into the sky, lifting away from him. He opened his eyes. They were still streaming with water, but he was able to see something even if it was blurry. Between the swirls of smoke he could make out the stars overhead.

He swung his other arm up, grabbed the guttering now with two hands, tried to ease an elbow into the ridge of the metal. He might have been out of a burning building, but there was a long drop onto the rockery below. It was too high. The landing wasn't going to be soft.

He could hear her – Leah, somewhere outside – crying out for him.

The sirens were much closer now, whirling lights of red and blue mixing with the tar-black smoke billowing from the windows, oozing out of every crack and crevice.

'Panis Angelicus'. The hymn. Why was he thinking of that now? Dangling from the guttering of his house, it was playing in his head as though his brain was wired with full acoustics. It had been Sophie's favourite.

Sophie, her ashes fallen, probably lost for good now somewhere below, scattered into the grass, the weeds. Was this the best he could have done for her?

'Sophie, I'm sorry.'

The guttering strained and creaked. It started to pull away from the house.

'Get that bloody ladder over here,' someone shouted from below. There were other voices too, frantic, yelling instructions.

'Hang on, Doc, just a few seconds more.'

The words to the hymn pounded through Sam's head as he felt his grip loosening.

Pauper, pauper, servus et humilis. The poor, poor and humble servant.

He stared up at the stars and began to weep, 'Oh, God. I am your humble servant.'

THIRTY-THREE

Julia stood over him, stern with worry. She'd been doing that every day for the last three weeks. 'You heard what the doctor said. It's too soon to be going home.'

'You forget, I don't have a home.' Sam used the triangle over the bed to pull himself into an upright position, trying not to grimace at the heavy ache down his leg.

'Stop being facetious. Sometimes you have to trust others to decide what's good for you.'

'Another day under these fluorescents and I'll turn into a Morlock.'

His brother-in-law came in with the wheelchair. 'Hospital regulations,' Paul said.

Anything to get out of the place.

'I could have done with a few extra days to get the apartment ready,' Julia said, helping Sam into his shoes and then the chair. The size of her, acting like a sergeant major. 'Not all the furniture is in, and I haven't had a chance to stock the cupboards.'

'I don't need much.'

'You and I can agree to differ on that one.' She brushed Paul's hands aside and took over with the chair. 'Don't forget his bag.'

Paul made a mock salute and Sam could only guess his sister's reaction. It made him smile.

Once they were free of the main doors of the hospital, Sam got out of the chair. Julia protested but he put his arm around her shoulders and kissed her cheek. 'You've done more than enough. And now it's up to me.'

'Don't be silly,' she told him. 'You should enjoy the fuss while you can.'

It felt good to walk, pulling his sister closer to his side, leaning on her just a little. And finally breathing real air, sunlight on his skin. Everything seemed so bright.

'We can stay with you if you like,' Julia added.

'And listen to me snore all night? You're better off in your hotel.'

'What about your physio?'

'All sorted. Now stop your worrying.' He kissed the top of her head and she wrapped her arm around his waist.

While Paul put Sam's bag into the boot of the car, Julia tried to convince him to take the front passenger seat. He waved her away and eased into the back. As they set off, Sam instructed Paul where to go.

'Not too soon?'

'I have to see the place.'

They drove up the long street and Sam leant forward to watch through the windscreen. The Cape Cod was gone and what was left of the lower floor was blackened rubble. Paul stopped the car out the front.

Sam reached for the door handle and cracked it open.

Julia twisted in her seat to look at him. She hesitated for a moment, her eyes mellowing as though she knew there was no point in arguing. 'Are you sure you're up to this?' she said.

'I'm about to find out.'

Sam got them to wait in the car. He went under the loose police tape as it flapped in the breeze from one neighbour's fence to the other. It wasn't safe to be moving amongst all of this debris and charred framework, but somehow he felt there was nothing to fear. A sense that the place could never affect him again. He wasn't sad to see it destroyed. But he wasn't glad either. Curious perhaps.

It didn't look anything like the scene his imagination had conjured in earlier times, when he'd wished it gone. Back then the image had been more macabre, as though the house would always leave a defiant and menacing scar. Instead, he found himself pitying it.

Sam went in under a half-fallen beam. Pungent odours of melted plastics and other unnatural substances stung his senses. He trod carefully over the mess, aware that his energies were already close to depleted. *Don't overdo it.*

Some of the walls were intact, particularly at the back of the house where his bedroom used to be. The spare room had also stood up, but the papers were gone, filing cabinets tipped and crushed like tin cans; desk legs protruding from under the collapsed ceiling.

He moved to the front of the house. A small portion of what had been the upstairs extension held at the top of the spiral staircase, perhaps where firemen had aimed one of their hoses. Sam went over and looked up from the bottom. Apart from the stairs being blackened, it seemed sound, except rather than reaching to the dark cavity of his memories, there was instead clear blue sky. Fresh and wonderful and promising. Sophie had tried to tell him many times about seeing so far out over the ocean, the beauty of the stars at night, cool breezes and more, so much more than just rooms.

He wandered outside and scratched around with his boot at some of the rubble, a mixture of bricks and burnt timbers, fragments of broken furniture, molten masses of unrecognisable objects that had once made up his possessions.

He was somewhere near the area he suspected he'd come down on. The ladder hadn't quite made it in time but it had broken his fall, or rather interrupted it. He didn't remember anything after that until he'd woken in hospital two days later. Strung up and braced. Wrapped like a mummy, arms and torso. Julia by his side, comforting.

Richard had come to the hospital when Sam was barely lucid. The older man had had trouble making eye contact, seemed wretched. 'Is there anything you need?' he'd asked. 'A doctor, nurse, water?'

'I'm okay,' Sam managed, stunned at the sound of his gravel-throated voice. 'I'm so sorry... Richard... everything.'

'There's nothing to be sorry for,' Richard grumbled. 'Nothing at all. Unless you die. I'll be angry if you die.'

The first time Sam had left his room for physio he'd found a type of police guard posted just outside in the hall. Not because he was under suspicion of anything, but because, for some unknown reason, the cops had decided they cared, and that he ought not to be disturbed by journalists, fraught patients or distressed stalkers.

He had a vague memory of Leah trying to make an appearance while he'd been prone in his hospital bed. Her dark head bobbing. Her scream as she'd been dragged away.

Sam had asked Richard to take care of her, get her some help...

The toe of his boot struck something, and it became partially visible a few seconds later as he dug around. He reached down and pulled Sophie's urn from the charcoal of rubbish and dust. Inside was some ash and other particles. He had no way of knowing if any part of it was Sophie's ashes. Maybe it didn't matter.

Sam headed back towards the car, bunching his sleeve over his fist to wipe the urn, Julia watching him from the front passenger seat. When he got in the back, she turned around and studied him further. He continued to rub at the urn like it was a genie lamp.

'Where to, buddy?' Paul said.

Julia shushed her husband. 'Give him a moment.'

Sam didn't reply because he was still thinking about it.

Julia eventually told him how it would be. 'I promised the doctor I'd make sure you rested up. That was the condition to let you go.'

'I know and I'm sorry. But I think I need to—'

Julia reached out and touched the hand that cradled the urn. 'Hey, I reckon we could bring that up to something of a shine. Maybe get a new lid fitted. It would be nicer that way, not all knocked about.'

Finally he nodded, and they drove on.

*

Paul and Julia deposited him into the apartment – a rented split-level that seemed unnecessarily extravagant. A bedsit would have done Sam. They showed him through the place and it was nice, overlooking Botany Bay.

'You should get back to the hotel,' Sam said after Julia unpacked his bag. 'I'll be fine here.'

His sister went to say something but seemed to change her mind, sighing as she reached up to touch his cheek. 'Don't forget, we're within walking distance. I'll bring you things every day.'

He didn't bother to tell her it wasn't necessary. After a while, he managed to get them to the door, pulling Paul back at the last moment.

'Can I have your car this afternoon?' Sam said discreetly.

Paul frowned. 'Where do you want to go?'

'Can I have it?'

Julia was moving down the hall. Paul watched her for a few seconds, then turned back to Sam. 'Sure, mate. Our secret. I'll leave it unlocked. The keys will be up in the visor.'

Sam closed the door and leant against it, taking in his new surroundings.

So, this was how it was to be.

He spotted a landline phone sitting in the charger attached to the lounge-room wall. He went over and picked it up, pressed the green button and listened. There was a dial tone. He'd have to get another mobile, but there was no hurry. The thought of his house burnt and his possessions destroyed had strangely brought a sense of relief, like he was no longer weighted or defined by objects. He was free and he intended to stay that way.

He dialled a number on the phone. A recorded message said the number did not exist. He thought for a moment, tried again. This time it was answered.

After the call, he returned to the kitchen bench where he'd placed the urn. He examined it, brushed away more of the dust. 'Let's see what we can do.'

*

Sam drove Paul's car to the lower mountain ranges of Kurrajong. Delia Wilde's house was a neat render with an uninterrupted view across the valley all the way to Richmond. Three hot air balloons hung in the distance like Chinese lanterns in shades of orange, red and yellow – a regular weekend feature. Sophie had urged him to try ballooning with her, but it had taken until their wedding day before he'd gathered the nerve. After the ceremony, as the guests wandered in the gardens of the reception house, Sam had whisked off Sophie for what he'd promised would be the biggest surprise of the day. And she'd loved it, even if he'd preferred to sink low and cling to the inside of the basket.

He smiled at the memory. Sophie with her inimitable zest for life, gripping her bouquet and squealing with delight as the photographer snapped away...

Finally, Sam reached into a folder on the seat beside him and drew out the small black and white photo. He placed it inside the urn, then got out of the car.

Delia was waiting for him on the front porch as he made his way down the white gravel path, a slight limp that he did well to cover.

She moved her fingers to her lips in the form of a prayer.

Then she closed the gap, and he stepped into her arms, the urn nestled between them.

THIRTY-FOUR

Tractor tyres ran in even strips along the beach – the sand swept and rolled clean. Sam thought it strange that for all the years he'd lived here, he'd never seen those tractors at work.

There was plenty of time; he'd arrived early to take in the sights. The surfers in their black wetsuits were just past the breakers, bobbing on the swell, while a stand-up paddle boarder weaved cheekily between them. A plane circled high overhead, too far away to give off any sound.

Sam headed towards the Kurnell rocks, but turned back, eventually stopping to face the shore. He thought of all the times he'd come here, those long walks, trying to reconcile his private agony. It had saved him; it had also cursed him. Strangely, it was the one place he'd yearned for the entire time he was laid up in hospital after his less than gentle exit from a burning building.

A flurry of seagulls landed, lifted and landed again on the sand, squabbling over some morsel or scrap. Sam turned away from them.

She was there, to his right, just out of reaching distance. Her smile was faint, gentle. There was something different about her. Sam realised it was her hair. Gone were the pale ends. It was now all dark – he assumed her natural colour.

'Hello, Sam.'

'Alice. I'm glad to see you.' He made no attempt to go to her, although he was surprised at how much he wanted to.

'I'm a bit early,' she said. 'Hope I didn't interrupt your thoughts.'

'No. I just... well, it seemed a waste to...' He faltered, took a breath. 'I hear your therapy has been going really well.'

She stifled a smile and tucked a loose strand behind her ear. 'Yes, Professor Camberwell has been great. Quite a character.'

'That he is,' Sam replied with a small chuckle. Good old Edgar. The man was underrated. After a long pause, he added, 'You look well.'

She nodded and pointed to his leg. 'You're all healed?'

He moved his left leg forward as though in demonstration, feeling awkward. He'd hoped to avoid that particular subject. 'Apparently I have bones that don't break so easily. They kind of bend. Maybe they're made out of rubber.'

She laughed lightly. 'That's got to be a good thing.'

He thought of the scarring under his shirt sleeves and on his back. The skin there still felt uncomfortably tight. 'Yeah, well it's all fine now.'

'I'm glad.'

They smiled at each other. Sam fought against the quiver at the corner of his mouth. He didn't want to get emotional, didn't want her to feel uncomfortable. And yet there were so many things he wanted to say.

Although everyone denied it, he'd been certain Alice had visited him in the hospital during those early days. He might have been half wrapped like a mummy and partially sedated, but he'd been sure of her voice, the blurred image of her features when she'd leant over the bed. Had she kissed his cheek?

'I'm thinking about moving to Perth,' she said, her gaze holding steady on him.

His stomach muscles tensed. 'Really?'

'I know, a bit of a surprise.'

'You sorted everything with your family, then?'

'Well, my medical retirement has come through. Luke, my brother, keeps nagging me to come over. My sister-in-law agrees – that was the biggest shock. My parents – well, they're another matter.' She rolled her eyes. 'Still, I'll get to spend time with my nephews.'

'I'm sure it will work out. It will be good for you to be with family.'

She sighed and scraped her teeth over her bottom lip. 'So what about you? Will you be able to go back to work?'

'Nobody has told me I can't.' He huffed, thinking of the stern advice Edgar had thrown at him. 'But I'm not sure I want to go back. Maybe I want to try something new, like travel around Australia. Explore the outback. Buy a pub.'

'You'll be seeing your sister in Queensland?'

He nodded. Julia and Paul had been home for several months.

It felt awkward again. Maybe because this was the part where he was supposed to apologise to her. He released a breath and dug his heel into the sand.

'You know, maybe on my way around, when I'm passing through Perth, I could drop in and... say hello.'

'I'd like that,' she said softly.

He wondered if she was merely being polite. It seemed she might say something else, but the moment passed.

'Well, I suppose I better get going. I wish you all the very best, Alice.'

'Goodbye, Sam. And good luck.'

'You too. Take care, won't you.'

He started to walk away.

'Sam,' she called after him.

He stopped, turned back.

A tremble on her lips; she took a few steps towards him, her eyes imploring. 'Why did you want to see me?' she asked.

'I needed to make sure that you were all right.'

A tear escaped down one of her cheeks. 'You could have found that out through Professor Camberwell. I know you asked him to take me on.' She took another step. 'Is there something else, Sam?'

Of course there was. He'd not stopped thinking about her. Not for a moment. Couldn't get the memory of her out of his head. The softness of her skin against his; he never wanted to forget it. Her wildflower scent that even now swarmed his senses. Those memories had aided his recovery – put him back on his feet. She was soothing to his nerves. It was the way she filled him up, made something whole out of him. He'd needed to see it for himself, to experiment with the wonder that all thought of her these past months only ever invoked the most loving feelings.

'Walk with me?' he said.

They turned to the south and headed along the shore. Slowly. The raked marks from the tractor made their path. There were no words, just those easy steps, side by side.

After a while she said, 'Are you really going to buy a pub?'

'Free beer. Seems too good an opportunity to pass up.' He looked at her and smiled.

An albatross swerved gracefully into view, taking Sam back to the first time he'd seen Alice on the beach – the sad and lonely figure. Now she walked tall and beautiful.

He took her hand, and she wound her fingers into his.

The End

ACKNOWLEDGEMENTS

They say an author's life is a lonely one. While the writing itself is undoubtedly a solitary practice, everything else comes down to a lot of talented people.

Thank you to Nicola O'Shea, editor, mentor and friend, who continues to be a shining light of guidance and wisdom.

Thank you Judith Flanagan, Antonette Diorio, and Jacqui Svenson from the Fic Chicks. And my original writing group: Sharon Ketelaar, Krystina Pecorari-McBride, Perla Del Pozo, Gill Cooke, Janice Dib, Pamela Cook, and Wanda Wiltshire. All wonderful writers who provided an eclectic range of feedback.

Thank you Rodney Ward (B. Psych M. Clinical Psychology) and Dr D. MBBS (Syd) Hons, FRANZCP for unswerving support, insightfulness, and answering all my questions, even the ones they didn't know I was asking. The story remains my own and liberties were taken for the purpose of a dramatic plot.

Special thanks to the devoted staff and volunteers at Writing NSW.

Thank you to Mon Cullen for insights into post-traumatic stress and medication. And to Janice Dib for her knowledge in pharmaceuticals.

Many thanks to Baz Radburn, Ian Gunn, Grace Heifetz, Annabel Blay, and Hayley Nash.

Thank you to Christa Moffitt for her fantastic cover design, Lauren Finger for final edits and an eye for detail, and Joel Naoum from Critical Mass Consulting, for everything else.

www.ingramcontent.com/pod-product-compliance
Lightning Source LLC
Chambersburg PA
CBHW050144120726
47903CB00002B/479